GW01458006

Diggers and Dreamers

Keith Walton

Keith Walton is from Lancaster, and was educated at Cambridge University and Leeds School of Art. He has worked as labourer, abattoir worker, carpenter and postman. He now writes full-time. He reads widely at poetry cafés and literary events in the South West and recently published a book of poems, *First Cut*. This is his first novel.

There is another world – but it is in this one.

Paul Eluard

Diggers and Dreamers

a novel

by

Keith Walton

Brimstone Press

First published in 2006
by
Brimstone Press
PO Box 114
Shaftesbury
SP7 8XN

www.brimstonepress.co.uk

Copyright © Keith Walton 2006

Keith Walton hereby asserts his right to be identified as the
author of this work in accordance with Section 77 of the
Copyright, Designs and Patents Act, 1988

All rights reserved

Author contact: kwalton@brimstonepress.co.uk

Printed in Baskerville by
Antony Rowe Ltd
Eastbourne BN23 6QT

Cover design by Linda Reed and Associates

ISBN 0-9548171-2-5

Some definitions

The Diggers were radical dissenters in mid-seventeenth-century England who cultivated abandoned land and advocated social and political reform. The name and philosophy were adopted by activists in the late1960s.

To dig: 'to understand, appreciate, experience (*informal, dated*)'. Concise OED.

Dreamers: 'unpractical persons; idealists'. Concise OED.

Contents

For

Sebastian Hayes

PART I:

RETURN TO THE HILLS

Chapter 1: Albi

I watch the cream and red train disappear slowly round the long bend. The last I see of Jane is her hand sticking out of the window, her fingers spread out like the ribs of a broken fan. I stare along the empty line until the noise of the train dies away and the rails no longer rumble and the humming wires fall silent, and then for some time after. I turn and walk through the dark station and out onto the dazzling dust area in front. It is midday and very hot and the white dust is endless. I stop, shadowless and blind, aware suddenly of the space all around me, aware that I do not have to do what I intended to do when she left, the thing I promised myself I would do for her, so that she can return, the one big thing. I stare up at the enormous sun. Then I walk quickly to the car and, instead of getting in and driving back up into the hills, I take out my bag and walk towards the centre of town.

We walked up this road eighteen months ago, rucksacks on our backs (Jane's was new and she wore it awkwardly), hand in hand, distant. We had left our trunks at the station.

As we passed this little house, I exclaimed 'Yvonne de Galais' house, that *le grand Meaulnes* used to stand outside!' and turned to her, laughing. She smiled a thin smile.

We stayed, that first night, at this hotel, an old place superficially modernised with plate glass door and Formica desk. We sat on the bed, beneath the aged flowered wallpaper and the picture of Jesus, staring across the red roofs to the hills, green, grey and white. I was excited, saying I hoped we'd find a place soon so we could start preparing the ground to be ready for spring:

'Shallots can go in in February, you know. And there's still time to sow broad beans. If you start behind, you never catch up. Imagine – our own place, growing our own food.

Two acres and a cow, Cobbett says that's all you need – and that's to feed a family! Of course we'll have goats instead. They eat anything. And you can freeze goats' milk, but not cows' – something to do with the cream.'

And on and on. Jane sat in silence. Then she got up quickly, went into the bathroom and was sick. Maybe we should have turned round and gone back then. But we'd emigrated, given away everything we couldn't carry, were making a fresh start. And for me there was more to it than that.

The next day we caught the bus up into the hills, to buy a place, to live, to be free. Within two months we had moved into our own house, with our own land, our own vines. And I had planted the shallots, late.

'You do still love me, don't you?' Her last words as the train began to move, her eyes searching my face. Or maybe memorising.

'Of course I do. Close the door.'

At the building site a crane turns slowly across the sky. An orange crane, a blue sky, the orange and blue complementary colours, of the same intensity, shapes that vibrate against each other; when I screw up my eyes I can't tell which is in front of which – I can fancy the shape of the crane to be an absence of blue, a cut-out revealing the orange beyond as it turns slowly, a moving absence. But what, then, is the orange? How strange to be alone! To stop spontaneously, to follow my nose, not having to explain or make sense of things, with Jane not here.

The train will be crossing the plain of Gaillac; she will be looking out over endless rows of soft green vines, where the woad once grew that built the towers of Toulouse, long ago. *Pastel*.

4

And now I reach the anchor, the huge anchor set on a plinth, eighty miles from the sea. I sniff it to see if I can smell the sea. It smells of iron and heat. How fierce the sun is! I cross the park and plunge into the public baths.

*   *   *

I stand in the white-tiled cubicle and let the hot water beat on me until I am almost senseless. Endless hot running water – imagine what it is like to someone who draws his water from a well and heats it in a black polythene bag in the sun.

I remember reading of South American women moved from squatters' shacks into apartments, showering a dozen times a day, astonished at this miracle, not knowing where it came from, not realising that, unlike a miracle, they would have to pay for it with more than faith.

At last I come to, and wash myself voluptuously, moving into and out of the hot cascade. I examine my hands, enlarged and roughened by hard work, no longer the hands of a student, an academic, a bureaucrat. I look at the scabs – each the fading record of an incident; at the scars – intensifying with time, as if growing confident of their permanence, fixing events. I feel my broadened shoulders and my thickened arms, the product of two years of carpentry, eighteen months on the land. At thirty I have grown into myself, filled the shape I was meant to be, ready at last to take my place with the other men of my family.

But now I have become hard and stiff. So much for the healthy outdoor life. Thoreau writes that the farmer, that image of the healthy man, is not healthy, because he has lost his elasticity; he has become an overworked buffalo, stiff leather in stiff leather. And Jane and I have become ox-like, starving our imaginations, blinkering our visions to the narrow world of our house and land. She is right to go back

5

to London; not just to earn the money we need, but for her own sake. And I am right to stay: for I must remain within this small compass until there is a resolution. And Thoreau's prescription for the farmer? "It would do him good to be thoroughly shampooed to make him supple". I apply the soap thickly to the sponge and rub myself all over. As I wash my soft, white places, I remember the softness of her body, our nakedness together, even in that last, fear-filled grappling. We have never been apart. As the water pours onto my head, drips like tears from my eyelashes, I realise the seriousness of what we have done; that what seemed a few hours ago sensible and rational, is a leap off the edge. We have acted as if we believe in fate. I wonder if we do. I grip the sponge and whisper her name.

I wash my hair, shave, clean my teeth, dry myself, put on white cotton trousers, a white collarless shirt, sandals. And – as I comb my long hair in the misted, rubbed-clean mirror – Thoreau's definition of health? "One sensible to the finest influence; he who is affected by more or less electricity in the air". Ah.

I stuff my dirty clothes into my bag, step out of the steamy cubicle into the cool, echoey building, and go out into the full heat of the sun.

*   *   *

Nothing moves. I can feel the surface of my damp hair crisping in the heat. The town sleeps, coshed by the sun; or spellbound. In front of me the war memorial, a triumphal red brick arch tattooed all over with the hundreds of names of the dead, set in rectangles of sharp white gravel and beds of vermilion flowers, bounded by low dark box hedges exactly clipped, a double row of black cypresses leading to and from it. The wide square, Di Chirico shadowed, empty. Nothing moves.

6

Except behind the buttressed walls of the vast red cathedral that rises hallucinatingly above and shadows the town. Within, the level of blood rising slowly, gurgling – spouts suddenly from gargoyles, bursts out through windows, pours down the walls darkening with crimson the scarlet brick, floods the narrow streets that now echo with screams and the crackle of fire, bursts in a foaming wave from the narrow streets, surges across the square, laps around the bases of the still black cypresses. I hold my breath as the roots eagerly suck in the blood. The tops of the cypresses, at first still, begin to vibrate, shiver – then burst open, flower, with a soft white oozing that shapes, re-shapes then fixes into the forms of heads. There is a head on the top of each of these black cypresses, and each the head of a hero. My heroes, the heroes of my life: long haired and shaven headed; bearded and fresh faced; composed and falling apart; gazing ecstatically still and chattering matily; singing; yelling angry obscenities; mouthing endless concentrated monologues – altogether a welter and babble of noise and movement that somehow makes sense, that is – my world. I gaze enraptured.

And then the tall orange crane turns slowly through the blue sky; the hook descends and lifts the great anchor high into the sky, turns again and the anchor rattles down and, with its arrowed barb, hooks under the arch and lifts. The arch, on its circular pedestal, rises, brick foundations falling, revealing a black emptiness; and down it swirls the blood, with maelstrom twist, gurgles, and is gone. The heads are silenced and stilled, turned to stone... begin to topple... smash to white gravel. The cypresses shiver and then are still. I close my eyes. "Oxidise the water-spouts", I murmur; "stuff boudoirs with the fiery powder of rubies". Such things I see, inside my head!

Out there, a creaking sound. I open my eyes. Everything – arch, anchor, crane – is in its given, habitual place. A cyclist in a big cap is cranking slowly across the square. A grey

7

shutter squeaks open and a man in a blue vest looks blearily out, scratches himself, yawning. The first car, a Dauphine, patched and particoloured like a circus car, appears in the street. The pendulum resumes and the clock ticks on.

Was it vision? Memory? Premonition? Or imagination, simply, long buried, emerging....

Smartly dressed figures appear and walk purposefully with briefcases. The streets fill with cars and motor cycles and the air grows blue with petrol fumes. Slim, trim shop assistants in white blouses wind open window shutters. A clock strikes twice. And then another clock, deeper. I run my fingers through my dried hair. Jane will be in Toulouse, waiting for the Paris train. I go to the car, stow my bag and walk into town, a tourist.

Chapter 2: The river

I go straight to the record shop and stare through the window at the record.

'How can you even *think* of buying a record, Kris,' Jane had said when I pointed it out to her; 'that's a month's petrol.' It was released the month we arrived.

'But I always buy his records.'

'You always used to. Past tense. Those days are over. This is the real world.'

'But *he's* the real world.'

'Grow up.'

I've waited eighteen months. I walk in, buy it, hold it, tense myself for the accusing voice. It doesn't come. She isn't here. I am here on my own. This afternoon I am living as if I am free.

I look around. The shop has changed a lot since I first came in ten years ago. The *proprio* is the same, but his once wild hair and shaggy beard are now trimmed to a perfumed neatness, his granny glasses replaced by executive gold rims, the saggy rainbow sweater discarded for a tight Fair Isle slipover, his whirling energy constrained to a nervous fastidiousness. The white paint, the gaudy posters, the scrawled messages are gone; now it is olive hessian and classical record sleeves on the walls. Albinoni plays; then it was Léo Ferré. And I was a boy with short hair and cycling shoes nervously buying a record I had heard playing in the youth hostel. "Le Temps de Vivre", by Georges Moustaki. I leave, clutching *Blood on the Tracks*.

*   *   *

I pass the smart shops. The patisserie, its cakes so carefully made, so highly finished – enormous red strawberries glowing through a magnifying glaze – that they resemble works of art more than food. The charcuterie, where thick sauces and gelatin moulds disguise animal and vegetable origins. The parfumerie, with its exotic and alluring scents, unhuman smells to swathe, disguise, transmute the human body. The *magasin de mode's* window of gorgeous fabrics draped upon impossible figures. Bourgeois France, in which everything, it seems, passes through a stage of artificiality (conscious mind? cultural sensibility?) before it is consumed.

How that intrigued me! I was ambling along, eating a *pêche* – a cake shaped like a perfect bum; I was sinking my teeth into the soft pink cheeks – all those years ago, when an attractive woman came out of this shop, clutching a large dress bag, her eyes bright with pleasure at her purchase (I imagined her trying it on), smiled absently at me as she passed, her perfume wrapping round me. Without thinking I turned and followed her. She wore no stockings, had slim brown legs, walked quickly in high-heeled slingback shoes. Beautiful brown hair with blonde highlights, smooth suntanned skin. She was slim and sleek and wonderfully middle-aged. I followed her without her knowing.

She reached her car, a white Citroën DS (*déesse*, yes), and, as she opened the door looked up and saw me watching her, half hidden. A frown passed across her face, followed by a smile – not directed at me but upwards, at the sky. Then she looked very directly at me. I was paralysed. Not frozen – no Medusa, she – but as paralysed as if she had opened her blouse and stood bare breasted in front of me. Then she turned and got into the car and turned the key. And it wouldn't start. She tried again. And again. I had an age in which to do something, if there was anything to do. I just watched. At last the engine roared into life and she drove away, her hand through the window giving a flutter of a wave, and then she was gone. I started after her helplessly, then turned, feeling strangely empty, and resumed my life.

Often I would remember, and imagine alternative possibilities, each of them forking ever further from my existing life into an entirely different present.

Such are my memories of bourgeois France. Now I live in peasant France. And I need to remember why.

*   *   *

An untidy bulk backs out of the bookshop, blocks my path, steps back into me, whirls round crying:

'*Boun Diou!*' Pieter often slips into *patois* when surprised; I still don't know whether from a genuine empathy with his peasant neighbours, or something wished for. Surprise is replaced by delight as he pumps my hand:

'Kris! How are you?' The rolled 'r' and the short 'yu' distinctively South African.

'Not bad. And you?'

'Good, good.' He taps the fat book he is holding, *La Terre d'Oc*. 'Fascinating. The parallels of land and belief, form and idea in a place. That bloody fortress, for example,' he points at the cathedral, 'every brick made with the blood of the broken Cathars. One day that blood will flow again, out of the bricks.

'And the springs – do you know of them, the *résurgences*? Even the name. Pure cold springs that bubble into the bed of the Tarn. Imagine, within the muddy, thick, warm river those separate, cold, pure streams. And hard, that water, hard and clear. The perfect image of the Other Way. And they have their effect – the river clears as it flows downstream. Does the Mississippi, or the Seine? No – but our river does. Parallels, you see.

'But you're alone – where's Jane?' I will have to get used to this question, invent the appropriate response for each questioner. He listens, his lined, tanned face grave beneath

11

the grey hair, says:

'Women live in the present – they see things as they are, not as they might be. And she sees that she has no home – she needs a home. But you have a vision. Now you must be strong, stronger than you have ever been. Work with all your strength. Make that vision a reality. Turn the damaged and neglected into a home, the wilderness into a garden. Then she can return.' We shake hands and he turns, then calls over his shoulder:

'Come and see us, soon. Hendrika likes to see you.'

'Sure.' And I walk on, wondering if it is what I want, any of what he said. The path leads, ineluctably, to the river.

*   *   *

I walk slowly down the steps, between the stones, into the noise, and stand, my sandalled feet an inch above the milky brown river. It is not so much the speed of the river I notice – although that's impressive, as a toppled tree speeds past, a bird still and sharp on its topmost twig – as its size. A hundred yards wide, of unknown depth; what volume of water? What power. The water piles against and divides around the bridge piers. The surface is marked by swirls and ribbons of movement and small conical holes like holes in mud. And are there really springs, bubbling springs and threads of clear water? The mill remains, empty now and boarded up. The terrace where we sat at long tables under the bamboo lattice is now a desolation of rubbish.

It was a youth hostel when I came, alone, a temporary one, open for the summer, run by a group of students from Paris. They boiled cauldrons of apples and we helped ourselves. They played chess and argued and drank, and giggled over small, shared cigarettes and caressed and – I suppose – made love. There was the pretty *gamine* with long hair and big eyes who would pass hours motionless and then instigate a sudden collective madness. There was the serious girl with short hair who kept it all going. The patient, methodical, bespectacled man, and the man all the girls fell for and who, you insisted, wasn't handsome but was, you conceded, attractive.

And the non-stop record player – songs of Cuba, Satie, Charley Patton, Bach, Dylan, Nina Simone, Congo drums, Brassens, *Misa Luba*, Monteverdi, Reggianni, Miles Davis, Milhaud, and more, and more. Most of it music I'd never heard, that I've only identified piece by piece in the years since, that I'll still be identifying years hence; the music of those three days (as I rested up) exists in a place inside me, waiting to be heard again to be recalled. Eighteen months later I imagined those students taking part in *les événements* in Paris. As I watched the savagery of the CRS on TV I hoped they were alright. Yes, the one I fell for was the longhaired girl; and the one I thought I should like, the shorthaired.

Abroad for the first time, cycling to the Mediterranean, crossing that line, that exact line that separates North and South, into a different world. I left the world I knew and entered a different world. The elastic connecting me to home stretched (how I missed home!), and snapped. (My bike broke miles from a bike shop, was repaired by a blacksmith – a different world.) I swam in the Mediterranean. I bought red espadrilles for the girl I wrote to every day. I spent three weeks in Provence and the Midi, in Roman Midi, in the Midi of Van Gogh and Cézanne and Petrarch and the Troubadours and the Cathars and olives and vines, that made me think of Greece, although I had never been to Greece (that I would one day go to Greece to find); in a different culture, in 'culture'.

I arrive in Albi, at what I think is the last stop on my sickle swing through the South, replete and, it seems, complete. I'm sitting here, at a long bench, beneath a vine-covered trellis, after a meal I've made myself, of rice, onions, tomatoes (those sweet, juicy, misshapen Southern tomatoes) and cheese (gruyère, all melted in), followed by goats' cheese and baguette. There is coffee in a glass by my hand, the hard sugar lump dissolving, and a glass of wine. It is evening, dark and warm, a Southern evening. The air is soft on my skin. The stars sparkle. I listen to the river's soft flow, and watch the last light fade from the sky. I am cycling fit, full of the books I've been reading (*La Nausée, Paroles, Thus spoke Zarathustra*), the experiences I've had (Mont St Victoire, La Fontaine de Vaucluse, the girls at La Ciotat). My diary (which is now 'a journal') is open in front of me. I am surrounded by activity that I am not part of, conversation I do not understand. I am ready to reflect on my adventure. I am warm and full and rather pleased with myself. Click. A new record. Georges Moustaki. "Le Temps de Vivre". I feel very, very happy. I write:

"I am surrounded by strangeness and activity, and I am at its still centre; in it but not of it. I am alone and unafraid. I am free." And then suddenly I know what I have to do. I have to go on. The next day, instead of heading north, retracing my journey here, I cycle up into the hills, into silence, towards nothing. The adventure I thought was ending is just beginning – or rather it is beginning a new, more dangerous phase. When I returned to England I gave the girl the red espadrilles and broke off our relationship.

Such moments happen to you when you are twenty. At thirty, maybe you have to make them happen. I look down at the thick water. I imagine the steps continuing, step by step, to the bed of the river. To the spring, the *résurgence*.

I step down, into the water. A smell of mud and weed rises. My foot sinks through the surface, disappears, and then grounds on the invisible step. The water is cool. It separates around my ankle. I step down my other foot, deeper, the water to my calf, cold now, tugging at my leg more urgently; my sandal touches, slips, I almost fall, recover, set down my foot. Step down again. And again. Each step takes me away from the bank, into the river, down, out, the water rearing up, filling my vision, the noise of it filling my ears, blocking out everything else, pulling at me. I stand, waist deep, divided at the *tan t'ien*, half in water, half in air, exactly between. Now. Decide. To descend, step by step, into the cool, muddy water, into the dark, descend into the stream, the silence, the single flow, seeking the spring. Or climb back, out of the buoyant water into the light, the air, the weight, and all that bloody complication….

Turn. Return. How the water plucks at me, clings to me, pulls me down, drags me in! Step by step, heavy with water, slipping, almost panicking, I heave myself up, out of the water, up the steps and stand at last on the stones, the water draining from me, fizzing to nothing on the hot setts, the quayside solid beneath my feet, the air hot around me. I'm panting, and shaking, shocked at what I did and have almost done. I stand and wait. Patient as an animal. Until I have somewhere to go, until a destination emerges into my mind. And then I set off, not towards the car, no, but across the bridge, over the river, towards the boutique, wondering suddenly if Sylvie will be there.

Chapter 3: Sylvie

Sylvie squeals with delight, cries:

'Kris! At last!' as I push open the door, the sheep bell ringing, and step into the shop. She throws her arms round my neck and her body melts against me. She is small and feels soft and smells sweet and I can't resist kissing her hair. She pulls away, eyes shining, saying:

'I'll be with you in two ticks,' moves rapidly round the shop switching off spotlights, stopping the tape (*Ziggy Stardust*), checking windows and doors, pinching out incense sticks – their fragrance hangs in the air and a thin line of smoke rises and twists from each and then stops – pushing her tarot cards and detective novel into her overstuffed bag. I stand, mystified, as she moves quickly, energy released, a creature suddenly liberated, in and out of the sunlight, talking all the time:

'I knew someone would come. What a day! Claudine abandoned me!! I was beginning to doubt – no, not really, but if you hadn't…. I'm glad it's you,' a quickly flashed smile, steady eyes for a moment. 'I'm really excited. Oh, here's the money, I sold two salt boxes,' of wood, that I had made and painted. It's more than the price of the record. 'What's the record? Oh, it's brilliant. "Tangled up in blue",' she warbles. 'I really sweated to sell them – remember that, won't you?' A West Country softness to her voice, short skirt, thin blouse knotted at her midriff, shiny skin, long hair pinned up in arabesques and folds, with just enough wisps floating free to look negligent. 'Why's half of you wet?'

'It's a long story.'

'Don't tell me. I'll have something to fit you at the flat. Okay, I'm ready. Yes, Cinders, you shall go to the Ball,' at the mirror, staring at her reflection then shaking herself free and clattering in her Minnie Mouse shoes to the door.

Outside, she locks the door and sighs, as if she is locking the door of a prison, and turns, free.

'But…' I say.

'Shsh,' she says, and looks down at me from the top step, waiting. The moment stretches, tears are at the edge of her eyes, when at last I remember:

'May the humble Bernart de Ventadour escort the Lady Eleanor to the *feu St Jean*?' Her face lights up, she curtseys:

'The Lady is pleased,' she says, gravely, and we walk a few steps along the street in stately formality, then she laughs and squeezes my arm and lays her head against my shoulder and whispers:

'I need this.'

So do I.

It is Midsummer, the eve of St John's day, traditionally a night of bonfires, a tradition abandoned by the locals, revived by Edvard and now, after three years, the main festival and gathering of the incomers. And I had forgotten.

'Jane's gone, then.'

'Yes. Midday. Glad to get away from me.'

'Not from you. From this place maybe, especially from up there, your situation, but not from you.'

'Mm. And Jean-Jacques?'

'Sodded off. Starts muttering about "sitting beauty in his lap" and "finding her bitter", and needing "to return to the soil, to seek a duty, to embrace rugged reality…". Then he sodded off.'

'Rimbaud.'

'What?'

'He's quoting Rimbaud.'

'Who the hell's Rambo?'

'Poet. Gave up writing at 19, became a gun runner and slave trader, died at 37.'

'Brilliant – Jean-Jacques's forty, for Christ's sake.'

'Rimbaud was a great poet.'

'Bully for him. I'm pissed off with being a muse, I really am, I really, *really* am!' Her voice is low, intense, angry. I want her to let go of my arm but she clings fiercely. I'm relieved when we reach her flat.

*   *   *

'How about these?' A pair of her trousers. How gorgeous to wear them. Far too small. I have to settle for a pair of Jean-Jacques'. She goes for a shower.

I look around, wondering again at all the things she has collected, or rather, accumulated. Sixties records – no record player – American books, French magazines, brass bells from India, mandalas from Tibet, worry beads from Greece, slippers from Morocco, postcards from everywhere, badges – a waistcoat covered in them, worthy of a Peter Blake painting – teak elephants, pottery incense holders, road lamps – red petrol, yellow battery – a white seagull that bobs slowly up and down when I pull the string, clockwork tin toys from Eastern Europe – a cymbal-playing bear, an acrobat; embroidered butterflies from China, Japanese paper kites. And the only time she'd left England was to come here. The walls are yellow, the ceiling blue, the shelves and chairs and table and doors and window frames are inexpertly painted in primary colours. It looks, I suddenly realise, like the room of a child living on its own.

An attic flat in the centre of Albi in a run-down block looking out over the red roofs. Maybe we should have stayed in Albi. Maybe we went one step too far. Because Jane too loves France. The difference between us is that I love being an alien in France, she loves being at home here. As I was experiencing solitude for the first time, she was here for a year before university feeling at home for the first time. We love different aspects of the same place; we love the same place for different reasons: therefore we love different places? The same thing experienced from two different angles is two different things. Is this true? It's as if it's true, so it might as well be.

'Now,' Sylvie says, 'what shall I wear?' Wrapped in a towel, hair wet and straggly, the shine washed from her, her face tired, she looks quite plain. Sylvie?

'Come on!' she commands.

'I know nothing about clothes,' I protest.

'Not good enough. You don't try. *Feu St Jean*. Midsummer. Fire!' She disappears and returns in a red dress, yellow shawl, large straw hat, radiant smile. She parades, crossing and recrossing in front of the window, turning round in the light, the dress crackling around her.

'No? No. Okay. The longest day. Fertility.' A green dress, long and simple, with a fitted bodice. A flower headband. She is slender and willowy, she looks like Guinevere, the Guinevere who never had children, waiting.

'Night?' Her face dead white, her eyes cold and remote as stars, a black dress with a red slash across the heart.

'No!'

'Too much, eh? Come on, there is something you want me to be.' I daren't even think. She pulls the dress over her head and stands in underwear, leaning against the door jamb, inspecting her fingernails, beginning to be bored. Stray hairs are trapped by the elastic of her pants. Her belly round and smooth. She spots something and walks over and moves a magazine. Her attention caught, she begins tidying up; or, rather, moving things around. Forcing books onto overstuffed shelves, throwing shoes into corners, making heaps of clothes. She does it impatiently, as if things bore her – she often says 'we have too many things', surrounds herself, buries herself in them. She moves lightly, her feet flexing expressively. Her skin is smooth, and although she is suntanned, she looks pale, as if the flesh beneath her skin is white. Her long hair flows over her face when she leans forward, hiding it. She finds a book of Jean-Jacques'. She stares at it with great intensity then walks quickly to the window, drops it out, into the river, and turns back into the room, dusting her hands, smiling in triumph.

'You should be an actress.' I say. She laughs:

'I am, I was. Better than you might think, my friend and I. You'll know her, she's famous now, gorgeous, you probably fancy her, maybe you've wanked over her photo. It's the eyes, men's eyes, they strip you till you're raw, or hard. It's not right. Now I perform my life. No spotlight till I find what I want to do.'

'Light.'

'Perfect.' She kisses me, her hands on my shoulders. Her lips are soft. I feel the heat from a body that is very close but not touching. My hands hang helplessly. She is gone for a long time. She comes in very slowly. She is wearing a long dress of thin muslin. Her face is white, with gold and silver dust sparkling on her cheeks and forehead. In her hair, which hangs long and straight, there is a large gold slide that frames her face like a halo. A moon pendant hangs down between her breasts. Long dark eyelashes. Her eyes dark pools in which two spots of light glimmer like pearls in the depths. She advances slowly, gravely. She is from another world. But it is in this one. As she reaches for the yellow shawl she says, her voice husky:

'The stuff's over there – do you mind skinning up? I'm feeling a bit shaky.' I reach for the *Capstan* tin. As I soften the resin over the match flame, I hear a song in my head. From *Ziggy Stardust*. As if the tape has been playing on in my head from the time Sylvie stopped it in the shop. I make a strong one. They are French papers, ungummed, and I have to tear off a narrow strip to make a fibrous edge that will stick. The tape has reached the final track. I light up and hand her the joint. She takes a long, deep drag, and holds the smoke in, eyes closed. She breathes out, sighing:

'That's better,' opens her eyes, pearls become diamonds. She passes me the joint. The words I hear, the last track, running through my head, "Rock 'n' Roll Suicide", as I inhale, she shakes her head, as I breathe out she says softly, in time to the music: 'such fools, what we do to ourselves,' and holds me gently as I burst into tears.

Chapter 4: Into the hills

The shops are closing, the streets emptying. The sounds of television, of voices low in conversation or raised in anger, of the scrape and tap of knives and forks on plates, come from behind half-closed shutters, worlds closing in on themselves.

We drive out of town through streets abandoned to dogs, through sunlight and shadow as sharp as knives. Past the cemetery, with its blank walls and black cypresses. Past the out-of-town hypermarket, looking gaudy and temporary in the middle of acres of empty tarmacadam. Across a no man's land of unmade roads leading nowhere, small factories built of grey concrete blocks and asbestos, plots of weed-infested land marked off by single wires, of part-built houses with raw concrete steps leading up to metal-rusting concrete rafts, of shacks in patches of bare, overused land with chickens scratching patiently in the dust. A zone of transition, for those on the way up, or the way down. Something American about it. A zone of hope and lost hope. And then we're through, across the level crossing, clear of the town, into the country, climbing into the hills.

The grass and wheat and maize glow in the late afternoon sun, the hayfields – some cut, some being cut – shine. The top is down and I'm with a princess. We smoke and laugh and wave wildly at the haymakers. They watch us pass; some wave ironically, some just watch. When the joint's finished, we fall silent. Sylvie becomes withdrawn. When I put my hand on hers she smiles, but it is quick and superficial. Yet the sky is clear and deep blue, and the sun is warm; the air is balmy and full of the scent of cut hay, and I am driving the princess of light.

And I am on a quest, for the first time in years, knowing, as I've always known but tried to pretend that it isn't so, that you can only begin a quest alone. We've stood too close, Jane and I, and she has blocked out the rest of the world. Now the only thing between me and the open road is an overloaded hay wagon, and when I've overtaken that and darted between it and the oncoming blaring flashing ambulance, the road ahead is clear.

'A year,' Sylvie says.

'Sorry?'

'I've been here a year. It was just before the *feu* last year. There was a terrifying storm. I was staying with Rosie. I thought I'd come to Transylvania. Is a year a long time?'

'It depends.'

'It is. Jesus, what am I doing?'

'You're driving along the N99 in a 1958 2CV at', I check my watch, '5.45 pm on the 23rd of June, 1976.'

'But I'm not! I want to be, but I'm not. I'm not going anywhere. I'm twenty five and I want to know where I'm going!' She's shaking. I put my hand on her arm and say:

'Let's stop for a drink.' We're driving through a village whose stuccoed ordinariness and emptiness Utrillo would have relished. I pull up at the small bar tabac, next to a large articulated lorry. On the side of the lorry is an enormous picture of a smiling Marianne in peasant costume, with the legends "*La Rouergate*", and "*produits de porc*".

It is very dark inside. An old man with a big white moustache and a beret like a large black plate is eating saucisse with an *Opinel*. At the far end of the bar the local drunk shakes over his rum. Between the coffee machine and the tisanes the *patronne* and the lorry driver are deep in conversation across the bar. She has short blonde hair, brown at the roots, a doughy face, moist, puckered lips. He is squat and hairy shouldered and has on a blue vest. Eventually she turns, looks Sylvie up and down, then turns back to the man, and serves us without looking again. We sit at a small iron and marble table by the silent jukebox. The marble is cool. From inside outside looks over-bright and bleached.

'So why did you come here?' I ask.

'Rosie was always writing "come on, you'll love it" – you know what she's like – and I convinced myself it would be a new beginning. The South of France looks inviting when it's raining in Bradford. It seemed a way out of an impossible situation – "with one bound she was free", and all that. A lousy teaching job, an affair with the wrong bloke – the married one – that was going nowhere. The usual. And here I really seemed to have landed on my feet at last. Within a week I'd met Jean-Jacques, found the job and the flat. But sometimes, when everything happens just right, it's wrong; it traps you. That's how I feel now.'

'Midsummer,' I say, trying to sound encouraging. She laughs and says:

'Let me tell you about Midsummer.' Again the West Country burr. 'When I was twelve I got up before dawn and washed my face in dew and changed my name to Sylvie because I wanted to be married to Johnny Halliday. When I was fifteen I sat on Cadbury Hill all night, waiting for King Arthur to ride out of the hill. He didn't. When I was sixteen I was up there on my own, in the afternoon, watching the clouds in the blue sky, dreaming my way along the horizon, when I saw a flashing light. It flashed for a while, then stopped. Then it flashed again, closer. It was coming towards me, across fields and hedges, up hill and down vale – towards *me*! When it got closer, I saw a man was carrying the light, a tall man with a golden beard and long, golden hair, wearing flowing robes, striding steadfastly. Merlin! He carried a staff with a silver top – that's what flashed, in the sunlight. He walked towards me, up the final bank, over the rampart. It was happening, all those dreams were coming true, I was the chosen one! Except he wasn't coming to me. He was coming

24

to where I was sitting, the centre of the hill. But that was near enough, wasn't it? He was walking a ley line, to Glastonbury.

'He had a thick Brummie accent, lousy teeth and acne. I went with him. Just took off. In the middle of 'O' levels. Can you believe it? But the world was Love, and I wanted to be part of it, and here was my guide. Up till then my dad had been my guide; but I'd seen that he was leading me towards what *he* wanted for me, what he had done, another step up the social ladder, more of the same – but it hadn't made him happy, so why should it me? I didn't want more, I wanted different.

'I sewed curtains into a kaftan, I wore beads and bells, we lived in a tepee. The bloke passed me on to one of his mates but I didn't mind. The men were bastards but the women were great. And after being so rigid, everything was suddenly fluid, and moving so fast. And no right angles, all curves – time curved, space curved. I smoked, dropped acid, seemed always to be on the edge of some marvellous revelation.... Jean-Jacques says: in the sixties there was alchemy; now there's just chemistry. Does that make sense to you?'

'Yes.'

'The police took me back of course. My dad couldn't speak to me. Maybe that's why I can't go back now – after putting it all back together, for him to see I've Humpty Dumptied again.'

She stares into her glass. The old man is eating tripe now, slurping it noisily through his moustache. The drunk tries to join in the conversation at the bar but they ignore him and he returns to his solitary mumblings. The *patronne* leans further forward, her folded arms pushing up her fat breasts, her lips mouthing the driver's words, her eyes adoring him. He smirks and preens, now spreading his arm expansively, now leaning forward to whisper intimately. Sylvie looks up at them, and her lip curls.

'They've all been bastards, the men. Except one. Met him when they brought me back. Almost my age, too. Robert. Amazing bloke – bright as anything, brilliant athlete – "headboy material", doncha know. Left grammar school at sixteen to become a carpenter. Headmaster mucho pissed off – visions of a golden entry on the Oxbridge honours board shattered. He's making a name as a sculptor now. His pals who'd stayed on in the sixth form'd ask him why he'd thrown away all this for a manual job. "To learn to think with my hands, before it's too late", he'd say. I liked that. We were good for each other – his steadfastness and clear vision, my quickness and flights of fancy. I really didn't want to leave him to go to college, but I had to, you know? Sometimes I felt like a kite, yearning for the string to break, wanting to snip it myself. I got involved with a lecturer. Et bloody cetera. Didn't know what I was doing, couldn't decide. Then I had a dream.

'There was an empty cottage we'd walk to, near Cadbury, Robert and I, tumbledown, overrun with roses and honey-suckle, very romantic. We'd tell each other stories about how we'd do it up and live there and have lots of kids. He'd do his sculpture, I'd write poetry – or do whatever I was into at the time. Anyway, in the dream I was outside the cottage, which was all done up as we'd planned, bathed in evening sunlight, roses and hollyhocks to the eves, honeysuckle round the door – I could actually smell the honeysuckle in the dream. From an upstairs room there came the faint scratch of a pen, from the workshop the tap of mallet on chisel, even and reassur-ing. Then there was a noise behind me and when I turned round I saw the whole side of Cadbury Hill had slid away and there we were, Robert and I, and loads of children and friends, music and dancing, all bathed in a warm and joyful light that glowed from the rock walls and the jewels strewn all around. Everything I knew, everything I wanted was there, clearer and deeper than ever before.

'Then I heard a click. I turned. By the side of the hill was a little gate, and holding open the gate was my lecturer friend. He wasn't smiling at me, beckoning me to join him; he was just the keeper of the gate. Through the gate led a narrow path that twisted through woods and towns and wastelands, a grey landscape sombrely lit, but with sunrays illuminating far mysteries, and the path a ribbon of silver leading to a fabulous city beyond the horizon, its light glowing in the sky. And however much I yearned for the cottage, for the place in the hill, all I wanted to do was to go through that gate, follow that path. Because it leads to – the place I never reach. I snipped the string – the jolt and leap when the string parts....' She sits in silence, head down, dark.

'Which you haven't reached yet,' I find myself correcting. Why do I do that? I don't know whether I want to save her or join her.

'Right, okay, why not?' lifting her head, voice bright. 'Come on, I want to be there when they light the fire – I want to *light* the fire! I want to have a good time. Come on,' and she's off. As she passes the drunk he sees her for the first time and his eyes are like saucers and he mumbles:

'Reine, princesse,' and giggles helplessly and his eyes adore. She stops, looks at him hard, kisses him on his ugly forehead, says:

'It's your choice, buddy,' waits, shrugs and is gone.

The old man is tucking into a big plate of green beans. The *patronne* and the driver don't even see us leave. I dash after her, into the dazzling light, the warm, expansive evening air. Into the car, on and up.

*　　　　　*　　　　　*

As the road rises and we get higher there are fewer fields of cereal and more pasture, fewer vines and more woodland. At last the road levels off and we are driving across the plateau. In the distance the land rises higher, to the dry hard centre of the Massif Central; but we are not going that far. Soon we reach the dolmen where we will turn off and drop down into one of the valleys that cut into the plateau, wherein dwells the secret life of the region.

I stop by the standing stones and switch off the engine. I'm about to speak when there is a commotion by the ancient grave. A buzzard rises heavily, driven by the sharp beaks and harsh cries of three crows. It tries to return but its curved beak is no match for the snapping crows, working together, hyenas of the sky. It circles a couple of times then seems to shrug and give up its kill and wheels slowly, disdainfully away. After a short distance it begins to glide in a circle, rising with each circuit, not moving its wings except for small adjustments of wing tips and tail.

'It's found a thermal,' I say. As the crows squabble over the tiny carcass the buzzard flies effortlessly and majestically higher in a medium that is its own, into the blue sky. As we watch it spiral upwards, I tell Sylvie of that first visit to France, of what happened in Albi.

'All I'd done, through travelling here, was exchange one set of clothes for another – more suitable, a better fit, of cosmopolitan cut, but still clothes: but I wanted to be naked. I'd heard more music than I'd ever heard before: what I wanted was silence. I wanted to see – what is. And in this unknown region, without history, where it seemed the only memory and meaning was in the rocks and vegetation and animals and people, for a few hours, or a few days – I've no idea how long, in my memory it's timeless – I lived. Just that – lived, in the here and now. And for the first time – how can I put it, words are so unreal – the inside and the outside touched. Nothing was the same afterwards.'

The crows have finished their meagre meal and are perched on a stone waiting for something to happen. The buzzard is now very high, a tiny cross spiralling upward.

'They have perfect vision,' I say. 'Imagine what the earth looks like from up there. The eagle's view. The only creature that can look into the sun without being blinded. When it's old and its eyes grow dim, it flies up to heaven and dips itself into a fountain that renews its sight. Maybe that's where that bird is going.' The vast blue sky, and the tiny speck, still going higher. Maybe it can see Jane's train crawling towards Paris.

'Later I read about tribal initiations, in which the young man leaves the tribal territory and suffers privations until at last he sees, in a vision, his totem animal. I suffered but – maybe there are no spirits anymore – all I saw was myself. But nothing was the same afterwards.'

Sylvie has listened in silence but I've sensed her growing impatience.

'But you came back!' she cries. 'You left what you call your 'tribal territory' again, and you came back to the foreign place, years later. And what's more you didn't come alone and naked, to the unknown; you returned with a wife; and you came armed – with money, skills, ideas. Why did you come back? To colonise it?'

'No, to share it.' That's what I say. It's what I believe. But I don't know if it is true. And now it feels raw and exposed up here, on the plateau, and I can't stand the eagle's pitiless eye. I start the car and turn off and head down, between two shoulders of land, into the valley. We drive through a village with red geraniums planted in old tins, where hens scatter and dogs bite at our wheels and widow-weeded women in crumpled stockings and carpet slippers stare blankly at us as we pass. I drive slowly behind a huddle of nervous, bell-tinkling sheep being brought in to be milked. Just before we reach the river I turn off, along the rough track that leads to Edvard's place.

Chapter 5: Approaching the *feu*

I park by the other cars, the usual mix of ancient and modern, of sensible, outrageous and clapped out, reflecting the inclinations and circumstances of their owners. There is no one about. We smoke a strong joint then set off along the track towards the house, weaving dreamily. Sylvie slips her hand into mine. It is small and bony; it is the only sense I have of her, her step so light and her movements so self-contained that all I am aware of is a disembodied hand, and the faintest rustle of her long dress. Edvard was our first visitor. (No, the second – the police came first, got us out of bed, to check our papers.) He knocked on the door as we sat on our trunks, paralysed by the strangeness of it all, aware suddenly that our intentions had been focussed on getting here and, now here, we weren't sure what to do, our dreams forgotten. He opened the bottle of wine he'd brought and talked about the area, the people, his work. 'Don't worry,' he said, 'it's all strange at first. But you'll find out why you're here. I promise. Everybody does. And it's never the reason you think.' He had been a sculptor. Now his place is his work.

Before we reach the house we come to a sign:

'AU FEU'

pointing into the wood and, a few yards further in,

'Antechamber'

'What *does* Edvard have planned for us?' Sylvie, from being languid and dreamy, is now alert and excited. She skips into the wood, beyond the second sign, turns:

'Come on!' she says, beckoning. I hesitate. Standing on the track, looking into the trackless wood, dependent on signs, at midsummer when the fabric thins....

'This afternoon I almost drowned myself,' I call to her.

'This evening is not for drowning – this evening is for *flying*!' Her voice echoing among the trees, her arms stretched out, her head back, turning on the spot, the golden woodland light diaphanous around her.

'Come on!' Hands touching trunks, leaves, she walks into the wood.

'I'm coming,' and I step off the hard track onto the soft woodland floor and quickly catch up.

Trees all around us, tall and slender, columns in every direction. Above us the high shimmering canopy transmuting the light like stained glass.

'Cathedrals are dreams of forests.'

We move and everything moves. We stop and all is still; and then a single orange butterfly peels itself off a sun-splashed rock and weaves its uneven path through our vision, our lives. There are sculptures among the trees – birds with spread wings, a mighty bear, strange abstractions. Each tree is a work of art. We examine closely the patterns of bark, look up at leafy branches spiralling into the sky. Mottled sunbeams shine down upon us, warming us and – illuminating us. Sylvie glows. There are briar roses and woodland flowers. Sylvie whispers. Leaning back against a rowan, arms spread, she sighs; and the tree embraces her as one of its own. I put my arms round an oak, press the side of my face, my ear against it, feel the strength and the pulse of it, from deep spreading roots to high-reaching branches. I exhale, and the long outbreath empties me of doubt; breathe in and the long inbreath fills me with certainty. My eye follows a fissured path up the trunk, and I climb the spiral of branches to the topmost leaf, leap out and breast the buoyant, light-filled air, descend a sunbeam as lightly as dandelion seed, enter the honeyed darkness of a funnelled flower.... Trees stretch endlessly in every direction. And among all this sensation, carved stones like sudden thoughts.

We might wander at will, hand in hand, enchanted, our footsteps soft on the leaf mould, our bodies bathed in light; except that we have somewhere to go. A single bird sings close to us, a short fluting sequence of notes. It darts away and repeats the sequence some distance off. We might follow that bird; except that we have a path to follow. A path not marked on the ground but indicated by signs: here a prayer flag, there a painted leopard flicking its tail, further on a manifesto painted on cloth: "Culture is our attempt simultaneously to escape from what is, forward, and to recover what was, backward. Hence the conflict. Nature is simpler. But to live in nature, you must let it be". A jewelled snake hanging from a branch, its red tongue flicking out and in. A motionless fox – staring at us, its triangular face a blank mask – that suddenly trots away, its fine brush parallel to the ground. We jump, then laugh at the joke of it.

We follow our path, weaving as unevenly and as apparently randomly as that butterfly, knowing that it too is responding to signals; and glimpsing through the trees other signs and knowing there are many paths and many other people in this wood, although we see no one.

And then the vegetation becomes denser, the path narrows. We pass beneath an old pub sign:

'HMS ENDEAVOUR'

I lead in single file, the path is so narrow. From being high and light the canopy has come down towards us and thickened, so that now it is a roof close above our heads, a tangle of intertwined branches and leaves cutting out the light. And instead of trees on either side, now there are banks of earth, rising as we move forward until they are head high and sealed across, over our heads, by tangled roots. Now I'm walking through the earth, and the air is cool, and smells of damp earth and mushrooms and roots, and there is darkness, and silence, and I feel the mass of earth on either side of me, beneath me, and the almost intolerable weight of earth above my head; and yet I am safe, might walk along this tunnel forever, not seeing, not hearing, not touching: 'Sylvie?' No reply, of course – sounds do not travel through a vacuum; I am alone.

Walking, I swell to fill the intolerable emptiness of the world all around me, to fill the world and become the world, and am at first exhilarated, and then sickened. Walking, I shrink until I am a spore, attentive but inert, waiting. Walking, I become once more human-sized, aware of the floor beneath my feet and the walls and roof close around me, and the sound of my breathing, and the presence of Sylvie close behind me, and of my precise lineaments, the outline, the surface, the extent of my body, its well-knitted-ness and precise functioning, the location of my thoughts within my head.

Ahead there is a light, long and thin, like a shining pendant sword, that grows as I walk towards it, that illuminates the strange signs on the walls, that becomes a portal between this dark world and that illuminated one, a portal between two pillars that is so narrow that in order to pass through it I must thin myself to a single atom's width, so that I can pass through the shining sword, cross the threshold; and then re-form, as a voice whispers: 'Realisation', entire, on the other side.

Senses assailed. Warmth, such bathing warmth. Sounds, the singing and chirping of birds, distant laughter, the sighs of breeze-moved leaves. Scents, of orange blossom, honeysuckle, pine. Shape and colour: an expanse of emerald velvet grass, flowered like a mediaeval tapestry; an immense chestnut tree, with a strong trunk and a vast umbrella of a million translucent leaves, on one side its branches merging into the wood, on the other arching over, as sure and elegant as flying buttresses, to touch the house that is as solid as a rock and as domestic as cheese. And light....

For within this frame, of grass and tree and house, is the river, below us, curving between limestone cliffs, a golden river turned gold by the enormous golden sun that hangs between cliffs themselves turned to gold by the light reflected up from the river of gold. As children we stand, fingers entwined. Edvard strides up, grinning, delighted at our astonishment.

'That's quite a trip,' I say, shaking his hand. He embraces us, says:

'Welcome – until the true mysteries return we have to make our own mysteries.

'But you're only just beginning – don't stop now, go on,' he points to the river, 'go on, bathe in gold – it's Midsummer Eve – bathe in gold!' and he leads us across the emerald grass to the beginning of the path down to the river, waves us on down the path.

We pass others returning, exchange greetings, but when we reach the river we are alone. At last, standing by the river, watching it flow, speech returns.

'I feel like a kaleidoscope,' I say, 'that's been shaken, and shaken, then shaken again.'

'He's a true shaman,' Sylvie says quietly. 'Inside I feel empty and clean. Now I need to swim, to strip off this old skin.'

I take off my sandals and walk across the warm clinted limestone pavement to the water's edge. The river flows steadily. The sun has begun to redden, the shadows are turning purple, the sky becoming mauve. Spread out on two great boulders are costumes and towels. Chalked on the stone is the single word: 'definition'. We change quickly.

The bathing place is an inlet beneath the cliff. The pool is very deep, its smooth stone sides disappearing into green depths. The water is very clear, very cold. I walk in, at first shocked by its coldness, then enclosed by it, my hot skin soothed by the water, my body shaped by it. I swim with long, easy strokes, dipping my head into and out of the water. Sylvie has climbed up the cliff. I see her above me as I lie on my back, brace myself as she plunges down towards me, feel the shock wave as she knifes into the water between my legs, watch her black and ivory form arrow down.

I follow her. We twist and turn around each other, naiad and otter, now descending into dark depths, now speeding upwards towards light and bursting into the warm, soft air.

Then we swim separately. In the depths I see a spring, Pieter's *résurgence*, bubbling into the pool; at the margin I see the silty river slide powerfully by: but I do not touch it. Swimming on the surface, looking down, I imagine letting go and sinking slowly to the bottom, watching the flickering light fade as I sink, lying on the soft sand staring up until something irrevocable happens. 'No, that's old stuff,' I tell myself, and swim vigorously until the feeling fades.

I lie on my back on the surface of the pool, at its centre, cold depths below me, warm air above, content to be where they meet. Maybe that's it. Maybe that's all there is. I swim to shore, climb out onto the warm rock, and lie in the sun, eyes closed.

I hear Sylvie sit down beside me. I hear fumblings of clothes. She sighs. I open my eyes. She has pulled the black costume down to her waist and she is lying on her back, arms stretched above her head, breasts tumbled either side of her firm chest, nipples pointing to the sky, absorbing the last rays of the sun. My eyes follow the lines of her, from her strewn fair hair to the tangle of black at her hips.

'It would be so easy, wouldn't it?' I say quietly.

'No, I don't think it would,' she says, eyes closed. 'It might be nice, and it might be good, but,' she opens her eyes and looks across at me, 'it won't be now.'

'But…'

'It's not just a matter of opportunity, you know. Is your life that accidental? Because if you've been planning this, I want nothing to do with it. We've brought each other here, that's what matters, that's the moon; us fucking would just be the finger. As for the future – who knows? Come on, I want to prepare myself before the bonfire is lit.'

Chapter 6: *Le feu St Jean*

We are standing in a semi-circle, around the unlit bonfire, looking out over the river, waiting for the sun to set. Edvard holds a burning torch in his right hand. As the red sun touches the river, he begins to speak:

'This is a special day, a day when we can renew old friendships and make new ones. When we, who most of the time lead isolated lives, can get together, share ideas and information, come up with more and better ways to cooperate. Because we're going to have to cooperate to survive – forget Darwin, remember Kropotkin! We each have our personal reason for being here, a personal vision, and to be strong we need to share these visions.

'And it is a time when we can remind ourselves why we're here, why we have come from different places, different former lives, to this abandoned corner of Europe. And it is this – this is the place we can do what we have to do, become who we are.' The sun sinks into the river.

'But there is more to it than that. We don't want just to escape from a culture that has had its day and is going down the pan – we want to show them a way of life that will work, a sustainable, ecologically-viable life, in which human relationships and art aren't peripheral, they're central. They call us *marginaux* – we're not, we are one of the new centres. Let us light a beacon to show them!'

The sun has gone. It is the night before Midsummer Day. The buzzard begins its long descent. Edvard is about to plunge the torch into the heap of sticks but then he turns and flings it into the air. Sylvie leaps high, catches it and, her face lit by the flames, radiant, plunges it into the heart of the pyre. We applaud, cheer, embrace those around us, wish each other well. 'Light catches fire,' Edvard murmurs, then out loud:

'Food! Drink! Let's enjoy ourselves!'

There are about fifty people here. At first, after extravagant greetings and embraces there is awkwardness; the fire is so small and the sunset so magnificent that there is nothing to draw us together. People stay in the couples or groups they came in, or soliloquise silently. But as the sunset fades and darkness spreads across the sky, as the fire burns up and lamps and torches (no electricity tonight) are lit, as the night closes around us and the stars begin to spangle the dome of the heavens, people come to the fire, relax, separate and mix, become involved in conversations. Expectations are gradually forgotten, the unexpected happily accepted. The *feu St Jean* is under way.

'Kris! Come and settle an argument!' Michael pulls me over and introduces me to his friends from England. Michael and Rosie always have lots of friends over during the summer:

'Willy says that Richard Fariña was married to Caroline Hester. I say it was Mimi Baez.'

'Both. He was married to Mimi when he died. And what's the greatest novel of the sixties? *Been Down so Long...*'

'*...it Looks like Up to Me!*'

'No, it's got to be *Gravity's Rainbow*,' Willy says.

'*Trout Fishing in America*,' Rosie says firmly. I sidle away, leave them to their nostalgia.

André is holding forth about the Tibetan diaspora being as significant as the Jewish:

'As with the Jews, an intense, inward-looking, religion-centred people have been driven out of their homeland – in this case the land of MU, centre of spirituality – by a materialistic invader. They will carry their religion and infect us with a new spirituality – for we are as unprotected against spirituality as the American Indians were against measles. As the Jews were the agents of the Piscean Age, so the Tibetans will be the agents of the Aquarian.' Marie-Claire listens patiently

38

with the others, looking respectful, loyal and bored. She flashes me a quick smile. André holds out his hand as I pass, we shake, he doesn't miss a beat.

Fred is sitting cross-legged, drawing the plans for a composting toilet for the serious young couple with the baby who have just bought twenty acres nearby:

'It's important to remember that it works aerobically not anaerobically,' squinting seriously at them through taped-together spectacles. 'Conventional sewage systems are anaerobic, hence the smell. In fact one of the central differences between alternative and conventional biological technology is that ours is aerobic based, theirs is anaerobic....'

Jean-Luc and the group of young French who rent "Carbonnière" are chortling over their latest supermarket scam: you pay for a trolleyful of goods, empty it into the car, refill the trolley with exactly the same goods plus a packet of biscuits, at the checkout you show the receipt and pay for the biscuits; half price shopping. It joins their 'hire a car and swap the engine' trick as a way of getting something without paying for it. How do I feel? They collect State handouts when they can, spend lots of time working out schemes to cheat big institutions, are always confronting, always getting busted. Are they freeloaders, or revolutionaries? Are these acts of guerrilla warfare against a political and economic system they want to destroy, or selfish acts that we have to pay for? It depends on where you put your politics. I realise, uncomfortably, that I want neither to confront nor to conform to the political-economic system; I want to be invisible to it....

George and Amanda walk by, their five children following like goslings. They live in a tiny barn, without electricity, a hundred yards from water. Their garden always fails and they live out of the local shop on the considerable family allowance the French pay to large families. His occupation in his passport is 'poet'.

39

I look around for Sylvie but she has disappeared, so I get a bottle of wine and some food and sit by the fire and look around. What do we have in common?

We are all *arrivés*, *installés*, strangers, incomers to a region which has known only emigration for hundreds of years, with a population less than half what it was in the fourteenth century – look at the number of empty buildings, at the hillside terraces, once cultivated, now buried under scrubby woodland. We are going against the trends by emphasising self-sufficiency in a community which is becoming ever more tied into the market economy.

Our self-sufficiency derives from ideas learned in the cities. We proclaim a modern self-sufficiency, based on scientific theories: the locals remember subsistence as back-breaking toil and grinding poverty. We say – ours is a way to a richer life: they remember shortages, privation, poverty, and see money as the only enrichment. We say – your life as peasants has been so hard because of politics, because you were exploited: they say – okay, it's because of politics – but who's going to change the politics?

And the locals are not here tonight; they're at home watching television, or at a dance listening to electric music. And we, with the electricity switched off, are an island, imagining the outside world away. But aeroplane lights blink among the stars, tractor headlights shine in the distance, cars accelerate noisily along the riverside road, and a train draws into Paris-Austerlitz, and a lone figure descends… don't look at the flames twisting, stretching, disconnecting, disappearing: concentrate, stare into the fire, seek your future in the white-hot stillness inside the leaping flames….

'What do you see?'

'Hendrika! I didn't realised you were here. No Pieter? Sit down, have some wine.' She is Dutch, a handsome, middle-aged woman, capable, tired. 'Flames, just flames. What do you think, about Jane going?'

'I think she was very sensible. And you think, what – that she's weak, she's betrayed you?'

'It was the only thing to do. We were blocking each other so. But I think maybe she's betraying La Balme, our ideal.'

'Perhaps it isn't her ideal.'

'Perhaps she has no ideals.'

'Steady, you've jumped a lot of steps there. Men are very good at having ideals – or ideas or fantasies or delusions – and dragging women into situations in which the women have to do the coping. And people do stupid things when they love someone. If they're lucky they realise how stupid and do something about it before they are irretrievably harmed, or all their bitterness is heaped on the loved one. You think she's being weak and selfish. In fact she's giving your lives a chance – she's giving you a chance.'

'To do what?'

'Only you know that. Maybe to examine your reasons for coming here. Maybe to be alone. Maybe to do something. Only you know – and if you don't, you have to find out.'

'Pieter says I have to make a home.'

'Maybe, maybe not. Hey, don't look so serious!'

'I want to get it right.' But all I want, at this moment, is for her to wrap her middle-aged arms around me and bury me in her bosom.

'Where's Pieter?' I ask. She looks across at the gorge and the cliffs, black against the sky:

'Out there. Looking for the cave. He thinks maybe the midsummer sunset will give him a clue.'

'The cave?'

'You don't know about the cave? Ask him to tell you some-time. In South Africa, when he was young, he found a cave. Now, after so many years in the Netherlands, he's sure there's another one, here.'

'What do you think?'

41

'The Dutch don't have caves,' she says, smiling.

'Maybe they should.'

'We don't have much choice. But maybe it's why we went to South Africa, and the East Indies, and South America. And the Aveyron, of course.' We laugh, then sit quietly watching the flames lick round the branches, the heart of the fire whiten. I feel safe with Hendrika. I ask:

'Are there different sorts of fire?'

'There is fire that burns, fire that consumes, fire that purifies. The fire that falls incessantly on Capaneus in Dante's hell is surely different to the fire of Donne's "Oh burn me O Lord, with a fiery zeal, of thee and thy house, which doth in eating heal". But maybe the fire is always the same, the difference lies in the thing being burned. Maybe it depends whether you are ore or wood. Or flesh. And which you want to be.'

'Thoreau writes: "I ask to be melted. You can only ask of the metals that they be tender to the fire that melts them. To nought else can they be tender".'

'Mmm,' she says, staring into the fire, lost in thought for a while, a peaceful time, then says sharply:

'But stop asking me such interesting, irrelevant questions and go and find someone young to talk to; go and *do* something! I'll be going soon anyway – we've a pregnant cow that can't be left too long.'

'Thanks for the chat.'

'Come over for a meal, soon. Pieter likes to see you.' I heave myself up and leave her staring into the fire.

*   *   *

Now the party is in full swing. Edvard plays the accordion and we dance energetically. There is a circle dance of changing partners, and when Marie-Claire whirls past she whispers 'see you soon', smiles and is gone. There is no sign of Sylvie.

When the dance finishes I drift away, to the edge, and look around. Two figures stand close together by a tree, silhouetted, talking earnestly. The French outlaws and the English trendies are in vigorous conversation. A looser group waits in gentle anticipation as someone tunes a guitar. The wine is singing in my head and my body feels good from the swim. The evening air is soft on my arms.

The bonfire is burning well now. How carefully Edvard has combined his bonfire ingredients, like an alchemist: cherry and apple for their scent, pine for the sparks, holly for quickness, ash for longevity; and the aromatics special to this night: thyme, rue and penny-royal. The smells of the bonfire smoke mix with the night scents of flowers and green vegetation and the resinous pine torches.

Shadows flicker extravagantly in torch- and fire-light. The Milky Way bands the sky, and the newly risen moon is a pendant pearl. There is the whisper of air in the trees, the murmur of conversation, the sound of guitar strings being plucked and strummed hesitantly. I can feel the still, dark woods all around us, the flowing river not far off, the rocks still warm.

It is a night on which I can begin to remember, and believe in once more, my dreams. It is a fine night, Midsummer Eve, to let all thought chatter, then fall silent, to allow a quieter voice, so often unheard, to be heard.

And then Marie-Claire begins to sing. Alone and unaccompanied, eyes closed, her voice at first flat, cracked, limping earthbound; we shuffle self-consciously: and then suddenly taking off, as if mirroring up from reflection to reflection of flickering light, from eye to decoration, along boughs to the highest leaf and then up with a rush to those still lights so far above us, across the face of the moon and from star to star. I don't understand the words she sings, but all I hear is 'why?' When she ends there is silence and then, as we collect ourselves, murmurs of appreciation.

Edvard sings, to a chunky guitar accompaniment, a lively song with many verses. From dreaming I'm suddenly wide awake as I listen to the unfolding story of the boy and the girl on Midsummer Eve. The girl says – dance with me, leap over the fire with me, unite with me, for our union tonight will be magic and blessed. The boy says – no, I don't know you, you might be a fairy, might give me ass's ears; tonight I must stand alone and await the revelation. And so he stands, proud of his vigil. But there is no revelation, and in the morning, when he searches for her she is gone, and the fire cold ashes. An old man now, each year he keeps the vigil, and sees only her face in the midsummer moon, and hears only her voice in in the crackling air echoing 'why not?'

Even as the sound of the guitar dies away and the applause begins, I am turning and heading away from the fire and into the wood. For suddenly I know why I am here, what today has been leading to. I know that she is there, waiting for me. I know Sylvie is at the centre of the labyrinth, waiting. 'Why not?' rings in my head; 'yes' I say, and plunge on. In spite of the dark I know exactly where I am going, guided by the trees – here a holly blocking my path, there a broom pointing the way, barriers, tunnels, avenues – and the attraction of Sylvie.

I burst through the final barrier between us – and am teetering on the edge of a long drop to the river. I curse myself for my unseemly haste, for not having watched carefully for the signs.

I move quietly now, observant, and soon I am in Edvard's labyrinth. And now I can feel her: when I follow a path away from her, I feel myself tighten and grow cold; as I approach her, I open and warm. Lights ahead. My heart beating fast.

I arrive at the small clearing at the centre of the labyrinth. Sylvie is there, I know. Sylvie is there, I see. Not alone, waiting. With someone. Being fucked.

Chapter 7: Midsummer dawn

I wake suddenly, stare up into black emptiness, happily empty; feel memories slowly precipitate in my mind; begin to sift them. Sylvie at the centre of the labyrinth, lit by flickering torches, leaning forward, her hands white knuckled, braced on the omphalos, her hanging breasts out of her dress shuddering with each impact, her skirt up over her white hips; Jean-Jacques, dark hands on those white hips, thrusting into her from behind. He bearded and yellow eyed, hairy buttocked. She pale victim – and yet grunting at each thrust, squirming on him, pressing back onto him when he is fully buried, gasping 'oh yes', 'oh more', 'you bastard', 'oh more'. Thrust 'bitch!', shudder 'bastard!', thrust 'bitch!', shudder 'bastard!', thrust 'bitch, Oh God, Oh Jesus, Oh Hell, oh....' 'Stay in, I'm coming, stay in, stay in!' I turned and staggered away as they sank entwined next to the navel stone.

I had seen – what? Two people, a couple, fucking. But I wanted, as I rushed away, through the grasping vegetation back towards the fire, I wanted it to be more than that: a mythological rape; a sacred ritual for which, if I had been discovered observing, I would have been hideously done to death. And when I reached the edge of the wood and looked at the scene around the bonfire, the flames leaping and the figures dancing, the couples standing and lying clasped and still, the cries and whoops and the brandished bottles, I saw an orgy, and looked around for the golden calf.

Then Rosie took me by the arm and sat me near the fire and gave me some wine; and the fire and the wine warmed me, and in the light I saw smiling faces, people dancing enjoyably, talking animatedly, good naturedly enjoying themselves. And after all, Sylvie and Jean-Jacques were lovers. And after all, I had come as her companion, her paladin, not her lover.

And so, gradually, I got drunk and began to enjoy the party. I remember dancing. I remember, in a quiet time, playing blues guitar to sprawled figures. I remember Edvard leading us in a long, serpentine dance, carrying torches, through the woods, to the river, along the tunnel, around the labyrinth. I remember us rolling the wheel around the fire, and dancing hand in hand around the fire, the joined serpent, and leaping over it, time after time, all of us, seven times. I remember that suddenly Jean-Jacques and Sylvie were among the leaping figures, and looking so splendid and happy I found myself embracing them both, saying 'sure' when Sylvie asked to borrow the car, giving them my car keys. I remember hugging people as they left, wishing them well, and, when they had all gone, crawling into this sleeping bag and falling asleep.

The memories fade. The trees are black. The embers glow faintly. All is still. So that was Midsummer Eve. And this is Midsummer Day.

I feel foolish that I had hoped to find a solution so simply, imagined that I had found the answer to a question I haven't even formulated yet. Yesterday, enjoyable, fun, was a trip; the journey is only just beginning. There are no answers here. The answers, if there are any, whatever they may be, lie over that ridge, in the saucer of land in which our house stands, in what I do there, and how I do it.

The memories have faded, and I feel deliciously empty. I slip out of the sleeping bag, look around, and jump when I see that I'm not alone. Edvard, in full lotus, eyes open but sightless, white. I bow to him. I taste the bonfire ash, rub a little on me, then make my way carefully down to the river, my path lit by the moon. There are delicate scents, of cut hay, elderflowers, and others too fugitive and subtle to name.

47

They waft around me like silk.

The broad, deep river moves noiselessly, as if on rollers, the fractured moon reflecting on its surface. I kick something that tinkles away. A small bottle. I write 'Are you there? I am here' on a scrap of paper, put it in the bottle, screw on the cap. I take off my sandals and step carefully from stone to stone, cool now, until I am well out in the river. I can feel the surge of the water around the rock, and coolness rising up from its turbulence. The river out here is active, noisy, turning, grinding like a machine. I trail my hand in its darkness and the water plucks at it. I bathe my face and neck, and drink. Each mouthful sharpens my senses. I launch the bottle, watch it jam against a rock, spin free and at last disappear into the night.

I see it floating down the deep, dark canyon; by the red walls of Albi; over the green and ochre plain; past the great wine city; across the stormy Bay; around the Arthurian cliffs; along the ship-busy cold grey Channel; and up the deserted Thames, to tap, tap, tap against Greenwich Steps, for Jane's hand to reach down, pluck it out, read the message....

*   *   *

By the glowing embers of the fire I perform the tai chi practice. In the slow performing of the one hundred and eight forms, the best thing that happens is the emptying. My feet – "bubbling springs" – grounded, Antaeus-like; the crown of my head – "thousand headed lotus" – attached by a thread to the pole of heaven; my attention focussed on the *tan t'ien* – "seat of heaven" – the body's centre of gravity, its earth centre, source of the chi power, three finger-widths below the navel, midway front to back. "Intention directs the chi, chi directs the body."

A sequence of slow movements, always moving, always on the point of being still, filling and emptying, inward and out-

ward, gathering and expressing; a pattern not of differentiation but of alternation; opposites always, at some point,
becoming the other. The names of the forms make of the
practice a poetic journey: crane cools its wings; strum the
lute; repulse monkey; look for the golden needle at the
bottom of the sea; wave hands like clouds (no beginning, no
end); part the wild horse's mane; grip the tiger's ears; snake
slides down into water; golden cock stands on one leg; and,
at last: embrace tiger, return to mountain. Embrace tiger,
return to mountain.

The moon sets. I am empty, without thought. My skin, my
senses connect outside and inside; I can look out, and in –
which is which? It doesn't matter. Enclose right fist in left
hand, feet close, bow once more to Edvard. He hasn't
moved. I turn to the path through the wood that leads over
the ridge. I hear a single note, low, continuous. The first light
shows in the sky.

*　　　　*　　　　*

But down here there is only blackness. And silence. So
silent that I feel as if my ears are blocked with wax; yet when
I move, my few clothes make enough noise to waken the
dead. I have to walk carefully, for I am enveloped in black,
suffused by it, there is only blackness, a thick black so close
that I reach out to push it aside, reach up to pull it from my
eyes; but my hand closes on nothing. Around me solid black,
above me depthless black in which the stars are mere spots of
less-black. I might be walking on the spot, for I have no sense
of motion, no sense of space in front of me nor behind me,
just outside and within. I find my way by touch, of feet, of
hands, of that sense of changing air pressure against objects
the blind have.

I'm approaching a farm, I can smell it, Lacombe's farm.
The rich, sour smell of the pig sty, the mustiness of rabbits,

49

the oily fleeces of sheep. The dogs are silent, for they cannot sense me; I am a wraith, a collection of senses without physical existence. I approach the warmth and smells and solidity and pass and leave them behind; they are my only relativity, my only certainty.

I walk on, my other senses tinglingly active although my eyes are blind, so that shapes, forms, including my own, are ever changing.

And then I am aware of light, a faint light that is hardly light, rather a first absence, in places, of dark. Darkness is divided; there is darkness and not-darkness: now there is location. I emerge from the wood. More light, and now I can see shapes; the hill against the sky, the dark wood and the less-dark field. And I too now have shape.

As I look the light increases and I can see planes; the nearer hills separate from the further, the solitary tree from the wood beyond. The world has the simplicity of a child's theatre. Sound, the first sound, a bird's tentative essay, just a few trial notes, and then silence; as I cross the dark field a lark springs, its song rising invisibly in the dark air, hangs, rises, hangs, rises, like a flag being run up a flagpole.

More light, and another change: now there is form – one side of a tree darker, the other lighter; some leaves catch the light, others are untouched; the tree has body. I have form, and the closer hills, and the hummocky field, and the trees of the wood. And with form comes life, as if the plane shapes have swelled with breath, life has been breathed into them; and with breath comes breathing and with breathing movement and with movement, change.

The land is coming slowly to life. The time of the undead is past. I can feel this life around me and inside me as I too, having grown into form, now feel the breath of life inside me. I swell with it. I examine my hand, curious at its new solidity. The closed-up daisies in the wet grass at my newly solid feet are bright pearls.

I walk on: time, I imagine, passes; and colour comes into the world – a hint of green in the grey hillside, a touch of blue in the grey sky. Now there can be harmony; or discord. More birds sing. Light is pouring out in waves, spreading across the sky, falling like rain, bringing everything to life. It catches on blades of grass, on leaves, on my skin. Now there is a play of light, light in motion, and enough light for every object, every part of every object to differentiate. Surfaces have texture. Now: there is a moment when there is enough light for every thing to be itself, while still sufficient dark for each to retain the memory of its common origin in black, a harmony in memory. I want this moment to stay. I want to cry 'enough!'

But light pours out prodigiously, prodigally, promiscuously, its single purpose to banish darkness and the very memory of dark from the earth. I hold out for a moment, for another moment: but am overwhelmed and everything suddenly brightens perceptibly and the moment is gone and differentiation has become separation. The sky is all blue, the grass all green, and neither contains anything of the other. Such sadness. Darkness gone.

But the brief regret passes and I let go and the waves of light lift me, waves lifting a surfer, lift me and carry me and fill me with their energy. The superabundance of light tickles me. The woods are a delirium of chattering, cawing, fluting, cooing, cuckooing song. This is a world alive, noisy, brimming and overflowing with light and energy and life.

I am at the top now, on the plateau, at the top of the world. And:

The sun rises. A fizzing, molten ball, dazzling and immense, heaving up from beyond the rim of the world to preside over the domain it rules. I fall on my knees. I have to. I am alone in a world empty of man and his creatures. I am the first man, or the last man – it doesn't matter which – and all this is for me.

The plateau stretches away into the distance, in ridges of ever paler blue-grey. The sky is a vast blue concavity over my head. The big valley to my left, steep and abrupt, is this morning filled with mist as thick as snow, that I could walk on if I chose. And there – it is almost too much – on the white mist (the sun behind me) am I, magnified, haloed in rainbow colours, nimbused, like a vision of a saint…. Almost too much – but I know it is not me. It is my image. My presence enables it to happen. My eye here, in me, registers it. I can live with that. And as for walking on the cloud, of course I can't. And if I could, it is not my way. This is my way, along the ridge above a smaller valley. My tiny shadow on the other side of the valley accompanies me as I walk, waves to me when I wave. I am a flea on the back of a giant elephant. I am tiny. And yet, now I know, today I contain multitudes.

Below me the village where I worked in the pig factory. There is the breeze block factory, ugly and drab. Above it the house the *patron* is building, a Spanish villa with a marble terrace and concrete statues, a half-finished swimming pool, each new extravagance paid for by our labour. There he is, pacing restlessly, checking his watch, looking up from the sunless valley to the light above the ridge to urge the sun to rise faster, for the working day to begin, so he can re-commence turning time into money.

I stand up here, on top of the world, possessor of all I survey, wave to him, urge him to come up and join me. He squints at me uncomprehendingly then, head down, resumes his pacing. I shake my head and walk on, my steps as light as if I am walking on hatching eggs, doing no harm.

At last it is the place to leave the ridge and scramble down into the little valley below our house. At the bottom I stop for a while by the stream, watching the water trickle between sharp rocks, slide over smooth stones.

I walk up the path through the chestnut trees, the leaf mould soft under my feet, foxgloves and columbines among the trees, the canopy pale green with the sun shining though casting a dappled shadow. Birds flit. I reach our meadow, enter through the gate at the bottom between the tall ash trees. I stop by the hen house, the hens safely put away by Gaston in my absence. I listen to their soft croonings and shufflings. I open the door and little heads, beady-eyed, peer out from the dusty darkness and fusty warmth. I broadcast a handful of grain, watch it patter onto the grass, hear it, then step back as the rufous creatures tumble out, scrabbling over each other, pecking sharply at the grains and flowing away from the house like rusty water. A buzzard wheels silently overhead. I leave the meadow through the little gate and enter the hamlet.

What was once a hamlet of half a dozen peasant families now comprises one farm of a hundred hectares, our little property of two hectares, and the smoke-dark cabin at the edge where the strange old woman lives with her stranger son. The neighbours' dogs come running up, eager to bark, then recognise me and trot back to sprawl vacantly in the dust. An alarm clock rings. It rings and rings, is beginning to run down before it is silenced. My bag and record are on the step. Good old Sylvie.

I go in, close the door on the hamlet, open all the doors and windows onto the sunlit garden, put on the record and lie down on the soft sofa. After I've heard the first few notes of the first track I smile and say, to the small bird pecking on the sun-warm step:

'Dylan's back.'

Chapter 8: A new day

I lie on the sofa and listen to the record through, then again. Dylan's back. I've waited years, through record after record, since *John Wesley Harding*, eight years, of disappointments and false dawns, waiting for the kick, the scrawny hand to grab me by the scruff of the neck, for the man, as he's done so many times before, to change reality.

I go to the door and stand in the sunlight and look out over the garden, the valley, the hills, clear and bright on this midsummer morning and now more alive in my eyes than it has ever been, because of the songs that are already weaving their way through me. What happened yesterday and last night is a dream; very clear, but a dream. This is real. This is where it will happen, and I have my first ally, this record, these songs, this vision. Dylan is on my side. The summer's record, the carrier wave.

I hear the heavy splash as Madame Bonafet throws a bowl of water from the top of their steps onto the cobbles. I hear the drag of Monsieur Bonafet's sandals as he makes his pigeon-toed way to the *bergerie*, the rising clamour of the sheep, his shouts and curses as he pulls the half-door shut behind him, the rattle of the pail as he lifts it down from the wall, the quieting to a murmuration of sheep noise as he squats on his three-legged stool and begins to milk. I can imagine, feel, the suffocating sheep heat in there. When he's finished he will go to the cow shed and milk a cow and take the warm milk to the house for breakfast.

I turn back into the house, comfortably cool, and walk slowly round, to see what it looks like when I am on my own. It is the bare structure of a house: bare stone walls, exposed oak beams and chestnut boards, the wooden ceiling of this room the floor of the room above, and beneath the boards under my feet a cellar half dug into the earth, a *cave*. I like the bareness. I like to be able to see the structure of the house; which are the load-bearing walls, where the beams are, and the rafters, the size of the lintels.

In our flat in London all structure was concealed and we lived inside a lining within a lining, where there were only surfaces and no sense of forces – of tension, compression, lateral thrust, the ever-presence of gravity. We lived on the surfaces of things. We stuck our pictures onto paint we had brushed over thicknesses of wallpaper pasted to plaster-skim that coated cement-render floated onto brick. We lived muffled lives; our feet on rugs over carpets on underlay covering linoleum over newspaper on concrete. Carpets are unnecessary – slippers are carpets that appear under your feet as you set your feet down. And the draughts that come up through the floor will warm you if, as the people here used to, you keep your animals in the cellar – a living, breathing hypocaust that stokes itself, comforts you with its domesticity.

Only when I know this structure will I want to begin to clothe its nakedness. There is too much decoration. "Before we adorn our houses with beautiful objects", Thoreau writes, "the walls must be stripped, and our lives must be stripped, and beautiful housekeeping and beautiful living laid for a foundation".

I like the bareness. And I like the old *cuisinière* that cooks our food, heats our water, proves and bakes our bread, heats our kitchen, at the cost of a few sticks and pine cones. I repaired it myself with fireclay I dug out from where the blacksmith told me it was, unused now, a bank deep in the woods, pulling aside the vegetation, digging.

I like the handpump that draws water by syphonic action up from the dark well fed by a spring (a *source*), the water splashing out to the rhythm of my pumping instead of gushing, as it does from taps, under pressure from afar. There is too much pressure from afar.

I am happy to shower outside under a watering can rose connected to a length of black hosepipe coiling across the wall, fed from a black polythene bag; although the water is sometimes too hot. I pee into a pot and shit in a bucket, the urine an excellent activator for the compost heap; and human excrement has, after all, fertilised Chinese vegetable plots for millennia, (often fed their pigs). But I am more fastidious – I compost it, all the bacteria incinerating in the vegetable furnace. I want to bend once more the linear into a circle – for isn't space curved, and hasn't the absolute notion of progress been shown to be pathetically relative?

I'm touched by our homely touches. Our rugs and wall hangings. The selection of records and the carefully chosen books. The flowers in the expensive vase bought in a moment of madness. (Too few moments of madness.) The little paintings we did for each other one winter's evening. I look at the battered old sofa. I lay my hand on the soft, feather bed. Surely we should have been happy here, if we had it in us to be happy together?

Of course there's work to do. The roof leaks – it has been too long neglected, it needs replacing. Jane won't come back until it is done. It is the big thing I thought I would return straight from Albi station to do. In the storm a couple of weeks ago, while I was still working at the pig factory, the rain poured in as through a colander, while Jane's old friends from college were here, stopping over on their way south on holiday, sympathising with her, looking accusingly at me. Shown up. The last straw. I should do the roof. I should start today.

But I don't want to, not now. I want to do something for me, something new. *Blood on the Tracks* confirms it – something new. And I don't want to work in the house, because there's too much of *us* here, too much conflict, too much bad feeling. Bothered by their opinion – what do they, comfy, trapped civil servants, know? Damn Jane, she's held me back, she's half-hearted, she refuses to commit herself. I'm glad she's gone, glad to be rid of her, glad to be on my own. I need to get out.

*   *   *

I sit on the low mound in the garden, where I like to sit and ponder. It is a peaceful place. We stood here when we first came to look.

The place was run-down and neglected, not just from being empty, but from the time the Combons lived here. At some point the heart had gone out of the place, so that even while they lived and worked here it was neglected, starved of energy, sad. "They ate crows", was Gaston's dismissive comment. The children left. When the old man died, and after the fire, the mother moved to her son's flat in Albi. They sold most of the land to the Bonafets, and the house was left empty. At first they returned each year to prune the vines and make the wine – whether from force of habit or the residue of a response to seasonal influences, I don't know. Then they stopped even that. In the cellar there are giant barrels of rotten wine. The place had a worn, broken-down feel, a fatalism, like a horse with a broken leg, waiting.

We looked round – the house, dusty, cobwebby, full of rubbish, a wine-stained glass still on the table; the overgrown meadow; the unpruned, grass-choked vines. We sat on this mound and Jane said "what do you see?" And I said – and meant it:

"I see a solid, traditional house in need of care and attention. I see it repaired and made self-sufficient with solar panels and a wind generator, composting toilet and rainwater storage. I see a good-sized garden thriving on compost, crop rotation, companion planting. I see two goats in the meadow, and hens scratching under newly-planted fruit trees, two cuts of hay for winter forage, the fringing trees

57

managed for fuel and timber. I see the vines revived, giving us wine, juice – which we can preserve by sterilising – and raisins dried in a solar drier. I see us standing there, side by side, hoes and rakes in our hands like pikes, new pioneers bringing a new energy, which is a marriage of the best of the traditional ways and new ideas for self-sufficiency, to a place abandoned because it was marginal to our urban-based economy. I see us converting what is marginal now into a place that will be central to the new world that comes into being when the old order inevitably collapses."

This was what I had brought from my studies in the city and my work on the buildings. And this was the vision that was so vivid to me that she too could see it.

But there is another vision. Does it grow within the first, like a worm in an apple, the worm of doubt, the devil's whispering voice as the Christian might say? Or does the existence of the first vision bring it into being, as everything brings into being its opposite – the Oriental pattern? Or maybe it is a previous vision, one that existed before, often submerged (and overwhelmed in the exclusiveness of my marriage to Jane) but always there...? I don't know.

All I know is that after we buy the place, and the problems begin – no money, so I have to work long hours at the pig factory leaving Jane on her own; isolation numbing us by degrees; our growing realisation of the size of our task, and the inevitable setbacks... in spring, digging the clay soil when it's too wet and watching it set to red concrete when it dries; the paralysing heat of high summer, the flies; Jane finding our first four tiny chickens headless in the meadow, victims of some invisible ever-present monster, the day of the geek; the invasion of rats at harvest time, their fat bodies slap slap slapping down the stairs in front of us, staring at us from the centre of the table; the featureless white of midwinter and a growing numbness... the first vision progressively fades and the other commensurately develops.

When things go wrong and she nestles against me and says "what do you see?", I can describe again the first vision, but each time with greater difficulty. The last time was the day before she said she was leaving. She asked "what do you see?" I told her. But I was telling her not what I could see but what I remembered seeing; she knew, shrank from me, and even as we came together in a last desperate act of lovemaking, there was a gulf between us. In my silence and withdrawal the other vision has been developing, becoming more real....

A tower. A tower made with my own hands, whose walls connect the inside and outside: filtering, refining, intensifying what is outside inward; amplifying and radiating what is inside out. A tower whose anticlockwise winding steps I climb to the wonder of the countless stars, the coldness of space, and the contemplation of ultimate meaning; and whose clockwise spiral I descend into inchoate darkness and the mystery and the heat of the root of being....

The tower is here, in the place I am sitting, on this very spot. And I must build it. Beginning now.

PART II:

BUILDING THE TOWER

Chapter 1: The idea

I level the site, laying a long board edgeways, my spirit level on top, this way and that until in all directions it is parallel to the surface of the earth, the curve of the glass tube mimicking the earth's curvature, and the bubble at the top as I am, on top of the world.

Then I range across the site until I feel myself at the centre, the point at which I am pulled in no direction, from which there is nowhere to go, and drive in a stake. Looping a rope the length of the tower's radius over the stake I pull it tight and walk slowly in a circle, scratching the circumference into the earth. Then I begin digging the foundations.

I remove a spade width of turf, cutting through thick grass, severing matted roots, and stack the turves grass-side down, where they will stay for a couple of years to compost. Then I begin to dig down, using pickaxe and spade.

I dig through ashes and rubbish: pieces of broken pottery and glass, rusty wire that snags the pickaxe, a fragment of cow horn, a rat trap, castrating irons, chicken bones, broken-bladed sheep shears, illegible newspaper – I wonder what date? How far have I dug already into history? So close to the surface there is no plastic, not even the indestructible twine you find everywhere on French farms; this site is already historical. I find a small bottle marked GIFT and some German words; I pocket it. As I dig I hear Madame let out the hens and ducks, Monsieur take out the sheep, Gaston unchain the cows and lead them off to pasture. Then there is silence.

I'm digging backwards, anti-clockwise: now I've completed one circuit and I'm through the level of human occupation into untouched soil. It is brown with humus, fibrous, alive with worms and centipedes and creeping things. I

63

unearth a larva the size of my middle finger, pale green, almost luminous, writhing slowly, wonder what creature this is destined to be. The sun rises higher, grows hotter. I hear Monsieur and Gaston return with the animals, the sounds of lunch, then silence as the family slumbers. The sun is at the meridian, pouring its full heat onto my bare head.

I have completed another circuit and now I am deeper than the animal and vegetable kingdoms – how shallow are life's roots into the earth! – into the mineral realm. Ochre clay, weathered rock. I'm digging into the substance of the earth, the earth untouched by living things, making a new connection to the earth as it was before there was life; as I go down in space, I go back in time. Digging the foundations. This is the place. There is nowhere else. My wanderings over the face of the earth cease here. Here I will strike down a root to the centre of the earth, to the earth's dark, molten core.

My brains are boiling in the helmet of my skull. The heat is a cloak of lead upon me. But I work on, through the heat of the day, the only waking thing in a silent, comatose world, the only sounds the hack and scrape of my implements, the only movements the rise and fall of my pick, the cut and throw of my spade. Everything else is held in the syrup heat poured down from the sun, like flies in amber. Only I, active in the fundamental particle-charge flashing between the earth's centre and the vertical sun, work on, possessed.

And then the sun passes the zenith, out of the zone of the meridian; the connection is broken, the heat begins to lessen. Paralysis becomes sleep, and from sleep there is awakening; the dogs shake themselves to their feet, the family scratch and yawn themselves awake, shaking heads at their strange dreams. They drink coffee and return slowly to their work. I strike rock, the living rock.

I clean out the trench, lay bare the rock. And then I step

64

out, stagger, almost fall, go blindly, wearily inside and put my head under the pump and pump until I can pump no more, wrap my head in a towel, crawl onto the sofa and fall asleep.

*   *   *

I awaken from a dreamless sleep. I lie, unanxious, staring at the ceiling, gazing in my mind's eye at the circle of rock I have revealed. Is it real?

I'm ravenous, need to eat – but there are things I must do before I can eat. I sit up. My back is rigid and sore, my hands red and raw. I walk stiffly outside. It is early evening, softer and clearer than when I went to sleep, the air, no longer trembling with fluid heat, still. The sun has set. The sky is clear, changing colour each second, darkening. I check the foundation trench – it wasn't a dream – then I begin my evening duties.

First to the garden. I inspect each potato plant carefully, removing the fat red Colorado beetle larvae from the leaves and squashing them, until my fingers are as red as if I had been picking soft raspberries.

I fill the watering can from the still pool at the edge of the garden. My back creaks. Watering would take less time if I used a hosepipe, but I enjoy the repetitions of the luscious slap and gurgle in the evening stillness as I fill the can with the dark water, and I have time to examine each crop as I water it, and it is good to do something of measured pace to end the outdoor day.

The garden is looking good – peas, beans, peppers, tomatoes, sweet corn, lettuce, onions all thriving. The root crops are beginning to suffer from the lack of rain, especially the potatoes, and the winter cabbage could be better, but the transplanted leeks have taken well in spite of the intense heat; I remove the leafy branches I'd shaded them with, and break up the soil where it pancaked when I watered them in.

I return the hoe to the pool where I leave it so the wood stays swollen and the head firm. I burrow into the warm soil for a handful of potatoes and pick some broad beans.

It is quite dark when I leave the garden. I pause to smell the fragrances of the herb garden, then I go to the meadow and feed and shut in the hens.

I switch on the light in the kitchen as I cook but I leave all the doors and windows open; it is still warmer outside than in. I put Monteverdi on the record player, the *1610 Vespers*.

I eat on the terrace, watching the last light drain slowly from the sky, the earth rise up. I eat the cherries I picked yesterday, those left over from the ones I gave Jane. I make strong coffee.

Then I get out the writing pad, and five times start the letter 'Dear Jane' and write one sentence, five times screw up the page and throw it in the corner. I open a book but close it immediately. I go upstairs and sit by the bedroom window, looking out at the dark world and starry sky.

My body is weary and inert, but my mind is active. I feel it detach from my body, in this unusual solitude and silence, and roam through realms of imagination, then return; together they slide into bed. I stretch. It is strange to feel this space all around me. It is very peaceful, alone in bed. I kiss the cool, still pillow and go to sleep holding it, smiling.

*   *   *

I dream of the girl in the red espadrilles. In the dream we make love sensationally. Waking, I lie with my eyes closed, not wanting to come out of the dream, amazed at how wonderful our lovemaking feels, how real. For we never made love.

She offered herself to me the night before I first came to France. I remember, in the dark of her front room, lit dimly by a distant street light, the dark triangle of her pubis, the whiteness of her skin, her shyness and defiance. She was seventeen. It wouldn't be right, I said, chivalrous – cowardly? Maybe we should have made love, given each other our virginities. We were such good friends. Maybe I should never have left her. Maybe, years later, I shouldn't have left all my friends, broken with all the women I knew, friends, to go and live with Jane. Maybe we shouldn't have been so exclusive with each other, an exclusiveness that eventually led us here. Things might have been different.

How that phrase shocks me. I've always imagined that my life has a pattern, a purpose, even if unknown to me. But maybe I am here simply as the result of the accumulation of many small decisions, actions, accidents, a pattern existing only in retrospect. "Is your life that accidental…?" The largeness of the implications disturb me, especially in relation to Jane. Forget them. I'm here, with a task to perform.

The neighbours' alarm clock rings. Eventually it is silenced. Their roosters are crowing madly but they are deaf to them; only a machine will wake them, for they are now becoming part of the machine. At first they defied Summer Time, but within a week they had altered their clocks. When I asked why, they shrugged and said – we kept missing our favourite TV programmes. I have a task, a vision. I prepare for work.

Chapter 2: Laying the foundations

Mixing concrete by hand is hard work; concrete is a heavy, unresponsive material. Throw a rock onto other rocks and it will bounce, elastic as a rubber ball, or shatter, the pieces flying with the energy of shrapnel. Throw a concrete block and it will land, and it may break, but that's about it. It is a sullen material, to anthropomorphise. Or maybe it is dead. Dead bodies feel heavy in a way that live ones don't (as I remember from working in a hospital). Concrete is an invented material, the calculated creation of the simulacrum of stone by the careful application of mechanical and chemical principles; it is an industrial material. Perhaps it is no accident that it was invented by the Romans, that most industrial of pre-industrial societies, forgotten, then re-invented in the Industrial Revolution. In its tightly-packed, economical structure there is no room for life; no crystals have grown here, there have been no fossilisings, no metamorphoses: it has no history.

But it has its value. And its value, its one superiority over stone, is that it can be poured cold. Stone can only be poured hot, and then only with difficulty. So it is excellent for foundations, for curved foundations. But it is hard work.

It needs a lot of shovelling. Which is why the labourer, whose shovel is the one tool personal to him, keeps it so well. Give him a new one and the first thing he does is get the angle grinder and take two inches off the blade. Is this a union thing, a class thing, his way of reducing the employer's pound of flesh to fourteen ounces? No. He knows from experience that the balance is wrong. He knows that although he will get less on the shovel, there will be more shovelfuls to the hour, and more work done.

And he needs no tribologist to inform him about friction:

he keeps his shovel so shiny he can shave in it; and I've often seen the old labourers frying their bacon and eggs on it on a frosty morning.

Four of gravel, two of sand, one of cement. Mix them dry, turning and turning until the sand (yellow) and the gravel (white) are randomly mixed, and every grain is uniformly coated with cement dust (grey), and all is grey. I flatten the castle and make a crater, an internal moat, and fill it with water. The minimum of water, much less than seems necessary, for this is a chemical reaction not a mechanical mix, and too much water weakens it: "you're not making mud pies", the foreman said. And then circling the crater I carefully collapse in the rim, taking care not to make a breach for the water to stream out. The hygroscopic cement sucks in the water like blotting paper. When the water is all gone I turn and turn the mix until it is all one. I pour it into the trench. I tamp it and level it. I've reversed the natural process and created rock from rock debris.

Except that the only property this material shares with rock is its hardness; its inertness is a barrier. To connect the living rock with the stones of the tower I insert twelve copper rods vertically at equal intervals.

Then I cover the foundation with wet sacks to slow the drying process; the slower it dries, the harder it will become. I wash the barrow and the shovel carefully, and then the cement dust and sweat from my body. I have lunch.

*   *   *

Through the heat of the day I barrow stones from the ruined barn to the site of the tower. Many of the stones are soot-blackened, some have been baked to biscuit, soft, cracked and useless.

The barn burned down: the Combons say struck by lightning;

69

the Bonafets say there was no lightning that night. By the time the dogs woke them it had taken hold and, with no telephone and only wells for water, there wasn't much that could be done. They opened the door, but the first animal to run hysterically out was a sheep on fire, and fearing for the hay, the other barns, the houses, they had to bolt the door and listen to the different cries of the different animals as they burned to death. The insurance money paid for the move to Albi. I wonder if there is still fire, still screams in these stones.

I make many journeys. Sometimes I overload the barrow and curse as I force it by force of will, straining, along the path. Sometimes I underfill it, and abuse myself for the waste, and feel my mind wander. And sometimes I get it just right, the weight and distribution of stones, I know, as I straighten my legs and lift, just able to lift, lean slightly forward and focus my attention on the single wheel and in my mind's eye see it beginning to turn and I begin to walk. I am walking a tightrope that the wheel is creating over nothingness as it turns, and it turns only because my attention is exactly on its moving surface. Is the tightrope unreeling because my arms and shoulders and back and legs are pushing this almost unbearably heavy wheelbarrow; or is the turning wheel drawing me along...? It doesn't matter. Intention is all. I watch fascinated as the stones fall and bounce and bound over each other, and then are still. One pile reduces, the other grows. One pile is gone, might never have been; this one is. By the time I have finished it is evening.

*　　　　*　　　　*

My whole body aches. I drink. Then I pull the lounging chair out onto the terrace, under the vines, and lie back.

The air is electric. Black thunderheads have built up and thunder rumbles around the horizon and there are distant flickers of lightning. The neighbours are scrambling for the tractor and trailer, hurrying to bring in the hay before the storm breaks. This is a nervous season, for the hot weather that makes good hay also creates the thunderstorms that ruin it. Tonight they are lucky; the thunder rumbles and the lightning crackles, but only a few fat drops of rain fall. They soon return. Three weeks ago there was a real storm, the one that decided Jane to leave.

I was still working at the pig factory. In the afternoon the storm broke, an apocalyptic one even for this area. The electricity went off while we were in the middle of slaughtering; the lights went out, the conveyor stopped, activity slowed and gradually everything stilled.

We stood between the dead pigs hanging head down from the conveyor, in various stages of dismemberment, swaying slightly. We were uneasy at being confronted by what we did, and our eyes avoided the steady, long-lashed pig gazes all around us. There was nervous laughter and silly jokes in the gloom among the swaying bodies as the rain beat on the roof and thunder shook the walls and lightning speared in through the windows. Eventually the power was restored and the conveyor jerked into life and we finished and got ready to go home.

A group of the younger workers stood at the door, hesitant. Out there it was another world, weird and alien: the rain fell in solid sheets, gutters spouted like gargoyles, the road was a swift-flowing river, a stream was busy gouging a new course across the car park; the whole valley was sinking under the rising water. They chattered excitedly, too loud. Then Marcel made a run for it, stopped, lost, as the rain beat on him, and rushed back in wild-eyed and giggling. Marianne ran out and back and shook herself on the others like a dog. Then they threw Yves out, and he stayed out, splashing in the water, throwing handfuls of mud in the air, dancing and whooping to the sky. He pulled Marie out. I sprinted for the car and dived in, rain thudding on the soft roof. Miraculously it started. As I turned the car I saw all of them, the gang, silhouetted against the open door, dancing and shouting, throwing mud and sliding each other around, soaked, mud-covered, primeval beings.

The road was awash. The windscreen wipers (connected to the speedometer: the slower you drive, the slower they sweep) were overwhelmed. I was driving blind, no idea where the road was, shocked by sudden trees and precipices, inching along, driving under water. And then the engine stopped. And wouldn't restart. I was seven miles from home.

I sat for a moment, dumbstruck, numb, feeling the rain pummelling the soft top of the car, aware that what a moment ago had been a speedy and cosy transportation capsule was now half a ton of useless metal. I got out and was instantly soaked to the skin. I pushed the car to the side of the road. There was no cliff handy. A sodden old man with a sack round his shoulders trudged across the road towards a cottage:

'Broken down,' I shouted to him through the noise of the rain. He stopped, looked gravely at the car nodded and said:

'Yes. It's because of the water,' and, satisfied with this observation he trudged on to the cottage, opened the door to reveal a heaven of kitchen sights and sounds and smells, and closed the door behind him. I couldn't believe it. And then I could. This is France. I said – okay, time to stop pissing about. I saw car headlights coming slowly, going my way. I didn't hitch or request; I stood in the middle of the road and demanded. The big new Mercedes with Paris plates stopped. A back door opened silently on perfect hinges. I got in. The door closed. The car began to move. It was quiet inside, hushed and perfumed and warm. Mozart played discreetly from multiple speakers. The seat was leather, soft and comfortable. The walnut panelling was elegant, even opulent.

Beside me was a girl of fourteen, long limbed in a short pale-pink silk dress, smelling fresh. I was scruffy and pig-smelling, rain beaten and soaked, but I was dry inside. She smiled at me with big dark eyes through a fringe of dark hair and recrossed her slender legs. She had very long thighs. She nursed a glass of amber liquid and had open on her knee *Salammbô*. Her eyes were bright and she breathed in short breaths as she read.

In the front passenger seat was a middle-aged woman in a black cocktail dress, her hair carefully and sharply styled, heavily and muskily perfumed. The driver, a small, grey-haired man, hardly touched the wheel; in front of him the instruments of the dashboard clicked and flashed automatically, sensing and adjusting, homeostatic, the car almost driving itself.

The storm slid silently by, picturesque, as if on a screen. I sat in silence. The woman half turned to me, looked me up and down, asked me about myself. Her lips were thin but shapely and red, her teeth yellow ivory. I told her.

'Interesting. We have a place, quite close. We must retain our roots in the land, mustn't we?' She smiled. 'We do what we can, but we really need someone to come in and help, with my husband so often in Paris. So difficult to get the right help these days. If you know of anyone…?' Another smile, very warm, then she faced forward again. Her neck was long and slender, the skin loosening.

The world slid by. I was warm and comfortable, bathing in freshness and perfume, wrapped up in the music. I felt like a vagrant invited suddenly into a box at the theatre. And then we were driving up into St Leon.

I got out. I was instantly wet, buffeted and deafened. The woman proffered a card with a manicured red-nailed hand. I took it. The door closed. The mobile, air-conditioned salon purred away. Long-nailed fingers waved languidly. I stood in the noisy rain, cold and wet again on the outside, but dry inside, and crumpled the card, dropped it, and watched it speed along the gutter and spiral down the drain. I stuck up a finger to the receding limousine and said 'up yours'; the softly waving fingers stiffened into a V sign. Bye bye, bourgeois France. I felt good as I went into the bar to wait out the storm.

There were the regulars, and a few trapped, nervous tourists. A young couple sat at a small table near the bar, the *Daily Telegraph* lying between them. I stared at it...

...and am, on such a night as this, walking to the lit-up house and the door opening to a billow of comfortable smells and my parents' greetings. Then there is tea by the mug and warmth and a hot bath and clean dry clothes that smell of my mother's washing powder (the smell that defines cleanness), and egg and chips, apple pie with evaporated milk, more tea, television.

Mum goes to bed and dad and I talk, warily, each trying to be other than a stranger; and maybe a little gap opens in our wariness and we flee from it and sigh and he goes to bed. I sit alone in the silent house, cocooned in its warmth, in front of the popping gas fire, reading the *Telegraph* into the early hours. Why the *Telegraph*? He should read the *Mail* or *Express*. He changed from the *Express* when I was eleven: why? For me, the right newspaper for a grammar school boy? To show solidarity with me? To demonstrate some hidden side of himself, that he was a cut above the station life had put him in? I don't know, I really don't know.

What I do know is that by two in the morning the sterility behind the cosiness is radiating from the walls and boredom oozing from the furniture and I know that by dawn I will be screaming to get away.

Don't even open it, that beguiling, disappointing newspaper. Let it lie. Two identical faces, bespectacled, intelligent, unimaginative, successful, dull; local government officers, the new bourgeois who'd come from the same working class, through the same grammar school system, as me. Traitors. Speak? Ask them for a lift? One look at their blank faces and I was back in the world I had escaped from; I emptied my second glass of rum and pushed past them and burst out through the door... as I had burst out of the office the day I left after that brief attempt to find a place inside (when the pain had eased a little and I had felt almost human again), ripping off the strangling noose of a tie as I ran, escaping to freedom, ready to face the worst the elements could throw at me... the rain had stopped, the night was fresh and mild.

I left the lights of the café behind and strode up the narrow twisting road into the night.

The thick cloud had gone, leaving torn remnants that moved quickly across a clear sky. But the thunder and lightning were still around and the air crackled with electricity. I passed the last house and headed onto the open plateau. Below me the lights of the village were patterned like a celestial constellation. Ahead of me lay black emptiness, crossed by the thin silver ribbon of the road. Booms of thunder shook the hills. Lightning crackled to the ground around me. The clouds were torn aside to reveal a waning moon, then its welcome light was buried by succeeding clouds. An owl flapped silently by and looked at me unblinking. There was something, someone behind me. Don't worry, there always is; don't look, let it be.

I strode on, terrified by the electrical night and exhilarated by it. For I was suddenly aware that I was envious of no one, that I didn't wish I was doing something else, that what I was doing was what I should be doing. If the lightning struck me, it wouldn't destroy me; it would transform me. "The healthy man is one affected by more or less electricity in the air." Conjure up devils, write in fire across the sky, I can take it, I am steadfast. I punched the air and yelled. Yes.

What a scene when I got back to the house: bedraggled, huddled figures, overflowing buckets, rafters dripping, water everywhere. Could I help it if I said 'what a brilliant night'? I went outside, stood on the mound, watched the departing storm, and said: 'this is a foreign land and I am a stranger here, with no roots, no rights, and that's okay. But now I am no longer a wanderer over the face of the earth. Home is not where you settle, it's where you do your work, whatever it is'. And in the last flashes of lightning I saw a figure striding along the ridge, saw him struck by lightning, saw him transformed.

*   *   *

Lying back in the lounger I smile at the recollection. For then the last bit of dream was gone and I was, at last, living here.

I had thought that moment ten years ago was the first step on the road; but that had been my first sight of the road, and since then there had been dreams, and the last eighteen months in all its weirdness and horror was the burning off of the last of those vaporous dreams that had covered the solid earth.

I hardly noticed next morning when the friends left and hardly knew what Jane, raw and tearful, was saying about how it made sense if I stopped working at the pig factory and worked here full-time while she went back to London and earned some money because anyway she couldn't stay a moment longer without going crazy. 'Okay, if that's what you want', I had said, and carried on staring.

The storm has cleared, the tremendous power departed. It is a calm, still night. In the hedge I see a glow-worm, a small, pale, pure green light, a promise. I go to bed.

*   *   *

But I don't sleep. I lie in bed wide awake. It is a warm night. The air is full of the scent of cut hay. And the night is no longer calm and still; the vacancy left by the departing storm is being filled, the stillness fractured, the air stirred, by a new presence.

Through the rectangular hole in the black wall I see the night air saturated by a suspension of white, almost silver, light, luminous. And the dogs are on the move. I hear their snuffles and yips, the pad of their loping paws, their pants and growls – and then a howl, a wild dog howl that hangs in the air and then is answered from across the valley and successively at greater distances, like a series of echoes.

I go to the window. The half-dozen houses of the hamlet contain between them a rectangular cobbled area. This area is lit up as if by white floodlights, so that it looks like a stage set. The dogs cavort, like unruly children allowed onto the stage before the performance. Mathilde, the bitch, runs restlessly this way and that; the two dogs follow her like fans, eager to touch, possess. They cuff each other aside, try to mount her, try to mount each other in their excitement, stand back when she sits back on her haunches and howls at the moon. For the moon is full. Then she is off again and the three of them are a tangled twist of whirling, hectic shapes. Gaston shouts at them from his room, and for a moment they are quiet, but then the stirrings within can no longer be stifled and they burst once more into motion. I throw myself back into bed. And get up immediately, pull on shorts and sandals, go out into the garden.

The moon is enormous. Its luminosity showers me, its rays beat down on me, its heatless light stirs and excites me. I walk through the garden, seeing and feeling the moonlight silvering my skin. Another howl – and I feel a responding howl forming in my throat. I climb over the fence, into the neighbours' field, where the hay lies cut. My heart is thumping in my chest as I trespass and recklessly intrude into a forbidden world.

I take off my sandals and run, kicking the hay, throwing myself down on it, grabbing armfuls and throwing it into the air. On this earthscape, lit by a moon (or am I on the moon and this light is earthlight…?) I feel the presence of Sylvie. The touch of her skin, the smell of her flying hair, the laughter from her flashing teeth. I grasp her, press her to me, run hand in hand with her. Sylvie, who is the moon on water – I dip my hand to scoop her up – Sylvie whom I want, desire, must have. I make a great heap of hay, armful upon armful of fragrant softness, and pull off my shorts and throw myself onto the hay again and again until I am breathless, exhausted, spent. I lie in the hay panting. Then I crawl under and, protected in this warm nest, I curl up and go to sleep.

I wake suddenly, as if a voice has called my name. Silence. Feathers of hay irritate my face and the mass of it suffocates me. I push it aside and scramble to my feet. Moonlight on a French hayfield. I feel exposed and absurd until I have pulled on my shorts and sandals. Then I rearrange the hay, as I might remake a bed I have used without permission, guiltily, aware of the moon eye upon me. Clothed, and with the evidence of my passion, my infidelity even, removed, I feel easier. The moon is high now, and smaller, a more prosaic moon. I gaze up at it curiously, examine its marked, round face with interest, a face at once familiar and newly strange. I address the moon as if I am speaking to Jane:

'Is it all gone then, the novelty and adventure? Have we become so set in our ways that one of us cannot change in response to change in the other? Must you flee from me as if I've become dangerous? Or do you see in me actions out of character, caprice? Maybe it is. Or maybe it's something long hidden, now emerging…? Three, almost four years. I suppose by now most couples have settled for what they've got. I never have. I've always been waiting, for something that's always been there, tantalising, elusive. Maybe now I'm beginning to grasp it.

'Did you flee because you saw me grasping, at last, my purpose, and feel left out? Or have you left me free to wrestle with it, Jacob-like, alone? I have no way of knowing; the best I can do is to avoid judging for as long as I can. You've gone, that's all. I have to make of that, and my life here, what I will. My love for you hasn't changed. It never will. Nor has my commitment. But remember – my commitment is not to you, but to something we share. I miss you. I want you to come back, when the time is right. And I pray that when you do come back, it is the right time.'

I wipe the tears from my face, walk sadly back to the house. In bed I cuddle up, as if to Jane.

Chapter 3: Building the wall

I set the door frame in position, plumb and level it carefully. Then I begin to build.

For seven days I work alone, speaking to no one: building up, and when the circuit is complete going round again, rising slowly upward, widdershins, a screw thread, Babel, the spiralling minaret at Samarra, slowly upward, a life of silent dedication. Tending the garden, feeding the chickens, looking after myself, are necessary but unwanted distractions from the steady labour of building and the slow mounting of the stone spiral. "Intention directs the chi, chi directs the body". Aspiration is all.

And yet within the general aspiration my moods change. Sometimes something happens and I click into a state of grace in which right stone after right stone comes naturally and weightlessly to hand, each fits perfectly into the rich and complex creation that is coming into being, the wall rises naturally, I am filled with the glow of the virtue of what I am doing. Sometimes I work in a mood of effortful but contented neutrality, sweating hard, in which stones are stones and mortar is mortar, and building this wall is simply the task I have set myself. And sometimes black depression overwhelms me, in which every stone I pick up is loathsome and alien and brutal to my hands, and every stone I lay is a stone of sorrow weighing out the futility of my life and the heaping up of this building is the culminating folly of a lifetime of stupidities.

And yet, strangely – for in free-stone building you see most clearly the signature of the builder – in appearance there is no difference in the look of the wall whatever mood I was in, and in structure all is sound.

I work on relentlessly, my life having purpose. A letter arrives from Jane, a doubting, questioning letter; I toss it aside dismissively and go back to my work. The wall rises, course upon course. I miss no one, I glory in my solitude. But the hard, unyielding work with hard, unyielding stone is making me hard, unyielding, stone-like. From the grey touch of the stone the greyness creeps along my arms; with the stone dust my blood thickens; my heart is turning, slowly, to… a commotion of dogs and the hooting of our car horn.

Confused, I think it's Jane and I tense myself for defence or flight, mute and neanderthal; but before I can move, Sylvie bursts in with such a swirling of energy, her arms whirling me round, her cataract of words tossing me high, the smell of her body heating my blood, her active hands touching my skin back to life, and a great, red cartwheel of a strawberry flan lifted high like a new risen sun, that I simply dissolve.

After an hour, of talking and being together, I am almost normal again, and we are in the car bouncing along the road to Michael and Rosie's.

Chapter 4: A 'Symposium'

I drive out of the hollow, my hands circling the smooth curve of the wheel, up to the top of the ridge – the sudden revelation of far horizontal sweeps of blue-grey, closer slabs of green and gold, a curved blue sky, and all around and above me space and air – and then I accelerate down the long hill towards St Leon, in control of the bouncing machine, curving through the bends, with barns and trees and open expanses of landscape passing at differential speeds, the wind in my face and vortexing around me, everything in motion.

'Thanks,' I shout through the wind. She smiles, a warm, pleased smile but a surface one. Beneath she is quiet, thoughtful, dark. Something has happened. I let it pass; I'm enjoying the slither of gravel, the bite of the brakes, the lateral motion through the series of tight bends just above the village.

And then we are at the STOP sign, engine idling, the rush of the wind replaced by the monotony of vehicle noise.

For the main road is nose to tail with caravans, vehicles piled high with camping equipment, cars with foreign number plates, a stream of strangers passing blinkered through the village, through the region. It is with great difficulty that I edge out into the traffic and take my place among the gaudy holidaymakers. I'm shocked at this sudden intrusion of the outside world; of what, I realise, I still automatically think of as the real world.

So many glossy new cars, such sophisticated equipment, such affluence. The accumulation of wealth, and the expenditure of it on dreamed-of holidays in far-off places. Each year a little more money, each year a few more possessions, each year another ambition fulfilled, another dream made to come true.

I think of Jane, in London, getting on with her life, resuming her position in the scheme of things. The notion of my aspiration falters at contact with this solidity and directed energy. My Zarathustran high-mindedness is shaken by the realisation that I am off the road, out of the flow; and the world doesn't give a damn – turn off the road and the cars close up, swallow your space as if you had never been; but try and get back onto the road, and see what happens....

'Yep,' Sylvie says, 'it's still there.' Linked into their chain, in my battered car and scruffy clothes, I cough in their fumes and stare at the rear window of the car in front, bicycles on the back, surf boards on the roof, my eye hooked on the yellow Smiley badge. Hypnotised, I almost miss our road, turn off suddenly, wave derisively at the honked horns.

Shaking myself awake I accelerate along the quiet road by the river. The jam of cars crawls zigzag up the hill, like ants, like refugees, like commuters, like a military convoy – rejoin that, the tourist route, the lemming rush, the broad highway, the chain gang of the technological imperative, the so many that death has undone...? I shake my head at how easily I am still affected. I drive moderately, along this quiet tributary of the Tarn, taking in the water meadows and the tall, slender, shimmering poplars, the dense chestnut woods and the terraced hillsides, the solidity. I remember again what Herman Melville had written: seek not to enlarge – rather, subtilise.

Soon we are driving up through Michael and Rosie's village. There are red geraniums in pots and, at this late afternoon hour, figures talking quietly, or working steadily in productive gardens, who acknowledge us with gentle inclinations of the head as we pass. Through the village to the top, where their beautiful house stands in its dominating position with its fine views. I stop the car. We sit.

'They're lucky,' I say, looking up at their house.

'I rather think they make their luck.'

'And you, how's your luck?' She is silent, looking away, looking across the valley to the far hills, maybe seeing nothing. When she speaks it is quietly, as if to herself:

'You argue, you fight, you get angry – hot with anger, blazing with it, burning up. Then it cools – it has nowhere to go, I suppose, you've blown off steam. You calm down and do nothing, decide to give it another go, until the next time. And then one day, over something minor, nothing at all, you say – that's it. And it's over. No argument, no fuss, no pain, no agony of decision. It's like you've turned through a hundred and eighty degrees so he's no longer there. Strange.'

We sit in silence. There is the sound of a distant tractor, of sheep bells, of a television set. And a flute, its fluid notes rippling through the air, almost visible, white notes in the blue sky, confident and reassuring. Nerving myself, I say:

'I saw you, Jean-Jacques and you, at the *feu*.' Looking straight ahead she says, quietly:

'I thought you did. It must have been uncomfortable for you. It wasn't…. I can't explain.'

'I…'

'Shsh,' turning quickly towards me, putting her finger on my lips, concern on her face. 'Please, don't say anything. I want us to be friends. I need friends. I can help, I really can, but… trust me, please?'

'I…' I say and put a finger on my lips. She laughs and squeezes my arm. The flute plays, the scent of honeysuckle comes to us on a gentle eddy of air. She turns suddenly to me, animated:

'Do you know why we're here?'

'No.'

'Firstly because Fred and Julie are leaving, and this is the last get-together.'

'No!'

'Secondly, because Larry's just signed the contract to publish his book.'

'No!!'

'Thirdly, because he saw Jane in London, and you can get the latest news.'

'Oh.'

'Come on!' and she scrambles out of the car, pulling me by the hand, overwhelming my reluctance. To the house, round the side, the sound of the flute getting louder, voices now audible, round the back of the house – and stop.

A *tableau vivant* illuminated by the clear, warm light from the sun which, while still radiating heat, is beginning to redden towards sunset, a pink light. A feeling of weightlessness, as if all that we see is about to rise up in front of us, in suspension. I watch, enchanted by the beauty, and yet resisting, after my raw working, this richness....

Perched on the large rock is the tall slender figure of Larry, one leg tucked under him, the other dangling, his long body curved around the flute from which he coaxes the music, the pattern of notes that holds them in thrall. Below him, at the base of the rock, Julie sits suckling Gemma, one large marbled white breast spilled out of her dress, a faraway look on her face. Close by Fred crouches over the beginnings of a fire, carefully floating shavings onto the low flame, adding thin sticks as the flames rise, breathing the fire into life.

To the side, further away, leaning precariously out from a slender ladder, Michael picks cherries, cherries over each ear, grasping the crimson globes from among the dark leaves and dropping them into the basket at his hip. At the edge of the garden, where the wood begins, three fair, naked children, garlanded with greenery, play, in and out of the trees.

And in the centre of the garden, in the middle ground, Rosie stands, tall and slim, hosepipe in her hand, watering the garden, the silver water inscribing a long, high arc and, in the falling droplets, a second separate arc, a rainbow. We watch. I let the richness fill me.

And then we are seen, and Larry slides down from the rock and Rosie walks towards us with open arms and Michael waves and almost falls out of the tree, and everything comes down to earth and there is bustle as we settle in.

*   *   *

As the women prepare the meal and Michael feeds the goats, Larry walks me round the garden, his long arm around my shoulders. I had forgotten how tall he is, how full of a strange energy, how disturbing his presence: an energy often dark and concealed, like radiation behind lead; sometimes spilling out like lava. Now he is radiant and clear. When I ask what he's been doing, he gives his habitual, smiling reply:

'Ranging over the earth from end to end, making ends meet.' Now he adds: 'and finishing the book.'

'And it's finished? And being published?' He nods:

'I was in London signing the contract. I saw Jane.'

'How is she?'

'Jane's okay. She's tired, because the life here has been tough on her. And she's shocked and hurt, because she was doing what she thought you wanted, but you sent her away. She trusted you to know why the two of you were here, and now she feels let down. But she's strong, and she'll soon sort herself out – London's her place. The problem is that she doesn't know what you want to do; and the question is – do you?'

Walking the rim of an invisible wheel, orbiting an invisible sun, or maybe a dark star, his slim, firm arm around my shoulder, I am eclipsed, dumb. Then he releases me, takes my arm like a nineteenth century student and, with me bathing in his radiance, we perambulate as he expatiates:

86

'I've been writing the book for five years. And I've probably wrecked Constance in the process. The first wife is the fuel, consumed in the fire of ambition; the second wife warms herself in the glow of success. Or you can have a marriage of equals – all our contemporaries have married women of comparable intelligence and education – and you each adjust your jigsaw edges to fit the other so you have that queer – sorry, odd – Platonic hermaphrodite.

'I knew exactly what I was doing when I started; I saw the whole picture, as if from a great height. And then I spent five years on my knees, my nose an inch from the ground, laying tessera the size of a thumbnail into a mosaic the size of a football pitch. Not knowing…. That's when the woman is consumed.

'If there's something serious that you want to do, do it. But know this; if you fail, you'll die. Better not to start unless you're sure you'll finish. There's a Japanese way to living Buddhahood. On his ten year journey the aspirant always carries a knife – if he gives up, he must kill himself; not as a punishment, but as a release, because his life would be over anyway.

'You know where you are, and where you want to be; and the work is the bridge. It's a bridge you're creating, piece by piece – from one end only. And the moment you stop, the moment you hesitate, the bridge will vanish from under you and you will plunge into the abyss.

'Do you know Milton's account of Satan's journey from hell to earth across the uncreated? I seem to have recited it to myself every day for the last five years. Now I want to give it to you.' He stops walking, stands, declaiming:
'"At last his sail-broad vans
   He spreads to flight, and in the surging smoke
   Uplifted spurns the ground; thence many a league
   As in a cloudy chair, ascending rides
   Audacious; but, that seat soon failing, meets
   A vast vacuity…"

'A vast vacuity. But he makes it through the "shock of fighting elements". And when at last he reaches the created universe, he looks back and sees:

'"Following his track – such was the will of Heaven –
    Paved after him a broad and beaten way
    Over the dark Abyss, whose boiling gulf
    Tamely endured a bridge of wondrous length
    From Hell continued, reaching the utmost orb
    Of this frail World…"

'And when you press the last piece into place, you get up, stiff-legged, and see a picture, quite different from the one you saw at the beginning, but complete. Complete.'

We walk on in silence, he lost in thought, me entranced. A woman's voice calls: 'Allez, venez les flâneurs! Nous sommes prêts à manger!'

*   *   *

We're about to sit around the long refectory table laid in the open air when there is an irruption of children. Two, a girl and boy, are baying eerily. The third is crying. He is crying because he is stumbling behind the others, barefoot, tugged along by a noose round his neck. No one moves. The girl announces:

'Hey Rosie, look, we're maenads!' Tamsin, Rosie and Michael's daughter, is seven years old. She has straggly blonde hair with leaves and flowers knotted in it, mud and berry juice streaking her face, a face at once angelically pretty and strangely old. She continues:

'We're maenads and we caught this man looking at our sacred rites and now we're going to tear him limb from limb!' She speaks in that breathless child way, the words and syntax correct, the pauses and inflections just off.

'My, my, you are having a fine game,' Rosie says, edging carefully past the aghast Julie towards the weeping prisoner.

'But I think perhaps Zack's a little tired now – maybe he'd like to rest with Julie?' and with practised speed and skill she interposes herself as Tamsin lunges for her victim, whipping off the noose and saying 'there, there Zack, it's just a game,' as the toddler leaps into his mother's arms and buries his face in her breasts.

'Hey, you can't do that,' Tamsin cries indignantly, 'we haven't torn him limb from limb yet!'

'Another time, Tammers dear. You certainly have made yourself look splendid with the leaves and flowers,' Rosie cajoles. 'And Digory, are you a maenad too?' The little boy, hair as long and blonde as his older sister's, nods vigorously. 'Wonderful – we mustn't be sexist, must we? Now, would you like something to eat?'

'Nah,' says Tamsin firmly. 'Come on Digs, let's leave him. Let's look for another man to tear limb from limb,' and they scamper across the garden and crash into the wood. Panic-stricken birds and rabbits erupt from it. Zack sobs quietly.

'Kids,' Michael smiles, 'they're brilliant, aren't they? So creative. What would we do without 'em, eh, Rosie?'

'Let's eat,' Rosie says firmly, and passes round the quiches and salads and home-made bread and baked potatoes and wine.

*   *   *

'So tell us, Fred,' Michael says, lounging back, post-pran-dial, wine glass cradled, 'why are you going back? With the referendum behind us, and Thatcher leading the Tories – I don't understand.' Fred chews methodically, brow knitted, chewing his thoughts as he chews his food, grinding small.

'I've realised it's not going to happen. I thought, four years ago, that just by doing it, by example, I could make it happen. After *Blueprint for Survival*, the "Club of Rome" report, *Small is Beautiful*, the Whole Earth Catalogs, Survival

Scrapbooks – even Government reports to the Stockholm Conference – I thought, okay, the time is right. Do it. Be an example. Show that what we'd been writing about, a low energy, intermediate technology, self-sufficient economy is possible, and desirable, and sustainable. And we've done it, Julie and I. And while we've been doing it, everything's been running in our direction – the oil price hike, the three-day week, the bombings in London, race riots, squatting, increasing homelessness and inner city decay, rising unemployment, hyper-inflation, evidence from all sides of an economic system – even a culture – in terminal decline.

'And what's the response been – city dwellers flocking back to the land, government encouragement for what we do, local initiatives, people taking back control of their lives? No – an increase in the nuclear power programme, a ghetto-ising of the inner cities, more repressive policing.

'There's no popular support for what we're doing, and no government support. A few of our ideas, the ones that can be commercialised, have been ripped off – solar heating, in Britain? It's a joke. And meanwhile we're marginalised. We're last year's fashion. It's over, I'm doing no good here.'

Michael: 'But your own good, the good of your family – does there need to be more?'

Fred: 'Of course! I'm a political animal.'

Me: 'But the political situation might change. If Thatcher gets in there'll be such a reaction to her extremist policies that there'll be a swing the other way and Benn'll be swept to power – and with his views on co-operatives and worker power....'

Fred: 'Maybe – and I want to be there if it happens. But I doubt it. These moments in British history, when the world's almost turned upside down – the Diggers in the 1650s, the Chartists in the 1840s – are always followed by repression and authoritarianism.

'We've shown that what we believe in can work. Lucas and

LIP have shown that co-operatives can work. But there's no pressure to de-urbanise, de-industrialise. Centralised power – the Thing, Cobbett called it – doesn't want it, because it would reduce its control. And it makes damned sure, with its control of the media, that the people don't know enough to demand it.

'And now, since the oil crisis, the Thing is drawing back into itself. The stones of the city are getting closer together; and I have to be a weed between the stones, a dandelion under the tarmac. Have to be.'

Silence, except for the shufflings at his adamance, and the soft warble of "White Bird" from the record player. Michael speaks:

'Don't you think that by confronting them, fighting them, you become like them?'

Fred: 'But I *am* like them. I'm their image in the blood pool, the antithesis to their thesis, their sinister side, Mordred. If I can't destroy them, I'll at least give them bad dreams.'

'But,' Michael persists, 'you can avoid them, ignore them, refuse to be provoked by them. Rip them off. You can build a separate world here, a new world, untainted. For a while a window opened, a window of opportunity, an eye opening on a possible world. Now that eye's closing, yes – but we've seen the possible world. We've seen it and they can't take that vision from us. We can make it happen. We can make it. We can be keepers of the flame in the dark times – what the monasteries were in the Dark Ages, we can be.'

Fred: 'That's a job for monks. I'm a soldier. I'll fight.'

Michael: 'I don't know whether to admire you, or think you a fool. After the failure of '68. After the moon landing. After the deaths of 1970 – I just want to be left alone. I really want to raise a family and cultivate my garden.'

Fred: 'Then that's what you must do. And I'll come and sit in it from time to time, and eat your wonderful food, and drink Kris' delicious wine.' Laughter.

'But Larry – you're just back from London – what am I going back to?'

Larry unwinds himself, begins in his plummy drawl:

'I'll tell you what it looks like to a Selenite – because the moon's been my habitation for the last several kalpas. There's a fashion among the wealthy, the new wealthy, for rural living – but that's nothing new. And among the chattering classes who've had to stay in town, a taste for things rural – stripped pine, quarry tile floors, floral patterns, practical clothing; at the weekend they dig allotments by railway embankments, and drive miles in practical cars to "pick your own" fruit farms to fill their electricity-guzzling freezers and collect wood for their Hampstead Agas. It's ghastly.

'Meanwhile their richer brothers, in the guise of environmental concern, are financing Trusts in the country – buying farms and letting groups of communards make a hash of being co-operative smallholders, when in fact the places are an insurance, bolt holes for the wealthy if the crash does come, so they'll be – with their private armies – the equivalent of the Roman villas, safe houses against the rising tide of barbarism.

'And in the inner cities, the joyless tower block children express themselves in joyless sex and joyless violence, and make joyless amphetamine music – two chord music, our beloved third has gone, and one note music is on the way – and jump up and down manically joylessly to it. It's called punk. It's very fashionable among Belgravia girls to have a Deptford boyfriend with spiky hair and slashed clothes and zips sewn into his skin who sneers and swears and gobs and knocks them about a bit – they've always liked a bit of rough. England's fucked.'

'So you're getting out?'

'Absolutely not! It's going to be like the fall of Rome – what material! I'm the *USS Enterprise* – observing alien cultures but pledged not to interfere. I can already see the ruins, and those who come after, like the Greeks to Mycenae, imagining only Titans could have built such walls. Or the Anglo-Saxon tiptoeing through the ruins of Roman Bath, in awe of the giants who built it: "Well-wrought this wall: Weirds broke it. The stronghold burst…." For we are giants. And we're about to fall – Spengler foresaw all this. We're living through the twilight of the giants. And right on cue, the Book of Revelation, the end of the Millennium.'

'We're not giants,' Julie protests, 'we're dinosaurs. Or rather our extensions, what we've built, are dinosaurs. But we're – human, and we can strip ourselves of them, junk them, return to the human scale.'

'Perhaps the Alternative Technology folk are the little shrews, those first tiny mammals, who wiped out the dinosaurs by eating their eggs?' Larry teases. 'Or maybe we're the ghost in the dinosaur brain, that leaves its body and renders its eggs infertile?'

'Foul!' Michael cries, 'overextended analogy, mixed metaphor – free kick to Julie!'

'I'm serious,' Julie says quietly. 'There is a chance. There *can* be an Aquarian age, emerging from the dying Piscean. What we need is more awareness, fewer clothes, more nakedness.'

'Teufelsdröckh. Carlyle would approve, and Montaigne. Rousseau certainly.'

'Larry,' Julie persists, 'you know too much. And knowing too much you can't separate the more important from the less; you can't rank your knowledge.'

'Ah, maybe all is rank,' Larry says quietly. There is silence. Then Rosie begins to speak. She has sat in silence, the silence of self-restraint. Now:

'Feminism. Women. No one has mentioned women! The Goddess, matriarchies, the earth as woman, woman as the oppressed majority, the feminine in each of us, the need for more yin less yang, more caring less exploiting,

93

more cooperating less competing…'

'More bloody hermaphrodites!' Larry interrupts. 'We need to emphasise the *differences*! That bloody, bloody picture of John and Yoko merging! Men have pricks, women have cunts; men invade, women enclose; men rape, women castrate; men wield hammers, women use knives…. Of course women should be equal – equal and different. But if they want it they'll have to fight for it – men will lose their way if they become less manly. The liberal conscience emasculates. The electricity of life crackles between opposite poles – the trick is to be as far apart as possible and still get the charge. But women will have to fight for it – as the Palestinians will have to fight the Israelis for their land, and the blacks the Boers. Only then will they be strong enough. Men can't give freedom to women – they must take it.'

'Prepare for battle,' Rose hisses.

'I'm looking forward to it!' Larry snarls. A dramatic moment. Or rather a moment of drama, contrived, as their faces soften into smiles and break up into laughter. But in this act of theatre – for they had read Drama together at university – there is, for the first time, real conflict, real pain.

'Okay,' Rosie says briskly, 'I'll bed the kids – who'll wash up?' Julie and I volunteer. 'The rest of you find something to do,' and off she strides, calling the kids, luring them to hand with titbits, hooding them with fairy tales.

Sylvie goes and sits at the edge of the garden, staring silently out over the valley. Larry and Michael retire giggling with the duty-free whisky Larry brought. Fred painstakingly repairs the flour mill, possibly wondering, as I do, what child-directed vegetable, or animal, passed, or rather failed to pass, between its impassive stones.

*   *   *

'Do you think Larry means what he says?' Julie asks as she fills the bowl from the solar heater.

'There's some rhetoric, but basically, yes.'

'I don't know if I admire or loathe him.'

'I'm sure he'd be satisfied with either response – as long as it's extreme.'

'Yeh.' She pauses, throws in a handful of washing soda, then plunges the little cage of soap pieces into the water and shakes it vigorously until the water turns milky. She washes, I dry.

'How do you feel about going back?' I ask.

'Relieved. I hadn't realised how much I was going against my nature. I grew up in London, and I've never got used to the silence here.

'When we went back for the interview – yes, I've got a teaching job; Fred needs to be free for his work – it all came back. There's always noise: the never-ending rumble of traffic – always people around: slamming a door, putting rubbish out, walking past the window. Whatever time you look out there are lights on in houses – it's a great comfort at sleepless 2am to look out of the window and imagine what's happening in those lit rooms, and wonder why that woman is walking down the street, what the stories are.

'And there's all the automatic stuff – fridges switching on and off, programmed central heating systems, traffic lights changing. Knowing that these human creations would carry on functioning even if there were no people – I find that comforting. Here, nothing's automatic, is it?'

'I suppose nature's automatic – the sun rises and sets, rain falls and plants grow, the seasons follow each other. But it's unfamiliar. The fascination is in becoming familiar with it. It's not what you do, it's what you become doing it.'

'There are things I've enjoyed – the garden, learning about herbs and healing, preserving, walking in the woods. I *will* miss the smells and tastes – they're disappearing from the cities, and they're the sensations that fix and locate memories. But who needs memories in the city, which is itself a vast information and retrieval system? Yes, I shall miss the smells and tastes.

'But the big thing is I've never felt safe here. Whenever I stop I feel the silence. I feel as though I'm being watched.' She shivers and plunges her hands deep into the hot water. We work in silence. I ask:

'Do you think that's how Jane felt?'

'I think it probably is.'

'Mm.' Silence. 'Still, you'll miss the company!' I say. She laughs:

'Everyone's so off-centre, there *is* no centre! It's wonderful. But from now on it's *The Guardian* with my coffee, yoga classes, and four books a week from the library.' She laughs again, a good-natured, relieved laugh.

'Come on, Kris, the chain gang's forming!' Michael's head bellows through the window.

'What for?' But he's gone.

'Go on,' she says, with a "boys must be boys" look, 'I'll finish.'

By the time I'm outside Michael, Larry and Fred are disappearing into the wood. When I catch up they are standing around a fallen tree.

'Our winter fuel,' Michael says. 'René's given it to us.'

'Why don't you get him to drag it down with his tractor?'

'I don't know – dryads, Fradubio, and all that,' Michael murmurs, head down.

'*The Faerie Queene*!' Larry roars. 'Una and Duessa, which is the true and which the false – that'll always haunt you, won't it? And you'll never see that it doesn't matter – because you are the only judge.'

'Do shut up, Larry. It just doesn't seem right, dragging it down – maybe we could carry it?'

'Like a warrior on his shield?' Fred inquires dryly.

'Well, at least – honourably.'

'Don't forget to talk to it as you're chopping it up.'

'Oh I won't need to – it'll understand the alchemy of transformation.'

'Which is more than I do,' Fred says, staring down at the tree. Then:

'I shall miss working in the woods, woodcutting. I calculated it took one day's work in ten to cut our fuel. Good time. Winter mornings, the axe biting into the wood. Thoreau talks of it heating you twice, but it's more than that. Yep, good time. Come on, before we lose the light.'

It is growing dark beneath the trees. We lift the tree onto our shoulders, form ourselves into pairs and, stumbling at first and slipping we set off down the rutted track.

Arms around each other's shoulders, and sometimes reaching out to the shoulder in front to steady ourselves, gradually we catch each other's rhythm, harmonise our movements, until we're moving together. The weight of the tree pressing on our shoulders increases the sense of unity; and in spite of the weight and awkwardness we're soon swinging along well together.

So that when we reach the edge of the dark wood, step out into the light garden, lay the tree down across the saw horses, we're flushed and bright-eyed, laughing in our breathlessness, and each of us contrives, however briefly, to touch the others, as if to reassure ourselves, before we collapse onto the grassy bank to get our breath back.

We sit or lie, with no desire to move. There is still a reddish glow where the sun set; most of the sky is a delicate lilac. It is very quiet. There are squares of warm light in the black house but we sit, quite happy not to go in. Joni Mitchell's "Blue" drifts from the house. We can see the women gathered.

'Why do we so rarely do things together?' Larry asks quietly. 'Is it biological, or just habit? Whatever, it sure makes for loneliness sometimes. We go to women for comfort, for satisfaction, for validation, for release. We invest them with such power. But *we* have the power. We should support each other. I think we're going to need it. Come on, before we go in, let's hug.'

We climb self-consciously to our feet. This is all new. We huddle, arms round each other. Then we embrace each other, awkwardly, like adolescents on a first date, made gauche by the unfamiliarity of the male body, unsure what to do with lips and groins. Yet there is something marvellous, sublime, about the feel of a man's broad shoulders within my arms, of his strong hands across my back. Arm in arm we walk to the house.

As we walk into the big room and the women look at us, we separate like guilty schoolboys, bravery become bravado, gone. Sylvie sits in the window seat, staring out. Rosie and Julie sit close together, heads almost touching, talking seriously. They fall silent and, barely perceptibly, move apart, looking at us warily. Julie holds Kate Millett's *Flying*; Rosie's hand is still on it, drops from it, leaving it in Julie's hand. Nothing can clear these cross-currents, and after a very little small talk, as the couples awkwardly recouple, we yawn and mumble and disperse to bed.

*   *   *

Sylvie and I are alone in the big room where we'll sleep. On one side is a bed which some romantic visitor has converted, with lengths of wood and Indian bedspreads, into a four-poster. On the other is the sofa, my bed.

'You're quiet,' I say. She nods and smiles tiredly.

'Thinking?' She nods again. She looks vulnerable, almost lost.

'Light out?' She nods a third time. As I flick the switch the windows spring clear into view, filled with starlight. I slip off my clothes and wriggle into the sleeping bag.

Sylvie is standing in shadow by the bed and I can't see her. But I can hear her undressing, hear each garment separate from the others, from her body. The noises cease, and I know she is naked. I can feel the heat radiating from her body. Then the nightdress slithers over her head and down her body and I can see her, pale and slim and cool. The curtains open and close and she is gone. The bed creaks as she settles, then there is silence. I cradle my balls in my left hand and close my eyes. I'm wide awake. There's a cough from one room, the brief moan of a child from another.

'Sylvie?' my voice too loud, cracking the silence.

'Mm?' sleepily.

'Are you alright?'

'Fine.' Silence.

'I don't think I am.' Silence, then:

'It wouldn't work, Kris, not now. There's too much – it wouldn't work. Sorry. But you don't need me. Imagine what you want. It's okay, really. Might even help you see more clearly. I might even join you. Goodnight.'

'Goodnight, Sylvie.' I am alone.

But I can see her, naked now, body smooth and brown, see her breasts rise and fall with each breath, feel their softness, feel myself embracing her, sliding up between her parted legs, she beginning to breathe faster and shallower… and then the bed in the room upstairs creaks. Just as I grip with my right hand, just as I enter, there's a gasp, a pause, and then the rhythm of fucking above me, the pantings, the increasing tempo, faster and faster – then silence, the long outbreath, the sounds of two people making themselves comfortable for sleep. I sigh and reach for a tissue and smile. I whisper 'goodnight'.

'Mmm,' she says, 'mmm'. I turn over and go to sleep.

I wake suddenly. The only sound is Sylvie's rough smoker's breathing. I go to the window.

In the bright moonlight I see two figures at the edge of the garden, by René's half-cut hayfield: one, short, stands upright, looking straight ahead; the other, tall, leans over her, whispering in her ear, a stream of words I cannot hear weaving around her.

Then Julie turns to face Larry, and they kiss and embrace for a long time. When they step apart and, hand in hand begin to walk, I step back, turn away, don't want to know which way they go, if this is the opening or the conclusion. I slide right down into the sleeping bag, pull it over my head, not knowing what I want them to do.

At breakfast, what happened last night seems like a dream. Sylvie sleeps. Fred and Julie talk amiably. Larry strolls in the garden. I go out to him.

'What are you going to do now?' I ask. He draws on his cigarette and stops:

'D'you know, I don't know? Is there life after birth? I think I'm only just coming out of some post-natal thing.

'I tell you what though – since I finished the book I've been feeling, almost physically, the energy, the spirit, the spark flowing from here to here,' he taps head and heart then groin. 'I've still got a lot to give. I'm going to have some fun. And remember – if you have to do it, do it. Good luck.' He turns and strolls on, puffing on his cigarette contentedly.

'When are you going to start the roof?' Rosie asks. 'You'll need some help getting those *lausses* off.'

'I don't know. I'm doing something else at the moment.' She looks at me sharply:

'I thought that was the deal? I thought Jane had gone to London to pay for it?'

'It's a bit more complicated than that.'

'Kris, I don't think you can afford to be more complicated than that.' She sits across the table, talking urgently to me, face to face:

'This is the frontier. There's just the two of you. There has to be lots of accommodating. There's no room for complication – you may have to give up some of your cherished ambitions – we all do. It's called maturity. It's not easy, but you have to stick together, believe me.' Oh Rosie, advocate of something I'm not convinced you really believe, but that you'll make damned sure works.

'I'll let you know,' I say evasively, then:

'Fred? There are a few things I'd like to talk about before you go – any chance of you coming over?'

'I'd like that – tomorrow morning okay?'

I take my leave of sleep-heavy Sylvie in her white gown in her four-poster. Embracing a dream has been a resolution.

'Thanks,' I say.

'Any time,' she mumbles. I kiss her and smile. She snuffles and sleeps. I take my leave of all, and drive off, towards La Balme.

Chapter 5: Fred visits

'A dovecot? – squabs are good eating. A sauna? Heat upon heat, to sweat out the fever. Something Reichian?' Fred surveys the wall of my tower. 'Nicely built. I envy you your time on the buildings.'

'A space. Just a space.'

'An important space, eh?' He points to the copper stakes. One evening, after an exceptionally hard day, I'd been wandering around the property, mind vacant when, walking between the house and the tower I had felt a tension, an unease. Splitting a hazel wand I had dowsed and found an energy line, quite a weak one but blocked now by the presence of the tower. The copper rods channel it round.

'Do they help? Did you dowse?'

'Not for the location of the tower – I found myself gravitating there. I'm sure it's a very deep hot spot, strongly connected. The Combons used it as a rubbish tip.'

'Typical. When they lose it, they really lose it. Julie's more into it than I am. It feels good. Very sensitive. Sited like a warrior's castle: "stream to the east, hill to the north, road to the west, open fields to the south" – isn't that it? Haven't forgotten all the feng shui. But I've got dull. A bit tired, maybe, too much work, too much thinking about the times....'

'Where is Julie?'

'Gone to Albi. With Sylvie and Larry. She'll stay over at Sylvie's. She's rediscovered "Art". Larry wants to show her the Toulouse-Lautrecs. He knows the *conservateur*, can show them the drawings, the extreme ones, supposed to be technically some of his best. So they say. God, I wish it didn't seem so Nero-ish. I feel like Ezekiel.'

'Have some tea.'

We sit sipping tea on the verandah in the green, leafy, vine shade. At first we're both ill at ease, unused to sitting like this, not working, at this time of day. But gradually we let the dappling shade soften us, we focus on each other, we listen to what we have to say on this important day of parting.

'I want to know more of why you're going back,' I begin. 'Why?'

'Because, of all the incomers, you're the one who most nearly shares my background. And because something's happening to me; I'm changing in a way I don't fully understand. And that's scary. I want to listen to other people, check if I'm as weird as I sometimes feel.'

'What are you building? What's it for?'

'I don't know. See what I mean? I feel like one of the blokes in the Bible God tells to do something but doesn't say why. Except there's no God, no voice, just a necessity. Not even that – I'm building it because I can't imagine not building it; I'm making material what is already there – though I don't know what it is…. And I'm sure the purpose will emerge.

'Something's happening to me, and I'm trying to keep in touch with it, that's all. For the first time in years, I'm on my own. There is silence again – not the blocked silence of two people who can't talk, but that silence in which, sometimes, real purpose emerges. Trouble is, you don't know whether it's purpose or delusion. Especially on your own. You just have to decide whether to go with it, or not.

'I'm beginning to see people, look at what I'm doing, without always thinking of Jane, without seeing it all as "us". I imagine making love to Sylvie and don't feel guilty. I start building this and don't feel guilty. Okay, a bit guilty – but stronger is the defiance. I'm talking about me, but I don't want to; let me listen to you.'

Fred sits, ponders, speaks:

'When I went to Town Planning School, I wanted to leave everything behind: family, neighbourhood; even the teachers who'd propelled me there with their visions of the grove of

103

Academe – one actually used that phrase! – and the endless possibilities of Ideas, were now prosaic, to be left behind, gone beyond. Onward and upward.

'We were the privileged group on the skyrocket to a new world, like in those '50's sci-fi stories. We were the products of the Welfare State, and its successors. It was our task, and honour, to bring in the Millennium. The war generation would complete the past – jobs for all, houses for all, health for all; our generation would inaugurate the future.

'Do you remember all those reports – of course you do, Urban Studies was just as much part of it – "London 2000", "Europe 2000"? Do you remember the Futurologists? We were no longer planners – we were Futurologists! Going to one of Bucky Fuller's five hour lectures and reeling out, my head exploding with 'synergy' and 'tensegrity' and 'geodesics' – and suddenly we weren't Futurologists, we were Comprehensive Anticipatory Design Scientists! Automata would do all the work – remember Bagrit's Reith Lectures? Soon we would all have endless leisure. Soon we would all be infinitely mobile. Soon we would all live in cities in the sky and the earth would be green and fresh, a combination of factory farm – what a compliment that was in those days! – and playground. Soon we would all be happy. A world without friction, energy – petroleum, nuclear power – the lubricant. An imaginary world, devoid of values, without a political dimension, that forgets that most people are always, always poor.

'We'd been seduced, we bright working-class kids, and sold a pup, the pup of the trickle down of wealth; when in fact we were a source of new energy being siphoned up into the middle class. The Third World bought the same pup.

'On seeing the pup for what it was, we said – we won't fight you, we're going to be different; we'll build an alternative society, an alternative economy, within yours – and one day we'll split yours apart and show it for the empty shell it is. You've given us the tools – now we'll take the power.

'We built domes in college courtyards, squatted, made street farms among the tower blocks, started co-operatives at street corners. Everything should be free – because everything we'd ever had was always free. But nothing's free. We developed new social forms, new technologies, that freed people from the control of government and big business – and government and big business ripped off the juicy bits, stamped on the rest.'

He stopped, stared into the distance, resumed:

'Seeing all this, my conclusion was that society had evolved into a state in which there was no sensible way forward, heading into a dead end.

'So I backtracked, searching through the anthropological record, to find the place I could start again – from high tech to low tech, factory to workshop, workshop to farm, farm to man the wanderer, man the gatherer.

'That was the place to start, before possession of the land, the need to defend, the loss of connection with the earth spirit… but I wasn't strong enough for that, not free enough. I almost lost myself in the ancient forests…. I had to accept that self-sufficient peasant was as far as I could go, as pure as I could be.

'So I married – all farmers need a wife – and we came here. For four years I've worked here. I was accepted by the locals because I started work before them, finished after them, worked side by side with them, matched them. I scythed hay, with long sweeps of a whetted blade. I ploughed behind oxen, stumbling at first over the furrow cut by the plough drawn by those gentle, lumbering beasts. I pruned vines and harvested grapes with a knife shaped like a new moon. I made a twenty foot ladder the traditional way, sawing a fir tree down the middle, by hand, two days of sawing. And as well I made solar collectors, a wind pump for the well, used greenhouses and hotbeds, composted everything, grew better vegetables than their animal dung, or more recently their chemicals, ever had.'

'But here,' I ask, 'away from your home, why did you come here?'

'Because it's a region still less than a generation from self-sufficiency. Because it has all the requirements for the community I had in mind: lots of woodland, good land undamaged by fertilisers, plentiful water, long hot summers, a rich ecology, many old buildings and terraces that simply need renovating. Because it's a region that for hundreds, probably thousands of years supported a much larger population than today, and could again because the ecosystem is undamaged, just abandoned; a rich area lying fallow. The chestnuts alone – hundreds of acres, uncared for, unharvested, food for men and animals, fuel, timber…. This area could be incredible….' His hands grip, his eyes shine.

'And yet you're leaving?'

'As I said last night, I'm finally having to acknowledge what I've always known – that it's all down to politics, and that means fighting on the side of the guy who hasn't and needs, against the guy who has and won't share. A shame, but true.

'But there's another, more fundamental reason. Sometimes I've walked these hills, feeling the grass beneath my feet and the wind in my face, and looked down at the settlements in the valleys, at our place, and seen how wonderfully homely it looked – and realised I'm an alien.

'There's something about the place you're born in, the place where you grew up – it provides you with your cosmology, your mythology. It's the place where the abstract and the existential meet. Doesn't matter whether it's Delphi, Dorchester or Deptford. No wonder ancient peoples are so disorientated if they're moved even a few miles, so strong is their connection with their place.

'I'm an alien here. As alien as the Inquisitors who burned out Catharism, the Catholics who tortured the Camisards into belief, the teachers who beat *patois* out of the children, the Germans who shot the Maquis, the EEC officials with their upland subsidies and bribes to "modernise" – in other words integrate more completely into the urban economy…. As alien, and as corrupting. My model smallholding is a wound in this land's flesh, a raw place through which corruption can enter. It's not a question of intention; it's simply that one can only be true to your own patch, your own roots.'

'So who will buy your place?'

'It's not ours to sell – didn't you know? I couldn't come to a foreign place and buy – it would put me in competition with the locals, be an attempt to possess. We rent it from the neighbours. Who will buy it? – and I guess they will sell, now we've "added value" – a trendy novelist wanting a chic rural retreat? A boutique owner from Paris remembering his origins? A philanthropist who centres a new community on it? All outsiders, all destructive.

'Driving through St Leon I was thinking about the wild boy of the Aveyron, the one Truffaut made the film about – he was caught in St Leon, did you know that? With the best possible motives Itard, that most enlightened of Enlightenment benefactors, tried to humanise him – softening his skin with washing, lowering his resistance by dressing him in clothes, insulating him from the earth in shoes, weakening his constitution with dainty foods. He tried and tried to teach him to speak. The boy learned how to eat with a knife and fork, but he never spoke. Maybe he had nothing to say, to Itard. Imagine how he felt, watching a thunderstorm, through glass. Itard should have been learning from him, not teaching him. The boy soon died.

'I'm going home. To the neighbourhood I left at eighteen. I'll work there for all the things I've worked for here, on my own patch, where I belong.'

Chapter 6: The letter

I lie within my wall of stone. The sound of Fred's car fades in the distance – oh to be a man of belief! Or opportunist, like Michael and Rosie who, discovering she was pregnant after their first date said – okay, let's live together and, with two small children left England in an old car and drove south until the car expired and rented a derelict house in the village they were in and, when a relative died and unexpectedly left them some money, bought the house and for whom friends suddenly appeared from England, masons and carpenters and electricians and gardeners, and transformed the place and as suddenly disappeared; who took an old wood-burning stove to England on one trip and sold it at a good profit, and returned with a dressing table which also made money, and bought a small van, and then a large van, and now were thriving antique importers and exporters. None of it intended, all of it accidental – and if not this, then it would be something else, equally successful. Why? Because at those sticking points, those testing times, they focus everything, risk everything; for they feel they have the right to succeed, and they cannot imagine annihilation…. Or Larry, building his defiant, monomaniac bridge over the abyss.

The midday sun beats down upon me. I lie on my back in this crucible of stone, spreadeagled, staked out by Apaches, my eyelids cut off, to stare at the sun until mad and blind…. O Sun, do not blind me, or burn me – give me sight, insight, heat; strike your heat deep into me, illuminate the diamond cave untouched by light, give me the strength for purpose without destination. Am I a loosed arrow without a target? A space craft slung-shot around the solar system, observing and never arriving, to end in the lifeless black of space or the fusion heart of the sun…? Don't think of ends; let the destination materialise….

'Don't wall yourself in.' Fred's last words. Is this a broken tower? No, a tower to complete, a tower to top out, to roof.

A cone of scalloped slates, as on fairy tale castles, Leduc's Carcassonne, Dordogne houses…? (How is Montaigne's tower roofed? Will I carve quotations on the beams…?)

A dome. A geodesic dome. The modern Gothic. Upon the firm foundation, lightness, the lightest of space enclosures, Buckminster Fuller's intricate pattern of carefully calculated triangles, aery dome, imaging the dome of the sky, the subtlest of skins connecting interior and exterior…. I see myself at my desk, chiaroscuro room with a single pool of light from my shell lamp in which I make my calculations. And at my bench, making the ribs, cutting and shaping. And on the scaffolding, fitting the network of ribs, building out the delicate lattice structure… the blast of a horn. The postman. A letter from my father.

I tear open the package. A newspaper. Good. I sit inside eating bread and cheese as I read the letter. Always such high hopes. Of what? A careful, measured letter, as always, in his neat, manufactured hand. Some news: "my leg's been a bit tricky, but your mother and I still get out for our regular walks". Words of advice: "you might try root-pruning your old apple trees – the shock to their systems will often rejuvenate them". His garden is like a parade ground. A little dig about a school friend: "We saw Martin the other day – he's just been promoted and says how worthwhile he finds his work" – buying components for Vauxhall production lines. The style, as always flat, controlled; but sometimes, as if to really express himself, a passage of purple prose: quickly suppressed, as if to conceal his real feelings.

So what *are* my hopes? That one day he'll reveal himself, show me the person who hides beneath the conventional shell. But maybe he's just an ordinary man pretending that really he is not ordinary. Or maybe he's just an empty shell.

And that he will one day treat me as an adult, rather than

an impractical, interesting thirteen year old. I'd hoped my letters from college would enable us to resume a communication that had stopped years before. How I poured out my heart! How they were dead-batted, stunned, stopped in their tracks. And I'd hoped, ten years later and a thousand miles further away, that my letters from here would do the same. I want him to be an enthusiast for what I do. Or at least use them as an entrée to telling me what he's an enthusiast for, even if it never happened…? But he both lives through me and is envious of me; an impossible combination.

I begin to stuff the letter back into the envelope, but it won't go. There's another letter, this one from my brother. I read it with quickening interest: "It sounds really interesting, what you're doing… the divorce is going through and soon the house'll be sold and there'll be nothing to keep me here… too many memories… I've never felt so low as in these last few months…. the last ten years seem like a complete waste… need to rethink things… thought of throwing my tools in the back of the car and coming to stay with you for a while – do you think that's a good idea…?"

My brother, coming here! Terry's a real carpenter, apprentice-trained. I've dreamed of us working together, dreamed of us getting back together ever since we were separated by the education system at eleven. I dash off a reply and begin planning.

We'll do the roof together – not the tower, the house roof. He'll enjoy doing that. He'll be surprised at how strong and competent I've become. The tower was a diversion, an indulgence to keep me from starting the roof until the circumstances were right. We'll do it together, and Jane will be pleased.

But now there is much to prepare, materials to buy, people to visit. It's a good job Jane sent the cheque. I know Pieter has some spare tiles, but I need more. And I need a flatbed truck. My first call will be on André.

PART III:

A DETOUR

Chapter 1: A bubble of light suspended in space

I haven't seen André since the *feu*, when he was talking with such certainty of the significance of the Tibetan diaspora. He is a man of certainties, a man of iron, a blacksmith, a clockmaker. He lives resolutely against the grain of the country, making his own life stubbornly. They live alone, André, Marie-Claire, and the boy.

I pull off the road by their house. It is a spectacular house, built on a steep slope high above the valley: at the back it is a cave cut into the rock; at the front a glass-walled room cantilevered out over the valley so that when you sit in it you seem to be in space; a feeling that exhilarates or unsettles, depending on one's nature and mood. He is the only incomer to have built his house from nothing. Around it are the terraces he has painstakingly constructed and is gradually bringing into cultivation. André does everything from nothing. I wonder what I have to learn from him.

One evening he told me his story. We were alone – Jane and Marie-Claire were in the kitchen. We began in the cave, by the spring that issues from the rock, lit by the low light of his ingenious hydroelectrics; moved through the main room where he showed me things he had made, objects he had collected on his travels; and finished looking out over the valley as the sun set, the light faded, and lights slowly appeared below us and above us.

"I was in the army, a regular soldier, and Marie-Claire was a soldier's wife. We lived in an army house in an army camp. I was a physical training instructor, without doubts, my life all of a piece. I was walking to the married quarters and had stopped to look at a new advertisement on the hoarding – the bill poster was up his ladder brushing out the last section; I love the way they do that, unfolding, pasting, brushing it out, the way the pieces fit together. It was an advertisement for a skiing holiday: sun, snow, laughing faces. I imagined speeding down the slope, approaching the speed of light. The tank came through the hoarding. First the gun barrel punched through a laughing face; then the hoarding exploded. Slowly. The man and his brush and pail and ladder arcing in separate trajectories through the air in slow motion. Then everything was spinning round, was upside down. And then nothing. Time ceased.

"I drifted in and out of sleep, feeling nothing, aware only of whiteness and the rustle of starched garments and an all-pervading hum. The only things differentiated were the red of Marie-Claire's hair, the low modulation of her voice. Gradually I came to. That was the worst moment. I couldn't move. I, who had always defined myself by my actions, who had never separated thought and action, now was swaddled like a mummy, connected to the world by two tubes. I was as helpless as a baby.

"And yet I was a man. I began to think, and slowly those large areas of my mind that had been bypassed began to operate. At twenty eight I had an adolescent crisis. I had questions and I could find no answers. They told me my leg was shattered, that I'd always limp, that I was finished as a PTI, that they could retrain me for an office job or discharge me with a pension. I wanted desperately to stay in the army, my only home, my only stability.

"I asked questions and got no answers. I wrote down lists of questions and lists of answers and tore them up. I wrote down everything I knew and tore it up – I knew nothing of importance, nothing of significance. I was just a set of habits. And all the time I was fighting the whiteness, the antisepsis, the mechanical droning hum, which I associated with annihilation. One afternoon it got too much for me.

"It was a hot day, and everyone else in the ward was sleeping, the snoring dead. Outside the cicadas rasped. A thin green lizard slid onto the wall by the window then vanished. In the little office the nurses spoke in low voices, with an occasional laugh, the rich, sexy laugh of the nurse from Guadeloupe. The whiteness, the hum seeped into me, all colour and shape were bleaching out before my eyes. I prepared, yet again to fight it.

"But I couldn't. I just let go, let it engulf me. I lay there, terrified, sure I was about to be annihilated. The nothingness swept over me, through me. I held my eyes tight shut, clenched my fists. And then I unclenched them, opened my eyes. I was still alive….

"There is an island in the Tarn. It's a low island, often flooded, but trees and grass and flowers grow on it. A couple of years ago the river was in spate, running stronger than I'd ever seen it, the island invisible under the raging surface of the water. When the river level fell I went to look at the island. It had been swept clean of soil and vegetation. It was bare rock. I was like that island: only those parts of my inheritance, my character, my experience that had been fully integrated into my being were left; the rest had been swept away.

"But there were two crucial differences between that island and me. The first was that I had self-awareness, the capacity to choose. Rock weathers, seeds are blown by the wind, kids light fires; things happen to an island, but it can't make things happen. I could. I could choose to accept or reject what happened to me. I could make things happen. I had only one thing, but it was the most important – a sense of myself. The second difference was this: a fire within me, an uprushing fire that burned along my veins and bones and flickered across my skin so that I was all on fire. Such a wonderful heat!

"Do you know the first word Pascal wrote in his night of crisis? 'Fire'. Do you know the test of an achieved Master in

115

Tibet? That he can dry, with his naked body, seven successive wet sheets wrapped around him as he sits in the snow on a winter's night. Inner fire. Each of us must refine himself, and then manufacture himself, in his own furnace...."

And so he began, day one of his new life, his life, testing everything and everyone, including Marie-Claire, in that fire.

With the pension they were financially independent. Sometimes they travelled, sometimes they settled. When he had learned enough to begin, they came here. They lived in the cave. As they learned new skills, developed new needs, he built out from the cave onto the ledge. And then beyond the ledge, into space. Was this defiance? No, a necessary extension, a new relationship with gravity, with air. Their house a combination of advanced technologies and traditional techniques: a sophisticated miniature turbine develops electricity from the small spring; the house is cooled by the same funnelling construction methods used in traditional North African houses.

"There are no useful patterns in the world anymore; we have too much knowledge, too little wisdom for that – and the two are related. There are no useful "isms" any more.

"You know the first sentence of *The Social Contract* – 'Man was born free, and he is everywhere in chains'. As important is the second sentence: 'Those who think themselves the masters of others are indeed greater slaves than they'.

"There is just the individual in his unique world. And there's no need to push back the frontiers of knowledge (anyway, as we learn each new thing, we forget an old thing, so what is gained – especially as it's the old things that are closest to us, that we need to remember...?) – there is plenty and enough knowledge and information.

"It's time to announce the closing of the frontier, time for each individual to hunt and forage through the world as it is, selecting, rejecting, choosing, learning only what he

116

needs to know, and thus building for himself his own unique relationship with the world, his own place, his own life. From now on, it's all *bricolage*."

It was dark. We sat in silence, in that bubble of light suspended in space. I remembered what Frank Lloyd Wright had said about the cantilever: "the most romantic, the most free, of all principles of construction". André's face was leathery and seamed, his eyes bright. He was tired, clean. A hero. And when Marie-Claire came in, her skin ivory, her red hair aflame in the lamplight contrasting with the blue of the sky, and laid a gentle hand on his shoulder…; his apotheosis. As I drove home I was, with Jane – as she rehashed her conversation with Marie-Claire – as hard and tight as a clam.

Chapter 2: The walking manikin

'André?'

I pad down the stone steps and across the small terrace paved with blue and white tiles, an endlessly intricate Islamic pattern; a pattern in which, André told me, the essence of being, the Pythagorean first level of number, can be seen by those with eyes to see. It is a strikingly beautiful pattern. I stop by the limestone rock at its centre. From it trickles cool water. It is very hot now, but a touch of the water to my lips and tongue refreshes me. I look around at the terraces, raw and unweathered, the soil yellow and inert. How will he grow things here? Will he? He will.

'André!'

A light tapping stops and André limps to the door of his workshop. He smiles a lopsided smile, holds out a hairy hand, says:

'So. Come in.'

It is a workshop like no other I've seen. Its white cave walls are covered with neatly- and carefully-placed tools, every conceivable tool traditional and modern for a range of trades, especially metalworking, arranged to André's own scheme.

Between the tools and boxes of parts are icons and beau-tifully-calligraphed quotations and enlarged monochrome photographs. The place is perfectly tidy, scrupulously clean, more like a chapel than a workshop. To the sides are benches with different sorts of vices. In the centre is a charcoal fur-nace, glowing red, the air quivering above it.

'So, this is Hephaestus' workshop?' I say. He pauses, pon-ders, says:

'Why not?', then: 'watch.'

On the bench is the model of a man, two feet high, dressed in a business suit and bowler hat. André touches the man on the shoulder, leans towards him as if whispering encouragement, steps back. The figure stirs into life, walks slowly along the bench.

There is something familiar about the way it, he, walks; not the jerky motion of a clockwork machine, not the clipped walk of a City gent. A fluidity, an evenness, a glide. When the model reaches the end of the bench, André touches it again on the shoulder, the manikin begins to walk backwards, and I see – Mr Chen, tai chi Master, who said: ordinarily, walking is falling; I will teach you to step. Forward or backward. Chi moves the empty leg, you place the foot where you want; until it touches the ground there is no necessity. Then it grounds and fills, necessarily; the full leg empties, becomes empty, can be moved by chi….

'It's astonishing,' I say, 'brilliant.' As I watch, André tells me how he studied Muybridge's photographs, pondered the Buddhist walking meditation, listened to what I had to say about tai chi:

'Imagine,' he says, 'a world in which businessmen walked like this. A Taoist Stock Exchange!'

'He's Mr Tao Jones!' I laugh.

As the figure walks, measured, balanced, intent, André opens the back to reveal a complex assemblage of rods, cogs, chains, cams, gears, working in different patterns at different tempi.

'There is only one primary movement – the stored energy in the spring released into the rotation of this central shaft. And this central axis is like the axis in tai chi, connecting the pole of heaven to the centre of the earth, through the performer, from the thousand-petalled lotus to the bubbling springs. And a gyroscope is like the inner balance; and hydraulics can mimic the filling and emptying.

'Do you see what I'm getting at – a Western technology applied to non-Western belief systems?' He gazes contentedly at the smoothly-operating mechanism, then shuts up the back and switches off. I follow him outside and we sit looking out over the valley.

'When I was a kid,' he says, 'I'd go to the museum at Neuchâtel and look at Jaquet-Droz's automata.

'There was a little girl who played the organ, actually played it, with articulated fingers. I was in love with her. I can still remember the tunes she played. And a boy who could write. He'd write a different message each day. One day he wrote my name – before my eyes, while I watched. "André". It was like a message from God. I believed that when I learned to write, the little girl would fall in love with me. Maybe everything I've done has been for that little girl….'

His head is down. He is turning a pebble over in his fingers, over and over. I hesitate, then speak:

'But those are museum pieces, two hundred years old. Couldn't you produce more realistic automata using electric motors, electronics, microchips?' He looks at me and smiles and lays a hand on my arm. Then he settles back, his hands behind his head, his face to the sun:

'The model itself is trivial – clever but trivial. What's important is what I learn, and can demonstrate, about mechanisms, machinery through it; and how I apply what I've learned to the task of living here. Sorting out our relationship to technology is fundamental to our chances of success. Most incomers are trying to escape from machines, while at the same time depending on them. That's frustrating. If you can live without machines, fine; if not, you have to establish a positive relationship with them.

'The problem isn't technology but its place in society. Look at the massive use of power, energy, especially electricity. Doesn't it bother you that we make and use, in vastly greater quantities and voltages, the energy that powers our bodies? And then hide it away so that it comes out of small holes in the wall, like magic? Look at the way invention has

120

moved away from the task in hand, using ever more industri-ally-processed materials – technology takes over. And indus-trial design processes – the intellect takes over. The Greeks performed plays in the open air to 35,000 people without microphones. In India there are superbly accurate observa-tories with no lenses. Everything in that figure I can make myself, with iron ore, a furnace, an anvil, my tools.

'Do you know the Islamic concept of *baraka* – that, through time, machines take on the qualities, good and bad, of the people who use them? So that a machine or tool used sensitively for a long time becomes more sympathetic. It's a good idea and should be basic to our society. We find Oriental ideas sympathetic – we should relate them to tech-nology. Doesn't that make sense?' I nod. I'm overwhelmed by his intensity.

'But you didn't come here to listen to me.' I explain the sit-uation. He tells me Marie-Claire has taken the truck to go swimming with the boy, Patrice.

'I'll bring the truck over this evening, take your car. As for tiles: I think Henry – the American who keeps goats, you know? – I think he may have some. I'll ask Marie-Claire. Good to see you.'

'Thanks. Thanks very much.' We embrace. Standing in the sun, he watches me for a while, then limps back into the workshop, his shadow dancing on the wall.

Chapter 3: Marie-Claire visits and brings news

I plan the work for the roof of the house; imagining the process of clearing the *lausses*, repairing the woodwork, making new dormers, roofing. At university I learned to think in concepts, a linear process. On the buildings I learned to think in images, spatially. For each step of the process I call up a picture into my mind: then I can move around inside that imagined world, change things, shift them around, until I'm satisfied I've forgotten nothing. Only then do I reach for pencil and paper and list the materials required. I enjoy visiting these imagined worlds. They are sensuous, non-linear, four-dimensional, rich. A richness I have experienced only since leaving the academic stuff behind.

I'm relaxing, wondering whether it's yet cool enough to water the garden, when Marie-Claire, not André, arrives with the truck. She swaggers towards me, smiling. Patrice hares off to the meadow, enchanted by the thick grass, clambering through the leafy trees, whooping in the soft greenness. Marie-Claire looks into my eyes, her eyes flicking from eye to eye. She pulls off her head scarf and shakes free her red hair, water-darkened, still wet from the river. She places a slender hand on my shoulder and kisses me on the lips. Her lips are thin but her mouth is wide and sweet. She smells of the river. She steps back, sighs, throws herself down on a verandah chair, pulls her feet up under her, looks up at me:

'That's what I was going to do,' she says.

I don't move.

'Have you got a drink?' I pour wine.

'That's what I was going to do after André told me you'd called. "Don't disturb yourself," I said, "I'll take the truck over". I'd no idea what would happen. Nothing was planned after that. And then Nathalie came.' She holds up her empty glass. I refill it.

'It's hardly ever the person; almost always the timing. What strikes me is not how rarely we hit, but how often we miss. Just before, just after. All that movement, all that gravity, and so few collisions.'

I'm standing, bottle in hand, struck dumb. She smiles, says:

'Sit down. Relax. Listen. Let me tell you about today.' I pour myself some wine, drain it, pour more.

'We went swimming, Patrice and I, you know that. I love the river. This is what I do. I float on my back, and let the river carry me. I become very still. There's a point – I know it well – from which it is just possible for me to swim back, against the stream. I'm a good swimmer, but it's a very hard swim to get back to the bathing place. Floating on the river is good – cupped in a watery hand, my head back, deaf, looking up at the sky, watching the birds fly across, leafy branches move by…. But the swim back, swimming my best, using all my resources of technique, reserves of energy, that's better. Usually.

'Today, I was approaching the point – it's not a physical place: where it is depends on the strength of the flow, how I'm feeling, lots of things; it's a locus of awareness. Anyway, I was feeling the delicious panic that brings me to life rising – and then, instead of intensifying, it faded, faded quite away, leaving an emptiness. And in that new emptiness I heard a voice, calm and caressing, saying: "don't stop. Go on. The river is your friend, it will bear you, carry you away to places you have only dreamed of. Let go". A delicious voice, whispering in my ear. How I wanted to trust it, believe it. Then I shouted "NO!" and turned over onto my front and swam back like one possessed, fought my way back against the flow, crawled from the river on my hands and knees. Patrice was standing there, terror on his face. We fell into

123

each other's arms.' More distant whoops from high in the ash trees.

'André doesn't swim, does he?' She smiles and shakes her head.

'But there's more, much more. When André told me about you and the truck, I was excited – I can tell you now, there's no need to hold back. And then Nathalie came. You know, Henry's wife. She didn't stay long, she wanted to get back. Henry had killed himself. I know, I can't believe it either. He went to the furthest corner of the garden – you know how overgrown their garden is – and cut his wrists, and then he cut his throat. His own throat. He bled to death. And I could see him lying there, staring up at the sky, listening to a whispering voice. I was furious – I was punching him in the face, shaking him, screaming that he couldn't get out of it like this, dragging him back. But it was too late. He'd gone. With a smile on his face. Bastard.' She's sobbing, shaking. I give her some rum. At last she looks up, eyes red-rimmed, pupils like needle points:

'You've just got to keep on – yes?'

'Yes.'

*   *   *

It's time to call Patrice, time for them to go. She has calmed, talked of Nathalie:

'She's keen that you have the tiles; she wants to carry on as normally as possible. Otherwise, she says, she doesn't know what she would do.' We've talked about Jane:

'She has to get away from your influence,' is her conclusion. We've talked of many things. We walk to my car, hand in hand. She puts her hands up on my shoulders. I place mine on her slim hips. We kiss for a long time. She makes a funny little noise, disengages.

'But....' She lays a hand on my forearm, shrugs, calls

Patrice, slides her lithe body into the driver's seat. Patrice comes running up telling her at the top of his voice of his adventures with the chickens. They drive away, Patrice's voice audible above the engine noise.

I touch my forearm, remember how her hips, her lips felt, shrug, and trudge to the garden. Watering the garden, the red sun setting, I feel a tremble, like a wind passing over the surface of the earth, and a shiver running up my spine.

Chapter 4: Surviving

Is suicide more common in rural areas? Not according to the statistics. But it is more visible in the country, and memories are long. "That's where crazy Bertrand threw himself down the well." "When was that?" "I don't know – my grandfather told me when I was a boy." And "Pujol hanged himself in that barn, there," and you hear the rope creaking on the beam, see the heavy swinging body, the kicked-away bucket sprawling in the strawy dust. Somehow it's never behind closed doors, always public. So much of life here is.

Facing the ill-repaired, rainbow-painted door, I realise how rarely I have faced death. A friend killed in a car crash a dozen years ago. Grandparents dying at a distance. I knock. It's not that he was a friend; Henry was erratic and disturbing at the best of times. The door opens. I stammer my condolences. Nathalie stands, her face empty of character and expression, shining white, seraphic. I stumble on, engulfed in this dazzling emptiness; a slight knitting of the brows, as if she's trying to comprehend one jabbering in an unknown tongue, and then as understanding dawns a terrific, radiant smile bursts upon her face:

'Thank you so much. Do come.' She half turns, as if to say something into the house, then checks herself, pulls the door shut and strides purposefully in her long skirt across to the barn.

'I'll help you.'

'Please, there's no need.'

'I have to.' She picks up tiles, heaves them onto the truck, working with a furious energy, an enclosed concentration, calling upon reserves of strength and stamina from who knows where in her slight frame until the sweat of her breasts wets her thin blouse, her chest is heaving.

126

When we've finished she throws herself down on the hay, pushes her long hair from her sweating face, lights a cigarette, draws deeply on it:

'That's better. Another half hour and I'd have gone crazy.'

'Who's there?'

'His mother and sister. They've come to take him back. They've got him back at last.' We sit in silence. Nathalie looks around as if seeing things for the first time. Her gaze settles on the tiles, tenderly:

'They were going to be for the new barn. We were going to have more goats. Lots and lots of goats. And bees. A land flowing with milk and honey. We would make cheese and yoghurt. Mm.' Her eyes focus far away:

'He always had a reason, for everything he did, for every change. In his family you always had to have a reason – they were so clever with words, they always sounded plausible. Him too. He thought he'd escaped when he left Boston and came to Paris, where we met. It was only partly to escape the draft. He said – how can I kill Vietnamese when the only ones I want to kill are my family? On one acid trip he thought he'd done it. He was so happy when he came out of it – until he found he hadn't. Until '68 he was a poet; in '68 he was a revolutionary; after '68 a rural utopian. Each change cogently and convincingly argued, with references to Byron, Southey, Thoreau, Hawthorne, Snyder, Bly…, annotated and footnoted…. After the community, we came here. Then there was nowhere to go.

'He'd watch television hour after hour, watch the aluminium coffins going home, the fall of Saigon, the last Americans going home. But he couldn't go home. The Khmer Rouge fascinated him: believers, smashing cars to slow movement, grinding watches under their boots to stop time, emptying the cities and levelling them to make all equal, peasants. Le May had said he'd bomb Vietnam back into the Stone Age; in Cambodia they were doing it to

127

themselves. "It's the only way," he'd mutter. "Even Angkor Wat. It's all got to go. Oh I wish I was doing this to Washington."

'And yet he was so good with the goats, so gentle with Joelie. I'd watch the astonished, stricken look on his face; as if someone was operating on him without anaesthetic. I could only watch, and then turn away. I kept trying to work out where I fitted, what I was supposed to do....

'I knew something was happening. Alarm bells were ringing in my head. But there was a voice saying: "it's out of your hands now. Live with the consequences". I knew I had to let him go. I'd pulled him back enough. When I found him, I stared into his face for a long time, trying to read the expression on his face, trying to find a message, any message, there. It was a complete blank. I suppose that was the message. Live with the consequences. When I stood up, looked down at He... He... Henry, looked round – I felt a pain, right here, as if two hands were tearing my heart open, an unbelievable, unbearable pain. I cried out, I know that; then I was desperately trying to wall off the pain, anaesthetise myself, fly away from it... and then I said: let it happen. It was like opening venetian blinds onto a neutron bomb. The radiation poured through me. I'm sure you could've seen my bones. And passed. And I was still standing.' She smokes in silence, then says:

'Have you ever stood at the top of a hill in a gale? You know that if you fight it, it'll knock you over; if you let it, it will pick you up and carry you away, wherever: but if you alter yourself, adjust the vanes, turn the slats so they're edge on to the wind – I can't think of another way of putting it – the wind passes through you, winnowing, cleansing....'

She grinds her cigarette under her sandal:

'Do you want some coffee?'

'No. Thanks. But I'll wash my hands, if that's okay.' As we walk across to the house, she says:

'It's warm today. Strange, I don't feel it.'

The kitchen is shuttered and airless. Joelie sits in the corner, talking secretively to her rag doll. A large, unformed girl of about twenty sits at the table, her head buried in a large book: *Coming To Terms With Death.* A middle-aged woman with long, iron grey hair pulled habitually back from her high forehead is scrubbing a shelf implacably. There is a pervading smell of disinfectant. Nathalie comes out with me.

'Don't worry,' she says, 'they're going tomorrow. They've got what they want. They're taking him back. All those coffins coming in from the West, and his solitary one from the East. Singular even in death. I have friends we'll stay with – we weren't married so they can't take Joelie, though they'd dearly love to. They won't take her. Good luck with the roof. They're good tiles. I'm glad they're being used.' She waves as I drive away, waits until I'm almost out of sight before she turns and goes in.

*　　　　　*　　　　　*

I stop by the black basalt Cross of Lorraine, amid silent pines, which marks the place where the Germans beat the partisans to death. I look back at the house, isolated on the bare hillside, the light harsh upon it. A loser's place. He must have embraced it when he saw it – at last, the place where he could fail. Nowhere to go. No escape. Like crazy Bertrand and old Pujols. Like facing a neutron bomb. I twist the mirror so I can see my face:

'And when will you open the blinds on your neutron bomb?' For a moment I imagine doing it; then I twist the mirror back so it reflects to my eyes the peaceful, empty road behind me. I smile at the illusion, and start the truck.

I drive too fast, carelessly. It's only when I almost hit a headscarfed old woman picking marjoram by the roadside that I come to my senses and drive more circumspectly. As I drive on I realise that I can't return, not yet, to the silence and emptiness of La Balme. I need comfort, civilisation, family. I set course for Pieter and Hendrika's.

Chapter 5: A Dutch interior

There are roses in the hedge near where I sit; single, pink, five-petalled, delicately scented, with soft green leaves, and thorns like a wildcat's claws. Roses of a time when a rose was *rose*, before there was red and white. Pale lanterns in a dark hedge. One perfume thread in an olfactory weave. I wonder if Henry – lusting after and yet nailed to the impossibility of the Celestial Rose – ever looked at a single wild rose, at its repetition of heart-shaped petals, its yellow-powdered centre, and said: "this is"; gazed upon its singular clarity, embedded at first in an unfocussed penumbra which gradually thins, fades, disappears; a single rose in nothingness. This is. I believe it would have saved him.

*   *   *

I climb slowly to my feet. I've no idea how long I've been sitting here, within sight of Pieter and Hendrika's farm, comforted by its presence without looking at it. Now I can look.

It lies below me, at the end of a curved white track, in its own small valley, a neat group of stone buildings set in a rumpled patchwork of small fields; the different textures and colours of pasture and lucerne, hay and sunflowers, wheat and garden, vines and woodland. There is even, on the narrow stream, a millpond and ruined mill. It is almost too pretty, too neat, like something out of a painting, for this rough region; although its prettiness is the reason they bought it four years ago.

The light is already draining from the land, intensifying in the sky as I bounce the truck down the rough track. Pieter looks up, lays down his hoe and hurries to meet me. He shakes my hand and embraces me and begins to talk

131

excitedly until Hendrika appears at the door of the dairy, then he scurries back to the garden without looking at her, works, head down. She walks to me slowly, smiling a weary smile:

'Come in,' she says, 'I'm almost finished.'

It is cool in the dairy, cool and with moisture in the air, a relief from the dry heat outside. Cool and clean and well organised. Hendrika's domain. Whitewashed walls, scrubbed flag floor, the polished sheen of stainless steel buckets, bowls, scoops. A milkiness in the air. Everything in its place. A high window frames a square of intense blue sky and a grey branch of shimmering green ash leaves. There is a wooden table, another inlaid with Delft tiles. There is a familiarity about this calm scene, a reminiscence. It nags at me as I watch Hendrika gruntingly heave buckets of milk – she brushes aside my offers of help – and move trays of butter. Then she calms. She reaches for a jug of milk and pours it into a creamy bowl. Of course. I see the way the falling ribbon of milk twists, exactly as it does in the picture, by Vermeer. A Dutch interior.

She pats the last block of pale butter into shape. She works carefully but awkwardly, her actions, I realise, an uninte-grated combination of childhood memories from her grand-parents' farm, and what she has read in books and learned on "small-scale dairy" courses. How hard she tries. And how rectilinear the result. She marks it with the farm impression, steps back, picks up a large pointed flashing knife and plunges it into and through the butter so it sticks quivering in the wood and the butter splits in two. I flinch and wait.

'We lost a newborn calf this morning,' she says, as she pats the butter back into shape, erasing the evidence of her vio-lent act, as if nothing had happened.

'I went to deliver the milk and yoghurt. I reminded Pieter to keep an eye on Saffron. When I got back she was

132

bellowing in the cowshed, a terrible, blood-freezing bellow, and Pieter was nowhere around. The calf was dead between her legs. The cow was tethered and couldn't reach to lick away the membrane and the calf had suffocated.' She pauses. 'Like a baby in a polythene bag.'

'Where was Pieter?'

She lays down the butter paddles wearily. She stands motionless. I see the way the skin sags from her arms, her throat. She is beginning to be old, the age when there are no more second chances, and she knows it. Then she wraps the butter carefully in greaseproof paper and clears up:

'He'd had a sudden intuition, a feeling, about that damned cave of his. He'd gone up onto the top to check an alignment or something. He thought he'd only be gone a couple of minutes. When he got back he was so excited, sure he'd made a breakthrough. Of course he was full of remorse. But we needed that calf. I don't know.' She finishes cleaning up and says, 'let's help him with the watering.'

*   *   *

The shared task of watering the garden lightens the mood, especially when Pieter and Hendrika jointly tell me of their latest application of biodynamic methods: boiling hundreds of slugs to make slug repellent.

'It was so disgusting, it was hilarious!' Pieter roars, doubling over with laughter.

'It was like something out of *Macbeth*,' Hendrika adds wryly, and Pieter roars again.

The watering done, I load the tiles while Pieter brings in the horses and Hendrika checks the meal she has insisted I share.

When I return I find them sitting on camp chairs on the small square of dried-up lawn in front of the house, looking for all the world like colonial settlers; if not harmonious, at least reconciled. I accept a drink and sit beside them.

The sky has turned peach. The first stars appear, seeming to arrive from a distance. The animals snuffle in the barns, the sound of the trickling stream comes up to us. Three crows beat across the sky homeward. The earth loses weight, rises up. Over all there is a great and welcome stillness. I settle in the chair, feeling calm and, as I often do here, with these older people, safe, at home. Pieter sighs:

'I never experienced this in the Netherlands. For years I never experienced it.'

'What?'

'Silence. And darkness.' I watch a star appear, brighten, and say:

'I remember during the miners' strike in England, when there were power cuts, cycling through the dark streets of London and looking up and seeing the stars shine with a brilliance that was so unfamiliar I had to stop and stare up at them. It was as if they hadn't been seen for years, like in that Ray Bradbury story. I expected people to come out into the streets and stare up in wonder, and marvel. Instead they stubbed their toes and swore.' Silence. Silence and the gathering dark. Pieter says:

'We had to go back to the Netherlands during the oil crisis. Do you remember the car-free Sundays they had there? You could stand in the middle of Rotterdam and hear nothing but the sound of bicycles and excited voices. Cyclists on motorways, liberated from the narrow cycle paths, suddenly aware of the width of the roads, the space they took up. No thud of pistons, just the whirr of rotary motion – the music of the spheres. I saw people walking along urban motorways, staring around them, seeing for the first time the Cyclopean, unhuman scale of the world that had been created around them, for them, in their name. They were shocked and silent.

'I stood on one of those complicated multi-level junctions, watching the colourful streams of cyclists weaving and counterweaving their way, and said to Hendy – "surely, now they'll see; now they'll open their eyes and realise what is happening". And for a couple of days things *were* different, people bright-eyed, talking of what they'd done on Sunday.

'But it didn't last. Because they never made the necessary connections. The brightness faded, and by Wednesday was gone. I felt sad. But at least it confirmed to me that we had done all we could there, that we had been right to come here.' The darkness gathers around us. Hendrika gets up:

'Dinner will be on the table in five minutes. Don't be late,' and walks quickly into the brightly-lit kitchen.

Pieter refills our glasses and continues:

'The Netherlands is an artificial society – stop the pumps and half of it would disappear inside a week – made rich by colonialism, and financed now by a bubble of gas. One day the bubble will be empty, the power will go off, the screen will go blank. It will be a new Dark Age. But it will be much darker than the last; for they've banished darkness from their lives, and they'll have forgotten what it is. It will have become for them the source of evil, not the necessary diastole. And the same will happen to Britain when the oil has come and gone.'

'But why is it different here? This is France, the Common Market, tied into the world trading system?'

'This isn't France,' Pieter snorts. 'This is Languedoc! They have their own language here, demeaningly called *patois* but still the language of the troubadours. This is upland Languedoc, the Massif. This place hasn't moved in fifty million years. Change has come in a succession of seas swirling around it, but only the occasional wave has broken over it. There are places here that haven't changed since Palaeolithic times. There's not one innovation of the last thousand years, and probably five thousand years, that couldn't be shrugged off and this area

135

still support double the present population. This place is solid. Solid.'

'Dinner!'

*　　　　*　　　　*

The meal passes quietly. Hendrika and I talk politely, exchanging news. There is a sticky moment when I mention Henry and she brushes the topic abruptly aside, saying 'foolish boy' impatiently and changing the subject.

Pieter, head down, eats and drinks noisily, brow furrowed, oblivious. From time to time Hendrika smiles apologetically at me, frowns at Pieter, but he doesn't notice. When he looks up it is to stare out of the window with a faraway look. It is only when we go into the sitting room and Hendrika puts on a record, Beethoven, and Pieter drinks his first brandy that he begins to talk.

At first his sentences are disjointed, separated by long pauses, unconnected, his mouth locking open when a word won't come. But gradually they cohere, into a stream, a river, a torrent of speech. It is as if he's now able to reach back across the unhappy incident of the calf to the awareness that drew him out of the valley onto the top this morning. I watch and listen, fascinated, as the words pour from his grizzled, craggy South African face.

'My father was a great hunter. I don't mean he had trophies on the wall and a leopard-skin band round his hat; but he was a hunter by nature, who loved hunting because he loved the animals he hunted. "When you hunt an animal", he'd say, "you share its being".

'We had a farm, but it was my mother who ran it. My father looked after the horses, but he was too restless for the repetitions of farming. He was no settler. At certain times of the year he'd be around the place, looking more and more sorry for himself; then he'd be gone. My mother's face would take on a hard, set expression and she'd yell at the men and tell us kids the story of the little red hen.

'Our Bushmen hands were just the same as my father – as the rains approached and the clouds built and the lightning flickered around the horizon, they'd become more and more fretful, would stay up all night chanting and dancing, and then one morning we'd get up and they too would be gone. We'd ask mother where and she'd say, in a heavy, sarcastic voice, "they've gone for a country walk, just like your father, gone for a country walk". I'd stare out from the farm to where they'd disappeared.

'There was only the desert, shimmering in the heat, the furnace heart of the Kalahari. I'd imagine what amazing places there must be to draw them into that desert, what oases and palaces and golden castles, what adventures. One year I resolved to follow. I made my preparations and set off before dawn on my little fat pony. I was twelve years old. It was a dawn such as you only get in Africa: vast, majestic, ancient. I was alone, with a mission, the only person to see that sun rise, and the sun greeted me benevolently, as its acolyte. I felt myself to be a real hero, and I kicked my pony into a short gallop in celebration.

'But as the sun rose higher, changed from benevolently warm to livid and angry; as the heat poured down and the air began to run like melting glass; as I left all vegetation behind and rode on through a desert of sulphur, I began to be afraid. I was alone for the first time in my life. My skin was burning alarmingly. All around me the land and the sky were breaking up in waves of heat – distant hills hovering, their bases dissolved by the running heat, strange twisted images of dunes and rocks and trees hanging in the sky; and everything rippling, distorting, changing, a world without certainty. And yet I carried on. I could have turned round and navigated out of the desert by the sun, but what had started as an adventure had become an ordeal, a test.

137

'I camped that night by a leafless tree, built a fire and lay back, looking up at the stars. I heard a lion cough as it paced around my fire just beyond its range. But above all I heard the stars.

'I lay there, staring up at them, aghast, awestruck. Countless stars. Sometimes I saw pricks and stabs in a velvet pall letting through a light immeasurably brighter than any I knew, a light that dripped down and spread in a silver sheen on rocks and vegetation. Sometimes I saw the depths of stars, from just beyond my reach to infinitely distant. Sometimes they were pulsing points of vitality, throbbing and shifting in a dance and clash of superabundant energy. And such a noise they made, low roars and sharp cries and a ceaseless oceanic hiss....

'At last I slept. In the night my pony got free and, very sensibly, trotted home. Now I was in real trouble.

'I remember little of the next hours or days or however long it was. Just moments. Of falling down on my face and opening my eyes and seeing a snake a few inches from my face, its smooth plated head, its curious flicking tongue, its impassive, unblinking eyes. It seemed to ponder long its decision before turning aside and sliding away. A hyena loping unevenly around me, squinting at me, sniffing the air. And a castle – or was it a palace, a cathedral? – gold and silver and pink, shimmering before me, shining.

'And then something cool and sweet trickling into my mouth. A sharp, animal smell. A wrinkled apricot body, a flat triangular face, slanting eyes. My head resting on a grimy, acrid-smelling thigh. The woman's shoulders heaving as she sucked the water up from who knows what depth in the earth through a thin tube, into her mouth, and down the side of a stick into mine. I have never tasted such sweet water. I looked into a face that was entirely neutral, non-judgemental. There was no question of right or wrong – she was doing the only thing possible. There was no soft expression of

138

tender sympathy, no sharp criticism. I gazed up at her and felt a contentment I'd never felt before, and have never felt since. I rested content. I'd been found, my life saved, by a group of Bushmen.

'My father, who knew them well, soon turned up. At first he wanted to send me back. But I'm sure he knew what would happen when I did go back, and he let me stay, sending a message to my mother that I was safe. And so I spent a season with the Bushmen, my first and last. I lived with them and shared their lives, insofar as a white boy could.

'Their shelters were made of bent branches and grass. They slept on the earth, scooping a hollow for the hip. Each family carried all its possessions in a single animal skin. Driven from their lands by encroaching blacks and whites, driven into the heart of the most hostile environment in Southern Africa, they lived the least stressed, the most harmonious, the fullest, yes the fullest, lives of any people I've met. I've never eaten better, slept better, lived better. They stepped lightly on the earth, and the earth responded. The most primitive people on earth.

'But not simple. They were complex to a degree we find hard to imagine, because it was a complexity without categories, without boundaries; though with levels. They were knowledgeable, their knowledge no collection of learned facts, but things learned from the world they lived in, the place they inhabited. Beneath an apparently featureless desert they could find roots and tubers, burrowing animals, water.

'Their senses were astonishingly acute and attuned – they saw, heard, smelled things long before I could. But they possessed more than these fine individual senses. At first I thought it was a sixth sense; but I grew to realise that it was as if they had a place within where the faintest hints from all the senses were brought together, integrated, so somehow

139

they knew. When they hunted, they ran with astonishing speed and stamina; when they killed it was with dispatch and an absence of pride; when they butchered, no part of the animal was wasted. Through their stories, about the first spirit of creation, I learned true religion. They had games, music, dance....

'I could go on. But you understand what I'm saying, don't you? That the so-called primitive man lives in harmony with the world, is of the world and in it. That his is the age of gold whose passing Hesiod lamented, which we place in the Garden of Eden. That science and technology and learning are attempts to compensate for a loss rather than being the measure of our gain; they are activities of the age of iron. No wonder the alchemists sought to make gold from base metal. No wonder the Spaniards destroyed South America in their lust for gold. And no wonder modern man draws around himself the Emperor's clothes of progress – his is a chilly world.

'And then it was time to go back. My mother must have seen a new look in my face, as my father had known she would, and within a few months I was packed off to Europe, to relatives in Amsterdam, to be "educated". Maybe she was right. Maybe the Africa I'd come back to, from the desert, was ruined for me – that all I'd see would be a battleground where the destroyers, the lost souls, black and white, would pillage the earth and fight each other to the finish, destroying everything worthwhile in the process. The only alternative would have been for me to go native, Bushman native; but that would have been an escape, not a solution.

'So, I began again in Europe. I was given a good education, a solid grounding in European culture. A culture of grandeur and nobility, intensity and individuality. A Faustian culture, sure – but what feelings were aroused in me when I read Dante, looked at Rembrandt, listened to Bach!

'And of course the familiar questions came to me: how, in a society of such civilisation, can there exist such evil; why have there been so many wars; how do you cope with religions and ideologies that torture people into belief; how do you enjoy fine buildings when you know they were built for the few and paid for by ruthless exactions from the many, who lived in squalor...? And behind these questions, sharpening them, was the vision, my memory of that society whose culture and harmony sang in the whole of me, leaving no doubts.

'For years the only way I could cope with these contradictions was by see-sawing between two extremes: at times a materialist socialist, advocating equality and iconoclasm; at times the mandarin aesthete, cultivating the senses.

'And then, in my reading and learning I began to sense an undercurrent in the great river of European culture. A chance word here, a veiled reference there. The numerology of Chartres; Hieronymus Bosch and the Brethren of the Free Spirit; the symbolism of Holbein's "Ambassadors"; Newton's alchemical writings; Mozart's freemasonry; Kandinsky's Theosophy. The sense of a dark body always accompanying the bright: of the Gnostic gospels behind the biblical; of heresies, through the Manichean to the Millenarian, behind the church; of astrology behind astronomy, alchemy behind chemistry; of Leibnitz's monad shadowing Descartes' dualism.... A subterranean stream beneath the great river of culture; like those earth-energy lines that dowsers detect. The road not taken.

'There's a word for it, of course: the esoteric. "The world will be saved by the few", Gide wrote. But I began to believe that it might only be saved *for* the few; who in their turn, by their survival, can bring in a new Golden Age.

'Throughout history man has faced choices; and the majority choice has always been for the outward, the material, the exoteric. The broad highway.

'But the other way has always been kept open, secretly, a byway, a secret path through the woods, to appear when the time is right. It was there in the sixties – vulgarised and commercialised, to be sure, but there: the counter-culture, the underground, the alternative.

'But then I saw that when it is brought out into the open it is bound to fail – partly because there is an inevitable, fatal coarsening; but also because it draws upon itself the full force of orthodoxy. The light destroys it. To survive it must always be shadowy, secret, eccentric. That's what I realised then.

'That's why we came here; to prepare in a bypassed place. And maybe that's why the others have come; to be part of this secret, life-saving community. We can do something here. Especially if we find the cave.'

He leans over and refills his glass and drinks deeply. Hendrika stiffens then shrugs. I hold my breath. Pieter's head begins to droop, as if he's falling asleep, then he snaps up, his eyes bright:

'The cave,' he says to me vehemently. 'In 1969, when the world was collapsing around me, when they set foot on the moon and I thought that's it, we've done it, the ultimate blasphemy, I had a dream. I was on my own, alone in a flat desert. In front of me was a hill, golden in the sun. I began to climb. There was no path, but I knew where to walk – something was drawing me upward: when I deviated from the way, the power diminished; when I returned to it, it strengthened. The sun was very hot and I was tired and thirsty – and there beside me was a pool in the rock. At the pool edge was a place carved or worn into the rock where I could kneel and drink.

'As I knelt a charge, like an electric shock, passed through me. I was frightened, but I rode the fear because I knew it

142

was right. I drank – it was like a draught of molten metal. I resumed the climb, becoming stronger as I climbed, more certain. I stepped out boldly, confidently – and stepped into nothingness. I fell, it seemed endlessly, through black space.

'I landed with a thud, the breath knocked from me. All was dark and silent. I struggled to my feet. I felt in my pockets; I had three matches. I lit one. The flickering flame revealed a cave, its walls and ceilings covered with the most astonishing paintings. I lit the matches one after the other, lighting up as much of these paintings, of incomparable vitality and holiness, as I could.

'And then the matches were gone. I had seen all I was to be allowed to see. I sat in the dark, letting the paintings etch themselves into my memory. I sat in the dark for as long as I could; then I felt myself floating up, towards a light, and I woke up at home, in bed.'

He pours himself another drink, clumsily, almost knocking the bottle over. Hendrika looks alarmed. I'm desperate that he says more before he falls asleep. His voice is slurred now:

'It reminded me. you see, of something I'd forgotten, suppressed; that I'd seen such a cave in the Kalahari, which the Bushmen visited, was part of their religious life. But this cave, the cave in my dreams, wasn't in Africa, it was in Europe. The desert was man-made, the sort of desert Europe might well become.

'Of course I knew there were Palaeolithic cave paintings in Europe, I'd seen reproductions; but I'd never connected them with African cave paintings. I was very excited and told Hendy that we must go at once to Lascaux. That was a disappointment – even though we managed to get into the real cave, not the copy everyone visits. They were too familiar, had been photographed, studied, stared at too much by ignorant, incomprehending eyes, over-examined.

'And then, when we were looking for a farm to buy in this region, I saw a hill just like the one in my dream. I knew that

143

here we would find a cave, a Palaeolithic cathedral, hidden since Old Stone Age times, secret, unspoiled, with its numen and message intact, a message from the first men, the first spirit; and that we could find our way gradually back to the first spirit, and bring it gradually forward into our lives, and illuminate our lives now with the spirit that I had experienced with the Bushmen. We have only to find the cave.'

He raises his hand dramatically, his eyes shine. And then dim, his hand falls, his head droops into his chest and he begins to snore. His craggy face has softened into the peacefulness of a child's, and he sleeps. Hendrika looks across apologetically and says:

'He gets very tired.' I nod and smile sympathetically. 'Coffee?' she asks.

As Pieter snores and Hendrika rattles the coffee things too loudly in the kitchen, I try to ponder what Pieter has been saying. But I can't get hold of it, the torrent of words still foams incomprehensibly. I let it go, and look around the room.

Another Dutch interior: rugs on a polished wood floor; framed maps and landscapes, discreetly spotlit, on white walls; a glass-fronted mahogany cabinet full of carefully-arranged china; polished bookcases with books in four languages; standard lamps creating pools of light; a walnut desk with framed family photographs on it. Objects, accumulated slowly, over a long period of time, charting a marriage, functional, aesthetic, talismanic. A world of objects. A room that reveals a belief in objects and the culture that produces them. And around it, dark now but there, beyond the reflecting windows a raw, uncultured world. A re-creation of urban Holland in rural France. Maybe more than a re-creation, maybe a transplantation.

How does this fit with what Pieter says? Is this his safe

haven from which he can sally forth and speculate? Or is it Hendrika's doing, her price for coming to live here? And while his ideas excite me, this comforts me. It's what draws me here.

*   *   *

Hendrika pours the coffee, puts on another record; Mendelssohn.

'Pieter loves to talk,' she says.

'I like listening to him. He's fascinating.'

'He – I don't know how to put this – you remind me of him, when he was younger.'

'Thank you.'

'No,' she says in alarm, 'I don't mean it like that. It's difficult. When you were talking, at Edvard's, it set me thinking, about you and Jane. You're clever. You pride yourself on knowing things. And you pride yourself on your independence. And those are attractive qualities, to a certain sort of woman. The sort I was, that Jane is.' She stops. I feel uncomfortable. She goes on:

'Pieter's read a lot and thought a lot, but he's never really done very much. He's always been full of ideas, of plans that somehow never come off. He was a photographer but he refused to do bread-and-butter assignments. He was a freelance writer but his articles never suited any of the publications. At one time I even found myself working all hours in a little corner shop while he was writing a book that never got finished. At last, when the third child came along, I put my foot down. He's spent twenty years working as a clerk in the council offices.

'What I'm saying is that he's a dreamer. What he likes about this place is not so much the opportunity it gives him to put into practice the things he's thought about, but the fact that he need never wear a tie, sit at a desk, call any man boss.

145

He can pee where he likes, and drink with the locals. This place could never pay on the amount of work we put into it. I costed our sunflower oil – it's ten times the shop price. I was left some money and that's what has paid for this place so far. But even that won't last forever.'

'But if you didn't think he could make a go of it here, why did you agree to come?'

'It's hard to remember now. Maybe I felt sorry for him, having watched him fret all those years in the office. Maybe he'd begun to sound plausible again. And maybe I was seduced by the air and the sun and the romance of the sound of it…. I like so many things about our life here, but there are so many things I miss: friends, social life, culture, just walking down a street. Here, there's too much space inside my head for my thoughts to chatter around in, circling thoughts.

'Now of course we have to stay – we'd never sell this place for enough to buy anything in Holland. And Pieter could never go back. There comes a time when there is nowhere else to go – but you and Jane aren't at that stage, you still have choices, and Jane is giving you the chance to go back.'

'You're presuming I can't turn my ideas into reality.'

'Yes, I'm afraid I am. I don't have a lot of faith in men's ideas. Men are fantasists, women realists. That is my experience.'

And that's it. The trade-off. I want to put my arms around her, lay my head on her breast. And she would stroke my head. But the price is to live in this cocoon, to wall out the darkness – you can sally forth, but always you must return to this.

But sometimes you have to let the darkness in, let it penetrate, into your house, your being, while you cross your fingers. And sometimes you have to go outside and stay out. This house isn't that different from my parents'. And Pieter slumped there, stunned by alcohol, quite like my father hypnotised by television; and Hendrika....

'Do you need any help with Pieter?'

'No, thanks, I'm used to this. You go. I'll be alright.' She shakes him, shouts loudly in his ear. Pieter grumbles and snuffles, then rears up in wide-eyed wakefulness crying:

'"The time of the hyena", that's what the Bushmen call madness. This is the time of the hyena,' and slumps back. Hendrika waves me away, saying 'take care.' Pieter struggles to his feet, Hendrika lifting him by the arm; I watch them move slowly across the room, then I turn and head out into the darkness, defiant.

Chapter 6: The second letter

But I don't feel so defiant in the night, nor the next day, even before the letter arrives.

I dream it was my brother who killed himself. I find him in a quiet corner of the garden in a pool of blood, ashen, his eyes wide open, the expression on his face exactly the one he had after his wife left him – guilty, terrified, lost. 'But why?' I say; 'you have so much skill, I'm the useless one, all talk. Why?' The flicker of a smile then the inexpressive movement of dry lips: to find out what's behind living. I watch life ebbing from him, watch him go grey.

And then he's hanging by his heels among the pigs, blood belching from his throat and I have a bloody knife in my hand, and he looks at first apologetic at the absurdity of his situation then aghast as he sees something I can't see. 'What?' I say, 'what do you see?' as his face deforms like putty until only the staring eyes and the grey lips remain and the lips mouth one word. Nothing.

I wake with a start, sweating. It's still dark but there is the beat of life out there, alien and strong. I'm trapped in the house which feels oppressive and strange. I think of Hendrika and say – yes, it's true, I am a dreamer. By what presumption do I think I can do what I say I'll do? I think of Fred and feel like an inept colonist, an intruder. I think of the incomers, one by one, and see meaningful, purposeful lives, all except mine. I fret. At last I sleep.

I awaken to an irregular wind blowing from the west, the Autun, a hot, maddening, dessicating wind. The sun is harsh and livid. One of the truck's tyres is flat, and the jack jams. Unloading the tiles I trap my finger which splits and I watch my blood stain red on red. The tiles become heavier by the

148

armful and fine dust comes off them and coats my sweating skin and thickens my lungs. I return the truck, expecting there at least a little sweetness; but Marie-Claire busies herself, keeping her head turned, until I'm leaving when she grips the two of them, André and Patrice, arm in arm, a family, and smiles defiantly at me. I drive away from something that has meaning towards something that has none. The postman's yellow van is just leaving.

I tear open my brother's letter – the details of when he's coming will get me back on the rails.

"Many thanks for your enthusiastic letter. I can understand about Jane – there aren't many women who can cope with that amount of disruption, they're all home birds at heart. You really sound as if you're getting it together. I too have some good news. As you know I was very low earlier in the year, feeling like chucking it all up. I hope you got my letter via mum and dad. Well, since I wrote to you I've met a great lady. She too has had a hard time and we understand each other. We are deeply in love and I feel that for the first time I am both loving and being loved. It's a great feeling. There's a real warmth in my life, after so much coldness. Now I have a new hope, and a renewed faith in human nature, especially the female kind, mine having taken a real hammering over the last year."

I force myself to read on, not wanting to read what I know he is going to say; that he isn't coming. Our one chance of working together, of being together, as we were long ago, of me working with the one who has known me from the beginning, ending. A door slowly, irreversibly closing. Closed.

I am quite alone. The world turns, people lead their lives, and I am quite alone. I doubt my existence. I must do something, anything. I begin to move some great baulks of timber, massive and heavy, heaving and grunting as I carry them one

149

after another until my muscles are solid with fatigue, my skin is running with sweat, the blood is pounding in my temples; and then I work on.

I hurl one onto the growing pile and watch it as, instead of lodging, it bounces off in slow motion and knocks me down and pins me to the ground. Panting I lie trapped. Then, summoning every ounce of anger and energy I heave it off my legs, lift it above my head and hurl it with a great cry onto the top of the pile. It stays. The cry echoes around the trees and hills and sky and I begin to weep. I work on, my vision distorted and made luminous by tears. I will work, I must work, I will show them. The sound of a car. Coming down the long road – could it be? Drawing nearer. Stopping. Stops. A door. I wait. For Jane. An unknown voice speaks to Madame Bonafet. Crushed I work, the world spinning and unstable around me, each spar of timber the only thing to cling to. My name, whispered, I whirl round, back away – no, don't find me like this – hands up defensively. There's nobody there. Nobody. But I stop, and look.

Nothing moves. Everything is imperturbable, ordinary, natural. The leaves shimmering on the trees. The soft vegetation and the hard stone. The way the light is on the wall of the house. Everything is as it is. And me. My bandaged finger. The downy, dusty hairs on my arms. The feel of my skin. The thoughts in my head. I'm here, and now. And this is the last piece of timber. I lift it carefully, almost tenderly, carry it slowly, place it precisely on the pile. I step back, and smile.

*   *   *

I shower and put on clean shorts. Then I wash all my clothes and my bed linen and lay it over hedges to dry and bleach. I clean and tidy the house, which I've let go rather. Then I begin to rearrange things.

I make up a different bed in a different room. I move the table. I pack things away that I don't want to see. The place is lean and spare, and organised in the way I want it, a place for me on my own; but, with its two chairs, a place I would be happy to receive David Thoreau into.

Before dinner I meditate, gazing at the candle flame, the first time for a long time. After dinner I write my diary; it is important to resume my conversation with myself, to exchange intimacies with that steadfast inner friend, rather than turning always to the fickle, mutable outer sort. Sometimes solitude is necessary so that the chattering voices gradually still and fall silent and the one persistent but often quiet voice can be heard. Sometimes solitude is the only way. Tomorrow I will resume work on the tower.

PART IV:

THE WORK RESUMED

Chapter 1: Pages from Kris's diary: mowing

7th July

I woke early this morning. The Bonafet bantam cocks had stationed themselves at the corners of the cobbled area between the houses and were engaged in a crowing contest. The first called his harsh "crack a doo da doo!"; the second repeated the call with interest; the third responded; the first augmented... and on and on, the sound swelling and becoming more vehement, the bantams puffing up, growing excited, oblivious in their excitement to each other, the rising canon disintegrating into individuality, the pattern of call and response breaking up into a cacophony that, amplified between the hard, reflecting surfaces of the buildings, shattered the still air into a thousand glittering shards. And then they stopped. I could feel, as I lay in bed staring up at the rafters, the vibrations of the air slowing, the air melting then resolving once more into a pure crystal stillness. I imagined the three flashy birds, with their red wattles and combs, the long iridescent curves of their tails, perched together on a fence rail, facing the newly risen sun, struck suddenly dumb by its incomparable magnificence and splendour. But sunrise was half an hour away. They had stopped because something inside had switched them off; it was time to do something else. The sheep shuffled in the barn. Birds sang. I got up, dressed, went out.

The air was sharp and clear, with the freshness that you get only in the very early morning at this season.

I walked along the twisting path, through the narrow gate, and stood at the edge of the meadow. From here the land slopes down into the valley. I could hear cocks crow miles away, an occasional dog. People here used to call to each other across the valleys, exchanging messages over a mile or more. You were never alone. Now, those who have, telephone, those without lead newly in-turned lives. I could see individual trees in the chestnut wood that fills the bottom of the valley, the hedges defining the fields, the cluster of buildings in the hamlet across the valley, all very clearly, each thing sharp and clear, as if there was no distance, only size. The sky was clear and pale blue, gold where the sun would rise. The chorus of birdsong echoed in the tall, slender ash trees that fringe the meadow. Their delicate leaves trembled slightly in a barely perceptible movement of air. The ash is called "The Venus of the woods", and they do have, these, a long-limbed, smooth-skinned, lightly-clad beauty and elegance.

The grass of the meadow, tall now and bending over, its green fading brown, splashed with the colours of meadow flowers, stirred softly. A field mouse, wary but unseeing, crossed in front of me in a series of rushes and halts, like a clockwork toy, and was swallowed up in the cathedral grass. Thoreau's words, "how much virtue there is in simply seeing" rose pleasantly in my mind like a bubble through water. But in doing, too, I suddenly thought – yes, in doing, for there is work to do, and is this not my meadow and does it not need mowing? Certainly it does. My meadow, my responsibility. I must cut the hay this year, at least so it can grow in good order next year; but also because I'll need hay to feed the goats over winter. I have no goats; but we planned to have goats and goats need hay. No time now for reverie. I returned to the house striding, my first task of the day decided.

I got out the scythe and the whetstone, the pitchfork and the rake. The rake felt fragile, and when I shook it the handle broke. The head and teeth, made of chestnut, were firm and fine, but the ash handle was wormed and dusty.

I got out the big-toothed bow saw and walked to the meadow to cut a new handle. I was wearing shorts and sandals and the grass was wet on my feet and legs as I skirted the

156

meadow looking at the ash trees to find a suitable branch. How to choose, among so many branches? (It must be a branch – a sapling has no substance to it.) Clean length, thickness, straightness, accessibility, balance of the remaining tree – don't look too hard, let the eye rove, rest on one: then dismiss all the others from your mind. There are many possibilities, each with its consequences; but once you have chosen, live with that and leave all the others behind, in the past, gone. There.

I scraped up a small ball of earth and shinned up the tree and made myself safe; drew the saw twice across the underside of the branch then sawed from the top, the rasp and hush echoing in the trees. The branch fell with a whoosh, landed with a clash, lay still. I rubbed the soil onto the cut surface and climbed down. I seemed to climb down into a bubble of extra brightness, in which everything was just right, in which I could do no wrong. I wasn't conscious of this at the time, only afterwards when it was gone, but I can remember how it felt. I had a very clear perception of the physical – the saw biting through the green-tinged white wood, the branch bending then falling, the clash of leaves and the soft thud as the branch hit the ground (that seemed to be what triggered it), the shivering after-sound and then the silence. The green smell of sap. The feel of the bark against my knees as I climbed down. The hushing sound as I pull the leafy branch through the wet grass. My footsteps.

Then preparing the handle – everything goes just right. Chopping off the twigs and the surplus length with deft strokes of the sharp axe; drawing my bright knife the length of the branch and peeling off the flexible bark. The wood is white, smooth, shiny, damp. It is like a long, firm bone. I run my fingers along the length of it, smell its green dampness. And then, again with the axe – an extension of my hand not an implement in it; this morning I could shave with it – shaping the

157

end, carefully splitting the first two feet, the blade searching out its destined path through the grain, pulling apart the halves and pressing the points into the ready holes of the rake head. A perfect snug fit. Two wedges hammered home to tighten it for a lifetime's use. I can see myself using this rake in thirty years, remembering this moment. I shake it; it is firm and responsive. And that's it. The bubble slowly dissolves.

I gathered up the ash leaves in my arms and carried them through the silent hamlet to the last small house. The door was open. It was dark inside, smoke-stained and bare – a rough table, two straw-seated chairs, a blackened cauldron hanging over a smoking fire, a paraffin lamp, a murky picture of Jesus. The old woman lives here, with her son. Often he sits on the wall at the edge of the hamlet, motionless: sometimes he's there, sometimes not, but I've never seen him move. He is a big man, thickset, sitting upright, hands crossed on the dog-head handle of his walking stick, his face stiff and expressionless, his eyes following you blankly, his mouth open as if he has just cried out. He sits, a stone guardian, petrified.

"Chid, chid, chid." I called but no one answered. "Chid, chid, chid." I walked round the side of the house to the garden. The old woman, in faded widow's black, in thick rumpled stockings and wooden clogs, thin, wrinkled, grey-faced, was mattocking the solid earth with long, fierce strokes. She shook at each blow; I expected the vibration to shiver her to pieces. I coughed and stood, in shorts and sandals, blond, long haired, my arms full of ash leaves. She looked at me, waiting. 'For the rabbits,' I said helplessly. She didn't move. 'Shall I put them here?' No response. 'Goodbye.' As I reached the road I heard "chid, chid, chid." I shivered and shook my suddenly-cold limbs as I walked back to the house, glad of the warmth of the newly risen sun on my goose pimpled flesh.

I had breakfast and did some jobs until the dew was off, then I went to mow the meadow.

I stood at the edge of the meadow and saw at first shades of green and brown with splashes of yellow and blue, purple and pink; a visual image, the ignorant city man's view, an Impressionist painting. On further looking I began to apply my recently-acquired knowledge: I saw feathery bents and furry vernal grasses, salmon-flowered sorrel and pink ragged robin, foamy meadowsweet and tall yarrow, brash buttercup and delicate forget-me-not. I've eaten green-apple sorrel, used yarrow for the I Ching…. Looking closer, pondering individual shapes and powers: the lion-toothed dandelion, dent-de-lion, diuretic *pisenlit*; the scabies-treating scabious with its devil-bitten root; the rock-breaking saxifrage, effective against bladder stones…. I was looking at a food store, a materia medica, a living encyclopaedia of pre-scientific culture in which form, function, name are related in a different way to ours, in which the homoeopathic principle is implicit, in which meanings overlap and interfold so there is no either-or…. I was looking at something which is rapidly disappearing, superseded even in this region by grass re-sown every few years, and cut green for silage: 'nutrient-rich', weed-free grass; even though it has been found that cattle fed on hay from old meadows soon become healthier and more resistant to disease. I was standing, holding a scythe, the grim reaper, about to mow down, scythe through, make hay while the sun shone – a whole body of metaphor now historical, unexperienced by 99.99% (and more) of those who use it…. I looked, and knew – but my knowledge was acquired knowledge; I was a folklorist. The only way I could begin to know this meadow was by mowing it. I stepped forward.

In my mind's eye I saw the long sweeps of the scythe and the neatly falling swathes of grass. Three times the point stuck in the ground; twice the blade slid over the grass and stopped a hair's breadth from my bare leg. My only wish was for a machine with a button to press. I tried swinging it like a golf club. I tried turning as in tai chi. As the point dug into the ground for the fourth time I heard a low, indrawn whistle. I whirled round. Gaston, Madame Bonafet's brother, man of all work on the neighbours' farm, was standing watching me over the fence, chewing as always on a sprig of mint, pushing his beret back off his forehead and scratching his head in wonder.

'What am I doing wrong?'

'Everything.'

'Can you scythe?'

'Of course.'

'Can you teach me?'

'I can show you.'

He felt the blade with a calloused thumb and pulled a face. He waved me back to the house, and checked through the tools the Combons had left. He picked out a cow's horn, a spike with a crosspiece and square head, a lump hammer. Back in the meadow, he struck the spike into the ground until it stopped at the crosspiece, then hammered several times along the scythe blade on this portable anvil, ringing blows:

'You do this – *enchapplez* – when you damage the blade on a stone. But you also need to do it regularly to temper it – especially a blade that hasn't been used for a long time, like this one.' Then he whetted the blade with long sweeps of the stone:

'You must keep the stone in water, in a horn at your waist. Hay takes the edge off a blade very quickly – though not as fast as wheat – so sharpen it often.' Satisfied, he felt the heft and balance of the scythe and nodded. 'This was old

160

Combon's wasn't it? It's not bad – wasted on him, though.' Then he spat on his hands, rubbed them together, and began scything.

With his right foot forward he swept the scythe back parallel to the ground, setting up the grass for the cut; the blade swept forward in a curve close to the ground with a hiss, cutting the grass so that it dropped on the spot with a sigh, neatly. A step forward, the blade sweeping back and then forward and the grass falling in a perfect crescent swathe. Balanced and rhythmical, an action that was never extravagant, always contained, that seemed almost too easy-going – until I saw the concentration on his face, the precision with which the scythe moved, the blade swept, the grass fell. He moved forward, inexorable, a light in his eye, a dampening of sweat on his forehead.

At last he stopped. 'See?' he said, a man in his element, but also a man in triumph, finding he can still do it. It looks straightforward enough I thought, and took the proffered scythe. I tried to keep the image of him working in my mind, to fit myself into it. I over-swung and fell over; I swung too little and the scythe stopped against the grass; I swung too straight and the blade hit the grass like a wall and wouldn't cut; I curved too much and it curled round without cutting. Gaston doubled up with laughter. 'It's alright for you, you've had years of experience,' I said angrily. He put his head on one side and said quietly, 'you're the one who's come to live here'.

Gradually I learned, and at the end of an hour, dripping with sweat, I could scythe passably. What I had discovered was how much physical strength, especially of hands and wrists and forearms was needed; that you need to have a constant sense of the plane you're working in so the blade is always parallel to it; and that there is a complex, but ultimately knowable relationship between the curve of the blade and the curve of the stroke. We talked a little.

'I used to scythe that bank,' he said, with a quiet pride, pointing to a steep part of the field beyond the fence. 'No one else could – they always dug the blade in. I could scythe wheat – the others had to use sickles.' He would like to scythe the corners that the mower and harvester can't reach; his nephew prefers to grub out the hedges, straighten the fields, so the machines can reach everywhere. He is proud of his skills. But often it is the defiant pride of one who knows he is being bypassed, and that his skills will die with him.

He looked up at the sun, said 'aye, aye, aye,' and went off to do the job he should have been doing, a new jauntiness in his step, whistling. A few minutes later he returned, with a bunch of dried mugwort. 'Fasten this in your belt: it'll help against backache. you'll need it.' Another smile, and he was gone.

And so I scythed as the sun rose and fell in the sky. I listened to the hiss and sigh of the grass, smelt the different scents of each plant as it was cut, saw the swathe of cut grass widen, lighter in the sun than the uncut. By the end of the day I could hardly move, and my swollen hand holds this tiny pen with difficulty.

8th July

I finished scything the meadow.

It was late afternoon, the great heat was past, the farm stirring into life. I sat in the fragrant hay and watched birds dart and butterflies flutter. Birds sharpen time; butterflies break it up. A bird flight is a swift mark on the firmament, a pencil stroke, *now*. The butterfly's bobbling movement, unhurried and indirect, makes a nonsense of the notion of the passing of time, expands 'now' into a multifarious, timeless dream. Once I was a bird. Then I became a butterfly. Now, maybe, I'm becoming a bird again. Or a butterbird. Or a birderfly…. Shsh.

162

I lay down by a few spears of uncut grass, beneath them so they towered above me in the blue sky. I smelled the earth, touched it, sank my nails into it, tasted it under my nails with my tongue, its sharpness. I shrank and became very small, an atom among molecules of earth, staring up at the heaven-reaching sky, at one with the earth – except I own it. It's mine, bought and paid for, and so, willy nilly, my responsibility. I might imagine that, like the Bushman or the Aborigine, or even to a degree the neighbour, I am as much possessed by as possessing, that some mystical relationship exists; that, as the phrase goes, I've borrowed it from my children rather than inherited it from my parents. But in reality all I've done is bought it, with money earned elsewhere, in a place where money is cheaper and land more expensive. A simple mercantile, capitalist transaction, supply and demand determining the price. I've bought it. And that's all I've done so far. Whether anything more develops is up to me and what I do here.

I got up and walked along the edge of the meadow, looking at the unpruned plum trees, unlaid hedges patched with rusty corrugated iron, invading brambles, the ruined barn, all the work that needs doing. A line of Thoreau's comes shudderingly into my mind: "how many a poor immortal soul have I met well-nigh crushed and smothered under its load, creeping down the road of life, pushing before it a barn seventy foot by forty"….

I walked across to our vines, four hundred of them, all pruned by me; I've just finished the last bottle from our first vintage. The flowers have set, the tiny grapes, now the size of grape pips, have begun to swell.

A house, a garden, a meadow, vines. We fell in love with a dream; but a dream we had in the city, that we brought with us. I had intended to return in order to discover something.

163

Instead I returned to own. At some point I had lost my nerve, the wish to discover replaced by the desire to possess. Was it because of Jane? Or further back, Melanie…? Perhaps the how and the why of my losing my nerve are the questions I have to discover the answers to, this summer.

I sat in the vines for a long time, tired and vacant.

I was about to go back to the house when a large bird rose suddenly into view. Below the vines there is a wheat field, golden in the sun; beyond it the land falls sharply, so the wheat forms a clear golden edge against the blue sky. The bird rose up between the the gold and the blue, a pale grey, almost white, hawk-headed bird, soaring on long, slender wings. A hen harrier. With easy confidence it saw off an ungainly buzzard, emptying this sector of the sky for itself and, after a few carefree solo soarings and plummetings, for its mate, which rose as majestically as itself from the valley. They turned and rolled, soared and dived, flew over and around each other, uttering heart-touching mews and cries, overlapping and interlocked in the same space though never actually touching; dropping into the valley, soaring high into the blue sky, sweeping across the golden wheat field, apart to the limit then as close as dancers, always together. I watched for a long time; and at last envy gave way to pleasure, and to pleasure was added gratitude.

Chapter 2: Pages from Kris's diary: the neighbours' farm

10th July

Midnight. A single bird song. Liquid, pure, beguiling. The song of a summer day in the stillness of the night.

I began cutting the struts for the tower roof, the geodesic dome, today.

I've had some lengths of chestnut machined to size and rebated by Lucien, the joiner in the village (I can't call him the village joiner because like all tradesmen these days he works over a wide area). He's a young man, about my age, who took over the workshop from his father. Although the old tools still line the walls, they're there to impress the city folk who've bought *maisons secondaires* and want them done up in traditional style. His pride and joy are the electric saws and planers and mortising machines he has installed. He wanted to know what the wood was for, so I explained, showing him my drawings and a couple of photographs of domes. He examined them carefully, but soon lost interest.

The older people here are against change because they know, intuitively, that life here is all of a piece, a complex interlocking system, and that once you alter one element the whole thing begins to fall apart. No, that's not quite right; this is a robust system, with lots of built-in redundancy, that has adapted to many changes over the years – the important thing is the rate of change. When that rate rises above a certain point, then the whole is unable to absorb it. The young, in contrast, are eager for change; they don't see the past (except critically), only the future. They want the latest, often leapfrogging intermediate stages, like Lucien going from hand tools to the latest Swiss machinery. But they are only interested in the new in a narrow way, examining it to see if it has any value in their work, for their clients, and if it doesn't, dropping it. They have ambition but no curiosity. The dome is something of no use, therefore of no interest.

I had some squares of flexible steel cut and drilled at the garage. More a machine shop than garage, he can do anything with metal, repair any machine – his father was the blacksmith.

It was good to be working at my bench again, with wood, with tools I understand and am familiar with; saw, plane, square, sliding bevel, chisel, mallet. The sweep and lisp of a sharp plane along a piece of fine wood, the smell of the curls of shavings, sharpening blades, the voluptuous delight as I push a tenon into a mortise and they fit together, snug and tight, and what was two is now one.

It's complicated, working out the structure and construction – but the combination of Bucky Fuller's abstract, stratospheric ideas and the down-to-earth workshop handling of wood is exhilarating.

Sunday 11th July

I was in my workshop when I heard my name called twice, urgently. I hurried out and from a third call located the voice in the neighbours' cowshed.

A cow was lying on its side, snorting, its great round side heaving, and Gaston was at its rear holding onto a tiny hoof. 'Pass that rope' he instructed. He knotted it quickly round the leg and, holding the rope tight, stood up, panting and wiping his brow. It was a rear leg; the calf was in the breech position and had to be got out quickly, before it suffocated. 'When she pushes, heave on the rope.' The cow bellowed and we heaved and the legs were out. She bellowed again and we heaved and the hindquarters emerged. Three, four, five times, heaving so hard I thought we'd pull the leg off or tear her open. One last pull, and the calf popped out like a stone out of an overripe plum. It was bloody and slimy, thin and still. Gaston quickly laid it by the cow's head and whispered in her ear in *patois*. In spite of her panting exhaustion she began licking the still creature with her long, soft, rasping tongue, licking and breathing her calf into dim, flickering life. Panting himself, Gaston watched intently as the life flowed and ebbed, sometimes sparking up, sometimes fading almost to nothing. Gradually life pulsed into and grew in and filled the calf. When at last the sparkings and fadings had settled to a low but even flame, when he saw that the little creature had its own separate, independent life, he sighed with relief, laid his hand on my shoulder and said 'we need a drink'.

Up the stone steps, into their kitchen, the room where all the living is done. A long trestle table covered with an old oil-cloth. Straw-seated chairs. A kitchen range, proudly converted from wood to oil just before the big oil price rise. A bottle-gas stove. A large open fireplace, hams hanging where they were hung to smoke through the winter. A freezer, into which they drop the larks they've shot until there are enough for a meal. A smart stainless steel sink – but the water to the tap comes from a spring, and the drain sticks out through the wall, emptying onto the cobbles. A large television set, up on a shelf as in bars, flickering permanently. Gaston snapped it off then heated the coffee in a small saucepan and poured us each a glass. Then he got out the eau de vie.

'Where is everybody?'

'Gone to Ernestine's, to see the baby.'

'Good job you stayed.'

'I had a feeling,' he said, tapping his temple and smiling his knowing smile. He is a bachelor, works on the farm all found and a little pocket money. He has a round, humorous face, unlined by the cares that have aged prematurely Monsieur Bonafet; but hardening now in late middle age with, I suppose the inevitable regrets – no wife to share his bed, no children to keep his memory, no land to nurture and pass on. But he is the keeper of the tradition. He looks after the vines and makes the wine, tending his *terroir*, his cellar with the pride and care of a Bordeaux specialist. The "progressive" farmers no longer bother with vines; our six hundred metre altitude is not ideal, and wine from the plains is so cheap that growing vines isn't cost-effective. Gaston says the altitude gives the wine a distinctive, light quality; and the commercial *vignerons* are more chemist than wine maker.

It is Gaston who yokes up the oxen and ploughs when it's too wet for the tractor, who ploughs and sows the corners the machines can't reach, who shakes his head at the hard-panning being caused by the new heavy tractor. He tends the garden. He replaces and mends the furniture, re-seating the chairs – though the straw from the new wheats is too short and brittle, he says, and anyway the harvester chews it up. He pollards the willow that grows in the damp hollow and makes baskets – last winter he showed me and I made a basket of willow and hazel, nothing fancy but sturdy and serviceable, in a couple of hours. In the autumn he gathers chestnuts by the sackful for the pigs. He finds the best mushrooms – cèpes and chanterelles as well as field mushrooms, but he'll touch no other, even though I tell him they're safe, and delicious. He knows where the walnut trees are, and will never tell me. He repairs the hand tools, using wood grown on the farm, and knows how to use them. He spends a lot of time just walking the farm, looking, being, a presence that the natural world seems to feel at home with. But of course that isn't cost-effective. The one thing he's not good at is making money – he planted some conifers five years ago, as his retirement nest egg; they're still spindly little things, three feet high, not even big enough to be Christmas trees.

We talked a little about the farm, the weather, Jane. He asked, in his roundabout way, where she was. 'London,' I

168

said. 'Ah,' he said, a voice of sudden comprehension, clouds of perplexity clearing from his face. He understands. He doesn't know why we're here, has never heard of the "ecological crisis", can't understand how we live producing so little; but Jane having gone to "London" – a place as mythical, as abstract, I'm sure, to him as "University" was to my parents – that makes sense. And now he has a little nugget of information, a secret that he can reveal, in his own time and way, to the family, in that daily remaking and reaffirming of the world that is their conversation. He is happy.

And so Gaston, who is central to the peasant tradition, the way of life that drew us here, is peripheral to what is going on now. For while the peasant way is to produce sustenance, the farming way is to produce money. They bring schools, and you need money. They bring electricity, and you need money. They sell you a tractor and you need money. They broadcast television and you and your family see things and want things and you need money. The man from Roquefort says – give me your sheep milk and I'll give you money. Then the big farmers specialise, mechanise (milking machines for sheep), the price goes down, you have to keep more sheep, specialise, mechanise. The price of wheat falls by two thirds in ten years, because of fertilisers and new seed varieties – so you have to buy bag fertiliser and new seed each year (because you can't re-sow the new hybrids), and pesticides because the new varieties are prone to disease.

But isn't it good that prices are coming down? Ignoring the global implications (of the exploitation of the earth's resources and primary producers in the interests of a few powerful, industrial states), the problem in this region is this – in a basically non-cash economy, each increase in cash cost is disproportionately high. The only way to make more money is by having bigger farms, fewer workers. More land means mortgages. Fewer workers means people leave the

169

land, so each hamlet, instead of having half a dozen families now has two, even one. The urban majority is happy – more second homes, empty for most of the time. The farm women are alone, go out of their minds with loneliness – they often leave the farm only once or twice a year – it's tedious making bread, bottling beans on your own; television breaks the monotony, makes them want things; the bread man calls twice a week with 'town' bread – he's someone to talk to. The brighter kids at school are creamed off into higher education in the towns; the less enterprising are left. The government says – here's some money, build a new barn. It's built on a concrete base, made of steel and asbestos, constructed by regional, even national specialists; the stone and *lausse* barn, built and maintained by the local *maçon*, specific in design and materials to this region, is abandoned. But the money wasn't a gift, it was a loan. You need to service the loan. You need higher productivity, more fuel, more fertiliser, more machinery, more money. Your son has seen flashy tractors with stereos in the cab, high tech. machines – Lamborghinis! – you buy one to keep him interested. More money....

No wonder Monsieur Bonafet sometimes beats hell out of his sheep in sheer frustration. No wonder he slouches pigeon-toed – trying to plough through all this, his feet are trying to walk in opposite directions, and tripping him up in the process. Monsieur Bonafet's life is no longer of a piece. Gaston's is. Monsieur Bonafet is central, Gaston peripheral.

This afternoon I walked up to the farm at the top to get some milk. They are commercial farmers – they kept sheep until the milk price dropped; they changed to beef, but disease ended that; now it is a dairy farm. They are specialists, efficient and profitable. They have no vines, grow no hay (too risky – silage is safer), the wife keeps battery hens, the husband spends five hours a day in the milking parlour. Their farm, with its Friesians, pasture and silage, could be anywhere

170

in Europe. The Bonafets have, still, a mixed farm, inefficient and unprofitable. I passed Gaston, muck-spreading. He was standing on the back of the ox cart, forking out the straw-rich, well-rotted manure. He sang as he worked; the oxen stood patiently, moved slowly forward at his command. The manure smelt sweet. The birds sang. The cart creaked as it moved. At the top of the hill the dairy farmer was muck-spreading – raw slurry spraying out behind a closed-cab tractor, radio blaring, the noise an uproar, the smell foul. Some ways of life venerate the earth; others insult it.

13th July. St Swithin's day. No rain.

The drought is now noticeable, more of a fact with each passing rainless day.

The animals are locked in at night, before the inhabitants bolt themselves in. At night the land is empty, abandoned to the wild, to ghouls, to – I don't know what; it's their night, not mine. In the morning there is a slow, sequential recolonising.

The hens are the first out. Madame Bonafet opens their section of the *cave* and broadcasts a few handfuls of grain and out they tumble, pushing and scrambling for it. As it disappears their frantic activity slackens, they slow, like mechanical toys winding down. For there is something clockwork about them – their jerky movements, their bead eyes, their expressionless faces, the way they seem to live in an eternal present. When the grain is gone, they spread slowly across the farmyard, scratching: looking straight ahead, the hen scratches the ground once, twice, quickly, then steps back and looks down, a look of great intensity that rapidly fades. Anything edible is pecked up, swallowed, forgotten. Hens don't eat, they peck up and gulp down; no lips, no teeth, no chewing, no taste. And drinking; not swallowing – beak dip, then a raising and a tipping back of the head so water trickles down the throat.

171

Among the hens strut the cocks. Especially absurd are the black and white bantam cocks, so small beside the red hens. Such self-importance; and such impotence. As if they know that they are superfluous, that the busy hens produce the smooth placid eggs whatever they do. The cock flaps suddenly onto the back of an unsuspecting hen, treads heavily, screws madly, then leaps off, wings flapping, and crows mightily. A fierce flash of life, a bright moment of conquest – followed by the dawning knowledge of its tinsel futility. The hen shakes itself clean of the the cock's impress and continues its industrious scratching without a backward glance. And the crow, when the cock rocks back on his heels, thrusts out his chest, throws back his head, the crow is not of power, of joy, but of self-importance and braggadocio.

Next come the ducks. They have finely shaped heads, are nobly formed, and even waddling on large webbed feet they retain a calm dignity. They are orderly creatures – as they walk from the shed they retain the order and formation they have on water, would have in the air if they were allowed to fly. Now they have only a tin bath to cool their feet in – the pond has dried up, the single frog silent. Later Madame will keep a couple in, force-feed, to fatten their livers. Not, as formerly, their webbed feet nailed to a plank, but gripping between her thighs and, with a long funnel, grinding maize down the gullet.

The pigeons flutter in their cages. They are easily caught – a handful of grain in an empty cage, the front dropped shut with a string from an upstairs window. The free pigeons and the caged blink at each other through the mesh, puzzled mirror images.

The caged rabbits are numb and dumb, warm bundles of quivering nervous energy, nibbling and copulating compulsively, waiting for the axe to fall.

The pigs grunt and guzzle in their sty. Once a month they are let out while their sty is mucked out, and they lumber about the farm, clumsy, curious, rather pleased with themselves. They look as if they think they've really got it made. What a shock when the pig finds itself in November suddenly roped and tied down to a board in a circle of grinning humans, and feels its throat cut and its life blood belching out into the bowl held by the kneeling woman. There was no kneeling woman to catch Henry's blood. Beatrice, the daughter, drives off to work at the pig factory.

Now Monsieur Bonafet takes out the sheep. They are nervous, stupid creatures, with bony, blank heads. They huddle together, bells tinkling, hurrying along, harried by the nips of the ill-trained dogs, eager to obey Monsieur's whistles and cries but chaotic because they don't really understand. The sheep are never left at pasture: someone is always with them, for they forget to eat, simply stand vacant, unless there's a human there to urge and chivvy them with trills and calls; then, heads down, they nibble anxiously. "Just like consumers and advertisers," Larry says.

Gaston takes out the cows. The rattle of chains, then out they come, one, two, three. Each skips a little as she feels the sun on her face. They are attractive cows, with lustrous brown hides, small shapely heads, large dark eyes, delicate feet. As the dogs snap at their heels the cows turn on them, heads down, strong necked, horns waving, re-enacting as ritual some dimly-remembered response from wild days. Then they order themselves and placidly follow Gaston.

He returns to the cowshed. More rattles of chains. I wait expectantly. The first ox emerges, then the second. They stand, unmoving, huge creatures with massive shoulders, but smooth and rounded, and somehow daintily proportioned. Eunuch cousins of great strength and peaceful disposition. They stand patiently as Gaston locks their heads together in the wooden yoke, tightens the strap across their brows, their long horns interlocked. He puts the light wooden plough

173

over his shoulder and leads them away, making chucking noises. They lean together, strange twins, balanced, separate but coordinated, their steps surprisingly delicate, but plodding nevertheless. He is going to earth-up the potatoes. Past the sturdy wooden frame into which an ox can be fastened – I imagined to restrain it while some hideous act was performed; in fact to support it while it's being shoed – an ox can't stand on three legs. Didier, the son, roars out on the tractor, stereo blaring.

14th July

I went to the *brocante* to buy a stove for my tower. There are wardrobes and beds, bread tables and bed warmers, yokes and old farm tools. The locals get rid of their old, solid, craftsman-made furniture, (they're embarrassed by the traditional) and buy factory-made veneered chipboard at the hypermarket in Albi. They sell reality and buy dreams. And the things they sell are being eagerly bought by the city bourgeois, to give a solid, authentic feel to their dislocated homes, although they have no experience of their use. The peasants want to live as if they are in cities, the city dwellers want the illusion of the country; the dreams of both are fed by magazines and television.

I bought a lovely art nouveau stove, a beautiful enamelled green-blue, Albi-made, for sixty francs. It fits well. I fastened the stove pipe in position and began building the stove in. Now my tower has a hearth.

It is dark now, a velvet night, warm, still and yet vibrant. There are occasional snufflings of sheep, but no bird song breaks the silence, no moon dims the silver dust of stars. I look up from where I write, at the white wall by the light bulb – dozens of small moths have settled. All colours and shapes: sulphur yellow, mottled brown, pale green, white, silver, sky blue; pieces of bark, tubes of straw, fragments of mother of

174

pearl; smooth wings and furry wings and gossamer wings –
and one with silver, silky, feathery wings shaped exactly like
Bleriot's monoplane that I saw hanging from the vaulting of
St Martin-des-Champs in Paris. It's called a White Plume.
Sometimes one bumbles around the light bulb, but mostly
they rest on the wall, bathe in the lamplight, delicate presences, not moths but *papillons de nuit*, on display for me in
wondrous diversity. Then something catches the corner of
my eye, I turn to the window – oh God, at the window, a
mask – a face!

15th July
It really shocked me. That window has mesh on it to keep
out the flies, and on it, wings spread, was the biggest moth
I've ever seen, massive, the size of my open hand, with a
large eye in the centre of each wing, the whole forming a
bizarre and terrible face. I knew it was a moth, knew it had
simply been attracted there by the same light that had drawn
the benign presences of the other moths; but there is something unnerving about a thing so out of scale with what is
familiar. The way it vibrated. The unblinking eyes. I suddenly felt alone, vulnerable, watched. I hurried to bed.

In the night there was another incident. I was awakened
by the sound of large diesel vehicles lumbering across the
fields towards the hamlet. It was 3am. They stopped a field
away, their engines kept running for a while then switched
off. There was a heavy silence. From the window I could see
white and red lights, large looming shapes, figures moving
silently. I lay in bed, frightened.

My first confused thought was that they were German
tanks from the war. (The war is still present here; the
Resistance was active, Gaston was a member, there were
atrocities, the café owner's wife in a nearby village is still
known as the German Commandant's mistress, had her

head shaved after the Liberation.) Or maybe I'd gone into the future, and the next war had broken out...? I've never lived in a place where there's been an invasion, a land war, people being shot. I felt very insecure. I pulled the sheet over my head and forced myself to sleep.

They are *moissonneuses*, harvesters, one red, 'New Holland', and one yellow, 'International Harvester'. They work on contract, 150 francs a day, a fortune around here, but for that they clear a twenty acre field. The drivers live in their cabs for weeks, driving between farms overnight, following the ripening grain north, barley this week, wheat in a fortnight – everything is early this year because of the drought.

I looked up the moth. The Great Peacock, *Saturnia Pyri*, the largest in Europe, found only in Southern Europe. There are 140,000 species of lepidoptera.

I gathered in the hay, a great flower-filled sunny heap in the *cave* under my feet – the fragrance rises up through the floor, warming and comforting. I imagine bony, shaggy, cunning yellow-eyed goats shuffling around.

Chapter 3: Pages from Kris's diary:
'every human being stands beneath his own
dome of heaven'

19th July

To the monthly market at St Leon.

The village square is prepared – extra stock in the shops spilling onto the pavements, special dining rooms opened with long tables spread with white cloths. Then the market traders arrive: at one end of the scale an incomer selling a few plants or cheeses from the back of a 2CV; at the other, great pantechnicon vans whose aluminium sides open up, let down, fold back to create illuminated stage sets on which are arrayed luminous polyester clothes, garish boiled sweets, nylon sheets, plastic toys, cheap records. At an intermediate scale the serious tool dealers, the haberdashers – here there are strangely-strapped pink undergarments, there Gaston buys his annual set of blues, an occasional beret – the nurserymen. This stall was the source of my one horticultural coup over Gaston. I bought some tomato plants at the April market; Gaston shook his head, said – there's always a frost later than this, I always buy in May. Ten days later the frost came. How are your tomatoes, Gaston asked innocently. Fine, I said, pulling back the polythene cloche I'd made. He scratched his head. This year I'll have the first tomatoes. I wonder what he'll make of peppers.

The stalls are laid out, the restaurants open, the bars busy, the crowds assembled for their monthly meeting. The men congregate according to age.

There are the over-fifties, in wide black berets and dark suits, tieless in buttoned-up white shirts, squat black figures standing in clusters, unmoving, rooted, laughing and easy in their groups but wary as they look out, watchful of the new. (I'd always thought of the beret as an item of folk costume;

in fact it's an interwar fashion item, especially popular in the 1920's, still being worn by those who were young when it was fashionable.) The middle age range, twenty five to fifty, wear caps and rolled-up sleeves; they're more active, individual, flexible, looking at what's new, remembering the old, trying to negotiate a path that takes account of both. And then the youngsters, under twenty five, in tight nylon shirts and flared trousers, bare-headed, hands caressing the glossy enamel of chainsaws and tractors, their eyes alive as they talk about machinery and speed.

I saw Gaston, in his best blues, watching the social goings-on with his cool, detached gaze, giving me the briefest of nods before retiring with his fellow bachelors to eat tripe in their restaurant.

A hand clapped on my shoulder: 'You'll never make a peasant, Kris.'

'Larry!'

'You're too light on your feet – I've been watching you move.'

'I'd forgotten you existed. This is where I need to be.'

'You can't hide here, you know. But tell me – are you building your bridge?'

'I'm building a tower.'

'To hide in? To the stars?'

'I'll know when it's ready.'

'You're taking a big chance.'

'I have to – I've let things go for too long. And you?'

'Passing through. Going south with Claudine, looking for stock for the shop. You're all half-asleep here.'

'And you're a kid poking a stick into the ant hill.'

'Just a bee among the flowers, doing no harm, trying to do good. Good luck.' A handshake, then an embrace. I watched him saunter through the market, exchanging words, shaking hands; watched tiny Claudine rush up, cling to him, carried along by his imperturbable progress. And then he was gone.

Meeting Larry had stopped me in my tracks. I found myself, instead of moving into the mass of the market, turning and walking along the narrow, quiet street that I hadn't walked alone for ten years. Past the old *vannier*.

Jane stood here once, watching him work, the quick, firm interweavings, the sharp taps with the hammer, the sense (I felt it too) of a basket waiting to come into being. She was fascinated.

'You want a basket?' he asked without stopping or looking up.

'I want to learn,' she said, firmly and boldly. I was taken aback. He worked on, then stopped and looked up at the determined, silhouetted figure:

'And what will you pay?' I saw the calloused thumbs, the knotted finger joints, the watery blue eyes fix-focussed at nine inches, the body bent like a steam-shaped chair. She saw too. And yet she was at the edge of saying (I know this, although she never spoke of it, never mentioned it), 'whatever the price', of stepping over the threshold, of disappearing. I almost grabbed her in alarm. She tipped forward, then sat back.

'Maybe one day,' she said.

'If I'm still here,' he said. 'Who will carry on when I'm gone?' and resumed his work.

I walked on, further into the past, along the shady street of old buildings, centuries old, grey with age, to the end of the village, the empty sun-filled square and the parapet high above the curved river.

Across the river is the chestnut forest through which the road zig zags down from the plateau, the road I'd cycled down ten years before, empty, naked, a boy on a bike. I stopped down there, by the river, and looked up here. And saw – what? A Potala Palace. A citadel rising from river to keep. In the harsh midday light I had taken note of all the blemishes – the peeling *crépissage*, the cracks in the masonry, the long stains from drainage pipes, the bare ribs of abandoned houses – but what I saw was something secure, solid, enduring.

Something to believe in.

The river flowed at my feet, water trickling between stones, deep still pools containing cool, silent fish, the sun shimmering on the water surface, shrubs and trees moving softly their green foliage, dappling shade cool and restful. None of that interested me. All I saw was the wall, the citadel.

I crossed the bridge and entered. It was one o'clock, hot and still, the shops shuttered and silent. I walked along the narrow street, my plated cycling shoes clacking like some bizarre alien, looking around me at the hard buildings, the blind windows, and felt – neutrality, impregnability. It felt safe. Having lost myself on the journey, I would find myself here. Yes, that's what I would do. This was my destination.

I didn't stay of course, I didn't dare – I had to get back for my final year at university. I probably thought I could return sometime – you do when you're young and something is happening for the first time; it happened once, so why should it not happen again? But of course it doesn't. The best you can hope for is that at some point, on another turn of the spiral, the various planes of circumstance and self will once more intersect, or coincide, or whatever they do, and that you will be able to take this new opportunity to change….

20th July

Gaston tells me that the drought is becoming serious. The barley's a fortnight early, the wheat will be too, and yields are down. The potatoes have stopped growing and so has the grass. In St Leon they're not allowed to water their gardens, and they're praying for rain in the church – his lip curls at this. I met him as he was going to cut ash leaves to store for winter fodder, to make up for the second cut of hay they won't get.

The tomatoes and peppers, peas and beans, and other plants I can water are thriving in the hot sun, swelling by the day; the garden is a colourful oasis.

But around it the grass is fading and bleaching, the wheat turning from gold to white, clashing noisily in the wind, and the fields that have been cut for hay are parched and bare, with no new growth. Monsieur Bonafet looks up anxiously. Clouds build, thunder booms, but no rain falls.

21st July

Monsieur Bonafet holds his hands under the stream of grain pouring from the harvester, plunges his hand into the sack, watches the grain trickle between his fingers. He gazes at the bounty, the pouring gold, delighted, his face the image of Avarice in a Brueghel painting. He jokes with his son, squints up at the driver; his breathing is shallow, his eyes bright, his thin tongue licks across dry lips from between yellow teeth. For just one day his farm is Las Vegas: the harvester is the fruit machine, and he has hit the jackpot. He no longer produces food. He is lost.

23rd July

I've finished making the struts for the dome. Tomorrow I'll start fitting them.

It is dark. I go out and step inside the wall of stone. I close the door, lie down. I am lying in a crater in the desert, where a meteorite fell millennia ago, a black stone. The sky is a velvet pall pricked by ten thousand pinpricks through which is visible the empyreal light. The points of light are suns, nuclear fusion furnaces millions of degrees hot, isolated in the absolute zero of space, moving steadily apart. The stars group into galaxies, the galaxies into clusters, the clusters into clusters of clusters, all relating to each other in a curved space-time continuum predictable within a chosen frame of reference. The stars resolve into heroic constellations that tell true stories, into zodiacal constellations which by their subtle powers affect our lives…. The sky, with stars lambent and lustrous, sharp and brilliant, is wonderful tonight.

24th July
Raise high the roof beams, carpenters…!

I don't know where to start. I've finished. The tower, the domed tower, looks great. I'm happy, a bit pissed – no – high.

It was tricky, building up the structure of struts – not struts, ribs, yes, ribs – into a dome. I suppose all roof raisings, no matter how small, should be communal affairs. But I wanted to do this myself, alone, starting from the curved wall plate, moving around, fitting ribs, edging out from the wall, in towards the centre, up towards the pole, gradually overarching space. I'd imagined a Brunelleschi mysterious almost mystical construction, spinning out an unsupported dome until it closes at the zenith ('how does he *do* that?'). In fact I had to support its gravity-heavy sagging as I pushed out over emptiness. Even so I felt wonderfully industrious, like a spider, or at least a spiderman, after mortising the first ribs into the wall plate, methodically bolting the ends of the ribs to the flexible steel plates, circling, constructing a pattern of triangles upwards and outwards yet inwards, over the interior space of the tower. It rested on supports until I was at the top of the dome, the north pole, fitting into place the last five ribs – and then there was no pole, just a seamless curved surface of triangles, the roof an integrated whole that lifted itself off, airborne. Weightless, self-supporting; rather than a structure to enclose or exclude, it is an aspect of space. It floats, an

182

idea. Like some tremendous metaphor of cooperation. Democracy, even. Bucky, you are beautiful – tough, but beautiful.

I stood inside it.

'Every human being stands beneath his own dome of heaven.'

I walked around it. I looked at it from every window in the house. I drove up to the rim to see it in the setting of the hamlet. It is perfect. Aesthetically, geometrically, geomantically perfect. I can feel its influence singing along ley lines to the seven great centres of the earth. At last I've done something.

I had forgotten, and now I remembered it all in a rush. (Isn't that what actions are for sometimes, especially actions you don't have a reason for but know are necessary – to remember, to open the door of a room you'd forgotten existed, a door from the present to the past, to allow the past to come into the present...?) That the geodesic dome's integrity is in tension not compression, so it weighs a fraction of any other space enclosure and hardly presses on the ground at all; that it derives from an icosahedron, one of the five regular solids, the one the Ancients said encloses the element water; that the geodesic sphere is found in carbon molecules (discovered after Bucky had *invented* the geodesic dome – they call them Bucky balls), viruses, microscopic sea creatures. Footballs. Fundamental geometry. Natural geometry.

When it got dark I went inside the tower and lay down and stared up. The pattern of ribs was black against the starry sky.

At first I saw triangles. Small triangles; large triangles made up of small triangles – and suddenly the Pythagorean "holy tetractys", the ten dot triangle or pyramid that represents position, extension, form, the elements, number, the triple

Goddess.... The triangles merged into diamonds, separated and re-formed into other triangles, other diamonds; and then hexagons – hexagons most of all, dissolving and resolving, overlapping and ever changing hexagons. Except at the top of the dome; there, where the Great Triangles (which are Great Circles) meet, there, uniquely, is a pentagon. A space that connects. An absence that creates presence. All around it is change, flow of energy: there, is stillness. My eye wanders excitedly over the pattern of triangles, as it would over an Islamic mosaic, or the face of a sunflower; and then returns to rest on the still eye of the pentagon.

I look at the stars, no longer free, through a mesh now, a net thrown over them....

When I went back to England, having not stayed in St Leon, things were different. How could they not have been? I had slipped out of my former life, like a tortoise out of its shell; or maybe a hermit crab out of the adopted home it has outgrown. (Metaphors! What use are they?) I had been into the desert. I had seen my vision. But for me no Beatrice, no Christ, no totem animal. For me, nothing – or at best (at best? What madness is this?) myself, my own face in the pool.... I was naked, aware only of my own nakedness. Behind me a family absurd – believing without questioning, speaking without thinking, living unconsciously. Ahead – nothing. To the side, around me? Ah.

For I had been handed over to the Masters at eleven. (I use this figure as an account of the way working-class children 'pass the eleven-plus' and are moved into the middle-class education system of the grammar schools, gratefully, no questions asked. As, in the Middle Ages, they were handed over to the church.) And now I was with the Superior Masters. I adopted their ways, dressed in their garments, wore the gown and goggles and hood. I was *educated*. Knowledge. Thought. The patterning of the world in the intellectual mode. Concepts. Paradigms. Models. Ideas as meshes through which to filter unknowable reality into the knowable, nets thrown over stars. Our knowledge – and therefore our society – evolutionary, progressing inexorably to its present height, and ever upward....

And although I had left St Leon, I had thought I could take it with me, in a crystal globe inside me. When I gazed inward, there was St Leon, brilliantly sunlit, warm and solid, with the sky as clear and blue as on that first day. On the grey days, on the days that felt already used up, the times when all meaning drained from my life, there, was the crystal globe, there, inside it, was St Leon. Everything went fine, with around me the gown and goggles, within me the inner globe, until I met Melanie....

She ripped the gown apart, tore off the goggles and hood. Unmediated experience, direct revelation. I was burned, blinded. The crystal globe exploded inside me. Inert ice comet, I had tried to throw a net around the sun....

Last week, sitting at this desk, I heard a buzzing at the light bulb. A wasp flew slowly round and round the light bulb, then settled on it, gripping it. The buzzing became louder, higher, rose almost to a scream, and then the wasp loosed its grip, slipped off, fell, flew slowly round in long, weary, wounded circles – and then returned to its tight orbit and again settled. 'No!' I cried. It did it three times. The last time it fell like a pebble to the floor – I heard it hit – and then crawled slowly to a corner....

Sometimes I sit here writing by candle light. Flies are drawn to the flame. Sometimes one crosses the flame; its wings vaporise with a 'ts' and a slight smell of burning, and the fly falls into the molten wax where it struggles fitfully until the wax entombs it. Sometimes there are four embedded in the wax.

I gaze at the pattern of triangles. But now my eye can pass through the net and see the stars. When there is no moon, the stars are brighter, their pattern more complex and interesting, their light more various. Jane moon gone. Moonlight drowns starlight, fills the night sky with its presence. Praise the moonless, starlit sky.

1st August
Jane's birthday. Happy birthday, Jane!

Last year, on her birthday, when I got back from the pig factory (I had left for work before she was up) I wished her 'Happy Birthday', and said 'you stay in the kitchen' and went into the main room and closed all the doors and shutters and hung draperies all around and lit dozens of white candles. I lit the fire (in August!). I laid the table: a crisp white cloth, china plates and cups, long-stemmed glasses. I filled a vase with long hay grasses and pale blue cornflowers, and placed a white bowl of red cherries beside it. I put on *Nashville Skyline*. We ate fish paste sandwiches and jam sandwiches and drank lemonade and tea. I blew out all the candles and brought in the candle-lit cake I'd made. Her face shone in the candle light as I sang 'Happy Birthday'. She made a wish and blew out the candles. The cake was in the shape of a bear. 'But I don't want to eat the bear,' she said. 'That's okay, he's holding a small cake – see?' We relit all the white candles. I gave her the triangular box I had made for her (my third birthday present) and we played pontoon for matches. We listened to *Imagine*, *Forever Changes*, *Moondance*, sitting on the sofa, drinking whisky, staring into the fire. She nestled against me. Outside the wind was rising, thunder began to boom, lightning flashed through a gap in the shutters. One of the shutters blew violently open and I could see the neighbours hurrying to the tractors to get in the cut hay. 'I must see if they need a hand,' I said.

'No!' she said, her face filled with alarm. 'I must.' She kept hold of me, then let go and slumped down, staring into the fire. I went out and helped. It hardly took half an hour; how my arms ached, how I sweated! Coming back towards the house, triumphant and wet, the door was open; the room glowed, incandescent with the mass of white, flickering candles. It looked like a saint's chapel, or a grotto where a miracle had taken place. Thunder boomed, lightning flashed, the rain slashed down, the candlelight shimmered and glowed and, by a wreckage of blue icing Jane sat, head in hands, weeping. I felt a sudden, aimless anger. I went in and slammed the door. Then we made a strong joint and got very stoned.

When I got up this morning I was going to ignore her birthday, in spite of the mirror in the square frame that I'd made. I fitted the first panels in the dome. I'll do some of wood and some of glass. I'll paint the wooden ones – it will be like Lascaux or the Sistine Chapel. This afternoon I went for a walk. As I walked, slowly, a bit dreamy, just looking, rather vacant, I found myself picking long hay grasses, and cornflowers. I climbed the tree and gathered some cherries. I laid them on the table with the mirror and looked at them for a long time. Then I arranged the grasses like hair, placed two cornflowers for eyes, and five cherries in the shape of a smiling mouth. I stuck a single lighted candle into a loaf and sang:

> "Happy birthday to you,
> Happy birthday to you,
> Happy birthday, dear Jane,
> Happy birthday to you."

I made a wish and blew out the candle and kissed the middle cherry. I ran to the car and drove too fast up over the ridge and down into St Leon and phoned her from the new public call box.

'Happy birthday, Jane!' I called excitedly down the phone.

'Oh, hello,' she said, 'I didn't think – you'd remember'. Wary, remote, a million miles away. I'd thought I was going to share; I'd intruded.

She was going out for a meal with Phoebe and Patrick and some friends. They'd been so good to her since she got back, letting her stay with them; they understood how she felt. She was really glad she had such good friends. I could hear the laughter, people getting ready for a night out. I could smell the aftershave and perfume.

'How are you?' she asked.

'Fine,' I said, 'have a nice evening,' and put the phone down.

I had a few drinks and it was dark when I drove back up. A fox crossed through the headlights and looked at me, red-eyed and defiant. 'Brother!' I yelled. It bared its teeth and trotted away. Am I too wolfish now? Into the house, the face on the table – I got a mug she'd bought me that I'd always disliked and hurled it out of the house as hard and as far as I could, crying 'Fuck you!' Then I climbed on the table and lay full length on it, gripping it hard, my full weight on it and devoured the cherries, chewing the sweet flesh and crunching the bitter stones. Another mug went against the wall and then, breathless, I sat at this table. I pondered long, wondering whether I dared, then wrote:

"Dear Jane,

I don't know where you are; I'm beginning to know where I am. I never thought I'd write that sentence. Or this: I'm beginning to relish saying 'I' instead of 'we'.

"I realise now that the self-sufficiency I imagined wasn't the *Undercurrents* kind, but a self-sufficiency of you and me, alone together, untouched by the world, Babes in the Wood

188

(complete with leaves), the Startrite kids. An attempt to hold onto what we once had in the London flat, that was beginning to slip away.

"Now we're apart and the cracks have appeared; the outside world, and the past have broken in, and... who knows?

"Maybe the big thing isn't going to happen to me. Maybe the magic word isn't going to be whispered in my ear. Maybe I will never be chosen. Maybe I will always be Billy Batson, never Captain Marvel. Maybe anyway big things aren't different; maybe they're just accumulations, combinations of small things; and maybe achievement is simply attention to detail.

"I've spent my life spinning threads. Maybe now it's time to get weaving – "the threads that we spun are gathered... the weft crosses the warp... the pattern is systematic", as the good Walt writes.

"I've said 'I love you' too many times when I didn't mean it. Maybe I'll never again be able to say it, even when I mean it.

"We're no further apart now than when we sat opposite each other across the table at which I'm writing this.

Happy birthday."

7th August.

The harvest is over, the barley and wheat gathered safely in, the harvesters have rumbled on northwards.

The land is bleached and bare, quiet and baking. The green fades from the pasture and the animals search fretfully for succulence. Ton Ton whimpers quietly. He is being punished for letting his wild nature through and ripping a sheep's throat instead of nipping its heels. After a beating they tied him up in the full sun. He's been there for three days. His ears droop, his eyes blear – yet when Mathilde the bitch comes close, he still tries to mount her.... The light is harsh, the air heavy and rippled and thick. An oven heat, the heat of molten metal. A Van Gogh sun, moving closer, getting bigger, hotter, scorching, the elemental balance upset, fire taking over....

I've worked steadily. I finished the panels in the tower roof and it stands empty. No purpose has revealed itself. Why did I build it? I go in and stand and look round and wonder what it's for. An orgone accumulator? A meditation chamber? A folly? At present, simply an empty space.

I've bottled tomatoes, salted beans, boiled cherry jam – stores for a winter I cannot imagine coming. I've made and decorated several salt boxes – strange designs, protean and arabesque, coming from deep inside, a new – or long-forgotten – place. I hope they'll sell. I lead a quiet, orderly life, as changeless as the weather. I'm happy in my solitude, but something inside aches. Jane's letters are bland and noncommittal, but at least they contain money. What is going to happen?

8th August.

I woke this morning and said 'today I'm going to start the roof.'

I drove to St Affrique to buy timber and felt and nails. I left as soon as I could – a rustic scruff, I felt out of place amid the busyness, the tourists, the soft-breasted girls. I breathed a sigh of relief as I drove over the ridge and saw our hamlet below. And jammed on the brakes. Someone sitting on my doorstep. Surely not...? No, a man, with a big rucksack. A visitor. I felt sick – I don't want to see anyone, speak to anyone, especially not some friend of a friend on holiday, or a chance acquaintance of Jane's from

London ("do go and see him – I'm sure he needs the company"). My heart was pounding. I turned and drove back down to the village, sat in the bar drinking, tempted to wait until they got tired of waiting and went. At last I summoned up the nerve to drive back and face this intruder. He got up and smiled and held out his hand and said, 'hi, I'm Richard'.

PART V:

*KRIS FIXES THE ROOF
WITH RICHARD*

Chapter 1: Stepping into space

I press the last ridge tile into place, and the singing stops. I tap the tile into the mortar with the heel of the trowel, smooth the mortar around it. I have finished the house roof. And the song that has been running through my head for three weeks stops, as if the tape has been snipped: "Fixing a Hole", Paul McCartney tum ti tumming, *Sgt Pepper*, dare we fix it, what's stopping our minds from wandering (wondering?), do we dare wander, (wonder)? (Such clean cut kids), "where I..." snip. The rattling spin of a disconnected spool, and then silence. Thoughts chattering up already into the silence; I let them, observe them, and slowly they too fall away, fall silent. Something has changed and I want to register the change. I sit astride the roof – a mahout on an elephant? Ahab on the whale? Ishmael? A man on a roof he has just finished making. The big thing is done. Now she can return. But something has changed.

The sun has set. It is very still. I am up high but grounded. The air is soft, caressing my skin. My muscles are strong. The sky is a shell of finest Chinese porcelain, the inside of an eggshell coloured rose and lavender and pale cobalt, pricked here and there by stars.

I watch the wavering headlights of the tractor, indistinct in the dusk, at the edge of a field of white stubble, hear the engine strain as Didier, ploughing out yet another hedge, rushes to get finished so he can race off to St Leon to be with his pals.

I listen to the whistles and cries as Monsieur Bonafet brings the sheep back from the dry pasture, bells tinkling, nervously bleating, their little hooves like pebbles on the cobbles, their jostling fleeces hushing against the stone walls and each other like a breeze through grass. Monsieur hustles them into the *bergerie*, looks up at the sky, a lingering gaze, then follows them in, kicking a space for himself, pulls shut the half-door, squats on his stool in the thick, oily heat.

Gaston walks quietly from the garden, a hoe nonchalantly over his shoulder, a few tomatoes nestled in his hand. He stops, steps back, looks up:

'Finished?' he inquires. I nod.

'Not a bad job,' he adds.

'I believe so.' A half smile, an inclination of the head – praise indeed – and he turns and walks up the steps to the kitchen.

'Good appetite,' I call. He half raises a hand, and is gone.

Sitting up here for the last time. The work that stretched into the future for so long is now finished – and begins to slip into the past, leaving the future empty. But where do I go from here?

A feather of breeze, like a cool breath, touches the back of my neck. I twist round. The moon, gibbous and pink, sits on the chimney pot. No distant object this, no mirror of light, but a veiled window, a circus hoop stretched with thin paper on which are marked the shadows of wonders beyond, and through which shines the dazzling light, as close as the chimney pot, within reach…. If there is no future, any future is possible. A few steps, a leap, and I could plunge through into who knows what….

I climb slowly to my feet and turn round. I am very high. Jane cried out when she first saw me up here, checking it over, cried out "don't fall!" Now, after weeks of working on the roof, I'm steady on my feet, nimble; but to walk along the apex of the ridge, like a tightrope walker, The Great Valerio….

I can feel the sharpness of the ridge tiles through my thin espadrilles, the empty air all around me, the distance to the ground. One step, two steps, eyes fixed on that window; three

196

steps, four steps, arms wide to balance, this is easy; five steps, six steps, almost there, prepare to dive up and through – my foot slips and suddenly the horizon tilts, a black chasm of cobbles is rushing towards me, and I am sliding down the tiles… one flailing hand hooks onto the ridge with three rigid fingers, the other stretches, grips; slowly I pull myself up, scramble back onto the ridge, grasp the chimney, chest heaving, body trembling, legs shaking. At last I can look up: the moon sails free in the sky, as solid as steel, a distant luminised object; and I hear tinkling laughter.

'Trickster,' I say to the moon.

'Fool,' I say to myself.

A sharp pain in my leg; the skin is stripped from my shin bone. Another scar, another souvenir of my time here – a sharp and precise one, this – that will last forever. Sitting there, relief at last floods through me and I can at last smile and shake my head and pick up the bucket and trowel and limp to the skylight.

As I descend the ladder I feel the warmth of the house envelop me, the thick darkness like a badger's earth close around my legs, my body, my shoulders. In up to my neck I stop, all below wrapped in warm earthiness and animal sharpness, and above – my head bathed by the blithe air. Who wrote that? Of course, Emerson. Emerson. And has all mean egotism vanished, and am I become a transparent eyeball, and do the currents of the Universal Being circulate through me? Well, no, not exactly. And so I sink into the thick heat, and pull the skylight shut over my head.

*   *   *

Richard is sitting on the doorstep, his broad, brown back bowed, his chin on his knuckles, staring out, as he often does, into the night. I lay my hand on his shoulder. He touches it

197

briefly, asks:

'How's it going?'

'It's finished.' He scrambles to his feet, face lit with pleasure, grasps me for a brief jig, hugs me:

'That's great, that's really great – on my last day, too. Now I can go back feeling I've done something. Hey, what happened there?' I look down at the dragon of blood:

'A strange encounter with the moon.'

'Ouch.'

'I'll clean up, you pour the rum – big ones.'

'Sure – then we can eat.'

The door to the living room is closed. I'm reaching for the handle when Richard says:

'Wait – look through the keyhole first.'

'What the…?' I look into a room transformed.

Sunlight streams in through the windows, there are richly-coloured rugs on the floor, exquisite paintings on the walls, extraordinary vases of exotic flowers, and a table piled high with the stuff of royal banquets: capon and sturgeon, pomegranates and pineapples, peacocks and venison. The centre piece is a swan carved from ice. And sitting opposite each other, glasses raised, smiling – Richard and me.

'By what magic is this thing done?' I breathe, falling to my knees. 'By what sorcery…?'

'Shall I say?'

'No – let me wonder.' I gaze tenderly at the soft bloom on the surface of the purple grapes, the light illuminating the room like the inside of a pearl, the look of fellowship on the faces of the two friends as their glasses touch…. Only the stillness of the candle flames tells me that this is a scene of enchantment.

'It's a marvel.'

'Let me look – gosh, yes, it is rather good. Do you want to see?'

'Do I have to?'

'No.'

'Okay – show me.'

'It's a perspective box – a *perspectyfkas* in Dutch – they were very popular in the seventeenth century. There's a rather fine one by Van Hoogstraten in the National Gallery.'

'You mean it's a painting?'

'Look.' Reluctantly I climb to my feet. He opens the door to reveal a box on a stool. There's an eyehole level with the keyhole, and a lamp shining into it, and everything I had seen is painted on the box's inner surfaces, the right angles of the box compensated for in the painting, and a new perspective, that of the actual room, created.

'It's brilliant. You're a genius. But you're not going to destroy this one…!?' He smiles:

'No, not this one. With this I'm out of the pool, back in the stream. Working on it has restored my faith in the value of lies and the truth of illusion. It's all a matter of viewpoint, isn't it? Enough. I'm starving. Let's eat.'

*   *   *

In the centre of the table is the chicken, roasted golden brown. At first we work around it, eating pâté and bread, tomatoes and green beans, potatoes. At last I say:

'Oh well, here goes,' and slice off a leg. Silence. I cut two thick slices from the soft breast. No sound. I bite into the flesh. Still nothing. 'It's okay,' I say. 'Have some.' I had killed the chicken this morning.

I had never killed anything bigger than an insect before, not with my bare hands. The book gives two methods: wring its neck, taking care not to twist too hard or the head will come off in your hand; push a sharp-pointed knife up under the beak and into the brain. I was already beginning to regret my suggestion that we have chicken for Richard's last dinner here; but it seemed like a necessary rite of passage towards self-sufficiency. I picked up my pig knife and walked across the sunlit garden to the chicken house.

It was a wonderful morning, fresh and still, with the air clear around me and the trees loud with the songs of birds and an early buzzard already soaring pleasurably high in the sky. I stopped at the hen house and listened to the flappings and scramblings, the purlings and cluckings from within; the hens were gathering at the door, expectant to be let out and fed. And soon all of them would be out; all except one. How would I choose the one to die, the one to eat? Ask them to draw lots? Pick out the one with the "gosh, I'm weary of life – I wish someone would kill me and eat me" look on its face? Feel among them for the plumpest and tenderest? Impossible. The impossibility of choosing. Unbearable power. I opened the door just wide enough to reach in, felt blindly around, my hand grazing feathers, claws, necks, each slipping away from me before I could grasp; and then one stopped for a moment too long, I grabbed, held, and pulled it out. 'It's your fault,' I want to say, 'you let yourself be caught. This is random death, nothing to do with me, I'm an instrument in the hands of more powerful forces. This is an accident. It's just not your day.'

I pushed the door shut and locked it. There must be no witnesses. I left them clucking plaintively and, with the victim crooked in my arm I hurried towards the house, furtive, concealing my catch, a thief.

I could feel its soft, downy warmth, the rapid beats of its hammering heart, the vibration of life in it. Its head was turning from side to side, its eyes round and bright, seeing, but as expressionless as jet and amber beads. I wanted to talk to it, reason with it. I wanted to explain that it was in the nature of things, that it had been well fed and cared for, that all good things must come to an end, that surely it must have

200

realised that there's more to life than two meals a day and a field to play in, that at some point someone's going to collect...? Its head twisted from side to side, its eyes stared. It alternated between wild, ineffectual strugglings and a waiting, palpitating stillness. At that moment it was the most life-filled thing I'd ever felt; its entire life force (a phrase only abstract before, now real) was dedicated to being alive – not staying alive, *being* alive. But it didn't understand. It was stupid. It deserved to die. I put the point of the knife to its throat, under its beak, prepared to push upward.

I couldn't. Not to a living creature I was holding in my arms.

I imagined its head exploding. I imagined its broken head turning to me with a look of reproach. The words of Balaam's ass rang eerily in my head: "what have I done to thee, that thou has smitten me?" I was helpless, and terrified of crossing this boundary, of direct, selfish killing. And yet I couldn't go back, couldn't say 'ho, ho, it was just a joke,' and return it to its fellows and drive down to the butcher's and buy a chicken someone had killed for me and dressed (what a word to use for something emptied and stripped so utterly naked!) and made carefully abstract. I had to kill it.

So I got a piece of string and tied its legs together and hung it upside down from a nail driven into the lintel of the wood store. Surely, now it was securely bound and all was lost, now surely it would accept its death with fatalism, stoicism, decorum.... It went crazy, flapping its wings wildly, twisting around, squawking loudly. 'Quiet, someone'll hear; please, be reasonable, your time's up; you'll hurt yourself. Accept your fate,' I pleaded. Its flappings became wilder, its squawkings louder. And then my concern turned to anger, the anger of one being defied, the anger of impotence, the anger of guilt. It disgusted me, this vain, futile struggle not to die; it lacked dignity. I picked up a stick.

I intended to give it a clinical tap on the head, to knock

it cold, neatly – instead my nervous arm unleashed a blow of terrible violence. The side of its head pulped; the creature smashed sideways, thudded against the wall; then it was swinging wildly, like a crazy pendulum, flapping and squawking. I had to stop it. In a red fury I hurled myself upon it, wrestled it to the ground and sawed crazily at its neck with the suddenly-blunt knife; I had to get rid of that accusing head, had to prove it was dead, make sure it wouldn't suddenly open an eye as I was plucking it, pulling its guts out.... I cut through rubber skin and tough gristle and hard bone, trying to slip the blade between the vertebrae but hacking through any resistance. At last the bloody head was off; with its one smashed eye and its one unblinking eye, it lay there. I grabbed it and hurled it out of sight, over the house – I heard the dogs fighting over it. Still the body flapped and spasmed. I held it down, my weight full on it, until at last its struggles slowed, and stopped. It lay still. I was panting, almost sobbing, my hands deep in its soft feathers.

At last I let go and climbed shakily to my feet. The orange-feathered form lay at my feet, peaceful and still. Bubbles of blood oozed from the raw neck and soaked into the dust, but slowly, ebbing. A moment's peace. And then the knife slipped from my suddenly-trembling hand and fell and stuck upright in the ground, quivering.

I was already sick of the whole enterprise, wanted to end it now, bury the corpse quietly and forget about it all. But I had to go on. I turned towards the house. Richard was watching me, horrified, the only witness. I picked up the knife, walked towards him, wanting to say 'tell no one of this', watched the horror turn briefly to alarm as I approached him, blade towards him, then brushed past. As I washed my hands, he set the rum down beside me. I said, roughly:

'They're easier to pluck while they're warm,' and went out to fetch it.

I picked it up carefully, held it in front of me, walked slowly. Richard began humming the funeral march in time to my slow steps. I shot him a fierce look. He persisted. I was holding it like an offering on a silk cushion. I felt something bubbling up inside me, something unfamiliar, long forgotten, a bubble that belched out. Laughter. I held it high, intoning 'In nomine patri, filii, et spiritu sancti'. He began to laugh. I flew it round the room, making aeroplane noises – 'bandits at five o'clock – help me, Johnny, I'm hit!'; flapping its wings – 'I can fly – look, Dad, I'm flying!' He fell to his knees, holding his sides. I set it on my shoulder, stumped unevenly round the room – 'quietest blamed parrot oi've ever 'ad'; sat it on my knee – 'at last, a dummy that doesn't answer back'. He keeled over and lay on the floor, arms and legs waving helplessly.

At last our hysteria quietened. We hung it up and commenced plucking. Soon feathers were everywhere, and suddenly we were laughing again, screaming with laughter, singing "the pheasant plucker's song" at the tops of our voices and throwing showers of feathers over each other – how slowly they eddied down, catching the sunlight as they fell. Once I glanced out of the door and saw Gaston watching; he watched, then shook his head and walked on. We were behaving like medical students. The other day Madame walked by holding a hen by the legs. It hung there, flapping intermittently as we talked of the weather, the drought. Is that dinner? I said. Yes, she said, there's something wrong with it, but – and with a sudden movement of great force she swung it against the wall and bashed its brains out and then held it as she had before – at least we can eat it, and carried on talking about the weather for five minutes before walking on. I emptied out its guts, cut off its feet and neck, and stuffed it.

We eat our way slowly through the chicken. It tastes okay. But as we clean each bone I can't get out of my head the picture of a chicken in the meadow with flesh disappearing from each of its bones as we eat, until all there is is a skeleton which stops pecking and slowly turns to me its damaged, reproachful head.

We eat in silence. Richard alternates between chewing mechanically, shoulders hunched, gazing into some lost middle distance, and sitting up suddenly and looking carefully around, as if memorising the room, me, the view through the window, the sounds, the smells. And yet I wonder whether, when he looks back on this moment he will see the room as it is, or his painting of it….

He has a handsome face, his rather small features having been given, I would imagine, a stronger look by the tanning process of long exposure to the Mediterranean sun. His clear blue eyes have a shadow of hurt in them, a look that some women – as I've observed in the last three weeks – find an irresistible sign of sensitivity, others see as uncharming self-absorption. But at least, now, the slickness has gone. His eyes catch mine looking at him and he smiles his crooked smile and says:

'Do you realise that a week from today I'll be sitting in a plastic chair, at a Formica table, eating soya bean pie with processed mashed potato and luminous peas? The canteen windows will be streaming with condensation on the inside, rain on the outside. I'll have wet feet and a red nose. All the girls will have spots. And all this will be a dream….'

'Ah, but for you this will never end. You'll leave tomorrow, and nothing here will ever change – the grapes will hang forever on the vines, the sun will always shine.'

'But drifting ever further into the past, a glowing island on a dark river.'

'Why go? Stay, paint here, why not?'

'Thanks, I appreciate the offer. But I think I need to go back. Unfinished business. And probably I need the security, if only to fight against. Anyway, it might be awkward when Jane comes back.'

'If she comes back.'

'I thought you said she'd come back when the roof was done.'

'No, I said she wouldn't come back before then. I don't know. Something has changed.'

*   *   *

We lie back in our deck-chairs on the verandah. The warm night throbs around us. Insects flutter around the light. *Blood on the Tracks* plays. I pass Richard the pipe. He draws deeply:

'I love this home-grown stuff – very friendly.'

'Grown to Soil Association standards. Take some with you.'

'Too risky.'

'I'll send you some.'

Soon after Richard arrived I put *Blood* on. At the first notes, those sprightly rising A's, he almost staggered and said:

'Oh shit, I'd forgotten this. The first time Flicky stayed out all night she brought me this the next morning, making excuses, apologising, trying to win me round – even took me to bed. When she left she took it. I bought a copy and smashed it and buried the pieces in concrete and sank it in the river. Shit. No, don't take it off.' We listened through it together – I even held his hand at "all your ragin' glory" – then, and many times after.

And now we're listening to it together for the last time. I draw deeply on the pipe. The smoke fills my lungs and, as I sniff in more air, floods along my veins and nerves, runs like electricity across my skin, tingles to my toes and fingertips, balloons in my head a black emptiness. And I see this:

The needle cutting the record; at the same time inscribing the sounds into the groove for the first time, and cutting through the vinyl, destroying it: as it is being made, so it is being annihilated. As it ends, on that rough, elegiac, open E, all that will remain will be a four inch orange disc and a pile of spiralised black plastic thread. The record ends. The needle lifts. The turntable stops. Nothing. I wait on the edge of nothing.

And then I step into space, into nothingness – and as my foot descends, is about to fall endlessly into emptiness, a stepping stone, firm and vivid, comes into being under my foot, and the world in which it is; another step into black space, another stepping stone. There is no future. That's what has changed. The future was finishing the roof and now the roof is finished, the future is finished too. The roof is finished but Jane's not here; so she's not part of the present. And there is no future. I no longer know where she is. My future now is the taking of steps into space, a future both terrifying and exhilarating, a future I embrace wholeheartedly.

'Come on, Kris – let's go and get pissed.'

Chapter 2: A night out

I settle into the passenger seat. The dogs' eyes glint as they slink in and out of the headlights. As the car moves they run with it, barking, biting at the tyres. The trapped headlight beams reflect off the planes and angularities of the walls and roofs of the hamlet and then are suddenly free, sweeping over broad fields and along the stream of road that curves up to the ridge. The snapping, barking dogs run with us for fifty yards then stop, panting, and trot jauntily back to the hamlet, their duty done.

At the top, instead of turning right towards the village, Richard turns suddenly left, towards the main road to St Affrique:

'The big city!' he yells. 'Lock up your daughters, the Goths are coming! Tonight I feel lucky. Serendipity rules, OK!' He's hunched over the wheel, eyes gleaming. I stiffen in alarm – I'm not ready for this, the careful orbit of my life, centred for so long on this house, being suddenly broken. Then I relax. It's okay. He can take me out to the wider world. And I feel an arousal of interest at the thought of women on holiday.

As Richard sings his way through the Rolling Stones song book, I lie back, feeling the wind blowing across my face, staring up at the stars.

*   *   *

Richard came into my life unasked and unexpected, an intruder.

On my own I had sometimes imagined people here, even yearned for it, had conversations, imagined a touch... but they were imagined, phantasms that would disappear on command, their existence dependent on my attention.

207

Richard was a real, physical presence. He got in the way, he confused me – my attention kept hitting him, like a bat's radar on a moving figure in its cave. I began noticing things I'd got used to – the loose floor board I habitually stepped over, the fault in the pump that meant it had to be primed for each use. As I showed him around I saw faults in the work I'd done, excused things I hadn't done, explained how things would be in the future. He looked and listened, this tall, self-possessed, confident, sophisticated representative of the outside world. Then he said:

'Kris, I don't know why you keep telling me what you haven't done – look at what you have done. This place – you're *doing* it.'

'Do you mean that?'

'I do. See what most of us do in a year, eighteen months. I'm envious.'

'It's time to water the garden.'

'Do you want a hand?'

'No, thanks. You – make yourself at home.'

The familiar task, the sluicing water, comforted me. As I watched and listened to him moving around in the house, I began to think it was okay having someone else here. When I got back to the house from watering, he had laid out the food he'd brought – expensive pâté, sesame-seeded bread, chocolate, brandy – exciting food for me. When I put *Blood on the Tracks* on, he almost staggered and said 'oh shit, I'd forgotten this….' We talked a lot, that first evening.

Richard is the brother of Suzie, a college friend of Jane, now married to Clive, her school sweetheart, who was an undergraduate in the department where I did my post-graduate work, one of the group I kept in touch with during my two years in the wilderness. I met Jane at Clive's party, and the following month went to live with her in London. I haven't seen any of them since. Clive and Suzie are on holiday in Spain and plan to pick Richard up on their way home. He had been at art school in the same city, but I had never met him.

'Wasn't it exciting, being an art student in the late sixties?'

'If you didn't want to be a painter. There was music, dope, sex. Students were taking 365 photographs of a plaster head and calling it *A year in the life of…*. Making four hour fixed-camera movies. Forming bands. Wearing "I am an Artist" placards. Making boxes full of mirrors or old socks. Robbing department stores dressed as superheroes. Shitting in official filing cabinets. Bricking up corridors. Their very own *Play School*. And the teachers were the worst of the lot – repressed wartime kids, I suppose, growing their thinning hair long, playing along, screwing around, not believing their luck.

'I wanted to paint and draw, learn how to handle materials, paint real faces, real places – like Vermeer, like Cézanne, like Freud. "Tradition is dead, Mr Jones!" they'd scream, "we've erased history, surpassed the past. Paintings are decorations on the walls of the tombs of the dead – we have smashed the walls, broken through, we are alive, we are free!" I was pretty lonely.

'One lecturer was sympathetic. He got me to Greece on an obscure scholarship in my last long vacation. I saw and felt so much – almost too much, the place so rich and vital. I found myself painting less and less.

'One day I went for a walk. I came round a headland. The sea was still and blue and as solid as lapis lazuli. Set in it was a steep, jagged rock, the shape of Mont St Victoire, pink and white limestone, with little patches of dusty green vegetation, shining in the sunlight. A boy, brown and clean limbed, was standing at the top, on the pinnacle, very still. Suddenly he dived off. I watched him plunge down through the air, clean as a picked bone, waited for him to smash to pieces on the solid sea – he entered it like a sword, there was a small white

209

splash, then the sea closed over him, the ripples spreading slowly and inevitably towards the farthest shores. For a long time nothing moved. Then he burst up through the surface with a splash, shook the water from his head, diamonds in the sunlight, and began swimming and turning and leaping like a dolphin, whooping like a Red Indian. I felt as if I'd been kicked in the stomach. And suddenly everything burst into life – the chanting chorus of cicadas, the clear threads of bird song, the smell of herbs in the heat, the sun scintillating on the sea, the far hills like carved smoke…. I walked back in a daze, crawled into bed, stayed there for three days. And then I knew I couldn't do the dipEd, become a teacher and Sunday painter, live in hopes – my life had to be painting.

'I got a job as a milkman, bought a tiny back-to-back for £300 in an area students avoid, put skylights in the roof and made the attic into a studio. I saw hardly anyone from college days. I worked. I drew. I drank in the corner pub. All I wanted to do was to draw the reality of things, their living presence, their *actuality*, without reference to anything else. To feel, to taste, to enjoy – and then to make marks on paper that said something about what I was seeing: back streets and cleared sites, the ruined abbey by the trash-filled river, flowers in a dustbin, drunks, tarts, children grievously damaged or miraculously untouched.

'There was a girl I knew. We always got on well, always imagined something would happen between us sometime, but it never did – we were always travelling in slightly different directions, you know? Well, I met her by chance, not having seen her for ages, and she said "I'm getting married next week". I said, "come and stay with me this weekend, I'll draw you". We spent the whole weekend together, even slept in the same bed, never touched. She talked, I drew. By the end of the weekend I knew every inch of her, knew her with an intimacy no one else had, shared her secrets. I put it all on paper; I possessed, kept nothing. As she left, she said "I feel clean, new, as if all the dead old stuff's gone". They were good drawings. It was beginning to happen.

'Then one weekend I went home to see my parents. It was a grey winter day, dead leaves under bare trees, misty perspectives, the park empty. Except for a girl on a swing, flowing hair, flying silk, Isadora at the circus.

'I want to draw you,' I said.

'No, but you can take me out,' she said, sweeping past me, on the bladed pendulum, up into the pearly sky.

'I may not want to.'

'You may have no choice.'

'One of those absurd conversations that either stop things dead in their tracks or start things going, depending.... Suddenly everything was different. My life looked narrow and mean. Here was a real person, lively, unpredictable, out of control. I felt very protective of her, saw her potential. She was bright but ragged, always heading for the edge. Lovely, of course. And when she turned towards me.... I focussed her interest on art, for which she did have talent. I got her to work enough through school to get a place at my old college.

'She lived with me and I taught her all I knew. She was full of energy, perceptive, undisciplined. As I took her to galleries and films, introduced her to books, showed her Paris, Amsterdam, gradually she matured.

'It was hard work; I found myself adjusting my life to suit hers. But it felt worth it – when we were at home, a record playing, me in the kitchen, she sketching, and I'd look through and see her bent over her work, illuminated by the edge of the spotlight, hair falling over her face – and suddenly she'd look up and give me the most brilliant, devoted smile.... Or seeing her in town with a group of friends – she was always the loveliest – she would suddenly break away and run to me and throw her arms round my neck and drag me over to introduce me as a hero, so proud.

'I was drawing less and less, but I was happy. I began to

211

think of the future and reapplied for the dipEd course. And then she brought home *Blood on the Tracks*. What a title. She took three years with her, wiped it away, there was no going back.

'Look Kris, I've spent months on the Med, "sitting by the flesh-pots, eating bread to the full". I've got soft. I need to be worked. I'll do anything.'

The next day we started the roof. First we had to strip off the *lausses*, the large, heavy flags of local stone that cover the roof. They're not fixed but laid onto boards with clay in between; as they slowly slip all the time, it's an annual job for the local builder to go over the roof malleting them back tight. But our roof has been left too long and can't be saved.

As we had no scaffolding, I began by punching a hole through the rotten boards, pushing aside a couple of *lausses* (dusty rays of light then a sudden flood) and climbing out onto the roof. I lifted the flags and passed them through the hole to Richard standing on the ladder who piled them until the space was filled and then we carried them downstairs and stacked them outside.

'The neighbours threw theirs off then bulldozed them out of sight. I want to use ours to make a new terrace.'

It took two days of hard, heavy work to strip the roof. Heaven knows what weight of stone we shifted. We could hear the roof timbers creak as we took them off, stretching, expanding, sighing, almost shaking themselves in relief. All the building here depends on weight and mass, strength in compression; no arches or trusses, just weight and the capacity to endure. I want to change that.

At the end of the first day, though tired we were elated at how much we'd done, how well we'd worked together. Richard beamed and said:

'This is work. This is real work. Let's make an early start tomorrow.'

But as the second day passed he became progressively quieter and more withdrawn, and in the evening he sat hunched and abstracted. I feared the work had been too heavy for him, that he might leave. I heard him moving around in the night, and the next morning he didn't stir. In the middle of the day I was on the roof cutting round for the dormer when his head popped suddenly up through the hole, sunny as the morning:

'Coffee?'

We sat on the verandah. Richard stared at the far hills.

'It was the record started it. And talking. Sometimes it just overwhelms me. Then all I can do is draw; like some fanatical anchorite telling his beads to keep the devils away, like Lucy Manette's dad cobbling shoes.'

'Where are the drawings?'

'Destroyed. I draw, I burn. Exorcism.'

'They might be good.'

'Doesn't matter. That's not what it's about. I'm not trying to produce, I'm trying to get rid. It's another way of cleaning up the world. We hold onto too much, we're too acquisitive, we're trying to breathe in all the time. Sometimes you have to get rid, breathe out until you're breathless and empty.

'Do you know that in Holland, if you're a painter you can become a salaried employee of the State? They pay you, and you give them all you produce. There are vast storerooms underground, below sea level, filled with these paintings. I imagine them getting damp, the sheets sticking together, the whole lot turning slowly to peat, becoming land, raising the land level…. It's appropriate for ninety nine percent of painters, ninety nine percent of paintings. Problem is knowing which ninety nine percent…. What you're doing up there looks technical – what can I can do?'

'I'll think of something. Oh, there's a letter for you.' It was from his sister Suzie; she and Clive would have to go home early because of family illness.

213

'I can leave now if you want, meet them in Toulouse. But I've three weeks before I need to be back in England – I'd really like to see the roof finished.'

In the evening he talked again:

'All I felt was an absence, an emptiness. No, lots of feelings – anger, frustration, shame, failure, self-pity, guilt – but all of them small, tiny perturbations on a vast emptiness. It wasn't *like* anything – there were no analogies, no metaphors, no images. I was an artist without images.

'I remember, at the end of the first week, lying in bed and looking out of the window and seeing the sunlight soft on the red brick chimneys, and the blue sky, everything so vivid and alive, feeling suddenly better and getting out my drawing stuff – and then a wave of nausea as I held the pencil over the blank paper. I couldn't open a book. The crassest pop song was like a knife in my heart. I'd be walking up the steps to an art gallery and an image of one of the pictures would come into my mind, and I'd burst into tears and turn and flee. Little flowers among rubble would have me blubbing like a kid.

'That went on for months. The only escape was in drink. Someone said learn to meditate; I felt good, mumbling my mantra. One day I opened my eyes after a particularly pleasing meditation and there, sat on the carpet in front of me, looking at me, was a large fat rat.

'Later I discovered revenge, quite by accident. A girl I took out, from raw loneliness, thoughtlessly. The look she gave me – hurt, bitter, broken up by betrayal. It gave me a sense of power, of control; a sense of myself. And the day before I left the Med, came here, I saw it again. But this time I felt sickened by my behaviour, thick with self-loathing. In between, countless times. I was the undead, bitten and infected, biting and infecting, passing it on. But no more, never again. I'd cut my dick off first.

'I was stuck with starting the dipEd in September because I hadn't the strength to get myself out of it, to do something else. I decided I'd at least try and have some fun first, so I've spent a couple of months down there, on the libertine shore by the sensual sea. I found, if I could no longer really draw, at least I could busk on the quayside, do passable imitations of cars, boats, portraits – the rich bastards' possessions. It felt good ripping them off and screwing their wives and especially their daughters into the bargain.

'But no more of that. I'm fat with vulgarity, thick with revenge exacted. I'm ready for a diet of hard tack.'

*   *   *

Street lamps like flying saucers pass regularly across my vision, lying back, and the orange branches of sodium-lit plane trees; the outskirts of St Affrique.

Chapter 3: Night life

Richard slides out of the car, snaps the door shut, pushes his cigarettes into one T-shirt sleeve, his matches into the other, says:

'Okay men, this is it – over the top!' Vaults the car bonnet, sticks his thumbs into his jeans' pockets and slouches cool-eyed towards the bars. I follow, excited, sure Richard has got it all organised.

But the bars are empty, the holidaymakers gone, the place reverted to a small, dull market town. We scout from bar to bar and find nothing. At last we find ourselves at the far end of town, standing in the middle of the wide, empty street, two gunfighters on the wrong set.

'Strange,' Richard says, shaking his head, 'I saw my fate waiting for me here. Let's get pissed.'

So we meander slowly back through town, zigzagging from bar to bar, drinking.

In a strip lit chrome and plastic place, all horizontals, the young men in their tight loud shirts and flared trousers with their shiny black hair play energetic games of table football and pool, while the girls nudge each other and give us the eye then dissolve into giggles and huddle together tittering. When the young men begin to look across at us and smack pool cues into their palms, we withdraw.

In a narrow dark bar, wood and iron, all verticals, with a zinc counter and signed faded monochrome postcards of fifties' singing and cycling stars (Edith Piaf, Charles Aznavour, Louison Bobet, Roger Wolkowiak...) we watch, on an ancient wood cabinet television, *Kind Hearts and Coronets*, dubbed into French. As the canoe disappears over the misty weir, with a French voice-over as portentous as in *Jules et Jim*, the effect is mysterious and surreal:

'Show this at "Academy 3", with subtitles,' Richard says, 'and it'd run for months. Weird.'

Sat outside the hotel in the main square, our heads turn together as a girl races by on her Solex – tight white blouse, billowy red skirt, long brown flying hair, bare feet up on the petrol tank, neat bum bouncing up off the saddle – we sigh. Our eyes follow her when she returns, teeth flashing, and we sigh again and feel old. But okay. For slowly the bright spark of anticipation, the sharp predatory sexual imperative, has changed into something calmer, mellower, more solid. Camaraderie.

'Why do we do it, Kris? Why do we believe they'll solve all our problems? Was it fed to us in our mothers' milk? Or are we so bloody lonely that we'll do anything for that soft touch…?'

We end up in the last bar in town drinking traffic lights and playing "Smoke Gets in Your Eyes", Brian Ferry, over and over as the patron, bullet-eyed, polishes the PASTIS 51 transfers off glass after glass. We go 'ooh…' each time the sax comes in; we play it so many times we swear we're beginning to hear the other side playing through ("Another Time, Another Place").

Thrown out, we weave our mazy way back to the car, arms round each other, singing and pledging undying love. At the car he turns to me:

'Kris,' he says gravely.

'Yes, Richard.'

'Kris – Fuck 'em all,' and collapses, hanging onto the side of the car, laughing hysterically.

'Fuck 'em all, Richard. Tell you what, I'll drive back.' The door opens, he crawls in, a twisted hand rises from the grave, holding the key. He subsides, then rears suddenly up, his eyes bright with sudden revelation:

'Serendipity lures – K.O.,' he announces, and collapses with a thud.

217

I drive studiedly, congratulating myself on my competent handling of the car as I proceed out of town, until a lorry the size of an office block, lit up like a building site, bears down on us, klaxon blaring, tyres squealing, and I flip over onto the right-hand side of the road. A can from the cab bounces noisily on the bonnet, and I am instantly sober.

Under the last street lamp at the edge of town a couple, romantically enclosed, embrace, the man thumbing vaguely. I broadside to a stop. The man, a boy of about sixteen, staggers up:

'Where are you heading?' I ask.

'Towards Montpellier,' he mumbles.

'That's the other way.'

'Great,' he says, kissing the girl inaccurately, fighting the door open and pouring himself onto the back seat. As I drive off I watch the girl in the rear-view mirror, her eyes brimming with tears, isolated under the orange spaceship light, give a wave, a tiny, secret wiggle of the fingers. The boy flails an arm wildly then collapses. I watch her as she shrinks in the mirror, as the vast night grows around her, engulfs her, she is gone.

The boy sleeps curled up on the back seat like a mouse. Richard sleeps sprawled across the front seat, snoring, mouth open. I am wide awake. The night is mild and very black. The headlights tunnel into the dark, shine sometimes on beady eyes and looming shapes, sometimes on the ribbon of road, sometimes on nothing. Tomorrow, today, Richard leaves.

*   *   *

Next we stripped the old rotten boards off the roof. While I continued with the dormer, Richard prowled around, doing odd jobs.

'What are you intending to do with the ceiling of the tower?' he asked, popping his head up between the rafters.

'Decorate it.'

'May I?'

'I'll have to think about it.' Alone, again I felt threatened, but now more intensely; for now my sanctuary, my empty room was to be invaded. I walked round it. I stood in it. I said again:

'What is the purpose of this place?' I touched the rough stone, ran my finger along a smooth rib, looked at the sky through one of the triangular windows, and answered, again:

'I don't know.'

'So its purpose isn't to remain empty?'

'Its purpose is to find its purpose.'

'Didn't you say the walls of the tower must connect and not separate, unite and not divide, be a medium not a barrier?' There was no rational reason to exclude him. But there were emotional ones: 'this is mine, and only mine'.

But sometimes you need to let people into your life. The question – is this the right person? Will he defile my inner sanctum; or bring to it a necessary energy? Will he despoil the room; or help me to discover its purpose? It was another day, and a singular incident, before I could say 'go ahead.' Immediately I felt lighter. He set to at once, looking through my books, walking round the farm and the places around, talking to me, sketching.

The next day I was sitting vacantly on the step when I heard Richard stumbling over some chords on the guitar, painstakingly repeating them until he could string them together, then begin in a quiet voice to sing: "If You See Her, Say Hello", she might be in Tangiers, and on, through the whole song, every word. And into my dark still mind came the image of Richard on his restless trail along the northern shore of the Mediterranean, the glitzy, thin strand of pleasure, and arriving at last at its western extremity and standing on the European Pillar of Hercules and staring across the narrow, uncrossable gulf to Africa – the gulf through which Dante's Ulysses had sailed, out of the known world, away from Ithaca, "following the paths of knowledge and excellence", to his destruction – staring across for a glimpse of one now lost to him, inhabitant now of another continent; and then turning and resuming his fierce punishing travels until glutted and sick.... And then another image, unexpected, as painful as a knife thrust, that I thought I'd learned to live with, made abstract, a pearled pain – that is still real:

A girl, hair flying, running through the city night in stockinged feet over wet pavements, from my neat flat to his, that other, unknown man's rundown house, looking over her shoulder, stopping at the door, looking through the window, hesitating; then opening the door – a flood of light, a man, going in – closing it.

Of course I had followed her. Of course I followed her a thousand times after, secretly, examining the pavement for signs of her passing, expecting flowers to have sprung up in her footsteps, doors to have burst into flames at her touch; journeys I plotted on maps of the city – the name of which I cannot speak, for what is to you just another northern city is to me saturated with her presence, inextricably linked to her: I would expect you to take off your shoes, cover your head, talk in hushed whispers in the presence of its name – plotted on maps to seek patterns, expecting it to make letters, spell out a word, to make sense, trying to make sense.... I was crazy, quite mad, without realising it, after she left.

And now I had to ask Richard the question I had avoided asking, had not dared to ask:

'Did you know Melanie X?' For they had been at the same art school. Sometimes it is a small world. He looked up startled, confused, for, having finished singing he had been sitting dreaming, and my manner was sharp.

'Melanie X? Yes, sure. Gosh, Melanie X, I'd quite forgotten her. She was quite a character. I almost went out with her once. She asked me. I'd just had a rough time with someone, been hurt – yeah – and said "okay, as long as it's not serious". She looked at me with utter contempt, said "it's always serious", and turned on her heel. I was surprised because, well, she got around a bit.

'I don't know what happened to her after college. I think she got a bit messed up, something about hospital. Quite a few of that crowd did – too much Velvet Underground, too many trips, walking on the edge too often. Why, did you know her?'

And that was it. To him she was quite a character, with whom he'd have gone out as long as it wasn't serious, one of a crowd, who'd got around a bit, got a bit messed up. To me she was everything.

In my final year at university, under the influence of a charismatic lecturer, I was drawn to the new modelling theory in urban studies, the idea that instead of just describing cities, you develop an abstract model of the urban system, into which you input data and theoretical postulates, upon which you test hypotheses about the subject's nature and functioning, compare it to the actual urban situation, modify, refine. It felt safer, having that model between 'actuality' and me – for things often had too much 'thingness' about them, inexplicably so. It was my way of coping with the emptiness I had experienced here, on that first visit to France. I was good at it, and I graduated well.

I joined a research team in that northern city applying General Systems Theory to the urban pattern of Western Europe, with the aim of developing a model of such predictive power that we could map thirty years into the future: Europe 2000. Laplace for the twentieth century. The scientific

221

method: to understand in order to explain, to explain in order to predict, to predict in order to control. Science the new theology, we its acolytes. (But who was God?)

I spent a year in a world of homeostatic systems, location analysis, nested hierarchies of central places, rank-size rules, stochastic processes, gravity models, game theory, regression curves, Monte Carlo simulations, electrostatic potential analogues…. Shuffling numbers and batting ideas back and forth, the group of us, always on the edge of some great discovery; the map of Europe at first still, then animating before our eyes, a robot version of the real thing, a simulacrum that we could understand and control because we had created it. The only place I felt safe was in the department, in the lab, among books, figures, maps, numerical plots. Outside, I tried to impose theories on everything, slid over life, lost touch with it; the simulacrum substituted, allowing me to not feel. And then I met Melanie.

It was my turn to cry out. I couldn't help it. The memory so strong, so vivid.

'Kris? Good God, what's happening?' I was crying my heart out. I could feel him standing there, hesitating, not knowing what to do. Then he sat down, put his arms round my shoulders. I held onto him for dear life, pouring out words and tears, feeling his arms enclosing me, feeling the strength of his body, at last no longer alone.

'After our first quarrel I cried, for the first time since I was eleven. What a relief, no longer dry, dried up – but God, the pain.

'Just to lie with her, touch her, wake early and look at her asleep, twitching sometimes and moaning, wondering what was going on inside her head.

'"What's this?" she'd say, looking at some file I'd brought home to work on. "This isn't something – it's *about* something. Look at what is – *this*!", slamming her fist against the wall; "*this*!", scratching her face, a tear down her cheek;

"*this!*", a Kathe Kollwitz self-portrait. I had become a Christmas tree bauble, smooth reflection on the outside, empty within. I was being swept by a solar wind. In a rage, she went on, "you think you're showing your best – I admit, I was impressed, at first. Jesus, you're clever, compared to me. But how I pity you – all your cleverness used not to reveal but to conceal yourself, to hide from yourself. Because you're scared of the real world, you'd rather have these 'simulations'", she spat the word. "Rather than seek Athene's true wisdom, you went to Medusa, Athene's maiden, made monstrous by her mistress for her falseness, whose false wisdom fills this," she pointed contemptuously at my work, "and you turned to stone. You feared you were empty, and decided you'd rather be stone than nothing. But you're not empty – you just daren't look at yourself; it's there, that spark of light, if you just dare look. Reveal it. Let it be. Be dangerous."

'I *was* empty. When she left, I fell from the Christmas tree and smashed. I flipped. Love's flint – lodges deep, covers over, is always there. I tore up all my work, took it in a sack to my team leader, who'd been kind, strict, encouraging, me his favourite. "But why, why do you do this?" "Because you lied to me, led me astray". Through the glass wall I watched him staring at the pieces. Like Bellerephon I'd flown – oh God, that time with her! – had fallen, was crippled. I made shrines to her, lit candles.

'At first I felt everything. Then I felt nothing. I dossed anywhere. Friends avoided me. I changed my name – not the sound, but the spelling, and the meaning – from Chris to Kris; the soft, breached, leaking C replaced by spiky K; not curly C but kicking K; the name now a Malay dagger. I tried writing her out of my system. I worked as a labourer to make money while I wrote, got good at it, liked working with my hands, trained as a carpenter.

'My family disdained me as an artisan, even though they were artisans – for one to choose to become what they were when you could be other was a betrayal of their dreams.

'On the bus to work I'd read aloud from *Leaves of Grass* – "are the rich better off than you? Or the educated wiser than you? … do you give in that you are any less immortal?" All eyes were averted. I'd hoped, among artisans, for the spirit of those who'd founded Mechanics' Institutes, co-operatives, the Labour party, read and discussed Emerson and Ruskin; the libraries of working men's clubs, once full of books, had been turned into snooker rooms, they drank, they watched popular TV programmes, they looked at pornography.

'I pretended to be normal, and had my disastrous time in the office.

'Then gradually I became more properly normal, linked back up with some of the weirder college guys, got into the alternative technology thing. I met Jane. Suddenly it seemed that my life had purpose. I gave myself to her, followed her, trusted her, tried to find myself in her, believed we could find ourselves through each other. This was our last resort.'

The next day I said 'go ahead.' Immediately I felt much lighter.

Richard set to at once, looking through my books, walking round the farm and places around, talking to me, sketching.

*   *   *

The dogs run to meet us, barking. When the car stops they form a wary circle. I help Richard out, drop him on his bed.

Chapter 4: Richard leaving

I wake early. Outside I'm greeted by the usual empty sky, the usual metallic taste in the air. The dog days, Sirius' baleful influence, an atmosphere of heaviness and exhaustion, and the period of a marked slowing of the farm's tempo.

There is little to do: after the harvest there must be rain before they can plough; and as the sheep dry off, all they can do, apart from taking them out mechanically twice a day to nibble at the hard, dry grass, is wait for the lambing to begin.

Monsieur Bonafet, instead of taking time off, slows, like a clockwork toy running down. He works on, in slow motion, an automaton, a torpid somnambulist.

Didier took his first ever holiday last week, a few days on the Med; he returned unnerved and stunned by the glitzy life and the undreamed-of wealth: 'we live on gold,' he says, fierce and uncomprehending, 'and eat shit'. "…How ya gonna keep 'em down on the farm, now that they've seen Antibes…?" He sits in the barn, under the buzzing fluorescent light, Radio Monte Carlo blaring, dismantling and reassembling oily machines.

Gaston carries on with the rhythm he always has, a rhythm that adjusts to the season: he tends the garden, cleans round the vines, works in the cool woods, prepares the wine cellar, repairs fences, tidies up – but he takes his ease too, in his secret, shady places by quiet pools or the trickling stream, where dragonflies hover and soft leaves dapple the light, lying, self-contained, his beret pulled over his eyes, dreaming who knows what dreams of slender dryads or fat tarts.

A vignette from this time: one afternoon, when the great heat was past, the air become temperate and mild, Gaston pulled out the ancient winnower from the shed where he normally worked it, placing it carefully on the cobbles to catch the last hours of the descending sun. The device is like a mangle, with additions; you put the grain into the hopper on top and when you turn the handle, a complication of rollers jostle the grain and paddles blow air through it, separating the chaff. For two vacant hours, humming quietly, he filled the hopper, turned the handle, watched one sack empty, the other fill, as the evening drew softly in. In the barn Didier was welding: blue arc light flashed, the lights dimmed as he overloaded the hamlet's power supply, his blank-masked and asbestos-gloved figure emerging only to pick up more pieces of rusted steel.

But this summer there has been an edge to the dry season, an edge of fear, almost of panic.

For the dry spell became a drought, and the drought has become very serious indeed, the worst for twenty years. But in that time consumption of water on each farm has grown many times, with more animals, more milking machinery, more washing machines, more bathrooms. But no piped water. The neighbours only have water from their own source; and so do we.

What do you do when the well runs dry and the nearest tap is five miles away and you have a hundred thirsty sheep? Each day Monsieur Bonafet came out first thing, sniffed the air anxiously, stared shortsightedly up at the sky for signs of a change, but none came; the high pressure remained steadfast, the air too dry even for thunderstorms. He became more than ever preoccupied and taciturn, short and gruff. Only the visits of his daughter with the baby mollified him, put a light in his eyes – the eternal hope that children represent, the possibilities of future generations. Last week their well ran dry.

What of our well? When we were buying the house we asked about the water; the Combons, with much pantomime astonished lifting of shoulders and spreading of hands, of poo-pooing, said: "worried about the water? – that's rich –

the well's big enough to turn a pair of oxen in". But I've no idea what the flow of the spring is into the well. Is it about to run dry; or am I sitting above a reservoir big enough to swim in? It's a strange feeling, not knowing. The answer lies outside the door, under a slab of rock I've never lifted. And maybe, at present, I don't want to.

Whatever, our pump still draws up pure, clean water; the neighbours' tap has run dry. Gaston tells me theirs is a new spring, found (as is usual around here) by the water diviner – *sourcier*, though at first I thought he'd said *sorcier* – tapped only five years before, when they needed more water. 'The old spring never dried up in fifty years,' he insists. 'Taps. Washing machines. Waste.' But they are relatively economical with water: they have no bath, no flushing toilet. More likely the increased demands and more powerful pumps of the neighbouring farms, such as the dairy farm at the top of the ridge have, over the years, lowered the water table.

Even here, I realise, you can't live in isolation; what you can do depends on what those around you are doing.

For a week now the Bonafets have been bringing water in by tanker from St Leon, and furiously lobbying the *mairie* and the *préfecture* to be connected to the mains. More money. And what is a reduction in isolation, an increase in security, is a loss of independence and relationship to the locality.

*   *   *

I take my ease at this early hour, leaning comfortably on the verandah rail, between the flowering rose and the fruiting vine, in possession, rather wishing I smoked to complete the effect, reflecting upon the three weeks of Richard's stay.

For us the dog days have been a time of decision and high activity. We have finished the roof. Richard has painted the dome ceiling. And we have spent three weeks in the same house; at first bumbling into each other like hulking adolescents, gradually finding our own space, accommodating each other.

It was strange to sit in bed at night, reading, self-contained, and suddenly hear Richard singing quietly to himself in his room at the other end of the house, as self-contained, and both of us aware of the companionability of shared accommodation.

'I hated school,' Richard said. 'Eight man buggery in a boat; put your arms round seven friends and kick shit out of eight enemies. Only if you were too thick not just for university but for teacher training college were you supposed to apply for art school. After that place, I wanted nothing to do with men when I got to college. I always shared with girls – all understood and platonic; until one of us got drunk, or had a row with the current. Very messy. Then I lived on my own.'

'I always lived on my own. Before Jane.'

Lying in bed in the early morning, conducting shouted conversations through the doorways and corridors:

'You see, "tangled up in blue" is exactly the same as "are birds free from the chains of the skyway?" back in '64. At least he's found that you can't escape your destiny in "love". So many tried that – back to mother. Like playing out – you stay out as long as you can, but sometime you've got to go back in.'

'There's got to be another way.'

'I felt really abandoned by our heroes – half of them fled into marriage, like an older brother giving up; others went away – Barrett, Green, Morrison, Hendrix.'

'It was like the Pied Piper had led us out of town – then vanished. Did he go on alone because he couldn't take us with him? Did "They" get him? Or did he join them – is he even now watching from his new house in the city, watching us stumble about, having a good laugh? Sometimes it seems

228

the only important question is: what do you do when the Pied Piper's led you out of the city?'

We took up table tennis, playing hard, sweat-flying games on the long family table. Sickened by too much competition at school, and discouraged from it by our women – "why are men always fighting?" – we'd both avoided such behaviour for years. It was good to rediscover the fierceness, the thrust and parry, enjoy the fine edge it gives you. We chalked the scores along the beams, prisoner style, and were soon into the hundreds.

We went to a party at Michael and Rosie's. I sat quietly, rooted in a deckchair in the sun, the party swirling around me, among threads of conversations and hand-touching greetings, reading *Journey to the East*. *Blood on the Tracks* had played through as I read; the last verse of the last track, "Buckets of Rain", was playing, "life is sad, life is a bust". I looked up, then wrote this in my notebook: "a harmonious gathering of people, happy together; sky, blue steel, soft as an animal's breathing flank, *mouton* clouds moving across, the view clear to the horizon; the last song, after all the anger and high-octane confrontation, meandering, reflective and, at the end of all hope, open; and this sentence in the book – "when something precious and irretrievable is lost, we feel we have awakened from a dream": sometimes life is so like this that it *is* this…."

Richard spent the afternoon, the evening, the night with the loveliest girl we had ever seen, not touching her and never taking his eyes off her, sleeping with her an inch away; she said she couldn't make love to him because she'd just had an abortion and couldn't be touched.

Coming away from Edvard's, Richard fuming. I said:

'What's wrong? His place is great.'

'But did you see the sculptures he did before he came here? They had the very devil in them, they were tremendous. Sure, his place is great, what he's doing is great – it always would be because he's a great bloke – but what's being lost? Think of the effect of his work back in the mainstream.'

'But look who buys sculpture, who sees it.'

'You're saying art can't change things. You're saying what I do is a waste of time. If a single person looks at a piece of art and sees a possibility he didn't see before, then it's worthwhile.'

'A lot of people may see new possibilities through his work here.'

'Maybe. But I sure as hell miss the art.'

Sitting on the roof, the sun on our backs, glazing the dormer. Plunging our hands into the bucket of putty, kneading the hard and soft together, pressing and squeezing, our hands sliding over each other's, until we'd massaged the stickiness from it and all was smooth plasticity; and all the time wreathed in the smell of linseed oil:

'This makes me want to rush to my studio. From being a little kid I wanted to be a painter – d'you know why? Because I loved the smell of linseed oil. I'd spend hours oiling my cricket bat at school – when I hit the ball it'd spray the close fielders. Now, show me how to glaze a window – hey, that's clever,' as I drew the slanted chisel down in a firm, sustained movement.

And now it's time for a last look at the ceiling of the tower, while Richard is still here.

The dragon and tiger twined together. Exact crystal forms. A spiral staircase, a coffin, a risen figure, the legend: "the badge of innocence and the band of friendship". A dark wood, illuminated by a flash of lightning. A tree in the sun, so real that I have to check that I'm not seeing it through a window. It's good. When he's famous I'll receive awed visitors, retail anecdotes; it'll become a place of pilgrimage, like the Schwitters barn at Ambleside. (When I'm dead they'll remove it to Albi, install it in a museum.)

But I'm no nearer knowing what this place is for, or what

elements I need to add before, in the alchemical alembic, the distillations, the transmutations, begin. Perhaps it exists to one side, an obsession that allows the real work to be done, as Bergman obsessively planned his staging of *The Magic Flute* while he was actually making his great films...? Judgment is all. And decision. A ringing chorus of "Oh, what a beautiful mornin'...", a swaggering cowboy figure, a waved coffee pot.

After breakfast, as he's packing, I give him *Blood on the Tracks*.

'I can't.'

'Please, it's done its job. I want you to take it with you.'

'Okay, thanks. Come and listen to it sometime.' He's lifting his heavy pack when there is a commotion at the front, swearings at the dogs, the door bangs open and the kid stumbles in. We look at each other and burst out laughing – we'd quite forgotten him. He blinks at us reproachfully. I offer him breakfast. Do you have any chocolate and coke? Coffee and bread, I say firmly. He hunches over his food, looking hard done by. Okay, we're going to Albi. Okay, why not. We bundle him into the back seat with Richard's rucksack, and set off.

Chapter 5: Return to Albi

'Let's go the river way.' An alternative route to Albi is by the valley roads; along the narrow, twisting tributary then joining the broader curves of the Tarn, a valley that alternately widens into cultivable tracts and narrows into spectacular gorges. Along its length are a number of villages, some of them unimpressive, practical places, one or two having the ornate, faded quality of Victorian resorts, with verandahed hotels and tree-shaded walks, where one can picture figures from Impressionist paintings, awninged boats upon water on which the light fractures, river cruise pleasures as on the Rhine or Wye. These days, apart from a few spartan canoeists, the river is empty. To avoid the gorges, the road uses the abandoned railway tunnels – a single track railway was opened in 1915, too late, just in time to close. Near Albi, where the valley opens out onto the plain, there is irrigation and market gardening, emerald plants in disciplined rows. The road enters Albi through an artisan quarter – past a metal-working factory, a bottle factory, and a working men's café with an art nouveau façade and Communist party posters on the walls.

'Goodbye to all this,' Richard says as we join the Tarn.

'Do you know what you're going to do?' I ask.

'I do, now. I'm going back to paint. I want to have an exhibition within a year, to be teaching part time in an art school within three. I feel strong. But you, what will you do?'

'I don't know. The future's still a blank. It's not there yet.'

'If you fancy coming back up North you can always stay with me. You'll soon find work, with your skills, even in these crappy times. Bear it in mind.'

'Thanks. It's a possibility. Can I show you something? Have you time?'

I turn off onto a narrow, twisting, rising road. The kid becomes restive, then slumps back. He stares vacantly. The only times he has come to life are when we pass a female, any female; his head shoots up like a periscope and he growls and works his fists.

I stop beneath a cliff, by some scrubby land with many beehives. The bees hum and the smell of thyme fills the hot air. The cliff rises in smooth surfaces of fractured slabs. High up, there are words painted on the rock face in white letters:

> *désire   réalités*
> *réalise   désirs*

Above, on a shrubby ledge, a finned bicycle wheel turns slowly and a light flickers.

'What's that?'

'A relic of the sixties, renewed in the seventies. Originally it said "We treat our desires as reality, for we believe in the reality of our desires". After '68 quite a few disillusioned students and activists came to this area, some jumping, some pushed. I imagine they painted the slogan and set up the wheel as their beacon, their eternal flame. Camisards of the twentieth century – except the authorities never pursued them, they weren't dangerous enough; just kept an eye on them, neutralised them. Some raise goats. Some drink and dream. I first saw it when we were driving to see a house. I climbed up to look at it. The tyre was perished and flat so the dynamo didn't work, and the wheel bearings were rusted and locked. While we were in England over the winter I got a wheel with a dynamo hub from a scrapyard and greased the bearings. When we came back, the first thing I did, the very first thing, before I dug the garden or pruned the vines, was to come here and rig it up. I fitted better fins, a directional vane, a governor. I put some bulbs and oil in a box beside it. Then I renewed, altered slightly, the parts of the slogan I wanted.

I had to do it hanging over the cliff on a rope. I think maybe that was when Jane began seriously to think about leaving. I'm very proud of it.'

*   *   *

In Albi we leave the kid in an amusement arcade, a black walled, mirrored, strobe-lit place, playing pinball, his eyes flashing in time to the machine, and go for a stroll in the old quarter.

Past Toulouse-Lautrec's house, between tall, crumbling tenements that smell of drains and cooking food and have washing stretched between them, where children play and women look at us suspiciously, into the reconstructed old town. They demolished the old buildings and built, with facings of Roman brick, large timbers, pantiles, a replica. Now, instead of the butcher and the greengrocer, the cheese shop and the baker, there are antique shops and hairdressers, chic clothes boutiques and gift shops. Instead of the smells of apples and cheese and blood, there are simply varieties of perfume. No children play in the pedestrianised streets, no families live in the expensive apartments. What we see are façades, not true.

'Terrifying failure of nerve,' Richard says, 'all this nostalgia, harking back. As soon as you have history, you lose something. Like with pop music – remember when you'd hear a record on Luxembourg for maybe a month, maybe just a couple of times, and then never hear it again? It was ephemeral, and therefore exactly attached to the memories of the times you heard it. Then the revivalists arrived. We're ever more concerned with recording, replaying, reconstructing. When is *now*?'

'Our culture is premised on the idea of evolution, progress. As that premise progressively fails, as the millennium approaches, what can a time-bound culture do? It will be more and more torn between those going for broke with the technological fix, and those yearning for, trying to recreate, a rosy past that never existed.'

'But isn't that what you're doing, Kris?'

'I believe that our culture is an evolutionary dead end. What I want to do is to recollect: through practical experience, through study and research, through reconnecting to the unconscious, the collective unconscious, the primitive; to recollect in order to be able to create a stable, no-growth, ecologically-mature culture. It will be quite different from other societies – we can't will ourselves to be primitives, if only because we've lost too many of the skills of the so-called primitives – but it will have one quality which it shares with them, and which this doesn't, because this is an imperial culture, of being sustainable.'

'A pretty speech – do you believe all that?'

'I believe it – it's what I've learned here. I'm just not sure I can do it, or even want to do it. That's the biggie. Until I know, each step is a step into the unknown, with no guarantee of a landing.'

'"Well, I just say 'good luck'". Hey, I bought you this.' He gives me Dylan's *Desire*. 'A step on from *Blood*, more in the world. I was going to get it – I couldn't believe it when you showed me the writing on the cliff. Such is life.'

We round up the kid, now with pinball eyes, and drive to the edge of town, the road to Toulouse, unload the rucksack and set it down at the roadside.

'Hey, I don't want you to go.'

'And I don't want to go. Stubborn buggers aren't we?' We embrace, genuinely, though already beginning to be awkward again, then shake hands.

'Good journey.'

'Good journey.'

I drive on a hundred yards to turn round. A red sports car

has stopped by Richard. He gets in. As we pass he shrugs and waves, the blonde-haired woman in dark glasses klaxons "La Marseillaise" and puts her foot down. I stop and look back and watch the car smoke into the distance and disappear. Serendipity rules, OK.

'Okay, kid, where to?'

'I know a place, not far south, a commune,' he says. 'I think there were some Swedish girls there, very pretty,' he adds hopefully.

'Why not? Why the hell not. Now,' I say as I slip the car into gear. Now.

PART VI:

STEPPING OUT

Chapter 1: Driving south...

...across wide expanses of orange earth and green vines, flatness spreading into the distance, past giant technicolor billboards set in the middle of fields – smiling faces, shiny refrigerators, barn-sized packets of detergent, along speeding naves of light-fracturing plane trees, through race-track villages stricken and grey with rubber and exhaust fumes, among glossy and brightly-coloured cars and heavy rumbling lorries, punching through air suddenly dense with the smell of aniseed, past sunlit fields of sunflowers whose faces turn towards the sun as mine does as I drive towards the sun exhilarated by driving fast, intoxicated by change, empty of destination, high on driving towards. The kid sits up beside me, gripping the dashboard, eyes flashing around him. Occasionally I look to the side and see distant villages – possible destinations – on the slope of the white ridge which keep pace with us for a while then drop slowly behind, the only measure of the distance I'm travelling; mostly my eyes are fixed on the road ahead, on the parallel lines converging on my destination.

At last, reluctantly, he indicates that it is time to turn off. As I drive more circumspectly up into the hills he slumps back, examines his nails, yawns. The landscape here is lighter, prettier, more of the Midi, less the Massif: pink cliffs rise up from mixed woodland of oak and beech, the scents of lavender and rosemary eddy in from the *garrigue*, the fields are small and walled with cream stone, the earth is red, there are silver-leafed olives, dark green orange trees, and ripe fruit on the delicate peach trees. This is the last ridge before the Mediterranean, the so-close sea I haven't visited in my twenty months here. Ahead is a village set prettily on the valley side, apricot-walled, pastel-shuttered, red-roofed, with black flame cypresses marking the cemetery and a white towered church at its centre. We drive in through an arched gateway. The houses have been daintily restored, *maisons secondaires* interspersed with modish craft boutiques and ateliers. The only dog I see is an Afghan on a lead.

We drive out of the village, up a rutted track, towards a tight group of buildings. Bouncing slowly down towards us is a yellow R4 with a Paris number plate. We stop side by side. The driver is a striking thirty-ish woman; she has an oval face, big beaky nose, arched eyebrows, large quizzical eyes, full red lips, alabaster smooth slightly freckled skin, an Afro halo of red hair, a long slender neck around which an extravagantly bright silk scarf is artfully tossed.

'Can I help you?' her manner imperious and proprietorial.

'We're looking for Gérard.'

'He's in the village. We're going to meet him there. Are you friends?' I indicate the kid, who gives his name.

'Ah, Gérard spoke of you. He enjoys having visitors. Go up to the house and make yourselves at home – we'll be back soon.' As she talks, controls, I'm aware of the woman in the shaded passenger seat, younger, smaller, dark-haired, with watchful blue eyes, sitting patiently.

'I'm Simone,' the driver says, holding out a long, slender, red-nailed hand. Gabrielle's is smaller, broader, softer. We say goodbye and I drive on and park by the buildings.

They are built around a courtyard, with a continuous verandah at first floor level creating cloisters beneath. The buildings are of grey ashlar stone, with carefully cut stone lintels and quoins, and slate roofs: alien materials. In the stone porch, by the nailed door, is a painted board:

NOTES FOR COMMUNARDS

To work for others is to work for yourself.
There is another world – and we must find it in this one.

5.45 Reveille
6.00 Meditation
7.00 Manual work
9.00 Breakfast
9.30 Communal discussion….

The timetable continues to midnight in this monastic vein. But there is no one about. Leaning against a wall is a stretched rabbit skin, inexpertly cured, hard as wood. An unwashed honey separator is covered in slow, droning wasps. The vegetable garden is thick with weeds. The group of buildings is enclosed within a low, unfinished elliptical wall.

'What's going on?' I demand of the kid. He looks embarrassed and evasive, then shrugs – what the hell, he's achieved his purpose, he's here – and confesses: there is no commune. There was, years ago, but Gérard's best friend went off with Gérard's wife and it all fell apart. Gérard lives here alone, with visitors who stay for a while and then leave. The kid's parents have a holiday home in the village, and his father had told him to be back today or else they'd leave for Rouen without him and he would have to pay his own fare. He'd got entangled with the girl, run out of money, been very drunk when he'd flagged us down… he spreads his hands, attempts a complicit 'you know how it is?' and dodges as I make to punch him. I shake my head and smile, and he looks rather pleased with himself. I walk up the steps and go inside.

*   *   *

Why? Because I've nowhere else to go as I act without volition until something happens. The steps are in front of me, so I climb them, one by one, and come to a solid closed wooden door; my hand reaches out, grasps the heavy metal of the latch ring, turns, pushes – and the door opens. It is as simple as that.

241

The kitchen is dark and empty. I drink some coffee. Outside the kid sits facing the sun, chair leaned back, eyes closed, an aluminium reflector under his chin. I hook the chair from under him. He scrambles to his feet blinking, says 'oh, hi,' and resumes his sunbathing.

'No hard feelings.'

'Okay.'

I root out a hoe from the gardening tools heaped under the carefully-marked hooks and go to the garden to rescue a few leeks from the overwhelming weeds. After an hour I look up: there are two rows of clear earth the length of the garden, like railway lines, heading for the kitchen door. The kid is gone. I clean the hoe and hang it, solitary, from its designated hook.

'Kris! We thought we'd lost you. Grab a glass!' There are flowers everywhere, blazing in the shafts of evening sunlight: Brel on speed sings "La Chanson de Jacky" very loud, the air is rich with the smells of spices and fresh herbs, of cut vegetables, olive oil, and good living; pots bubble, vapours spiral among the sunbeams and Simone swirls purposefully from chopping board to stove, singing, a large knife flashing in her hand. A silent Gabrielle patiently fills the spaces. I wonder whether they live together, whether, even, they are lovers. Simone takes me by the arm, thrusts a bottle into my hand, whispers:

'Stay, at least for the meal. So few people come here. Take the bottle, share it with him.' She steers me through the door and closes it firmly behind me.

Gérard sits at the far end of the main room, silhouetted in a doorway that opens onto nothing. I pull up a chair warily, fill his glass and mine, and sit down. We're on the edge of a twenty foot drop to sharp rocks. Gérard's foot taps on the threshold. He is about sixty, grey-bearded, chin on chest. In front of us the sun is about to set.

'You're English? I'm Belgian. What draws us here? Oh, I know, it's the only country that never had a population explosion, so there's space. The only people who don't breed like rabbits when the grass grows. Rational? Cunning. Like foxes. Drought still bad in England? Kids still getting nitrate poisoning? Men still growing breasts because of the oestrogen in recycled water?' He has bad teeth. 'France is no better – just bigger, with more space, where you can lose yourself. I got this,' he points to a white scar on his forehead, 'protesting against nuclear power stations.' His eyes, from being vague and empty are now flickering with life as thoughts bubble up in his mind. 'Protest is useless. Authority feeds on it, grows strong on it – how they loved '68! But at least here I can live secretly, work silently, away from the corruption. The summer's ending. Soon you young people will go back to the cities. You'll remember for a while, but then it will deafen, blind, coarsen you. But I'll still be here. I'll always be here. That,' he points to the bladder sun puncturing on the ridge, disgorging its bloody redness over the land, 'is the future'. His thin stretched arm and pointing finger quiver.

'Oh, isn't that beautiful!' Simone and Gabrielle stand arm in arm, their heads together, their eyes bright with reflections of the sun. 'Dinner's ready.'

*   *   *

As we eat, Gérard's spirits revive, stimulated I'm sure by the excellent meal and the presence of engaging women. Certainly the rich sauces, the fine wines, the animated conversation awaken aspects of my senses that have slept for a long time, open doors of rooms long closed. We are a convivial company, sitting around a table upon which candles are progressively lit as the night gathers around us until their flickering dense light is our only illumination and their waxy smell fills the air.

Once, when there is a lull in the conversation, a few moments of rest and digestion, when the only sounds are those of cutlery on plates and muted sighs, Gérard sits back, beaming, looks from face to face, raises his hands:

'It's good to have people here. This is how it should be. Thank you.' The momentary awkwardness soon passes. At the end of the meal he says:

'Excuse me, I must do my weaving.' He goes into the next room. Soon we hear the rhythmic treadle of warp and weft, the slap of the shuttle flying.

'What does he weave?'

'His destiny, he says – some literary reference, I think. Night and morning. It's his meditation. He measures his life in woven centimetres and an old woman in the village reads signs in the fabric.'

A trio, two cosmopolitan women and me – I like it. They live in Paris, but not together:

'Oh no,' Simone says. 'We hardly knew each other before the summer. We met through a friend. We both wanted to see France, look at what's going on. You work in Paris, work hard, head down, doing what you can, living day to day. We wanted to step back, slow down, see the alternatives.'

'Where have you been?'

'Everywhere! A Celtic festival in Brittany, drinking cider, meeting great Irish people, dancing, dancing, dancing. We saw Pink Floyd in the Roman theatre at Orange – that was magic. We rafted through the Tarn gorges, Romantic tourists. We stayed with Langue d'Oc liberationists in Toulouse – they write love poetry in Occitain, like the troubadours – don't they Gabrielle?' She grins at Gabrielle. Gabrielle looks down.

'We went to Montségur,' Gabrielle says quietly. 'It's impossible not to cry when you see the dove. The whole future changed there. You look around and say – what if…? And then – one of those amazing things that happens – I was

244

looking through the stone dove, and a real dove appeared – within the dove-shaped space created by the stone a real, living, flying dove. And I'm thinking – is this a sign? What does it mean? Tell me.' She looks at Simone questioningly, then down, her back bowed, a back which seems to carry the weight of the world, that one wants to lift off. A brief silence, then Simone resumes her itinerary:

'We supported the workers at LIP. Did you know Voltaire financed a workers' co-operative of watch-makers? We campaigned at Larzac, weaving children's clothes into the fencing. We went night-clubbing in Marseille.' Again the grin at Gabrielle. 'We've visited lots of *installés* – there's such a buzz in the country now. We've just come from L'Arche. Lanza's a saint. It's so austere, yet full of joy. He says – if you think you need a machine, don't use it, don't have it. It turns logic on its head, and it makes sense.'

'So how do you come to be here?'

'You don't know about this place?' Simone is amazed. She prepares herself, then launches into the story.

'Imagine,' she begins, her slender arm extended dramatically, the candle light catching the red of her lips, inflaming her hair, 'a vast building of metal and glass, constructed like a musical instrument – "a wind instrument combined with a stringed instrument" – which recreates the harmony of the spheres; a building that moves with the sound of that harmony, which we would hear as silence, a sound as soundless as water is tasteless. Imagine a building constructed according to the ancient sacred geometry, the secret canon of proportion that has come down to us, hidden, from man's earliest creations, through Neolithic stone circles, the Temple of Solomon, the Gothic cathedrals. Imagine – but first, a little history.

'The ideas were contained in a visionary poem by the Saint-Simonian Michel Chevalier, written just before the authorities

245

closed down their first Utopian community in 1832. They actually began to build it, their temple, at Ménilmontant, a village near to Paris, but the police action stopped them. The poem was forgotten until it was rediscovered by another visionary, a well-known architect, in that pivotal, pivoting year, 1961. His obsession, through the '60's was to realise the poem, at first as designs on paper, then in a building.

'Everything seemed to conspire towards the realisation of his dream in that decade in which anything seemed possible. It was his Project Apollo: new materials – anodised aluminium, plastics, carbon fibre; new construction methods – especially the application of tensile strength; the scrolls discovered at Naj Hammadi, with their insights into early Christianity; new observations of the fundamental structure of matter revealed in the particle accelerators; studies of sacred geometry; the limitless energy potential of fission and fusion; electricity use doubling each decade, filling the world with light and sound; the accelerating growth of electronics and computers; the mind-altering power of hallucinogens, enabling him to see the form of sound and the shape of colour…. He was convinced that, just as Babbage invented the computer, which couldn't be built until the technology was available in the 1940's, Chevalier's vision could only be realised in the 1960's. Through the decade he worked on his drawings. These drawings.' Dramatically she unrolls a horizontal scroll of paper along the longest wall, pinning as she goes. 'And then the perfect site came available: Les Halles.'

I walk slowly along this astonishing exhibition, at once a complex, brilliant work of art, and a precise blueprint. It is grand, grandiose, seductive. Some of the pictures are vivid watercolour sketches, of a crystalline and yet organic structure. Some are meticulous architectural drawings of construction details. There are plans and elevations. There are quotations from Chevalier's poem, circled and arrowed to drawn details:

246

"The spire, erect like a lightning conductor,
seeks electrical power in the clouds:
storms swell it with life and energy,
as a man's aroused senses swell his member."

"The sun lives here in light and fire,
the Earth
in its mystery,
through electricity and magnetism
brilliantly."

"In towers and pyramids
savants observe the paths of the stars."

"Underground there are labyrinths and furnaces,
silent squares
in which the marvels and treasures from the bowels of the earth
have been placed with infinite skill,
and where other wise men experiment,
shrouded in tranquillity and darkness."

"The harmony,
when structure, pillars, vaults speak!
How magnificent,
the ampleness and variety
of its space!"

"Between the Circus and the Basilica,
in the middle of the nave,
an immense plaza,
surrounded and divided by serpentine waters
and transparent lakes
dotted with islands, mysterious refuges of pleasure."

*"In the nave, he is one, and they are two
the man and the woman,
and they are three."*

*"Division of the sanctuary, 2 and 3. Division
of the right side 5, of the left 7,
number pi and e…."*

'Look!' she points out excitedly, 'lenses and mirrors, coloured glass, light fractured and reconstructed, lasers and flames. Galleries and grottoes, plazas and verandahs where man's creations are exhibited, which in their very construction and form *represent* knowledge. The spire, drawing electricity down from the sky – have you ever seen that astonishing photograph of the Eiffel Tower being struck by a dozen lightning bolts? Absorbing and transmuting natural forces; not an earth but a battery, an accumulator. The pyramid meditation places where the form amplifies the practice. Deep underground, places of initiation and transformation…. Imagine such a place!

'And look at the actual location in Paris,' another map, the familiar city with this new creation at its heart. 'Its underground places enfolded in a labyrinth of *métro* lines, secret tunnels and communication links; between the Hôtel de Ville and the Élysée Palace, at the very heart of government; the gut of the city; between Notre-Dame and the Templar temple, centre of the mysterious Order so brutally liquidated by the French king on that Friday the thirteenth, 1307 (– and where, ironically, Louis XVI's son and heir was done to death). For a while in those heady days he had the ear of some in the government – there are always initiates of secret societies close to those in high places.

'But his message, that this would be the culmination of our knowledge, the high-water mark of our culture, what we

248

would leave to posterity, to be read as we read the Pyramids or cave paintings; that was too much for those not ready to believe that progress would not go on forever. He tried, and he was rejected.

'Instead, we got – the Pompidou Centre; a legoland creation with its outdated paintings upstairs, onanistic music in the basement: and next to it, a hole in the ground that, having thoughtlessly created it by disembowelling Paris, France even, they don't know what to do with.

'And like many a neglected visionary he cursed the city, shook the dust of it from his heels and headed, with his disciples, into the wilderness. Here.'

'Of course it was different here.' Gérard has come quietly into the room, speaks. He looks sardonically at the grand schemes for the Paris Temple, more affectionately at the smaller, quieter set of plans:

'Even "the master" realised that. But the location was good: a Catholic seminary, built on the site of a Cathar house – the standard method by which one religion replaces another. More interestingly, there are caves beneath the crypt, hints of deeper caves, of prehistoric wall paintings.

'We began by copying the ground plan of the temple at Ménilmontant, an ellipse, enclosing the whole fabric, the whole history of this auspicious place, intending to neutralise the malign forces, amplify the beneficent. Our glass would cover solar panels, the lighting conductor would be replaced by a wind generator. We would descend once more into the caves, follow the clue to our own hearts. Our energies would once more balance....'

His voice, soft and quiet, fades to nothing. His eyes fill. And then he begins to laugh. He laughs until tears run down his face:

'One winter! One winter he lasted! Then he went back to Paris, to his air conditioned office, his cushioned job – the

249

arses he had to lick to get back in! With Juliette. My Juliette. Pah. Take them down. I don't know why you pin them up. Utopia. Nowhere. *This*!' his fist slams down on the table, 'is somewhere! Take them down.'

Chapter 2: Gabrielle

Gabrielle and I are in the kitchen washing up, Simone having gathered Gérard up, taken him away to quieten and soothe him. The water had been heating slowly in a large iron cauldron suspended over the fire in Gérard's room. I carried a slopping bowl of it carefully across the main room, the door onto blackness now closed, the wall cleared, but still a knot of perturbed energy disturbing the atmosphere.

The kitchen, softly lit by an oil lamp, silent except for the soft swirl of water in the bowl, the low clash of cutlery, the light sound of a plate being carefully placed onto wood, is calm and peaceful. It is a relief after the excitement.

Gabrielle washes. She washes with the absorbed concentration of a child, revolving the mop on each plate then lifting the plate from the water and examining it before handing it to me. It makes me smile. I want to say 'you're so caring', but of course I don't. Anyway 'careful' would be more the word.

'Why do you think he stays?'

'I wondered that. I asked Simone. She says he has nowhere to go. He can't go back, and there's nowhere to go on to. This is the only place he's ever wanted to be. If it doesn't work here, it won't work anywhere, his life. He's had offers for this place, good ones – the kid's father wants to turn it into a high-class therapy centre for stressed over-achievers. But he'll stay. He'll wait. The world will turn. Maybe this place's time will come, maybe it won't. It's the chance you take when you really go for something. But he'll stick it out. Maybe that's all you can do at a certain time in your life? I don't know.' All this with her head down, washing diligently. Then:

'She's amazing, isn't she?' looking straight at me, her eyes wide, as if she's suddenly thought: who are you?

'Remarkable. What does she do?'

'She's a lawyer. Surprised? Very radical of course, ardent

251

feminist. Does a lot of work with North African women. She's brilliant. But she has a hard time. A Jew guilty at surviving – she was born near here, her mother on the run in the war. And she has her own needs. Divides her. But she makes things happen. What do you do?' I explain as best I can, mentioning Jane circumspectly, saying that really I'm not sure where I'm heading.

'But you have a place, a home, a commitment!' she says, her eyes bright with enthusiasm. 'I'd love to live in the country. Especially after this summer. The cities are finished. Life in Paris is terrible now.'

'But I don't think it's enough, for me. I realised, as Simone was talking, how exciting big ideas are. It's not easy not to be seduced by big ideas – they make one feel big.'

'I don't like *anything* that's big.'

'"The youth gets together his materials to build a bridge to the moon, or maybe a palace or temple on earth, and at length the middle-aged man concludes to build a woodshed with them".'

'Is that a quotation?'

'Thoreau, an American philosopher.'

'A man. Man's talk. Think of all the resources that go into those materials, all the grief he causes gathering them, and then all the waste. The woman's way is different.'

'Oh.' Silence. The soft swish of soapy water, and a stab in me.

'Sorry.'

'It's okay. You can say what you like.'

'I was sharp. I don't want to be sharp. Sorry.'

'It's okay. Let me scrub those pans.' As I burnish the heavy iron I ask her what she does.

'I teach. In a nursery school. Little ones.'

'Good?'

'Very. Although it's hard – the classes are too big, there's nowhere to go to outside, but yes.' She stops her careful washing and stares at the window, at the blackness or at her reflection, and speaks in a soft, musical way, as if to children:

'I like their world – imagination, dressing up, fairy stories. They live in a world that is at the same time absolutely fixed and entirely limitless. And they are either perfectly good or monstrously awful; and there's no connection between the two states, so they're never smug and never guilty. They live without reflection, in a world without mirrors. They're brilliant animals. Sometimes – it makes me shiver to remember – I'll be talking to a couple of them, telling them a story, sitting on the floor with them. I'm absorbed in the story, out of myself, and slowly I'm aware that the other children close by have stopped what they're doing and are listening. They slip off their chairs and move silently into the circle. And then the children further away. They crowd round – they love to touch. They sit with rapt, upturned faces. The only sound is my voice, or rather the voice that's coming through me, because I'm only a medium, and the story is telling itself. Then I feel magical.' Swirl and swish. Examination of the plate. Hand it to me, a quick smile, then hands plunge decisively into the water:

'But I won't teach much longer.'

'No?'

'I suddenly knew, this summer, for the first time, what I'm to do.'

'Oh?'

'I shall teach for another year, then I shall go to South America. And when I return I shall have a child.' Just like that. So simple, so certain, that I believe her.

*   *   *

Simone again asks me to stay; there's a spare room. I have been drawn in, squaring their circle, the symmetry of four. I have no reason to leave.

We sit in Gérard's room, baking potatoes in the hot ashes of the fire, passing the wine, talking. Gérard says that of course Western industrial society is doomed, that it has disregarded the natural limits governing man's actions, that nemesis necessarily follows hubris, that we are living out the last scenes of a Greek tragedy, victims of the gods we tried to believe were dead.

I say my fear is that scientific thought and technology, the chosen means of postponing nemesis, will irrevocably harm our humanity; that we will destroy the rain forests of our souls. 'My fear is not just that we will make the world uninhabitable; but that we will then learn to live in it. We are too adaptable.'

Simone says that she believes that we are each sparks of the Sophia imprisoned in flesh – but that what one believes is of little importance compared with what one does. And that for her the way is to work within the system, helping the helpless, working to balance the always unbalanced scales of justice.

Gérard says – no, for to work within the system is to be inevitably corrupted. The only way is to isolate oneself, like the Desert Fathers.

Simone says that while the Desert Fathers were being godly, talking with God, the Catholic church was taking over Christianity.

'But simply by *being*, the Fathers were influencing,' Gérard says. 'The first duty is to keep the flame. And whether by telepathy or even a cosmic mind, their thoughts and actions strike sparks in certain individuals. The most isolated individual, if he is true, is influential.'

'I like that,' Gabrielle says, looking up suddenly. Simone snorts and says you may like it but it doesn't stop female circumcision and slavery.

The discussion goes round and round, in that heated, inconsequential, comforting way of such discussions.

254

Gabrielle says little, sitting, back bowed, head down, crocheting. When Gérard says, 'is that the time? I must go to bed,' she looks up, pleased with herself, and gives each of us a small panel of crochet work with today's date picked out in red. 31.8.76.

When Gérard has gone, Simone spends some time tidying up, fussing with the fire, gathering up her things before she leaves.

Gabrielle and I sit on the old sofa, quite close together, saying nothing. The room stills. The silence gathers around us. Maybe one of us is about to speak when Simone puts her head round the door, smiles sweetly and says, 'are you coming, Gabrielle?' Gabrielle rises immediately, says goodnight, and goes out.

*   *   *

I feel her absence. I have become interested in her: I have included her in my space; and now I feel her absence. I look at the shapes where she sat, imagine their warmth. Solitude closes slowly around me, and I feel cold and lonely. I stare into the cooling ashes. I look around this lonely room. I sit until long after all sounds of movement have ceased and silence has settled upon the place. Then I write in my notebook:

"I fear what I see in this room. I fear it for myself. A loom like in Van Gogh's paintings, threaded with dark yarn, that reminds me of the execution machine of "In the Penal Colony". Rows of dusty, long-unopened books. A damaged straw hat. Rouault and Van Dongen prints, helpless and hopeless. A small arched niche containing, instead of a household god or votive offering, a rotten apple. A broken sofa. A worn car seat. Two rough wooden stools. Bits of tree root. An old string puppet with an Ensor face hanging twisted. A pot of last year's lavender, faded, its scent gone. A yellow-faced bakelite radio with all the old stations on its dial. Everything covered in a layer of dust. Nothing personal of now; all memories of a person. The place of one who has overreached himself, lived too much in dreams, detached too far from reality. Gérard Laval." A long pause, and then:

"Meanwhile. It's 2 a.m., and an event which I cannot make happen is hanging by a thread – as the women prepared for bed and Gabrielle might have, why not, tiptoed back – illuminated and taut, about to fall… falls, smash to the ground. And all the steps into nothingness and the magically appearing stepping stones, and all the serendipity I'd thought was unfolding towards a conclusion, have only brought me to a beginning, to the messy place of choice and decision, of taking risks and putting things at risk." Another long pause.

"She feels safe. I want, just for a brief time, to unfasten the knot that holds me together. In a safe place. I want to be with her."

Chapter 3: Mushrooming

I get up early, very sober (I hadn't realised how much I'd drunk last night) and dress quickly. Outside, although the sun is bright, the air is cool. I stop by the yellow R4: there is a brightly coloured poncho thrown over the passenger seat; the car is full of womanly things; it seems to give off a faint perfume. I run my fingers slowly along the smooth roof, then smile at my involuntary action and turn away, to my car. It would be easy to step in and drive away. How it would simplify matters. And maybe it's only the thought of the embarrassment I would feel if someone came out as I was starting the car that stops me doing it…. No, there's more to it than that, much more. Occam's razor is folded shut, Alexander's sword firmly sheathed. I get my jacket from the car and set off down the track towards the village.

Narrow streets carved into angular slices of light and shadow by the bright sun. Brightly painted shutters, pots of brilliant flowers, wrought iron balconies, next to low, peeling, crumbling hovels. I look up at the deep blue sky wedged between apricot walls. I cross the wide square, past the elegant fountain at its centre, dry now, carved with mythological scenes – the Triumph of Zeus? The Labours of Hercules? The Judgement of Paris? – and stand at the parapet.

A long, rocky drop to the valley, dark with trees, soft in the haze, and the air dense and viscous and pure. Gardens and smallholdings carved out from the woods; squares and rows of light green and dark green, lengths of thin, snaky hosepipe, rabbit hutches and pigeon coops knocked together and patched up, men working before they go to work. A cock crows, indignant and defiant. Birdsong echoes up from the trees. My eye follows the stream between tree-clad bluffs, out across the hazy blue plain that stretches away until it is lost in the distance, towards the Mediterranean.

I draw my eye back. The sun is warm on my face. Although birds dart and leaves shimmer, everything is still. And then my head begins to swim and I have to hold on to prevent myself pitching over the waist-high parapet. I turn abruptly and go and sit in the bar.

I stare at my coffee. Each tiny decision produces such manifold consequences. I feel a book in the pocket of the jacket I haven't worn in weeks, haven't needed to. Rimbaud. I think of Sylvie. And then I open it at random: "As for me, my life is not weighty enough, it flies and floats far above action, that dear point of the world". I try again: "Oh, to rise up again into life! To look hard at our deformities!" Thanks a bunch, Arthur. I look around the quiet bar. I would like to sit here forever, the saucers (if they still did it) piled to the ceiling, not moving, watching the world moving, past me. But I can't. I make my decision: if there is no one about, if I have seen no one by the time I reach the car, I will get in and drive away.

I am placing my hand on the car door handle when Simone appears round the corner and says:

'We're going mushrooming this morning. You must come.'

*　　　　　*　　　　　*

In the mirror, as the car bucks slowly down the rough track, I see her watching, then slowly turn away. I curse myself, grip the steering wheel hard, but don't stop. I pass through the gateway – and as the stone gateposts close together behind me the period I have spent there closes up, finishes, ceases to be the present, becomes memory, part of the past. I turn north and drive fast, reviewing it all, thinking furiously until I know what I will do.

We set off mushrooming, with Simone striding ahead full of purpose, Gabrielle and I trailing along, distracted by little things, like wayward schoolchildren. Down the lane, over the road, across the wide flat valley, with Simone calling out the names of every plant and tree and bird in sight. Gabrielle whispered one word to me: 'coquelicots', the large red poppies in the hayfield; the word echoed in my mind all day, became the word of that day. Coquelicots.

On the narrow path across the hayfield, with the grass high on either side, we waded through a fragrant, shimmering sea, to the wooded slope on the opposite shore.

We climbed slowly up through the wood, Simone poking around in the undergrowth, consulting her book, muttering. When we walked in single file I watched Gabrielle's narrow bowed back, the way her heavy dark hair fell away from her slender white neck, wanted to reach out and touch her, just touch. Sometimes she would turn and give me a quick, uncertain smile. I wanted to walk by her side, take her hand in mine. I began to hum "Le Temps de Vivre", the Georges Moustaki song I had heard in the Albi youth hostel, the record I had bought in the Albi record shop, the song maybe I should have sung to someone all those years ago but hadn't, that I was humming now, singing the words in my head, hoping that by some magical process she would hear, not my humming but the words, in her head: now, we can take hold of this moment, now, to be free; we can dream our lives into being. I'm here, waiting for you:

"tout est possible,
    tout est permis…."

I felt awkward, foolish, seventeen.

We reached the top and looked back across the valley. The wind was in our faces and scattered clouds were being driven across the sky, their shadows moving over the ground. 'Look,' Gabrielle said. The shadow of a cloud shaped like a dragon was moving down the opposite slope exactly towards us. Swiftly it came, over rock and stubble and grass, absorbing the light, darkening all it touched, up across the trees towards us. I held my breath. I felt suddenly naked and defenceless with Gabrielle, children helpless before this dragon bearing down on us, about to devour, me for being with another, for being unfaithful, for wanting – I suddenly realised it and as suddenly was prepared defiantly to express it – to have an affair with this woman; her for being with me. I held my breath: the shadow engulfed us; and passed on. I breathed again, almost laughed; everything was brighter.

Mushroomless we walked back, down through the woods, across the wide valley, up the craggy hillside, back to Gérard's.

I said goodbye to Gérard and Simone inside, and then I was standing by my car, with Gabrielle. We had, elliptically, referred to our situations: she lives with a boyfriend from whom, she has come to realise over the summer, she must separate in order to live once more on her own.

And so we faced each other, not knowing what to say, not knowing what each wanted the other to say, somehow close but suddenly helpless strangers separated by a narrow, bottomless gulf. We talked awkwardly aimlessly. At last, running out of nothings to say, I said, 'well, good-bye,' shook her hand and grabbed her by the shoulders and kissed her quickly on both cheeks. What I wanted to do was enfold her in my arms, hold her to me, whisper 'come with me' through her hair, in her ear. I didn't dare. I prayed for a sign from her, a signal, a touch. None came. The moment passed. I got into the car, closed the door, and with a wave set off, cursing myself.

In the mirror, as my car bucked slowly down the rough track, I saw her watching, then slowly turn away.

*   *   *

I will write to her.

Standing in front of her, looking into her face, I found myself staring into a void. This was no dream, no imagined situation in which the future already exists; this is the real world, where actions have consequences, consequences unknown. Standing, looking into her face, the ground shifted under my feet, unbalanced and unnerved me. Now, safely in the car, moving, alone, I can condemn my loss of nerve, my missed opportunity; I can imagine. And so the future, once more, exists.

Every few hundred yards I curse my cravenness and pre-pare to slew the car round, drive back, leap from the car, rush to her, and say – what? That's when the future stops. Not: I love you and can't live without you. Not: I want to make love to you. But: I like you, I feel less lonely when I'm with you, I want to spend some time with you…. But. What of Jane? Is this a brief detour in my relationship with her, or the first step out of it? And anyway, be practical, what if Jane is back – imagine climbing out of the car, with Gabrielle, and Jane standing at the door….

I make my decision: when I get back, if Jane isn't there and there's no word from her that she's coming, I'll write to Gabrielle. A short, prosaic letter. And then it will be out of my hands. I spend the rest of the journey relaxed, content-edly composing the letter, draft after draft.

*   *   *

The house is empty. No Jane, and no letter. It's over a week since I wrote to her telling her the roof was almost finished, the house soon an ark proof against any flood. Instead of being present she is absent; it is she who has absented herself, maybe even removed herself from my life entirely; it is her fault. With shaking hand I write the letter. I write in English:

"Chère Gabrielle,

I just wanted to say how nice it was to meet you, and that if you and Simone want to visit, or stay, on your journey north, please do, I'd like to see you. And of course if you want to spend some time here after Simone returns to Paris, you'd be more than welcome. There's plenty of room here, and it is very peaceful. If I don't see you, please write soon; I would like to keep in touch".

I copy Gérard's address carefully from my notebook. I read and reread the letter. But still I don't send it. It is Wednesday, and they are leaving Gérard's on Friday: I won't post the letter until Thursday, giving Jane one more day to write, and lengthening the odds on Gabrielle receiving my letter and being able to act on it. Another throw of the dice. On Thursday I meet the postman; he has a card and a letter from Jane. The letter says: good news about the roof but I'm still confused, I won't be coming yet. The card is from Amsterdam, where she is spending a much-needed holiday with friends. I swear at her, seal my letter and hand it to the postman.

On Friday I arrange, rearrange, clean, wash, tidy, cook, wait. At five o'clock I suddenly decide to make up a bed in the tower, which I frantically do, sure they will arrive at any moment. Then nothing happens, and by sunset all hope has faded.

In the evening, after dark, when I'm thinking of going to bed, there is an uproar of dogs and a commotion of vehicles.

262

Simone and a man stumble out of her R4, laughing and all over each other. Gabrielle steps slowly out of her car, a 2CV with rainbows and sunflowers painted on it. She is calm, self-possessed, smiling. We shake hands, kiss cheeks, and I, heart thumping, say how marvellous it is that you came. After the meal, at which Simone and Paul are outrageous and uproarious, and Gabrielle and I quiet, indulgent towards them, exchanging satisfied looks, Gabrielle says:

'I'll get my bag.'

'I'll help.'

At the car I put my arms round her; she is slimmer than Jane. I bend to kiss her; she is shorter than Jane. She reaches up to be kissed; Jane always waited. We kiss; her lips are thicker than Jane's, softer. She tastes different. We stand, pressed together in the dark; she feels different. I look up at the trees, the stars, the lights of the house. Everything looks different. Enfolded in my arms, holding me, held to me, I whisper through her hair, in her ear, 'you came'.

'Of course.'

'Where will you sleep?'

'With you.' Of course. She has come to sleep with me, to be with me. Of course. Arms around each other, we walk slowly to the tower.

Chapter 4: Gabrielle visits: 'La fossiure a la gent amant'

I'm sitting at my desk, thinking about Gabrielle's time here, writing a letter to Richard, trying to make sense.

> "10th Sept
> Dear Richard,
>   The kid was the clue."

I look around: vases of autumn vegetation and an appliqué hanging complete the tower. Write on:

> "She stayed for five days, nights of the full moon."

I made this desk from a thick slab of sawn chestnut wood and two wine barrels. I like its roughness. While I was cutting wood one morning she placed the decorations. The rain hushes onto the glass above my head. I write another line:

> "She has been gone two days. I might have killed her."

Two days of terror. The water is running again across the cobbles, everywhere there is movement and flow; but I want to hold it all still, what happened, until I understand….

We undressed each other by star light, stroking and kissing each other's hot skin. Her hair was black and heavy, her skin soft and pale – how light she was, how easily I lifted her – and the light shone in her eyes and on her teeth as she laughed her delight, and then she became quiet and serious, head down. We held each other, our bodies contoured together, a long meeting of skin and skin, the beginning of a melting. Then we slipped into the white bed.

Out there, was light and music, all the lights on, record after record, changed capriciously, and cries of laughter, interspersed with groans and silences as Simone and Paul pursued each other round the house, into the garden – Simone's loud 'shsh, everyone's trying to sleep, God look at those stars – bastard! I'll get you for that!' – back into the house, bodies banging against walls, heavy breathing silences.

In here, in the dark, two relentless, blind creatures exploring one another silently and limitlessly with mouths and hands and hips and feet.

Out there, in the house, the watches of the night marked by crescendos – the quickening rhythm of the bed, the insistent rising slap of flesh on flesh, the grunts of giving and the groans of receiving, the breathless cries of pleasure and the sudden gasps of release.

In here, we pored over each other endlessly, insatiably touching, smelling, tasting, and at last holding each other heart to beating heart, me inside her, she around me, minutely moving, often still. We lay in each other's arms through the unmeasured hours of darkness, slipping into and out of sleep, waking, kissing, murmuring, sinking back. How calmly she slept, like a child. Dawn came softly.

Sandbagged by sex, Simone and Paul snored noisily.

Awakened by sensuality, our skin electric, we lay, arms around each other, whispering sweet words, talking gravely, giggling suddenly.

As the waves of light filled the dome with light, she looked around – at the rock walls, the diamonds, the windows, the paintings – and declared:

'This is our "fossiure a la gent amant".'

'Our Cave of Lovers? You like the Tristan story?'

'I love it. I love their crazy love.' Amour fou, crazy love: as evocative, as thrilling, in both languages. We spoke our own language, a mixture of both.

265

'But they love only because of a potion.'

'Oh that's just an image, a way of excusing an unsanctioned passion. Anyway, as an image it rings true – sat across a chessboard on a hot day on a long sea voyage, you share a drink and – wham.'

'But the effect wore off after three years.'

'And that's right. Love, passion, that intense, all-consuming thing, can't last. It's a madness. You have to decide whether you have other reasons for staying together when the effect wears off, or whether you move on. I love that moment when Mark comes upon them asleep in the woods, ready to kill them – and sees them lying just a little apart, with Tristan's sword between them. Then he knows the crazy love is over and he can take Yseult back to wife again, he doesn't have to kill them. That's how it should be.' All this said with certainty, as if it was obvious, logical, incontrovertible, entirely without notions of guilt or shame, shockingly un-Anglo-Saxon. Wonderful.

'But it all ends tragically,' I persisted. She pulled a face:

'Because of possessiveness, and jealousy. Which is why Tristan's wife tells him the sail is black. And why Mark chops down the rose and the vine that grow from their graves and entwine. But three times he chops them down, and three times they grow again.'

She gripped my hand. As the silence grew, she said:

'Tell me a story.'

I told her the story of the wounded man looking from his pale house and seeing a place in the distance – at first an illumination among shadows, then a place coloured by the end of the rainbow; at another time sparkling like crystal, and then a reflection off gold; of how, ill, he imagines a fairy queen there who will heal him, and one day sets out through the tangled, untravelled country and at last reaches the place; and finds a tumbledown cottage, and a sad and lonely

266

girl who is certain that, could she but meet the happy man who surely lives in the white marble house that she sees in the distance, looks at each day, all would be well.

Then she told me the story of the boy who visits the puppet theatre and falls in love with the puppet princess, and she with him. He persuades the wizard to change him into the puppet prince. At last, after many adventures he reaches the sleeping princess; he bends down to kiss her; it is not the princess he fell in love with. He looks up, across the lights, and sees, in the audience, a girl, his princess.

Strange tales to tell in bed together for the first time in the luminous dawn. And yet, I remember now, how one can tell one's fears, be painfully honest, at the beginning, before you, the two of you, have vested interests. And how, too, the whole pattern of a relationship is established in the first few hours. Suddenly she said:

'Cover me. Make love to me.'

We got dressed quietly and went for a walk. Clear and bright, the world empty and still and full of life.

She walked carefully, reluctant to crush anything, even to put her full weight on the ground – and she so light. From time to time she would let go of my hand and drop to her knees with a little cry and cradle in her small hands a tiny flower – a scarlet pimpernel maybe, or a blue speedwell – and look up at me with big brown eyes. In the wood she stood still for a long time, finger on lips, so still I began to wonder whether she was, Daphne-like, turning into a slender tree; until a green woodpecker, its red cap ablaze, suddenly flew across, left to right. 'There!' she cried in triumph, giving a little jump, and looked at me with vast pleasure and took my hand and led me down to the stream. Looking carefully into the trickling transparent water, she at last picked out two pebbles. She showed me how, apart, each was entire, but that together their qualities enhanced and intensified each other. She expressed all this with a cool certitude, as if she was demonstrating a logical proposition or a mathematical theorem, then she said: 'there', and pressed one of the pebbles into my hand. It lies on the table in front of me.

Simone was on the verandah, dipping bread into a large bowl of milky coffee and eating with relish. She smiled and waved.

'Where's Paul?'

'Oh,' dismissively, 'I got rid of him. Have some bread. It's fresh from the village. I'm starving.'

Memories. I resume the letter to Richard:

"When it comes, it's nothing like I expected. While it's happening, I'm aware all the time of the difference between what I'd expected and what is. Afterwards, it seems to have been inevitable.

"Something has happened, but I don't know what. Suddenly, after all the stepping into space, there was a landscape, a real place, all around me. But what do I do now? I told you that Jane and I have a lot of shit to go through. Maybe we don't. Maybe we won't. Maybe we'll just disattach ourselves, drift apart, make separate lives. Maybe the unthinkable has already happened.

"I read and reread Jane's letters and they're from a stranger – no, from someone trying to make herself a stranger. You said: "don't let go easily. If you do you'll always regret it – I know". I want to believe that but I don't know if I do. Maybe our love was an invention. And if it can be invented with one, why not with another? How is one landscape, place, better than another? Has it all become relative? If it has, I don't know how to cope with it."

I stop writing. Remember.

We went down to St Leon together. While Simone bobbed here and there, taking photographs, talking to people, end-

268

lessly curious, Gabrielle and I walked quietly down the main street, hand in hand. I took her into shops, hand in hand, gazing steadily back at the curious back and forward looks. It was important to do it. But why? Maybe I wanted witnesses. By the keep she said:

'There's a castle where the mortar is as hard as stone, the walls impregnable, because the people added their blood to the mortar. Do you think that's terrible (again that thick 'r', so beguiling), or magnificent?'

'Terrible – our blood should be for our lives not our buildings.'

'I think it's magnificent – you must be prepared to defend what you hold dear with everything you have.' Her voice was fierce.

On the drive back, Simone said:

'I went to the house where the Wild Boy was captured. If only Itard had tried to understand him, learn from him – but of course it was the Enlightenment, the light that exists to obliterate darkness, that says darkness is the absence of light and progress is the increasing of light and the shining of it into further and further corners until at last darkness is eliminated. Instead of seeing that light and dark are defined by each other. Darkness can never be eliminated: it can only be hidden or held at bay; or it must be included.'

Simone left that evening. She would journey north overnight, a pile of cassettes beside her, a bottle of amphetamines in her bag. 'I love driving through the night.' She would arrive at 8.30, see her first client at 9.

As we were saying goodbye, embracing, I suddenly realised – and she made it clear that she saw that I had realised – that it could have been with her that it had happened. Having kissed me with her soft lips and pressed me to her larger softness, she grinned in reaction to the sudden astonishment on my face. Then she gripped my arm and said: 'please, be seri-

269

ous, don't mess about, look after her, I mean it, please.' She spoke for a while with Gabrielle, then she was gone. The last we heard was "Heroes" drifting on the wind.

'What did she say to you?' Gabrielle asked.

'Be careful. And you?'

'Be careful. But I don't want to be.'

'Neither do I. But maybe we should.'

'Let's go to bed.'

*   *   *

We spent four days alone together, the days and nights of the full moon. How happy she was, how contented to be here. For her it was a culmination, a fulfilment, what her long, extraordinary summer had been leading to, its fruition. That's how she saw it, how she expressed it. At the end of a summer of many people and many places, of a slow shaking off of the city, of the cracking open of the greyness of her given self and the flowering through of her real self, a place, a man, an arrival.

'"Three days of happiness already".'

'Sorry?'

'I saw it painted on a wall at the Sorbonne in '68. Actually it was "ten days", but that's how I feel. "Under the cobblestones, the beach". "Be a realist – demand the impossible". "Freedom is the consciousness of our desires". "The purpose of the enemy is to break our bones; our purpose is to defend the collective imagination". "Society is a carnivorous flower". All those slogans. But not slogans – truths.

'I was only a child, but I went to the Sorbonne during the occupation, talked to people. Everything was so exciting, everyone so happy. A whole new way of life coming into being before my eyes. There was a grand piano in the courtyard and someone always playing – Chopin at dawn, ragtime at midday, the blues as darkness fell, Scriabin at night. Ten days of happiness already. The happiest days of my life. Until…. So much love.

270

'But then the *flics* came, the CRS, shining black armoured beetles crawling over the barricades, beating, maiming, crushing the flowers underfoot; then the dinosaur bulldozers, breaking down the barricades, letting that awful world rush in.

'I talked to my father. He was one of those on strike – seven million at one time – just before the workers were bought off, just before they realised their power, that they alone turn the wheels and that without them the wheels stop. He said – and he'd been a Communist all his life – "the union preaches revolution, teaches resignation. This is the last chance to change things, and they've allowed themselves to be bought off with a few francs, a few pieces of silver". No more union meetings for him. Now my parents spend every day of their holidays building their own little place in the village they came from, to retire to. But I need to act now.'

Happy, she helped me gather in the harvest. Together we salted beans, dried apple rings, bottled tomatoes, strung onions; each activity having a different quality, a different rhythm, the shape and feel of the fruit in our hands, the smells on our fingers changing from task to task. Lifting potatoes, me forking them up, Gabrielle hunting for them in the dry soil like a child searching a bran tub.... I resume the letter:

"We were digging potatoes. There's a mystery about digging potatoes; you don't know, as you sink the fork in, what you will find – the top growth gives you no clue. The feeling, when you lift the fork up from within the dark earth and the potatoes cascade onto the surface, or lie half hidden, like nuggets of gold or mystical eggs, is extraordinary.

"Suddenly Gabrielle sat back on her heels, looked around, and said 'it's so beautiful here'. I looked up and suddenly saw – for a moment I think through her eyes, unattached, without the habitual weight of responsibility – the beauty. Seeing, it was like a punch between the eyes, the blow of the

271

Zen master's stick. I'm here. For a reason, but for none of the ostensible reasons. All summer I've felt watched; I thought by others, but in fact by myself, my selves, all those threads spun, the warps fixed in place, waiting for the first throw of the shuttle. Gabrielle has brought me back to the surface of things. I can see, feel, touch. Anxieties have receded, dark thoughts sunk back down, and I have risen up. I have returned to the surface of things.

"We made love many times, but I came only once, a momentous event."

I want to tell him everything; not to boast but to share, explore the mystery of sharing, with a man – already I can feel that reluctance to tell, that complicity of man and woman that excludes his friends. But I must write:

"For three days we played like children – or rather, like adolescents. Do you remember those times, before you'd done "it", with your girlfriend, parents out, an empty house; or maybe with another couple there, in another room, everything sexual but, because you'd decided not to do "it", not heading towards anything? Do you remember the days before foreplay, when there was only play? Am I romanticising? Of course – for years all I wanted to do with my virginity was lose it. And yet….

"We sang Joan Baez songs together – she knows all the old ones, from the early albums that used that same photograph, the one we were all in love with, learned painstakingly, by ear, hardly understanding them. We'd quote Prévert poems to each other, alternating French and English lines, poems about painting cages with open doors and waiting for a bird to enter, wait years if necessary, and when it does you close the door then carefully paint out the bars and paint in beautiful foliage and the wind's freshness and the dust of the sun and the noise of insects and wait for the bird to sing; and when it sings, you can sign the picture with one of its feathers…. We spent hours doing very little.

"We had gone for a walk in the afternoon. I watched her walk, alert, absorbed in the moment; or was she focussing on the moment, trying to absorb it? A question – after only three days, already the beginning of my detachment. I felt blocked, frustrated, wanting something to happen. I took her hand, put my arm round her, trying to feel her presence. I guided her to the vines, my most peaceful place.

"The grapes were fat and black, with a soft bloom on them but still a little hard, with an edge of bitterness, not ready yet to harvest. We lay down among the vines, the earth warm beneath our backs, staring up, looking at the clear-edged, soft, bright green leaves – leaves you can wrap food in and eat – the thick clusters of grapes, the twisting curling tendrils, all clear against the blue sky. It calmed me a little. We got up, walked, sat down in a broad field to watch the sun set.

"Directly in front of us the fat red orb sank slowly onto and then began to slip down behind the hill. As it sank the shadow of the hill moved slowly up the field towards us. 'Look,' she said, pointing at its slow approach. She unbuttoned her blouse and leaned back on straight arms, eyes closed. I stared at the small roundness of her breasts, the soft nipples that I had tasted, the pucker of flesh at her waist. I felt suddenly fierce. The shadow advanced. It touched her naked toes and she twitched. It moved slowly up her bare legs and her breath shortened. It crossed the hinge of her splayed thighs and she held her breath for a moment then, as the shadow slowly climbed up her body, breathed with long, slow breaths. It crossed her lips. The moment it touched her eyelids her eyes sprang open and there was a look of triumph on her face. I felt unsettled. I scrambled to my feet, needing to move, feeling choked and blocked.

"I needed to move, and I didn't want to go back to the house, for that was suddenly a place of disturbing memories. I wanted to stay away from the house, be outside it, but to keep within the rim of hills, to traverse in curved walks this saucer of land, with the hamlet at its centre and the cultivated land and pasture and woods around it, as night came on. The sky turned violet. The light was pink, a pinkness spreading across the land. She whispered 'rose', and the word spread across the land, filled the air. The sun had set.

"And now the moon rose. A full moon, exactly opposite the place the sun had set, like the lighter rider on a cosmic see-saw. As we watched the balloon-like orb rise into the sky, I told her of the time I was on a boat crossing the Mediterranean, from Africa to Europe, having slept on deck and awakened early. I lay, quite alone, listening to the regular throb of the engine, feeling the firm deck beneath me. I felt the smallness of the boat, the vastness of the sea stretching to the distant edge of the earth all around, a perfect circle, the darkening, densening depth of water beneath me. Alone, tiny, unafraid. Turning my head to the right – the newly risen sun, a finger's width above the sea, solid, radiant, golden, fiery. Turning my head to the left – the full moon, a finger's width in the sea, setting: the moon under whose rain of cold fierceness I had spent a troubled, momentous night; now opalescent, translucent, benign. I felt, at that moment of symmetry, at the centre, the fulcrum, of – what? The world? Creation? My life? Just at the fulcrum, the pivotal point, just there.

'You mean you were the fulcrum?' she asked eagerly.

'No, exactly not that; I was quite incidental – but uniquely privileged to be there, in that place, at that moment, a witness.' Her eyes, from opening wide as she listened, narrowed a little, as if it had not been the story she wanted. We walked on. I was aware of the tiny separation between us. And I was aware that I had not told her that Jane had been lying beside me, asleep, inches away, our first holiday together. I wondered whether they were parenthetic, that dawn, this dusk.

"Still restless, still looking for more. We walked through the dusk into the night, inscribing heaven knows what parabolas over that darkening saucer of land.

"We arrived at last at the edge of the hamlet, drawn by the lights but unable to enter. I fastened up the chickens. We stood in the meadow. Everything down here was dense black; up there were stars. I felt blocked, thwarted, clogged with trapped energy. I took hold of her, kissing her hard on lips, face, neck. She looked surprised. I pulled her blouse open and kissed her breasts, her nipples – she said 'ow', they hardened, I didn't stop – her belly. I fell on my knees and fumbled with the buttons of her skirt, pulled it down; she wore no pants. I waited for her to stop me – no, to resist. She didn't. I could do anything I wanted with her. I buried my face between her legs. Her hand touched the back of my head very lightly, then fell away. I licked until the sweaty mustiness opened into salty wetness and I entered her with my tongue. Her legs were bent, her hands were behind my head, pressing, she was moaning. That moan opened my ears – a bedlam of noise, of birds, cicadas, stars. A thousand eyes watched – animals, trees, rocks. A million stars pricked my back; and trapped, half blinded by the trees, the moon watched. Everything remote and cold, the only warmth between her legs. I pulled her down and pushed in hard. She gasped. She stretched her arms wide, at first sinking under me, then gripping me with her legs, pressing herself onto me, digging in her nails, moving urgently. I wanted her to stop, pressed harder down, moved harder to get her to stop; she moved more, more wildly. I was in a cave, in the dark, lost and cold; and yet a light there somewhere, low and flickering, in her to find, in me to ignite. On, on – she clutched me as if I was hurting her, I carried on, didn't care, wanted to, it was what made me come, I came.

"I pulled off and lay gasping. I had been unfaithful, for the first time. I had lost my fidelity. Gabrielle made noises beside me. I'd been selfish, didn't know if I'd hurt her. In gasping, wondering whispers she told she'd come, for the first time with a man; she was happy.

"We lay on our backs, close, staring up. Many stars, although the sky was milky with moonlight. Many stars, all still – and then one unhitched itself and moved slowly across the sky, bisecting the heavens above us. 'Look,' she said. No shooting star to wish on, no portentous comet this: a satellite. Even here. 'Probably carrying a spy camera.' We stuck out our tongues, humped our hips, waved 'up yours' fingers. It continued its imperturbable course and passed on. The heavens did not fall in half. We held each other, kissed.

"At last we got up. Standing brought the moon rearing up from behind the trees into the clear sky. We fastened our clothes. By the time we reached the house I had a raging headache. I lay with a wet towel wrapped round my head, looking around and thinking how ordinary everything looked. Gabrielle massaged my neck but the headache persisted. She was angry with herself, frustrated: 'I want to have powers,' she said. Ah, don't we all?

"That night, in our cave, we held each other, feeling apprehensive, even afraid, not knowing what had happened, each the sole source of the other's warmth. By morning we felt better."

I stop writing. The crack of a knot, the flare of resin, then the fire settles to a warm orange, visible through the mica windows. Above the stove, the wall hanging she had appliquéd assiduously on the fourth day, the sun and moon carefully balanced. A quiet day, both of us thinking about what had happened the previous evening – my act of will, or maybe defiance; hers of surrender that might have been self-realisation – of her leaving the next day. A golden day, with a movement of air, a clarity of light, a brightness of sun so different from the hazy summer heat. We were closer, and yet warier. We drove to the river and swam. We sat in cafés. We ate prune tart. We visited a church where there was a rose and a lily carved in wood which we both noticed and neither commented on. We touched each other often, nervous hesitant touches, accompanied by quick looks. We went for a last, quiet walk, ate dinner in silence, she looking up, around, often. We went to bed early.

"The last night the weather broke and it began to rain, with a symbolism almost laughably neat. But why do I write "laughably" when it *was* so? Kneejerk hard-boiledness, Richard, when I write to a man.

"The long summer was now, definitively, over. And when the end came it was quietly, in the night. No violent, shattering thunderstorms like I'd seen at this season in Spain and Greece; no epic battle, no titan clash of weather systems, maritime conquering continental; no trumpeted victory of melancholic humour over sanguine. The summer slowly weakened, the autumn slowly strengthened; the time of one was over, the time of the other had come. That's all. But what now was beginning?

"We awoke to a different world – grey sky, the steady patter of rain, long-forgotten scents, temperature down ten degrees. The pond is beginning to fill and everything is sodden – but there's still a dryness underneath. The landscape is like a man in a raincoat – the coat is soaked, the rain pours off, but underneath he is still dry. The soaking in, the percolating down of rainwater to groundwater, all that will come later.

"When Gabrielle checked her car, she found a tyre flat. 'See, even my car doesn't want me to go.' I replaced it with my spare. I was just lowering the jack when she came out to me and put her arms round me, inside my coat. I carried her inside.

"At last, much later than she'd intended, she left. I stood in the rain in my shirt sleeves watching her car climb to the rim, softening with distance. It stayed there for a long time

277

then slowly tipped over and disappeared. I stoked up the stove and sat in front of it, remembering the things we'd done, imagining her driving romantically north through the rain, her tear-stained smiling face peering ever forward through rhythmical wiper blades, but her eyes often flicking to the rear-view mirror. How warm.

"And then cold. As I replayed, time after frantic time, the moments by the car. I let down the jack; she embraced me; we went in. I put the hubcap on, singing… without having tightened the wheel nuts. Another film loop, of wheel nuts unscrewing one by one, of the wheel drifting slowly off, of the helpless mummied figure in the hospital bed. I had no address for her. She carried no evidence of my existence. I would never know.

"I rushed to the gendarmerie. The gendarme was sympathetic, shrugged – what could he do? – returned to his newspaper. I drove back up with a voice over my shoulder saying 'see? This is what happens when… – will you never learn your lesson?' And me agreeing, wanting punishment, penance, without forgiveness. But WHAT LESSON?"

This is what I want to share with him. I think of those two days of terror. Then her card arriving – everything fine, new flat great. A funny thing… just before St Leon… rattling noise… wheel nuts… mechanic fixed them…. See, you didn't want me to leave either!

I read the letter through. But I don't send it. It's too private. The old loyalties remain, after all. What I do is cut a gun-shaped space from the pages of Vian's *J'Irai Crâcher Sur Vos Tombes*, fill it with plastic-wrapped grass, write 'the mouth kisses the barrel of the smoking gun' and send it to Richard, care of the college.

PART VII:

SUMMER'S END

Chapter 1: The first days of autumn

The summer is over: the hotel in St Leon has closed, the holiday homes are shuttered; even the last of the Dutch and English are straggling home, and there are just two tiny coloured tents marooned on the flooded campsite. The wind sweeps in from the west, the clouds churn, change predominates.

The farm has struggled into motion: potatoes lifted, fields ploughed, lambs dropping, milking resumed. There is a new green bloom on the shaven fields, and fresh brown earth in long contour lines turned by the shining curved ploughshares. Figures loom from the mist, guns fire, birds plummet into the deep freeze. Gaston whistlingly sulphurs his wine barrels. Monsieur Bonafet has come back to life – all he needed was a good soaking.

The summer is over but nothing is resolved. My two tasks completed – the tower, the roof. A form given to each of my visions. But to what end? Chance allowed to unfold until the moment I chose to intervene, to make a decision. Of course I'd always wanted an affair – looking into the future and seeing myself sleeping forever with the same person (any person) always panicked me. The exclusivity of marriage panicked me. And yet I relish the involvement, the Platonic two into one. I'd expected the affair to have resolved something; to have satisfied my curiosity; to have shown me definitively whether I did or didn't want to remain married to Jane. Something. Instead it has added complication.

I gather chestnuts by the sack. I've plenty of firewood. My storage shelves and root cellar are well stocked. Soon there will be wine. With a sack of grain, some sugar, tea, coffee, I could spend the winter here for next to nothing. But for what

purpose? Thoreau moved to his hut to "transact some unfinished business with the fewest obstacles". I came here to live
with Jane.

I write to Jane, listing garden yields, then: "there's been a
girl. I won't say more unless you ask. Tomorrow I'll go grape
picking, to make some money. After that – I don't know". I
can't spend her money now. And what I earn in a month will
enable me to live here for the winter, if I choose.

I pack my rucksack, ask Gaston to look after the hens. I'm
about to leave when my brother's letter arrives. "Never been
so happy… her kids accept me as dad… some great news".
I don't need to read on. She's pregnant. Freedom, so seductive, terrifies him.

At Michael and Rosie's, Sylvie asks for a lift to Albi. I
watch her climb into the car. It's been a long time. And she
has changed. As we reverse our journey of midsummer eve,
now with the roof up, the weather grey, occasional scuds of
rain, I ponder the change. Gone is her edginess, her volatil-
ity. Now there is a firmness, a fullness, a solidity about her.
And a different, but still wonderful, loveliness.
  'It's been a long summer,' I venture.
  'It has.' She smiles, a secret smile.
  'Do you want to tell me?'
  'Oh look, crocuses – in autumn!' She points excitedly at
the pale purple, gently involuted flowers in the fields we pass.
  'Meadow saffron,' I say. 'An autumn flower. The rain's
brought them out. But yes, like crocuses.'
  'Crocuses,' she murmurs, and settles back complacently,
watching the road.

Outside her flat she sits in silence.
  'Do you want me to come up?'

282

'What for?'

'You seem…'

'I'm *preg*nant.' The way she says it, the first syllable high, definite, surprised, the second lower, drawn out, ending in mystery, a word she hasn't yet got used to speaking, but is very pleased to be saying. Pregnant.

'What does Jean-Jacques think?'

'Jean-Jacques? Oh heavens no, he's not the father, no. Larry. Larry's the father, but the child is mine. At last I've found what I want from a man.' She laughs and strokes her belly. 'I'll tell him one day. Maybe.'

'What will you do?'

'I'm going to a women's commune in Wales. Julie's coming too. We'll have our babies together. We'll bring them up in a women's world. It's the only way to change things. Rosie put us in touch.' I remember Rosie saying, fiercely, to Jane: "how different we'd be if there'd been feminism when we were at college!"

'We don't need men, you know. 'Bye.'

I remember their faces as Jean-Jacques ejaculated inside her; his twisted with power and yet loss, hers strained at his invasion yet bright and alive as she took from him. I think of pregnancy, of the growing of a life within, the coming to term, the bringing forth of a human being. I wonder how many of the actions of men are the result of his envy, helplessness, inability to do what for a woman is so simple. I ponder parenthood, family – thirty years old and never thought about it before. I think about Larry, his years of creation, his summer of procreation – I imagine his seed hot, robust, brilliant – his exclusion from the results of his fertility, the fusion, the growth, the coming into being.

At the Gaillac employment office, where the North Africans, with their cheap suits and cardboard suitcases, are routinely "tu toi'd", pushed around, insulted, as they wait with dignity and patience, I'm told there are no grape picking jobs, but there's work picking apples at Cavals, a few miles north. By seven o'clock I'm settling into the little cottage by the apple orchards where we three pickers will stay.

Chapter 2: Picking apples

I've come out of the wild hills, descended to the domestic plain, in search of money. Whether as brigand, as supplicant seasonal worker, or to give myself up and, amnestied, to go straight, I don't yet know.

The alarm clock wakes me with a start, and I have to get up. I'm back in the world. I imagine a horse that has run free all summer in a flower-splashed meadow feeling the first touch of the collar on its neck, the forgotten taste of metal in its mouth. I feel the tremble, the twitch, the snort; and then the familiarity, the resignation as the harness settles. And for me, it's something to push against, somewhere to dream.

I'm in a little house with two French lads. I look out of the window; a barn owl flaps silently past, a scrap of cloth in the blue early morning light. After breakfast we go out. We're in a wide flat valley between white cliffs. A roof of thick white mist, of cloud, is a few feet above our heads – the tops of the apple trees catch it, melt into it, and we will climb into it when we reach for the highest fruit. It is quiet and still among the trees, but cars pass frequently along the road at the side of the valley. The grass is thick and wet and our feet, soon soaked, leave deep prints. Moisture drips. The trees are symmetrically planted so that wherever you look they stretch away in straight lines until they disappear in the mist. They are pruned identically, and with their tight polls of leaves look like army recruits' heads. Perfectly-shaped, light green apples glow invitingly among darker leaves.

'Have one,' the farmer says, selecting, plucking, polishing, offering, a smooth innocence nestling in a rough knowing hand. It is glossy and blemish-free, a clear green with a hint of yellow, and it settles solidly in my hand. I bite into it. Its texture is perfect – crisp, clean, juicy. I chew, wait for the taste. It tastes of nothing. It has no taste. It tastes of absence of taste. The farmer waits eagerly. 'Fabulous,' I say. He beams.

We begin to work. I will work for three weeks, six days a week, nine hours a day. I will fill six boxes an hour, with sixteen kilos in a box and nine apples to the kilo. That's an apple every four seconds. 139,968 apples. Approximately. An apple a day for 383 years.

We pick in silence. There are no birds, no insects, and nothing moves. The only sounds are those we make as we pick (twist so the stalk stays on, otherwise the apple won't keep), fill the boxes, move our short ladders. The apples are consistent in size, grown to a particular grade to command a particular price. But there are exceptions: sometimes an apple identical in form and colour but a tenth the size; and on each tree one apple size, apple shape, but brown, soft, white speckled, rotten. I christen them strange dwarves and scapegoats.

The first French lad, very young and pretty, long-haired and self-obsessed, lasts a day. At first resolved, saying the money will get him to Amsterdam where he's been offered a job in films. But he trips over the ladder, complains first of the cold and then the heat, wails 'look at my hands!' and after a desultory day and unsuccessful attempts to entice us away, slouches off saying this is slave work and he's no slave.

The other stays a week. A good worker, talking only of Soft Machine, Pink Floyd, his son Syd; he says on Saturday, with a grin 'that should satisfy the *Agence d'Emploi*; I'll say my wife can't cope without me. It'll keep them off my back for a few weeks while we're rehearsing.' So most of the time I'm alone.

At first everything is new; what I see, hear, my actions – placing the short ladder in the thick grass, leaning it into a firm forked branch, climbing it carefully, reaching around for the apples, emptying the basket into the box, moving the ladder. I experiment. I acquire a technique, not necessarily the best but one that will fill the quota. Soon the technique fixes, becomes automatic, a habit, and I cease to be aware of it, unhitch myself from what I'm doing, sink into myself and my mind lives its own life. It's a method that allows me to work without involvement in what I'm doing, to say the work doesn't touch me, that I'm selling only my time, not myself. I'm no longer sure it's true.

Occasional events intrude. A single drab butterfly flutters around me, the only moving thing, stays with me for a long time, eventually lands, folds its wings slowly, expires. The sudden smell of mint crushed underfoot in the lush grass. The cloud lifting, the cliffs rising higher, the sun breaking through, sudden colour transforming a grey world. The Morrocans working in the next field, families of them who, as the sun begins to shine sing, calls and responses, songs that endlessly meander, that move from pain to yearning to joy to sadness, songs that both create and reflect the changing moods of a long, repetitive working day. It is Ramadan, and they work the whole day without eating or drinking. We work in silence, once the boy has left with his infernal radio.

The first evening I write in my diary:
"I pick in a day more apples than I'll eat in the rest of my life. But they're not apples. They're mirages, with the physicality of holographic images. They don't smell of apples – at the end of the day my hands smell of rubber. They don't taste of apples. When people buy them in supermarkets – see them piled high, pyramids and mountains of "Golden Delicious", so inviting, such abundance – I think: they're not

287

buying apples so much as the *idea* of apples; sanitised, blemish-free memories. But they are to real apples what the rebuilt quarter of Albi is to what was there before – an idealised, predictable, safe replica. They are the image of apples, but with too little "appleness".

"I remember, last autumn, climbing over a broken wall and taking an apple off an old tree. The apple was scabbed and misshapen, even had a caterpillar that I had to shake out: but when I bit into it, the taste, the time – climbing the wall, the changing formation of the clouds, the way the birds darted – fixed themselves absolutely, and because it was so specific, so exact, that apple bite connected me to, enabled me to remember, other specific, quite different apple bites. The taste of these apples, in contrast, is blurred – they're blurred in taste, so memories are blurred.

"In the supermarket, people remember apples, buy memories of apples. They're dissatisfied, but they persist because they can still remember – although they wonder why the memories are blurring. But what happens when we've forgotten apples, when a generation grows up which never knew apples? We'll continue to grow them and eat them and call them apples. But something – appleness – will have gone; our lives will be irremediably diminished, and people will experience a nagging sense of frustration and dissatisfaction, and not know, amid all this apparent perfection and abundance, why.

"Because they're produced by a process concerned with number of units, it's as if, somehow appleness is diluted, spread too thin through the whole number. The process is the problem because as so often – always? – the process and the product are inseparable. The farmer here isn't a specialist, he's a monoculturist. The specialist focuses all his knowledge and all the knowledge of the world into a particular activity; his specialism is a lens which both focuses the world and through which he sees the world; his activity and what he produces are everything, and one. The monoculturist applies certain general principles to the production of a particular item. The nature of the product is subsidiary to the productivity of the process. And here I'm part of that process; I learn nothing, contribute nothing, nothing happens. Time passes through me, and I sell that time for money. My justification is that I can live for a week at La Balme on what I earn in a day here. And I wonder if that is sufficient justification."

For three weeks I pick apples, read, walk. On the surface my life goes on uneventfully. But deep down things change and eventually erupt.

*   *   *

Often I walk to Cavals. It's a pretty village, and in the soft evening I imagine walking hand in hand with a girl. But the girl keeps changing. One space occupied alternately by two women, different, with each of whom life would be entirely different, but no obvious reason to choose one or the other; and not wanting to choose, as one transforms into the other. I've never before had a relationship with two women at the same time. Always a pattern of relationship, solitude, relationship, solitude, a cartoon sea serpent. The decision (yes) to be with Jane deliberately breaking that pattern, which was becoming a habit. An affair, when it came, would somehow, I'd imagined, be contained within the relationship, not create a tension, a need to choose, between the two. I begin a letter to one and it becomes a letter to the other, so I tear it up and turn with relief to *The Pursuit of the Millennium* and imagine all that happening now.

And then, on the Monday of the second week, the eruption takes place. At first a letter to Gabrielle, a simple letter but one that starts subterranean tectonic shifts; the earthquake, the landsplit, follows. At lunchtime I write to Gabrielle:

289

"After a morning picking apples (more apples, more and more and more apples!) I'm sitting outside the little house, eating bread and cheese, with a glass of red wine. The sun is warm, gentle, the times autumny. I saw you this morning driving to work, thought of the days getting shorter, your suntan fading. I think of you at La Balme, and realise that will never fade.

"Last night I went for a walk in Cavals. Birds were gathering to fly south, city people making their last visits, securing shutters, packing their cars. There was a young woman putting things into a car just like yours, personal things – photographs, a vase of grasses, a bamboo birdcage with a single red rose in it. She smiled at me as you might smile and I smiled back. And then you were with me.

"We walked, your hand nestling in mine, up the narrow darkening street and stood on the parapet of the ruined castle at the edge of the overhanging rock looking out at the patchwork valley, the white cliffs, standing at the edge of space. Birds dart, eating insects; the high black falcon hovers motionless, pivot around which the world turns. An exotic orange bird squawks past, a feather falls like a leaf in concave sweeps and slow spirals, into your hand. You wave it mysteriously and roll out the orange carpet with its strangely swirling pattern across the void and we step on, walk out into space, several steps before we stop and turn. We could easily unhitch it, fly wherever we wish. Instead we walk slowly back and step lightly onto the hard rock. The sun sets. I embrace you, you fade and as the last ray is snuffed you are gone and I am alone.

"I listen to the sounds of the stream next to where I write. Willow leaves trail in it, lady's slender fingers from a drifting boat. Now the stream is loud enough, so I no longer hear the rattle and buzz of the cold store; it always is of course but sometimes it's easier to let the buzz fill my head. Same in the city – the stream's murmur is always there if you listen. The

290

white clouds that you look up at are the same ones I see. There is much that we share. I kiss your fingertips".

It pleases me, this letter. The feelings are real. I feel full. And then, as I work alone through the afternoon, I empty. And into the emptiness comes anger. Because I've written a letter to Gabrielle that I should have written to Jane. But Jane vacated my life, left a space, and now Gabrielle occupies that space. I feel betrayed by Jane, by what she hasn't done – for, by her absence, her extended absence, she has allowed accident into what was deliberate. I write:

"You stayed away too long, Jane. I waited for you, expected you, but you never came back. And now it doesn't matter. I worked to keep things going, to make things better, saying – this will surprise Jane, Jane will like that. Even when the roof was finished, even then you didn't come. By staying away you've walked away from what we've done together.

"Things weren't right between us, I know, we needed a break – but there came a time when truths could be told and fears shared and honesties laid bare – now it seems that time is past, and those things lie between us unspoken and unresolved, and will until they slowly decay. When you see me again, you will see a stranger, a mystified stranger who doesn't know why".

Tears splash onto the pages as I write, chest heaving, not daring to read it, rushing to the village and dropping both letters into the yellow box at the same time – letting go, grabbing, hearing them hit the bottom, wondering which is on top. Then through a blurred world to the parapet and one step from endless space, terrified at what I've done, at having smashed the glass bubble in which Jane and I, lovers, lay; shaking in the cold rushing air, terrified.

291

Chapter 3: Vendange

Mostly I feel numb, but each day I pick my quota of apples. On Saturday afternoon I start for La Balme for the weekend, to pick my grapes, but go to Pieter and Hendrika's instead.

On the way I pass the mobile distillery, polished and steaming and wheezing, where the *paysans* bring their grape pomace to be made into eau de vie, a strict quota for each so they can't sell it and disturb the commercial spirits trade.

Pieter and Hendrika welcome me, feed me, and I drink too much. They say I should stay but I insist I get back for the grapes. I feel a sudden sense of freedom as I drive up the track from their illuminated warm safe haven into the dark, space all around me, unattached. I drive too fast along the narrow lanes, like a kid, chasing the headlamp beams, throwing the car around as I'd never dared do with Jane beside me, for now there's no one beside me, I don't care, I'll take my chances. And then I run out of road. The headlights, from reflecting off trees and walls and the road, are swallowed up by darkness and I'm plunged into darkness and ahead of me there's nothing. I swear, hit the brakes, skid, curse myself, wait as the car slides. Now you've done it, a voice says to me, my voice but someone else's really, in smug satisfaction; now you've done it. I wait. The car stops. With its nose over a precipice. I stare into the abyss for minutes, at first obscurely disappointed and then, as a bubble of well-being grows inside me, I laugh, reverse, drive on, gravel spurting, just as fast but now driving with precise control.

The next morning I find Jane's telegram: "Alarmed by your letter. Please please telephone Tuesday evening. Distraught. Jane". I crumple it and throw it into the cold fireplace. And a letter from her. That she'd written the same evening I'd written mine, maybe at the same time. The coincidence is bitter, reading this after a week's numbness.

Out with friends as usual, then sitting alone with a solitary joint watching a silent flickering television screen. Feeling nothing, the usual carapace. "And then it began, the waves of feeling, of misery, like retching, your name inside me, inside that shell, trying to get out, me holding it in; then it burst out, like a flint from a festering wound, bursting out, a name, your name that I say over and over again sobbing, oh Kris, oh Kris…. The waves subside, the pain easing to a throbbing ache – then up again, searing, no waves this time but a fire of misery annihilating and yet illuminating me. Afterwards I almost laugh – after this the only way is up. I've never known such pain – but your name was on my lips, is on my lips, at last, again, now." She wants to know how I feel about her coming over, probably will anyway, she wants to see me, me to see her.

I look at the letter, try to imagine her writing it, can't. I wonder what it means, that we were writing our letters at the same time – the measure of how we share the same space…? The moment of sundering…? Two planets once twinned in mutual orbit passing once more close together, affecting each other tidally whilst travelling in opposite directions…?

But now she is a person to me again, not just a circumstance. I feel her hand upon me; I don't know whether it feels good or bad. I feel a forgotten heaviness inside that both reassures me with its substance and weighs me down.

*　　　　　*　　　　　*

It is grey and wet as I drive the car over the stubble to the vines. I pick in silence and alone, cutting the bunches with the small curved *serpette*.

Last year we did all the grapes together, the neighbours' and ours, a dozen of us, uncles and aunts and cousins swelling the numbers on this, one of the gathering days.

293

I remember the youngsters, gamesome, squashing grapes into each other's faces, high spirited and flirtatious. I remember cutting my finger and Madame holding my hand tight and pressing grape juice into the wound with a surprising fervency. I remember standing on the swaying trailer among overflowing baskets of grapes, adjusting my weight to keep my balance without holding on as the oxen towed us slowly back (a creaking ox-cart of old wooden grape-filled *comportes* and youthful pickers, the cousins so briefly blooming), Gaston at their heads, half turned all the way so he can gaze contentedly, proprietorially, a mild Bacchus, at his harvest – and the sun suddenly breaking through the mist and spreading a soft light overall, a warm glow, a glowing mystery among leaf-thin trees, and a bloom on the purple grapes. I remember the meal around the long table, the many dishes, the wine, the eau de vie, the bawdy conversation – bright, flushed faces, brought to life, aroused even, by the grape picking, the soft squeeziness of grapes, the splitting skins, the dripping juice.

This year, on this grey foggy Sunday, I work alone. And when I've brought the grapes back to the house, instead of pressing them with Gaston's mangle I take them straight to the *cave* and put them into the big tub, set barrel-high on bricks, a tie of bracken inside over the corked bunghole, rustlings of nesting creatures, and the scents of dry hay, faded flowers and damp earth; take off my boots and socks, roll up my trousers, and climb in. Yes, I'm about to tread the grapes.

I'd thought that treading was to squeeze the juice out; in fact it's to break the skins and release the juice so the yeast, naturally occurring on the grapes, can begin the fermentation (Dionysus trampled and torn apart). At first the grapes are hard under my soft feet, like marbles, and small twigs prick my soft skin; but as I tread and squash and as the grapes break, I sink deeper at each step and soon I'm tread, tread, treading in fruit-filled jelly. At first cold the grapes, then warm the juice, pressing, squeezing, bare-footed, very sexy.

At last I climb out and dry my feet and legs with handfuls of scented hay. I dip a cupped hand and drink. I imagine blood-stained legs and feet, Jesus' as he carried the Cross, the spear thrust mixture of blood and water, Madame catching the pig's belching blood. But juice is dying blood; wine is living, fertilised, inspirited by fermentation. Doors open back generation through generation to the beginning, the first winemaker. I stare in awe at the dark liquid, at what it will become. Then I pull on my socks and boots and go upstairs.

The following morning I drive back to Cavals for my last week of apple picking. On Tuesday evening I phone Jane.

Chapter 4: Talking to Jane

'Kris?'

Her voice anxious and hesitant, speaking his name to the person whose name it is, for the first time for a long time, unsure of the response; and then sensing the echo off the other person, familiar, as of old and, no longer flailing in space, saying again:

'Kris?'

Stronger, more confident, more proprietorial. My heart tightens. That almost-forgotten familiar feeling; as if she is holding a thread attached to a hook in my heart and has tugged it slightly. I want to pull away. I want to be reeled in. For good or ill the attachment, wanted, willed, desired, is still there.

I close my eyes as I speak to her down the telephone, and see her down a long, dark tunnel, her face clear and white and sharply outlined in the blackness. I've no idea what I say – at some point I say 'I love you' and wish I hadn't and she says 'you don't have to say that, you know'. I leave the farmhouse, stumble down the concrete steps. As I near the little cottage a phrase clears in my head: "Some things you need to walk away from; some you have to go through". Lying in bed later, I say, out loud:

'Problem is, knowing which.'

I went to the farmhouse this morning to ask if I might phone from there this evening and they said, 'sure'. It is a big house, new, set in the middle of the orchards like a citadel, a watchtower.

The farm is run by two cousins and they, with their families, share the house, so that when I'm shown into the large living room it is awash with nimble, shy, dark-eyed children. When I first came here I was almost touched by their uncomprehend-

296

ing alarm that their careful scheme was collapsing at the last, vital stage. Having planned everything to the last detail: location, land, EEC and French agricultural subsidies, marketing, varieties, spacing of trees, spraying programme – fourteen times a year, herbicides, pesticides, hormones, to make the flowers stay on, the fruit set, the little apples drop off, the big apples stay on, a preserving coating… – they had pressed the button on the production line; for this is a production line, a temporal rather than spatial sequence of programmed operations. And now, at the culmination, the trees laden with perfect fruit, green on these trees, red on those, each apple representing, in the difference between the cost of putting it there and the price someone will pay for it, the unit profit – there's no one to pick them. The locals are too busy at this time of year, and the unemployed the *Agence* sends are too slow for them to make a profit paying *SMIC* (minimum wage) rates – for the only available French are unemployable city kids, *déclassés*, who care only for music, dope, highs, fixes, trips; and the occasional *marginal* like me. Their solution is to pray, in the long term, for the invention of an apple-picking machine; and in the short term to employ North Africans illegally on piecework, picking fifty per cent more than I do for the same money. Which is fine as long as the Moroccans meekly return home after the harvest and the pruning. But now they're leaking into the cities, forming yet another underclass…. The alarm on the farmers' faces made me feel sympathy, for they are as much trapped in the system as the *Agence* lads.

But now, having seen their house, the satisfied smiles on their faces – they must be getting the right numbers out of their new computer – the fat sofas and cherrywood sideboards, the shining hardwood floor, the picture window, the balcony with its Italian ironwork and Spanish pots, the carefully chosen, commanding view, my sympathy is less.

I imagine when they stand on the balcony and look across their orchards, they feel not attachment but possession, not stewardship but ownership. And there's fear behind the success. But they put money into my pocket. And when I ask how much I owe for the call they raise mutual eyebrows, smile, and say, with magnificent benevolence, 'that's okay', and grow misty eyed at their charity.

*   *   *

The next day I write two letters.

To Jane:

"Hearing your voice. Since you went, nothing of you has meant anything; no letter, no memory has penetrated; just a long fading. Then suddenly – Jane. Such a shock. Jane. Your name suddenly means something, is someone, is you, you are Jane. Memories flood back… and then fade slowly away and there you are, just you, name stripped away, very white in the blackness of space, just you, looking at me. A connection, good or bad, real.

"You will come, I know that now. And our hearts will once more interlock, for good or ill, and with who knows what outcome. Last night I almost saw your body".

To Gabrielle:

"The full moon. One month. I wish I could hear your voice, see your face, touch you. Driving back here early – sun warm, air clear, sky a soft autumn blue. Leaves turning golden, fields growing green, rich brown of ploughed fields, firm destiny of furrows, tractors everywhere, autumn energy. Two more days of apple picking.

"Jane is coming. I don't know what will happen.

"You asked what "keep in touch" means and said what a beautiful phrase it is. I want to keep in touch".

Suddenly I know that I will not allow a renewed Jane-and-Kris to blot her out; I add:

"p.s. I will come and see you".

298

*   *   *

At the end of apple picking, with a pocket full of paper money, I drive to the hypermarket and fill the car with all manner of goods, like a trapper on his autumn visit to the trading post.

Back at the house, I light a fire in the house, light the stove in the tower. I pin up, in the tower, Jane's painting of a long-haired figure – male? female? – flying a kite. I eat an enormous meal, play *Desire*, get very drunk, go to sleep in the dark in the tower.

The next day the world has disappeared. I hear noises, people moving around, but I can see nothing. A dense fog all around, the world blotted out, this place lost in the clouds.

I sit at my desk, surrounded by evidence of Richard, Gabrielle, Jane; alone. There is a pile of paper at my right hand, an empty space at my left. I take a sheet of paper and write "1999" at the top, then commence to write.

PART VIII:

JANE RETURNS

Chapter 1: "Europe 2000: a Tale of the Future"

"His foot slipped again and he almost fell. He swore. Everything around him was dark and indistinct, but the sky was still full of light; the dusk hour, *entre chien et loup*, the time of transformation. He did not want to reach the lip, leave the valley, climb out onto the plateau, had to, was there.

"Behind him lights moved urgently back and forth in the community below; and along the valley, advancing, ordered and implacable, more lights. He thought of Miller, his clear blue eyes troubled, puzzled that it had come to this; of McGregor's fierce preparations, his murderous mantraps; of Leah, fiery and energetic, sharpening yet another blade; and of Rachel, calm, stroking her belly reflectively, the urgent cells dividing and multiplying within her, the form taking shape, another future, possibly. He had wanted to stay, share their fate, have a hand in it.

" 'This isn't your place to fight,' Miller had said. 'You've more journeys yet before you face your moment. You have a purpose – go and seek it. Take what you have learned here. Use it well.' He had felt exhilaration when Miller had said that. Now he felt only desolation. All around him the black featureless plateau and the blank grey sky, two daubs of paint laid on by a pitiless hand. But now he must move, before the two merged, became a directionless one. He heard cries from the valley, but didn't turn round. The wind blew cold. He shivered. He held up the crystal pendulum in the shelter of his body, stilled himself, observed its tremblings and, with a deep breath, set off in its appointed direction, striding out."

. I put down the pen. I read the last page, then pick up the pen and write:

"THE END".

I put the sheet on the pile at my left hand and cap the pen with a snap. Hands clasped behind my head, I lean back in my chair. Above me a triangle of blue is slowly covered with white and slowly revealed again. A thin branch, sunlit on one side, shadowed on the other, trembles. The leaves are yellow, beginning to curl. I feel the wall of the tower, the shell of the dome around me. For a week it has protected me as I softened to formlessness to write what I have just finished. Now I must leave it, to find out what has happened to me in this week.

I open the door, shiver, close it. I look around, at the glowing stove, the sturdy stone walls, the painted panels, the rumpled bedding, the space on the desk where the blank sheets were and the place where the pile of written pages now is. I sigh. I was happy here. I put the pages into an old Research Department file marked "EUROPE 2000" and place it in the middle of my work table. Then I go out.

The sun is bright and at first I have to screw up my eyes; then slowly I release them and open them fully as I attune to the vastly greater illumination. I will have to get used, too, to a low sun that strikes at the eyes rather than the head, that is light without heat; now it has a soft, comfortable warmth and I bathe my lidded eyes in it pleasantly.

The air is cool and clear, with a sharpening clarity. I look upon an autumn scene, of harrowed fields and trees blazing yellow and the first dark ribs and thin high cloud, and feel a movement of cool air and the shivering premonition of winter winds. A moment's emptiness – and then the sounds and smells of the neighbours' farm tumble in; a vigorous scrubbing, the clang of a metal pail, the mixed babel of animal noises, boots squelching heavily through mud, the dry scent of hay, the smells of damp animals, but mostly the smell of shit – how much shit there is on a farm!

I look at our house, see what is: a solid place, lacking amenities, perfectly habitable, neutral. With a garden, meadow, trees, vines. In the middle of nowhere. Somewhere. Here. Three images, long merged, slowly separate, like the three colours in printing. Self-sufficiency. Domesticity. Isolation. Which do I want? Any of them? None?

Slowly I walk the whole property. It looks both less and more real than it has ever looked before. Less real because I am no longer adding what might be; more real because I am seeing what is. No waves, just quanta. Almost something more....

I enter the house, and am stunned at its ordinariness; and moved by it. All my dreams have been consumed within the crucible of the tower. Inside, an empty head. Out there, just – what is. Nothing moves. Why should it? When it has somewhere to go, then it will move. I walk around the house, to make things move, to make a movie out of the single images, and then I stop. I've no need to make movies. When I have somewhere to go, then I'll move.

An unopened letter. Familiar handwriting. Happy anticipation, or dread? I open it. I begin to read, slowly, as if it's written in a barely-comprehensible foreign language, my eyes screwed up at the sunlight reflecting off bright paper. A shadow falls across it. A figure in the doorway, dark against the light, fuzzy round the edges, a familiar form, and yet different.

'You got my letter, then,' Jane says, and comes in.

Chapter 2: Jane arrives

Coming towards me out of the sun, blocking the light, arms around my neck, coming closer, blurring, lips kissing mine – a remembered kiss – face drawn back, into focus, eyes looking right into mine, she smiles, says:

'Hello.'

'Jane,' I whisper, and draw her to me, unready yet for the intimate distance, kiss her on the side of the face, avoiding her eyes, mumbling as I scramble to make sense of what's happening.

I hear the familiar noises in my ear, feel the familiar width and solidity of her body, the way she, fractionally, concaves her hips; but now thrusts them to me: and her body is slimmer, her hair now short and coiffured, she wears a new city perfume, musky, her clothes are unfamiliar. She pulls back, stands in the light so that I can see her sleeker body that wears confidently the expensive casual clothes, her highlit hair an artful conflation of feminist defiant and executive efficient. She likes what I see. She smiles. I stutter:

'You, I – how did you get here?'

'With the postman,' she says briskly. 'There's a letter for you.' Holds it between thumb and forefinger. From Gabrielle. I take it from her as if it's an unexploded bomb and put it on the table. She looks from it to me. I try again:

'You're – I don't know what to say.'

'Say you're glad to see me.' Matter of fact, with shades of seduction and pleading. Still I do nothing. She takes hold of me, puts her head on my shoulder, presses herself to me, whispers:

'Oh, I've missed you.' Her hands are moving over my body and I have to stop her because I'm not ready for this, because there's a bubble in my head and inside the bubble there's something very important, and the bubble mustn't burst.

306

'Come on, I'll show you what I've been doing,' I say as I pull away. For a moment she stands, as if she doesn't know what to do. I suddenly realise that she's rehearsed it all, and now I've departed from what she had imagined. She sags slightly, almost shrugs, then quickly braces up:

'Sure, why not?' I take her arm and lead her outside.

'I did the roof with Richard.' Relieved that my voice is now just one among many sounds and I can back away, gesticulate, lecture. 'He's a good bloke. You should meet him.'

'I saw it from the road. It looks good. I like the red. All I remember is grey.'

'Do you like the dormers? They were tricky – especially cutting those Bedarieux tiles They're really hard. Old Condamine in the village showed me how – you score across with the trowel, then – bang – just like a karate blow. But it's worth it. Takes a weight off the house, lets it flex and breathe, lightens it.'

'The roof looks great.'

'I was bothered about being untrue to the area. But this area needs lightening up. That's why we're here. And of course it gives us two extra rooms. I'll need to make some stairs, but that's no problem. Wondered about a spiral – interesting technically.'

'And it keeps the rain out?'

'Tight as Noah's Ark. "Pitched within and without". Good for another hundred and fifty years. Five generations.' She nods, her face expressionless, but I feel her tighten. She turns abruptly and points to the tower:

'You didn't tell me about that.'

'I didn't know what it was until I'd done it. Difficult to explain in a letter. It does wonders for the geomantics. Puts fizz into the place – this place needs fizz.' She smiles a thin smile and mimes an explosion, then pushes the door open and steps warily in.

There is a single sunbeam shining in, onto the folder marked "EUROPE 2000" on the rough wooden desk. She looks at it, then turns deliberately away.

'Nice paintings.'

'Mostly Richard's.'

'Nice stove.'

'It was a real bargain.'

'Nice flowers.' I say nothing.

'What's that?' pointing at the folder.

'A story. About the future.'

'Whose future?'

'That depends.'

'I thought you had that sort of thing on hold until we were sorted out.' Her eyes have hardened. All I can do is shrug.

'Is it any good, the story?'

'I think so.' I want to say: 'it's bloody marvellous,' but I don't.

'Am I in it?'

'No. It's a story.'

'What will you do with it?'

'I don't know.' An inbreath of impatience, then:

'Well,' as she sweeps out, 'you've certainly been busy,' beginning to breathe more easily only when the door is shut. Five paces away she stops, looks around, amazement on her face.

'Shall we walk around?' I ask, eager to keep moving. 'There's not much left in the garden, but it's been a good year, in spite of the drought. The meadow's in fine fettle – I got a good cut of hay and the hens are almost ready to come into lay. The *vendange* was good. I – '

' – can't believe I once lived here,' she says, in a perplexed, faraway voice. 'I've never felt so helpless in my life, so unhuman. I'd look around and say – this is nice – then remember that I was chained to it, like an animal chained to a wheel, going round and round, without even the mercy of a blind-fold. How could you? How *could* you!' There are tears in her eyes, anger in her voice. I flinch.

'It doesn't have to be like that. We can work something….'
She's already heading indoors, her words trailing behind her:
'I need coffee. I need walls around me.'

*   *   *

'I'm sure I can put a tank in the roof and hand-pump enough water each day to have a bathroom. I can link it to a solar panel – hot and cold running water in every room if you like.'

'There will only ever be cold here for me.' I plough on:

'And I've been refining a design for a composting toilet – you see, by using bracken, and exploiting the *cave*, I could –'

'You still don't understand, do you?' She's thumped the table and is leaning over on her fists, eyes blazing. 'I haven't come here to talk about running water and composting toi-lets! I've come to save our marriage! If that's possible. This, all this, it's ridiculous, Kris. We're in the second half of the twentieth century! I want to live like other people,' her voice a wail, 'who take flushing toilets and running water for granted. I want to turn on a tap and pull out a plug; all I'm bothered about is the water in the bowl. I don't *care* where it's come from, or where it goes to. I'll pay someone *else* to deal with that, and I'll earn the money to pay them.' She's walked across the room, stands facing the blank wall, then turns to look at me. I stand, astonished at her outburst.

'But Jane, I don't understand. We've talked about this – don't you remember?' I begin patiently. 'The whole techno-logical thing is unsustainable. To use your example – the sew-erage systems are collapsing under the city streets at this moment, there are water shortages everywhere; technology, with its ever greater demands on diminishing resources, can

309

no longer guarantee the future. We have to pioneer a new way. Even more important is that we take control of our lives; stop treating everything as black boxes, on which we depend but which are opaque to our understanding. The only way we can regain control is by simplifying our lives, by starting from basics.'

'Is the peasant in control of his life?' she asks angrily. 'The nomad? Are *you* in control of your life if you've no money? If nobody wants what you have, you have no value, without value, no power, without power, no control. Scarcity determines value, value determines price. It's all down to *money*.'

'I don't want to control my life, Kris. I want to find my place, take my place in life, *live* my life, and, where possible, enjoy it.' The anger softens, her voice quietens. She looks at me as she continues in a quiet, reasonable, modulated voice:

'I didn't come back here to live, even to see it – except maybe to confirm how necessary for my sanity it was that I left. I came back to see *you*. I want to live with you again. I want us to be lovers again, to share our lives. I love you. Please, please, stop talking. And....' Her arms drop to her sides and she looks down and tears come into her eyes.

I want to tell her about the bubble in my head that a summer of things happening and a week of solitude and concentrated work and being in the tower have developed; of how I want to wait, just wait, to allow to appear in it the revelation that I was on the edge of when I left the tower. I say nothing. I see her standing there, the one who has travelled six hundred miles to see me, who has left a safe world and returned to a perilous one, a world in which her sanity had been threatened, to save us; who has reached out and stretched, but cannot at last reach me for I am untouchable; who stands now, head down, arms at her side, defeated because I will not take one step, that single step, towards her.

I look at her; and then, whether it's from gratitude that she has travelled so far, pity for her helplessness when she is so near, faith that she knows what's best for us, for me, desire for the remembered pleasures of her body and the happiness I've known with her, or terror at what might happen if I break my pledge to her, never know her again – I take the step.

The membrane around the bubble splits, the world rushes in, I'm holding her and she me and our hands are all over each other and we're tugging off each other's clothes and the bubble is filled with passion and desire and, as her hand closes around it, I have the biggest hard-on since – the last good time with Jane; and body to sweaty body we're lying on the heap of clothes on the kitchen floor in front of the glowing stove screwing madly, screwing until for both of us the dam bursts. We laugh and gasp and cry and are briefly still. Then we do it again.

We lie entwined, our bodies glued together from shoulder to toe, the familiar reciprocal of hump and hollow, our faces, tear-stained and sweaty, an inch apart, our eyes at first roaming across each other's bodies and faces in astonished recognition and at last coming to rest and sinking deep, deep into each other's eyes.

Chapter 3: A fight with Jane

We dress in silence, make lunch in silence, though contriving, as we prepare it, to squeeze past each other, for our hands to meet as we reach for the same item, to touch; and then each looks at the other, unsure until reassured, and we can smile, even laugh. After lunch I look at her, and she says:

'Why not?' But as I head for the stairs she stops me and fetches down a mattress from the spare room, a feather one, and the spare duvet, and makes up a bed in the front room. I close the shutters and light the fire, and we sit watching the licking flames, the shavings curling and the logs beginning to catch. Then we undress slowly and make love slowly.

At first it is all new. The short hair, springy and blonded, that reveals her long neck, her warm ear.

'Your hair's so short!' I laugh. 'I'm not sure I like it.'

'It's for me,' she says quietly. 'The one who's in me. And yours is wonderfully long,' running her hands through it. 'Wear it in a pony tail when we're out together.'

'I may have it cut.'

Her body, newly slim and sleek and active:

'Aerobics,' she says. 'And stress.' A body over which my hands – too hard, I wish them softer, although they are still soft under the calloused skin – rove, exploring a once familiar form, now memorising a new shape.

The new perfume, like a smell on other women, in towns, that she wears sensually, erotically, in places I've never known her perfume. I'm with another woman, I think, as the flickering light casts strange shadows, changes her – but then suddenly, stabbingly, reveals Jane. And I remember what I'd forgotten, remember from long ago, from too long ago: that she is endless, her skin extending forever ahead of my touch, a landscape that curves and folds, a planet, a Venus of mountains and plains, of jungles alive with agile blue monkeys and

312

flashing birds of paradise, of fathomless lakes and silent caves, of limitless animal-rich savannahs and icy peaks, of porpoise-leaping seas and crab-still pools, of windswept tundra and fern-quiet springs…. I'd forgotten what it's like to lie on her and feel her strength (such strength), to look into her eyes and see vulnerability, certainty, curiosity – so much life! – flickering across them. I'd forgotten what it's like to be inside her as we hold each other, breast to breast, arms wrapped far around each other, lips suckered, eyes locked, not knowing where I end and she begins, whose arms clasp whom, one. To hear again in me that little voice that cries 'I'm me', to feel again that little figure who pulls away – until a single movement of her hips, a simple response of mine silences him, dissolves all tension and separation and signals our surrender to that which encompasses us.

*   *   *

Covered by the duvet, eating chocolate and sipping whisky, staring into the fire as *Still Crazy After All These Years* plays, she lies back against me, her head on my chest, my hands cupping her heavy breasts.

'I flew,' she says.

'Me too.'

'I flew to Toulouse.'

'Bang goes the goat.'

'And got a coach from there. Do you want to know why?'

'Er – yes.' She adjusts her position so that my prick is no longer between her cheeks, is flat against her back. She slides my hands down onto her ribcage, stops them when they head for her belly:

'Because I didn't want to retrace one inch of the journey I took when I left here in June. I didn't want to recall any of the guilt and uselessness I'd felt, the sense of being a failure, the feeling of rejection.'

313

'It wasn't rejection,' I soothe, kissing her hair. 'It was just the most sensible thing to do.' She shifts again so that she's sitting next to me:

'It certainly felt like rejection. And you made damned sure I felt like a failure. I was shattered. It took me weeks to recover, to value myself again. And you were instrumental in that loss of self-esteem. And though I blame you for that, I'm glad it happened, because without it I'd never have done what I've done this summer, wouldn't have had the crisis, and without that I wouldn't have found out what I can do, begun to find myself.

'People helped, right through the summer. People are great – d'you know that, Kris? People are great.' She's shuffled round so she's facing me, duvet tucked around her, eyes on fire. I sigh:

'Okay, people are great. I happen to like my own company.'

'Your own company?! You're a self-obsessed, misanthropic wanker!' Her voice now is loud, she's beginning to hit her stride, pulling on her pants, saying:

'I don't know why I give a damn about you,' as she hooks up her brassiere.

'Let's agree to differ, shall we?' I say, reaching for my underpants, feeling more naked with each unfamiliar garment she puts on.

'"Agree to differ"? And I suppose we should "agree to differ" about that letter. Who's it from?' as she buttons her blouse.

'From Gabrielle,' I say as I grab my trousers.

'I know it's from Gabrielle,' she spits the name. 'The French very conveniently write their names on the backs of envelopes. And she's…?'

'The girl I mentioned in my letter, yes.'

'You wrote "has been", "there has been a girl", past tense,' stepping into her skirt.

314

'Yes, that's what I wrote,' realising at last what's going on, pulling on my clothes fast, getting angry:

'I didn't write "there's been someone but it was just a fling and now it's all over and I've had my fling and got it out of my system and I'll be a good boy from now on". No, I didn't write that. I wrote "There's been a girl". So – what do you want to know?' Her face registers alarm, and anger, but her voice is calm:

'I have to know, Kris – is it serious?'

'What?' I say, suddenly furious, 'what do you mean "is it serious?" Do you mean – was it serious while she was here? None of your damned business. Is it a serious friendship now? Yes. Has she come between you and me, is she a serious rival? You selfish bugger – *everything* I do is fucking serious!' I raise my voice, say "bugger", put in the "fucking", because they are ways of hitting her without touching her. She flinches, but she doesn't crumble. And from some place she draws a strength I'm not familiar with. When she speaks, her eyes are dry, her voice even:

'I simply want to know where I stand.'

'You stand exactly where you want to!' My loud words bounce off rafters and walls, shatter and fall slowly, in pieces, to the ground. I try again:

'And you, what about you and your "helpful friends" – how many of them "helped you make it through the night?"'

'You really are vile. It wasn't like that, and you know it. They're friends, good friends. And you're a bastard.'

'So you had a celibate summer, you and your vibrator?'

'Stop talking like that. Why? Why are you talking like that? As a matter of fact there was someone, right at the beginning, just one – we didn't plan it, it just happened, it was incidental, it's long over, it – '

' – doesn't count? Creative sexual accounting? Well, do I know the lucky prizewinner? I'd like to know, so I can compare notes with the man who fucked my wife.' I don't

315

remember ever, in my life, calling her "my wife".

'Kris, you're pathetic. Larry. It was Larry. I thought – I don't know, I thought you'd know.'

'Why? – because everybody else does? Strap on the horns, Kris, you're about to enter a crowded room. Larry. So, the playboy of the western world got to you, too. I hope he handed out certificates. You could have reunions. "Old Larrovians. Summer of '76". In the Albert bloody Hall!'

Her first blow is a stinging slap across the face that shocks rather than hurts, and my surprised, angry response is to cuff her round the head. Her second is a beauty; a right hand punch that travels up from her toes, gathering frustration, fury and venom on the way, and is delivered to the side of my jaw, through a large silver ring, exploding like a shell. I stagger back, sit down, stare up at her amazed. She's wringing her hand, in pain, but she's looking fearlessly down at me, legs apart, jaw firm. All my anger has evaporated. I don't know whether to cry or laugh.

'Jesus,' I say, flexing my numb jaw, 'where did that come from?'

'I've done it a thousand times in my imagination.'

'I wish it had stayed there.'

'No way – upfront Jane from now on.' She winces and shakes her hand.

'You'd better get that ring off before your finger swells. Where did you get it, anyway?' She tugs at the ring but it won't come off. She goes into the kitchen to rub soap under it. I follow. She's got the ring off and sunk her hand in cold water. I splash water on my face, look at myself in the mirror. There's the livid imprint of a lion on my jaw.

'I'm branded.'

'Larry. Larry gave it to me.'

'Great. Branded with the sign of my wife's lover.' I roll the words round, testing them on my ear, wonder what the small blank patch inside me is.

'Don't. Please. It's not easy for me, especially with that letter, the postman giving it to me. I suppose you'll creep off somewhere and read it.'

'It's mine, not ours. Private.'

'Secret. How can we have a life together if we have secrets?'

'Throw that damned ring away.'

'No. Not before I know.'

'Okay, you keep your sign. I'll keep my secret. Maybe we haven't had enough secrets, maybe we've tried to live too openly, too much in each other's pockets. I don't know. God, I hate this.'

'I do love you,' she says.

'And if I knew what it meant, I'd probably say I love you. But maybe it's not enough – eh?'

Chapter 4: They walk

A quiet, weary cup of tea later, I say:

'Can we go for a walk? I need to get out.' She seems about to say no, then shrugs and says 'okay.'

She picks up her cobwebbed wellingtons reluctantly, shakes them out warily, pulls them on wearily. She lifts her old duffel coat off the peg and puts it on and stands, arms hanging, weighed down.

It has turned cold and grey, a raw wintry day, the sky solid grey with a dribble of red where the sun has set. The fields are drab and wet. A cutting wind blows from the east, rattling dead leaves on the trees. A crow is swept past, nailed to the wind. I want this wind to blow away what we say to each other; it seems our only chance.

'I made it, somehow, onto the train at Toulouse. I was huddled in a corner, trying not to shake in case I fell to pieces. Then Larry was there. And suddenly I was in a movie, a movie he and I were making. Do you understand?'

I understand very well. It's Larry's special quality. He did it last Christmas. The snow came early, and everywhere was white and still, everything muffled. We were isolated and marooned, hardly talking to each other, living by habit, down to our last bag of flour. I was chopping evergreens, to decorate the house. The only movement was my mechanical chopping, the only sound my axe. Then I chopped my finger – I knew it was my finger because it sounded different; but I didn't feel anything in my frozen flesh, watched fascinated as the blood bubbled from this alien thing, bright red, fell, as red as holly berries, onto foliage and snow, melting the snow, spreading, lots of blood. A light touch on my shoulder. A quiet voice:

'England for Christmas?'

He drove forty-eight hours straight, with Jane in a sleeping bag in the back of the van slowly thawing, me in the passenger seat staring along the headlight beams, radio on – "Bohemian Rhapsody", "No Regrets" and "Born to Run" were played a lot, I remember – watching ghostly smoke ooze across from burning fields, seeing white-fleshed plane trees like severed limbs felled by the side of road widenings, gazing over Paris from the *périphérique* at dawn, the city smog-dead, the sun blood red, Monet gone apocalyptic.

And in my head the script of the road movie I was part of – driving through a collapsing world, immune.

And now for her another journey north with Larry, but a different movie. From desert to oasis, from isolation to society, with Larry so full of life, across a fertile land of meadows and crops, forests and gardens, wide shining rivers and prosperous towns, to Paris. A few summer days there, then on to London.

'It wasn't important, the sex. It just happened, it was incidental – except it was central too, because I was a woman again. What was important was being with him, talking, getting around. I learned how to enjoy myself. I began to get my self-confidence back. I've worked really hard this summer, I've got a good job, a great flat, I feel established again.' Even under the dead weight of the coat she looks alive, well-knit.

'There's something about Larry – I couldn't live with him, it wouldn't last five minutes, he's too – completed, that's the word. He knows what he's doing, is entirely self-possessed, won't allow anyone to deviate him from that. He'd be impossible to live with; but he's great, at times in your life, to be with – he's so certain, so lacking in doubt, like a rock, a natural force. He can give you what you need when you need it. You and I are different, we're not fanatics like him, we're still developing. And that gives us a chance – not balancing each other up but helping each other develop – doesn't it?'

As she's telling me this, it is as if she's rummaging around in my guts, tugging on bits of me I never knew existed, finding new places to inflict pain. It is with difficulty that I begin to tell her of my summer; but I soon warm to the task, and am gratified by the stricken look on her face, her silence.

I'm aware of how different our stories are. Hers a story of focussing, mine of diffusing. Until the week in the tower, the bubble in which something of great importance was about to precipitate. Of Gabrielle, she says, 'I thought there would be someone. But I expected it to be someone we knew. Sylvie maybe. But it probably simplifies things, an outsider.' As we walk and listen to each other's story, we make our calculations. It is important, crucial, to feel we are breaking even. We go back to the house and stoke up the fire.

*   *   *

'That evening I wrote to you,' she says, 'I felt a great liberation – the net you'd cast around me dissolved, and I was free to love you.'

'Something snapped;' I say, 'the thread connecting me to the sense of obligation I took upon myself when I first said 'I love you'. 'I love you' became relative, therefore meaningless. But I still want to know you.'

We sleep side by side in separate sleeping bags in the fire's glow. In the night we unzip, make love, zip up. We awake the next morning side by side, having had the same dream, and lie together drinking tea.

'I'd like to go to St Affrique,' I say.

320

Chapter 5: To St Affrique

'You see, by 1999, the end of the millenium – and of the Piscean Age – it will all be collapsing. The US will have turned its face to the Pacific, its back on Europe. The Russians, or the terrorists, will have taken out the Middle East. North Sea oil will be running out, and the gimcrack French nuclear reactors falling apart. Western Europe, deprived of colonies and energy, will be suffering increasing entropy, approaching heat death. The expansion, the long outbreath, will be over – and there'll be no air to breathe in. Listen to this:

"As he walked along the guarded streets, past the fortressed shops, Terry remembered something that had happened that summer, long ago, with the girl, that brief period of happiness before he let her go and he got Anita pregnant and began the long slide. They'd lived in one room, by the park. It was the great hot summer, and the sun shone every day. Often they would spend the whole day in bed; then at night, when the park became a pool of oxygen, a lake of coolness, they would gaze at it, often play in it like young animals.

"One day they watched a troupe of players arrive. They unloaded an enormous rainbow bladder which they unfolded carefully on the grass. They attached a pump, switched on a motor, and gradually it inflated. It was a tent, a play palace, a pleasure dome, held up by the air pumping into it. They had workshops, performances, exhibitions, dances. Terry and the girl were soon involved – he made junk sculpture with the local kids, she learned and performed mime. At night they would dance together and, in the buoyant air, with the bubble-like surface flexing above them, the lights, the music, the joints, the feel and smell of grass under their bare feet, it was magical.

"Then one evening the motor stopped. Instantly the air lost its buoyancy, its expansiveness. The molecules closed together, the air pressed on them, the dome wrinkled, people were pushed together, there was anger, blows, the beginning of panic, almost a riot, even though the dome had hardly deflated at all by the time everyone was out. It was the sudden change, from expansion to contraction.

"Later, living with Anita, it became one of his nightmares: the plastic collapsing slowly on him, suffocating him, and him trying to punch it away – but his fist, his whole arm would be enveloped by, swallowed up in the plastic, held, and the plastic would mould over his reaching hand, close over his nose, his mouth…. 'The motor's been switched off', he said suddenly. 'And society's collapsing in on itself.'"

I read on silently, enjoying what I'm reading; then I remember and turn again to Jane:

'There'll be no more of the fixes that keep cities and agribusinesses going. Everywhere'll be cold turkeying.

'Except here, and in a few places like this. The Reserves. Protected by sympathisers among the power elite, it's developed into a working, post-industrial society. You should see some of the things André and his group develop – brilliant low tech stuff. The whole area basically self-sufficient agricultural and craft communities – differing, depending on the people involved: some a revival of local peasant cultures – chestnut-based for example; others taking advantage of all the knowledge we have of such societies, and modern ideas – an austere, Zen-type community here, a hearty, belly-centred Kwakiutl place there, science-based centres using all the knowledge of science but applied to a small-scale, low energy, renewable-resource situation; pastoralists; hunters; New Age centres. Saved from isolation, energised with the stimulus of ideas and the arts by the travellers – entertainers, traders, educators – and by the gatherings on the Great Days. All sharing the same principles of attunement to their precise physical environment, man as part of the ecology, not outside it, a non-exploitive, cooperative relationship with the natural world.

'And having in common the great cathedral. Because Pieter *does* find his Palaeolithic cathedral – he dies doing it, dies fulfilled. And with that connection back to pre-lapsarian man, it becomes a place of initiation and renewal, a place to go to remember, and to foresee.

'But the sympathisers can no longer protect the area and the Black Ones, the excluded, are gathering on the borders, beginning to break in.

'One young man,' I continue, 'Terry's unknown son, the child conceived that summer, a member of one of the dissident groups that exist in the cities, starts from London to reach this place, in a search for one man. He sets out in an armoured vehicle, completely self-contained, intending to make it through the hell that is England and France – starvation, pollution, disease, radiation sickness, marauders, Millenarian flagellants, the Middle Ages but worse – untouched. And he loses it all. Listen:

"He made it to Paris on a single gulp of air. Onto the *périphérique*, stilt-walking round the city. Eiffel Tower in the distance, bent. Road the racetrack of some crazed demolition derby. Sliding through chicanes of bivouacs and wrecks, vapourising barricades, eyeballs out there, gobbling up the miles.

"Then he fell for it. The oldest trick in the book. The unbreakable rule: never stop. A white-faced girl, eleven or twelve, naked, eyes the pits of hell, holding out a hand – except there was no hand, just a bloody stump, dripping. It was the stump that did it. The world he'd held at bay, through terrible visions, for so long, suddenly hit him. It was as if the windscreen had dissolved and the world poured in. He stopped. Stupid.

"They rose up slowly, parts of the wrecked landscape

coming to life. Foot down – wheels spin, too late, jacked up – neat. He got out and gave them the keys. They stared. He emptied his pockets. They stared. He stripped naked. They gathered up his things, lifted the girl almost tenderly over the parapet, dropped her – she fell without a sound – and drove off.

"He watched his world moving away from him, an alien world swallowing him up, came suddenly to life, running after it, fists punching, screaming 'bastards!' It slowed, he made an almighty effort, leapt for the rear crash bar, almost missed, grabbed – and flew twenty feet through the air, hair on end, blasted by his own electrical protection. They waved and accelerated away, laughing. He bounced on the concrete, slammed into a wreck, blacked out."

'He's alone, helpless. But he learns how to survive, and eventually he makes it along the underground route, from bead to different bead, following the thread, sidetracked only once, to Sardis, the place of the pyramid builders, who seem to have the answer.

'Their leader, you see, is a physicist he'd known in London, a dissident. They're building a pyramid. You know that the top sixteenth, 30'4", of the Great Pyramid of Khufu is missing? Well, they're building that missing pyramid, to complete the work begun so long ago, on an intersection of ley lines that corresponds numerologically to Giza. They're building it of concrete, the rock of our age, omitting the top sixteenth which will be a truncated pyramid of silver 1'10" high; this to be capped by a pyramid of gold 1.4" high and, at the apex, a perfectly cut, flawless diamond pyramid less than a tenth of an inch high. Four levels. Plus the Great Pyramid itself, makes five.

'But seven is the sacred number of aspiration – the seven-stepped Ziggurats, the seven terraces of Purgatory, the seven levels of wisdom, the seven spirits of God. The first level is the earth itself. And the seventh? What can surpass diamond, the hardest, purest matter? The abstract. This age's equivalent of the unspoken name of God – the General Unified Theory of matter and energy. When that formula is engraved on the diamond, at the molecular level, and the diamond placed at the top of the pyramid at midday on 29th February 2000 – a day that doesn't exist because every four hundred years a day has to be left off the calendar to keep it in time with the earth's revolution, and that's the day chosen – a cosmic connection will be made and a revivifying energy drawn down which will spread along ley lines across the whole earth, thus inaugurating the Aquarian Age.

'There are hundreds of acolytes working on the pyramid, doing everything by hand, even generating electricity for the necessary computers on a treadmill. The young man is almost seduced by the logic of it, by this bringing together of ancient wisdom and modern physics, by their certainty – but realises, just in time, that it's a false way: attempting to achieve the spiritual *through* the material rather than expressing the spiritual *in* the material. A mirror image of the rush for a nuclear fusion breakthrough that's consuming so much of the remaining energy of Europe. The physicist is the False One, hardly distinguishable from the True One. But the young man sees just in time, passes the test, goes on.

'He gets across the plain, past burning red Albi, into the hills. In spite of being poisoned by the treated apples at the boundary to the Reserve, he makes it – guided by the flickering light on the cliff near the river – and arrives (after another detour, this time to an 'over-spiritual' community) at the Centre he's seeking. He stays there a year, a whole cycle, learning from the man he's sought out, who becomes his father (who is in fact his uncle, Terry's brother). "The father gives the name and the set of arms": that's what it says in *The White Goddess*. He learns, sees his future within himself, and, when the Black Ones come, is sent on, the mustard seed, a spore, a hope for the future. Do you see?'

I close the file with a snap, well pleased. We're almost at St Affrique, Jane driving the long-undriven car circumspectly. She doesn't reply, stares through the windscreen, jaw set.

Chapter 6: In St Affrique

I leave Jane and go and buy nails. As I'm walking back I see her from a distance, sitting at the café table in the autumn sun, an elegant scarf tied carefully at her neck, sunglasses pushed up into her hair, still, observant, poised. I hardly recognise her. I stop and watch.

Is she the same person I met four years ago? The tiny wire-rimmed glasses that made her look like an anarchist are long gone, replaced by contact lenses. Her long hair, that she used to plait into a single thick braid, strong enough to climb up, cut off. The leather headband with the single pearl.... Of course we change our clothes, our accessories over time; but what's important is whether those small things, that drew our attention to someone, were incidental or essential, decoration or hooked into something deep. If they were incidental, matters of fashion and circumstance, they can't be trusted as indicators, expressions of the deeper person, the being that is a slow, dark, subterranean stream, moving in the way it has to.

Physically – how long does it take all the body cells to be replaced? Seven years? She's more than half way to being a different person. So am I.

But something shouldn't have changed. There should be a connection. Maybe we've both changed too much this summer. Maybe we'd stayed too close for too long – that's what I'd meant about having secrets – damming up the changes taking place in each; and now we've changed with a rush, apart. She's right, one reason we were drawn to each other was because we were both unformed. But it seems to me that this summer, in London, she's been definitively forming, into a professional career woman. Whereas I…?

But the past is over. I *am* looking at a new woman. Maybe the only sensible question is – what do I think of her? Things clear, I'm pleased – she's smart, attractive. I walk quickly, almost run to her, her gaze far off, her face quite vacant, and kiss her full on the mouth and look intently into her face, then kiss her again, more gently, and sit down opposite her, smiling. She looks surprised, confused, pleased. I feel suddenly happy.

'I love this view,' she says. She's leaning over the stone parapet of the bridge, arms folded, foot over ankle, tapping. I have my arm round her waist, attentive lover, smelling her hair.

'I want, one day, to be able to come and visit and look at it with pleasure. But it will be years before I come again, if ever.'

'Do you mean that?'

'Oh yes.'

*   *   *

At last she speaks, still staring out of the window as I drive back.

'The locals find it hard enough to make a living, and we're strangers. It's us who're disturbing the ecology.'

'But it should work – they have the experience, we have the knowledge.'

'But it doesn't happen, does it? And the incomers, they're crazies, escaping from the real world into their private worlds. Without roots, cut off from the mainstream, where will the energy come from? They'll run down like clocks.'

'But that's the whole point – from the underground, the esoteric, from the place, the *résurgences*, the ley lines. From an exact, detailed observation of and living in this area; talking the routes, singing the horizon. By living in this landscape, sensitive to it – but changing it where necessary, the feng shui way. Don't you see?

'And as to the crazies – Pieter's farm is the core location; André contributes the technology; Edvard understands the landscape and social interaction; and of course it's Pieter who believes in, and finally discovers, the cathedral. And I…'

'But Kris,' she says with a wail, looking helplessly at me, 'it's a story! It's just a *story*! You made it up! It's only happened in your head! Don't you *see*? Where are you going? What are you going to do here? How are you going to live? Of course you've reduced your consumption to an absolute minimum – but what are you *producing*? Where's the revenue? What'll you do when the car breaks down, you get toothache, you're ill? Why are you here? When I look at you, I don't see the man I was married to. I see someone who's beginning to be a madman. And that scares me.' She stops, as if unsure how to go on, sighs, says:

'I'm going back tomorrow. Come with me,' pleading. 'I've got a good job, a flat. You could find interesting work. No more working on the buildings. I know someone who's starting an ecological publishing imprint – it would suit you.

'And when we've got ourselves sorted out, built ourselves up, lived like normal people for a while, even thought about starting a family, maybe then we could do something with La Balme. It'll be a different proposition when the mains water comes in two years – it's settled, the postman told me. We could do holiday lets, use it as a second home. We might even start our own business, could run it from here. There are so many possibilities. Come back with me now, before it's too late. Let's start again.'

Mains water – oh no.

Chapter 7: Jane Leaves

We lie naked under the duvet, in each other's arms. Long after she's asleep I lie awake, watching the shadows cast by the fire flickering on ceiling and walls, listening to the wind and rain outside, feeling her warm and solid against me, in my embrace, thinking of being on that plane tomorrow. And I realise that never again will I feel so secure, and so safe.

I wake suddenly. It's dark. The fire is cold. Jane is heavy on me, and as I try to wriggle out from under her she follows me, her breast heavy, her arm like a bar across me, mumbling a childlike complaint. I stop at the edge of the mattress. "Come back with me now". I've never imagined going back; only staying here. Or going on, further out. "Build ourselves up". "Live like normal people". I can hardly breathe she's so heavy. I'm angry with myself, resentful of her that I've softened up so much in the brief time she's been here. I'll be glad when she's gone. I hold myself stiff.

*   *   *

'Come back with me, now.' I see myself on the plane, sitting next to this smart woman, long haired and tanned, an exotic, a primitive, a runaway being taken back, a wild boy being taken to be civilised.

'I can't. I have to barrel the wine. There are things I have to do.'

'Come soon.'

'I have to go to Paris.'

'You *don't* have to, you *don't* have to go to Paris! You *don't!*'

'I promised.'

'Break your promise to her. Remember your promises to *me*. Remember them.' A horn sounds.

330

'There's the postman.' She kisses me as awkwardly and I hold her as clumsily as when she arrived.

'You're a fool, a bloody fool,' she says. As she turns to go, I say:

'Jane – I'll never love anyone like I've loved you.'

'Me too – but maybe it's not enough – eh?' and she shrugs, waves from the doorway, and is gone.

PART IX:

LEAVING

Chapter 1: Last pages of Kris's diary: pig-killing

Tuesday 12th October

I saw a film once of an underground nuclear explosion. The land surface heaved slightly and shivered, then settled back. There was a muffled roar, then silence. Nothing had changed, except deep down. I saw a dark, secret, subterranean stillness changed suddenly to molten incandescence, blinding brilliance, chattering radioactivity. But on the surface nothing had changed.

Where did it go, that emptiness, that moment? So near, so near. I feel as though she's taken my summer. Like women do. Mothers. Wives. They try to stop you having those moments. "Close the door, it's cold". "Be back before dark". "Come down and eat something, you must". "Come in, silly boy, you're getting soaked" – rain beating on you, drumming on your stretched skin, as you watch a cat in a doorway, twisting and turning, its eyes steady on you; you wait for it to appear in the vast emptiness: "I can't, I'm waiting for something". "Silly boy, come in". And when those moments come they try and take them from you, before you can act on them, because they're frightened of them.

If I know what "Europe 2000", the work of that week, is, I'll know what this tower is, and the whole summer.

Is it a story, a piece of literature, the first flagstone of a path?

Is it the summation of what I've believed these last years, the 'something' that filled the 'nothing' after my breakdown, the extension of it into the future, in words, which allows me now to leave it in the past, the end of the past that allows me to begin again, now?

Or is it the blueprint for my future, the desired objective

towards which I'm meant to continue to work, a setting-out of my life's work, to be made to happen?

I want to say – she has taken my summer. But that's too easy. Be strong. Be still. Be dark. Be quiet. A cave, fifty degrees constant, where cheese ripens, where wine matures, where you gradually begin to see paintings on the walls.

Sunday 17th October

I sulphured the barrels – it fizzed like a fuse when I lit it and I felt like a gunpowder plotter in cobwebbed catacombs as the rain dripped outside. I poured in the wine and banged tight the bungs. Priestly purple. Double last year's – amazing, given the drought. Gaston predicts a landmark vintage because of the sun. The locals drink the first bottle at Christmas.

As I ran my hands over the fat barrels, I remembered back over all that's in them:

The mist when I picked the grapes, and my loneliness.

Tasting the first grape – a pebble in my mouth, solid and round, as I suck it and taste what's around me as if it's imaged on its surface; pressing it between tongue and palate until it splits and the first gorgeous sweet juice floods my mouth, followed by that necessary sharpness that cuts through the sugar; chewing the flesh and skin and seed, fleshy, nutty substance, and at last an edge – or is it a centre, the seed? – of bitterness….

The sun and the moon opposite each other in a lilac sky.

The hen-harriers, dancing.

The white petals falling as the fruit set.

The flower buds like bunches of tiny green grapes.

The leaf buds, already swollen when I pruned in March, sap oozing like blood plasma, the east wind cutting through me, freezing my face, as I absorbedly worked, the endlessness of the mass – and then a singular event: the wind dropped, the air was suddenly still and mild and empty; I looked up, and into the silence and stillness irrupted a flock of linnets, at least fifty, all moving together in dipping, bounding flight, twittering clamorously, their pink caps and breasts flashing, landing and instantly taking off, incessantly searching, a swarm but each bird an individual chip of bursting life and the whole a cloud of brilliant energy. And then they were gone, and there was emptiness again, but different; and even when the wind came up again and everything settled back into its average functioning, it felt different. I had lifted my head, and now I saw before me the tangle of overgrown vines choked in brambles and grass, and behind me the vines I had cleared, pruned, liberated. I was a carver, a sculptor. And was this, I wondered timorously, my *terroir*?

The upturned claw of Gaston's hand as he showed me the shape of the well-pruned *pied*, the shape to strive for, my first day in the vines.

Monday 18th October

I checked my stores. The potato and carrot clamps are fine. I looked along the rows in the store room:

The crocks of salted beans, the jars of jam. The bottles of tomatoes and ratatouilles, softened glowing fruit pressing against the glass of the preserving jars, suddenly experiments in the generation of new forms of life by some solitary natural scientist, benign.

Marrows hang in their nets, strings of onions wait to be plucked.

Dried apple rings, leathery on the outside with a fruity tang when the teeth bite.

Heaps of chestnuts, lustrous and such a satisfying deep brown; boiled they are a sweet and nutritious food – it could be a noble culture that has as its staple the sweet chestnut. I boiled some in sugar to make *marrons glacés*, as gifts.

I remember how laborious the work was at times, how tedious, how I would wish to be doing something else; but that's imperfection in me, I'm still corrupted by too long a life of work as a means to an end. Through my education, learning in order to score well in tests, pass examinations, gain qualifications; since, working to earn money.

It is a different world when you work for the work itself. I sowed those beans, watered and tended them, staked them, harvested and cut them and packed them in salt; and when I could, when things were right, all I was doing was working on those beans, so that the beans would grow and keep, so there'd be beans for me to eat. But when I'm working for money, when the end is money, which is purchasing power – so I'm working to amass power – then my relationship to what I'm doing is blurred and indistinct. So often I've worked in order to buy things to compensate for the pain of working; the work, which is of necessity at the centre of our lives, taking up as much time as it does, is at best blurred, at worst a hole. Terrible things follow from that. I don't want to go back to it.

I dug a patch of garden and sowed broad beans. Gaston said – why not leave it until spring, I'll put the ox plough across. I just shrugged.

Tuesday 19th October.
I finished the brooch for Gabrielle's birthday. Jane had seen it. She just stared. I've only ever made such a gift for her until now. I made a card too. It is the end of something, this summer. But the beginning of what?

A letter from Richard. Back three days late after his dalliance with the blonde in the sports car, and since, frenetic activity; on one side a series of drawings expressive of his summer in France – "they just keep coming, and they're good" – on the other a busy personal life as he succumbs, again, to being attractive to women. An exhibition already arranged for spring. A nostalgia for single-minded days at La Balme. Unease at his social life. "But – there's a girl I've seen around, haven't even spoken to her, but she looks so sweet and gentle, so young…."

He's spoken to Clive. There's a joint scheme by university and local authority to convert a terrace of condemned houses into an ecological showpiece – insulation, renewable energy, allotments, the whole thing. "Clive says it's a perfect opportunity for you, and you'd be just the man to do it. Think about it". Oh to be back. Oh the loss.

Thursday 21st October.
The neighbours killed their pig today. There's often a pig-killing in country tales: soon I will write about a massacre; today was just an execution.

A dozen were there – the men clumped together, silent and dark, clenching and unclenching their fists, talking quietly; the women voluble and shrill, bustling busily as they cleared the kitchen and scrubbed the surfaces and boiled water, as thorough as for an operation or childbirth. It was a grey still day, the hamlet hidden in cloud.

The men went for the pig, we heard the noise in the sty, they soon reappeared dragging it, stumbling, the pig lunging and squealing, a tremendous force held in the constraint of taut ropes. They threw it down on its side on the killing board and tied it firmly down, tight bindings criss-crossing it, digging into its flesh, so that in spite of its heaving it was helpless. At first it struggled and squealed; then it just watched wild-eyed the circle above it.

The butcher had drunk his glass of rum, had sharpened his knife and, with a single measured movement he thrust the shining blade into the pig's throat up to the hilt, twisted and pulled out – dark blood poured out, over his hand (I could feel its warmth), spurting as from a fountain in a thick arc. The pig struggled frenziedly, squealed desperately, heaving against the ropes as its blood gushed and flowed into the large white bowl that Madame held; she knelt at its head, whispering quietly as the red blood stained the white china, filled it foaming to the brim. The force of the pumping flow diminished, its eyes dimmed, its struggles became feebler, muscular movements gave way to nervous twitchings, and at last there was an out-breath, a sigh, and its movements ceased. Its long-lashed eyes slowly closed. One last spasm, and then stillness. The pig was dead.

There was a moment's pause, as if everyone moved back slightly, then they fell upon the body in a rush of activity – ropes discarded, a knife in the belly pulled down like a zip and the guts tumbled out by the handful and carried away by the women to be squeezed empty of partly digested food and unevacuated faeces and to be washed out for sausage skins. The men poured buckets of boiling water over to soften the bristles, and worked vigorously amid clouds of steam, scraping off the body hair.

Soon there was a soft, smooth, naked, baby-pink body; and the butchering began. Head cut off. Body split in two, gradually dismembered: bacon to be salted, hams to be smoked, tongue jellied, trotters boiled, slabs of fat, sausages, blood pudding, pâté, stock. Salting, smoking, boiling, freezing. The bubbling and industrious processing in the kitchen would go on for hours, but outside, in the misty darkness, the pig was gone, a shape on the board marking an absence. The larder was filling, the women chattered as they worked, the men talked as they drank, and for a day, as on all harvest days, there was abundance and plenty.

I'm still shocked by the sudden violence. But it's not brutal. Gaston snapping a pigeon's neck with his thumb, like a matchstick. Madame slamming the hen against the wall in mid-conversation. The sudden focussing of energy on an act of violence, but with no anger. I can't imagine violence without anger; that's the difference. I saw my first pig-killing on my first day's work at the pig factory.

The day had passed quite reasonably; a frantic hour of emptying frozen boiled hams from metal moulds in the cold store, followed by hours of boning hams, repetitive work but okay.

Then activity ceased and all the workers disappeared from the cool tile and stainless steel place where we worked. I'd taken the job not knowing what the job was. We'd been desperate. The foreman beckoned me and I followed him along labyrinthine breeze block corridors and up a rattly metal spiral staircase. A final dark corridor: 'pigs don't frighten you, do they?' Pretty pigs? – of course not. Around a corner and there were four of them, inches away, each hanging by a single heel, eight foot long from heel to snout, immense, flailing, twitching, belching blood, bloody, dying. I wanted to scream. But I didn't; because I also wanted to pretend it wasn't happening. No – I wanted to pretend I wasn't there. No – I wanted part of me to be there, part not. I felt a wrenching inside as I separated myself from the person standing there watching, so that I was outside or inside that person, but not the same. Then I didn't have to scream. A rubber-aproned, bloodstained faceless man swung a hanging, twitching pig round the corner on the overhead conveyor and plunged his knife into its throat and pushed it on, blood gushing, with a whirr of wheels so that it hit softly against the others and they hung there swaying slightly until the measured cogs would engage and move one slowly round the next corner. We waded in our wellingtons through the blood bath – a shallow, tiled bath, like you paddle through between changing room and swimming pool – calf-deep in foaming blood, and round the first corner.

341

A dark concrete and asbestos building, lit only by shafts of bloody sunlight, divided by metal crush barriers, echoing with blows and cries, the whole a seething mass of squealing pigs. Pigs squeal like babies. They squeal like torture victims going out of their minds. (Why do I write that? I have no way of knowing. It's what I imagine.) The scene, hundreds (it seemed) of frantic pigs, wild-eyed, crushed, struggling, squealing, a heaving soft dirty pink mass, smelling of piss and fear (that I can still smell and taste in the bacon I eat), should have been intolerable. And yet I stood and watched. I watched the swarthy little man, like a figure from a depiction of Hell, driving them from pen to pen with kicks and curses and hard thwacks with a length of hard black hosepipe. I watched him corner and grab one pig by a hind leg and loop a chain around the ankle and hook it onto a slowly rising conveyor. I watched the chain tighten and drag the pig up as its trotters scrabbled ineffectually for a foothold until it was hanging, kicking and lunging, head back, squealing. The squeal was shrill, hysterical (I can think of no other word); it was as if it was being strangled and the scream, locked inside, was squeezing out through the constricted throat only with enormous effort. I watched the man dip electric tongs into water and yoke them behind the pig's large, twitching ears; the pig stiffened, convulsed, then relaxed and trembled and slavered and pissed and shat as the conveyor carried it round the corner.

Sometimes he missed the nerves and shocked the pig instead of stunning it and it squealed even louder and banged through the metal gate twisting and lashing the air with short, helpless legs. The man with the knife shrugged but stuck it just the same; the pig, conscious, eyes open, flailing madly, dying just the same. I watched a worn-out woman plod into the blood bath and fill a bucket with blood, pushing the turds and froth aside, and carry it heavily away, for *boudin*, blood pudding.

Only when the foreman offered me the black hosepipe did I react; I shook my head. And when he held out the tongs I said 'I don't want to do that', and he shrugged and tried it himself and shocked the pig. But I didn't walk out. In the space of a few moments the unimaginable, the unbelievable, the intolerable, had become acceptable. If not for me to do, for me to accept that it happened, that it was part of a process that I would allow myself to be part of.

The foreman shrugged and led me past the gasping, sighing, dying pigs, already quite normal, round a corner into the butchery, a long room with a long perspective of hanging pigs in progressive stages of dismemberment. He led me the length of the room, which became calmer and quieter and less bloody and the meat less recognisable the further we got from the living pigs. Until we got to the end of the line. There was a man with a blowtorch. Severed heads were thrown onto his table and he burned the bristles off, working with the concentration and attention to detail of a fanatical barber determined to remove every last hair; although, incongruously, leaving untouched the long, curved, feminine eyelashes. When satisfied he threw the head into a vat of bloody water where it steamed and bobbed and sank.

My job was to retrieve the heads and set them in a row on the cold room floor, a row of smooth pink heads with large flexible ears and rubbery flat snouts, each with a crocodile grin and an expression of insanity. Then I punched the sharp point of my knife through nostril and cheek and pushed a hook through and hung the head from a rail until there was row upon row of swaying, grinning heads. The cold room, with its rows of long slim half-carcasses and impaled livers and severed heads was a calm place.

When the last part of the last pig was safely in the cold store, we washed down the entire factory and went home.

*   *   *

So ended my first day at the pig factory. I worked there for six months, a whole summer, even went back after our Christmas in England. Why? It was a job, the only work available, we needed the money – I left the day we paid off the house. Small principles didn't get a look-in set against the large principle of owning our own house and land. I hated the job; and yet it fascinated me. It was like being there at the beginning of the Industrial Revolution. It was a system, and it worked, a system of transformation with its own fascinating internal logic. It was a manufactory.

Each day pigs, the raw material, were collected from farms all over the region, a dozen here, a single pig there (welcome cash), and carried in big lorries to the top of the slope on which the factory was built and disgorged into the mouth of the factory (most staggering, disorientated by the switchback journey, sometimes one or two dead, stifled in the heat, or heart-attack victims – pigs react badly to stress), which ingested, digested and processed them into all manner of saleable products which, packaged and labelled "fresh country produce", left by the door at the bottom of the factory in juggernauts for distribution to supermarkets nationwide.

I started work at seven. Sometimes it was like driving through the fog to prison.

But sometimes, driving over the top on the empty road through the woods, I'd see things. Columbines, pretty as fairies' dresses; foxgloves, so secret and velvety I could see the silent fox slipping his paw out when he heard me coming. Horse mushrooms the size of dinner plates; puffballs, edible white spheres from outer space. Wild strawberries, their taste, sharp and instant, the essence of strawberry without all that unnecessary fleshiness. Hedgehogs trotting along the road, up off the ground, quick prickly piglets. Once a hare lolloping along ahead of me, so long-legged and unrabbit-like I thought it was a dog. Even a hoopoe, pink, crest up, curved beak, looking like a cockatoo – where was I, the East Indies? Tarzan could have swung through the trees and I wouldn't have been surprised, or a boy running with a pack of wolves, or Morgaine la Fée. The mysteries of ancient forests, messages I didn't quite understand, undecipherable clues, a world lost to me although buried deep inside. Once, driving home in the dark after rain, I saw something in the headlights and stopped and walked back with a flashlight. On the road, quite still, were seven black and yellow lizards, coal and sulphur, like something from the Amazon jungle or the Mojave desert or a moon of Jupiter. I looked them up. They were salamanders. Salamanders! Why not cockatrices, phoenixes, gryphons, unicorns!?

Elvish mornings as sweet as a nymph's breath. Nights as black and protean and bulging with life as a sack of blind labrador pups, or the creatures in the belly of Sin, or the moment before the first moment of creation – I'm grasping at images in a ragbag of knowledge. I have only history; no prehistory, no mythology. Maybe in a lifetime here, a life as in the manuscript I wrote in the tower, maybe then I would discover the mythology that is in the landscape and, maybe, inside me....

Sometimes I'd stop at the top of the hill and look down at the solid old stone houses of the village curled like a snail around the castle, the stream running through creating its own silver track, the gardens terracing up the hillsides giving way naturally to pasture and plough, vines and wood. And there, squat and square, on a site hacked out of the raw hillside, the breeze block and asbestos factory, where I worked. Then I'd take a deep breath, drive down, walk in.

I have two views of the pig factory. The pig factory as seen by my two separate, unconnected eyes. (I'd always alternated;

as the Catholic church alternates between fat and thin popes, and me between wild and steady girls. I thought I'd overcome it, developed stereoscopy with the Green vision; as I'd thought Jane was my syllogistic salvation. Maybe there's no resolution; maybe the best you can hope for is a ceaseless alternation – as the hand can endlessly describe the yin yang image.)

One eye. You see the products in the supermarkets. Tins of pâté and ham, shrink-wrapped saucisse, paper-collared saucisson: "Charcuterie du pays", with a picture of the pretty, smiling, Marianne peasant girl, *La Rouergate*.

I asked the sausage man in the factory what goes into the sausages – he used to be a real butcher, killing and butchering animals one by one, as needed, until 'hygiene regulations' restricted killing to big concerns and he went out of business and had to come and work in the factory. His eyes rolled up to the heavens, his hands spread, "*une pharmacie*", he wailed, "*une pharmacie*". Jars of dried additives, strange powders, bright chemical colours.

The place is a machine; when the electricity's switched off, it stops. It is run from an office buzzing with computers. It is served by enormous lorries that squeeze through country lanes, for which roads must be straightened, bridges strengthened, trees cut down. It requires new sources of water, new sewerage systems. At its centre is the *patron*, a man driven, who is ceasing to exist, who is becoming pure will. Each step of progress diminishes the workers, as the job is broken down into ever greater specialisation, ever thinner slices. Each innovation (technology, management system) increases the input of outside intelligence (designers of machines etc), diminishes the input of the workers' intelligence and skill. They're becoming 'hands'.

When I started we boned hams six around a table, chatting. Then a conveyor track was installed and we all faced the same way, each at a small table, hams arriving and departing by continuous conveyor. We mumbled and grumbled, our faces hardened, but there was nothing we could do. The *patron* is converting a peasantry into a proletariat, in the 1970s; and economic conditions are driving them into the factory as surely as they did the handloom weavers of eighteenth-century England.

And the youngsters like money – their ambitions are those propagated by television. Capitalism works. Or at least, the challenger to capitalism – socialism – seems to have failed. Maybe ecology can be the new challenger? Or maybe it's just a Bluebell Line next to the main line electric....

The other eye. I started work at five past seven, always got shouted at for being late – I liked that.

In the cold room, the air dense and frozen, emptying hams from their moulds, frozen in, banging them on the table edge, fingers without feeling, sometimes smashed. Remove them from the moulds, pile them on the trolley, feel the cold penetrating; imagine being locked in here, naked, water sprayed over, skin icing, blood congealing, ice crystals forming in the blood... I'd rush out and gulp the warm air and be amazed at the southern heat.

Then four hours of boning hams. Repetition, boredom, broken only by the occasional careless cut and the gush of blood. I cut myself so often they gave me a chain-mail glove. And yet sometimes the knife slipped through, part of me and part of the ham, followed every subtle contour of the bone and the bone came out completely clean; and I would hold it and look at it amazed. And sometimes, instead of fighting time (watching the minute hand of the clock, looking away, guessing how much time had passed), I would find myself carried along on a wave of *being*, and the work became a meditation and I could imagine boning the perfect ham, so that for a timeless moment I would experience the nothing, ecstasy, nirvana, perfect peace....

I ate my sandwiches in the car, reading newspaper stories

about Beirut, the Khmer Rouge, the oil crisis, hyper-inflation.

Three more hours of boning hams. Boredom. And yet stories all around me. Bonacasse the simpleton, who is everybody's butt (is there, you feel, to be the butt, the reason he's employed – so we don't feel we're the lowest of the low) and who disappears on three-day drunks every full moon. And Claudine, the dreamy girl who stands by the tenderising machine, feeding and serving it, a machine which sometimes, with its repetition of mechanical sounds seems relentlessly to be ticking away the fruitless seconds of her life, with its motion squeezing the breath from her body, pulping her being; and sometimes sounds with intricate polyrhythms that enliven her blood, pulse in her veins, cause her to skip with tiny, involuntary dance steps. I imagine Bonacasse and her in a love story that goes horribly wrong.

Then we trooped upstairs to the killing floor. My station was by the rectangular vat of boiling water. As the conveyor rattled a blood-dripping pig around the corner, gasping its last, we threw it into the dimpled water and after twenty seconds operated the giant ladle that lifted it steaming from the water and fed it between pummelling rollers that stripped off its hair. Fifty. A hundred. A hundred and fifty. Sweat poured off me. My day had begun in the frigid zone, would end in the torrid. I'd practise mental tricks to pass the time – reciting the alphabet backwards, doing complex mental calculations.

Sometimes a hanging pig struggled from its chain and fell to the ground and staggered and slithered around, blood pouring from its throat, until at last it expired. We cursed as we manhandled its vast soft bulk into the vat.

Sometimes the knife had missed the artery and the pig was plunged into the water alive. It would thrash and lunge, boiling water flying everywhere, eyes staring, squealing when it could. We'd hold it under until it boiled to death.

Sometimes I would look along the line of corpses and imagine them human and myself working in an extermination camp; and could imagine it. Why had the intolerable become, so quickly, acceptable? Because it was acceptable to authority, and to the other workers. That realisation chilled my blood. But on I worked.

At last we cleared up. How good I felt, mopping and polishing and leaving everything clean and tidy and walking to the car in the evening sun, virtuous at a day's work done, a day's pay earned.

Driving home I would maybe stop and pick some flowers for Jane. Or fill the car with bracken, for the compost heap, and drive drugged by the heady scent. Or I'd think suddenly – my life's been all spinning threads, when will I begin weaving? Or driving into a low, dazzling sun, squinting, hardly able to see, I would look in the rear-view mirror, at the clearly illuminated, perfectly visible landscape behind me, in the past, and say – life's like that.

Nowhere have I spent more hours of misery, nowhere has time passed more slowly, nowhere have I seen so clearly into myself. I saw that my ideas, morals, ethics, were all theoretical, abstract. I learned that the two eyes cannot unite, that if you attempt it all you get is an unsatisfactory mix; that the weaving begins when you choose one way and follow it wherever it goes; that if you don't choose, circumstance will impose its way and you will have lost the opportunity to make one of the few choices we have.

The pen has stayed poised above the paper for the last ten minutes as I digest what I have just written. I write this, then I put it down.

Friday 22nd October
The oxen went today.
'Where are they going?' I asked Gaston as he watched the lorry go. He drew his finger across his throat. Behind his

nonchalance, I saw a man stricken.

'But why?'

'They eat too much.'

'What will happen to them?'

'We'll eat them.'

Sunday 24th October.

I've begun the process of closing down La Balme, of mothballing it, because I don't know how long I will be gone. In the meadow I looked at the fences that need mending, the hedges that need laying, the trees that need pruning, winter jobs. The vines too are best pruned in winter. I looked at the view, russet now, glowing autumn fire. Soon it will be bare. Where will I be when the leaves have all fallen?

In the cellar I checked the wine barrels and turned the hay, disturbing field mice – sorry. At the top of the house I examined the new flashing, locked the skylight, fastened the shutters.

I sat in the tower for a long time, trying to remember how I felt a month ago. I looked at "Europe 2000"; I don't know what it is but I will carry it with me, a sort of talisman. And I don't know what to do.

I thought it was past, my life of choosing, thought that all it would be, from now on, would be doing. For so long I'd lived at the edge, on the seashore, not knowing my destination, so not starting. Then I came inland, to the heart of the continent, and to the heart of love – or so I thought – just to do. Now I seem to be all at sea, dog-paddling around until my foot touches something other than slimy jelly fish, something solid. I might land on an island and find that it's a whale....

A letter from Jane: "I think I understand why you have to go to Paris, although I'm very hurt by it. But afterwards –

there's really no reason why you shouldn't come to London. It will take a lot of working out, but I'm sure we can do it. We owe it to each other at least to try".

Monday 25th October.
A letter from Gabrielle.

I read through all her letters, the record of six weeks back in Paris, adjusting to that life again, after the summer, in close harness, in the city.

She awakens on the first morning and, with her eyes closed, imagines that she is still at La Balme; until a police siren sounds and she hears motorbikes and cars outside. She mourns Mao's passing, "a giant". She returns to her old flat, where her boyfriend is preparing to leave to go and spend the winter with Gérard at the place we met. On the first day of school, when the alarm clock rings, she says to herself: "be strong, because this is your last year".

She says that when she was at La Balme it was like a dream because it was so wonderful, but now she sees that it was real life; she tells me about *Encore Heureux Qu'on Va Vers L'Été*, in which the children leave everything behind – parents, authority – and go and live their own life in the country, living a dream that is real life. I imagine it as a film, with "Le Temps de Vivre" the soundtrack.

She finds it hard as the days shorten and the light diminishes. She's certain that the bad air, like the summer's drought, is the result of world pollution; she's upset that man has so, and maybe terminally, disturbed the global equilibrium, and wishes we could turn the clock back. She's rereading Breton's *L'Amour Fou*.

She says, come for *Toussaint*, when she has a week's holiday. She says, stay as long as you like – she knows someone at an agency for English teachers, and they always need people there.

And why wouldn't it work? Living in Paris during the winter, living here for the whole summer, Gabrielle visiting for the holidays…?

I don't know what I'll do. I have no one to talk to, just this journal. I write it like Captain Scott, for others to read; although maybe the other is me, a future me…. When I go, maybe I'll leave it open on this desk, to gather dust. Maybe stop in mid-sentence, or in mid-action, as in "MS. Found in a Bottle":

"Going down!"

I read Rilke's "Autumn Day", Rimbaud's "Farewell".

Tuesday 27th October. Evening.

The house is all shut up and shut down. I sit and keep vigil. This place, which has been my work, an extension of myself, for so long, is separating from me. I am becoming atomic, a spore. Soon I will leave it to the mice, the spiders, gravity, time. Soon I will blow away.

Thus begins my going down….

Chapter 2: Kris leaves La Balme

It is dark when I wake. Dark and cold. I switch on the light. It makes little difference, fails to move the dark back, lies thinly on its surface.

I dress and eat. I eat a lot. I've noticed this, that I have a tremendous appetite before a journey; not knowing when I'll eat again, a primitive storing-up, I suppose. My rucksack is packed.

I look around. In the night the house has become distant and alien, turned away from me, concerned with its own affairs. I feel put out. I had imagined a leisurely, affectionate farewell, an evocative wander through the house, a gentle touching, to fix things in my memory. I had imagined sitting on the terrace, with my breakfast, singing Dylan's "One More Cup of Coffee (Valley Below)".

It's ending like an affair: not, as one would like, with caresses and sad looks and "if only's"; but, as they do, abruptly, because one at least of you is already out of it, gone. So I hurry round the house checking that everything is secure, pull the heavy door shut and lock it quickly. I hide the key in the usual place and stand on the step. The hamlet is still and uncommunicative.

I shoulder my rucksack and set off across the damp cobbles. The neighbour's alarm clock rings and rings. The dogs sniff at me, then turn away and wander off. "Chid, chid, chid" from the widow's garden. Her son sits, as hard and still as stone, holding his dog-headed stick, his eyes following me, his mouth open in that soundless cry, his face blank.

At the edge of the hamlet I meet Gaston sauntering home, gun over one shoulder, a rabbit over the other, beret pushed back, sprig of mint in his mouth.

'Going on manoeuvres?' he asks, indicating my pack.

'I left you a present.'

'A present?'

353

'Paris. I'm going to Paris.'

'And then?' I shrug. Expressions flit across his face, more expressions than I've ever seen him display; and then his face settles back into its habitual stoic blandness and he shrugs.

'Have the hens, any eggs.'

'They're all cocks.'

'Eat 'em, then.' We shake hands. He seems about to say something but doesn't and saunters on, head up, towards the house. I watch him pick up the package, disappear inside, close the door. Then I turn and face the road that winds up between the open fields.

The sky is lightening, colouring, the grey turning to yellow and peach and pink. At the rim I turn and look back. The sky explodes vermilion and crimson, red engulfs La Balme, the new red roof glows; and at its centre, glittering and shining, a cut ruby in flames, containing the flames, is the tower's wondrous faceted dome.

And now is the moment, if I dare. I close my eyes. I reach out and pick up that ruby; I hold it and put it into my mouth, feel it fill my mouth, hot and sharp – too hot the red, too sharp the faceted surface! I want to spit it out. No! – swallow, swallow, gulp it down this thing so hot and hard, searing and tearing, swallow it down to the *tan t'ien*, the midpoint, the centre.... And there it detonates, explodes through me. At last.

I open my eyes cautiously. The world is still there. I see Gaston in one of his private places looking at the figure I'd made for him, the figure carved in wood of the man scything, turning it over in his hands, examining it.

'Gaston!' I shout. He looks up. I wave, shout:

'Thank you!' He waves, his short, half-wave, then turns back to the figure. I turn and walk over the rim, leave it all behind, take it with me.

*   *   *

354

I stride out, stretching my legs, glad to be travelling on my own two feet, pack on my back, wondering how far I will walk, pleased with the air in my lungs, the pressure of the blood through my arteries and veins, the sound of my boots on the road.

The sun rises up from behind the ridge. My shadow stretches out in front of me. I stop. There is a grand silence. I wait. And then walk on.

Notes

Some definitions. For more on the Diggers, and other activists in "the other revolution [in mid-seventeenth-century England] which never happened, though from time to time it threatened" (Hill p15), see Christopher Hill's *The World Turned Upside Down: radical ideas during the English revolution*. The parallels with the ferment of ideas, often expressed in pamphlets and other ephemera, in the 1960s and 1970s, are worthy of note.

p7. Arthur Rimbaud in "Delirium II", from *A Season in Hell*.

p87. *Paradise Lost*: Book II line 926 et seq.

p91. LIP was a French watch-making factory, occupied by the workers and run as a co-operative.

p136. Pieter's story owes much to *The Lost World of the Kalahari* by Laurens van der Post.

p183. 'Every human being…' from Robert Musil's *The Man Without Qualities*.

p189. Walt Whitman.

p220. *The Divine Comedy: Hell*, canto XXVI.

p229. *Journey to the East* by Herman Hesse.

p245. Lanza del Vasto was an Italian follower of Gandhi whose 'Community of the Ark' still exists. Author of *Return to the Source*.

p246. The information about Michel Chevalier, including the text of his poem "Le Temple", is from "The Palace and the Temple: two Utopian architectural visions of the 1830s" by Ann Lorenz Van Zanten, in *Art History* Vol 2 No 2 June 1979. The translations from the poem are mine.

p255. "In the Penal Colony" by Franz Kafka.

p265. "La fossiure a la gent amant" is in Gottfried von Strassburg's *Tristan*.

p266. The first tale is "The Piazza" by Herman Melville. I can't recall where I read the second – apologies for not crediting.

p289. *The Pursuit of the Millenium*, Norman Cohn's fascinating study of millenarian and anarchist movements in medieval Europe.

p324. A misreading by Kris of John Michell's *The View over Atlantis* p90 et seq.

p325. *The White Goddess* by Robert Graves.

p351. *Encore Heureux Qu'on Va Vers L'Été* is by Christiane Rochefort.

p352. "MS. Found in a Bottle" by Edgar Allan Poe.

Song lyrics. It is difficult, and expensive, to get permission to reproduce song lyrics – otherwise the book would have been full of them. The best place to find the ones referred to but not quoted is on the internet: search – artist's name, lyrics.

An appropriate soundtrack album for this book would be:

'Rock 'n' Roll Suicide' - David Bowie
'Tangled up in Blue' - Bob Dylan
'Nisi Dominus' - Monteverdi *1610 Vespers*
'White Bird' - It's a Beautiful Day
'Blue' - Joni Mitchell
'Fixing a Hole' - The Beatles
'Idiot Wind' - Bob Dylan
'If You see Her, say Hello' - Bob Dylan
'Buckets of Rain' - Bob Dylan
'La Chanson de Jacky' - Jacques Brel
'Le Temps de Vivre' - Georges Moustaki
' "Heroes" ' - David Bowie
'One More Cup of Coffee' - Bob Dylan.